He May Wear My Silence

He May Wear My Silence

Zdravka Evtimova

galaXy

First Trade Paperback Edition

This is a work of fiction. Names, characters, places, and incidents, either are the product of the author's imagination or are used fictitiously. Any resemblance to actual persons, living or dead, events or locales is entirely coincidental.

ISBN: 979-8-9886342-0-1

Editor and Publisher, Justin Sloane
Cover art: *Storm Coming* © 2023 by Bob Eggleton
Book design by F. J. Bergmann

an imprint of Starship Sloane Publishing Company, Inc.
Austin–Round Rock, Texas
starshipsloane.com

TABLE OF CONTENTS

FOREWORD

My publisher friend Justin Sloane got in touch saying he was working on a novel by Bulgarian author Zdravka Evtimova that he thought might interest me—given my preoccupation with mythology and folklore. "I thought it might be right up your street," he said; and he was completely right.

Knowing next to nothing about Bulgarian folklore, I found the story fascinating from the outset. To begin with I wasn't too sure where the story was taking place. I kind of assumed it to be America because many of the main characters have very Anglo-sounding names—John Cole, Philip Mill, Jacob Harvey—with a sprinkling of more exotic-sounding ones—Sara Eutim, Boya Bagd, Ivan Georg—as happens commonly enough in the States. The action also begins in the town of Dusk, capital of its region, which conjured an image of some place vaguely out in the West. But no: it gradually emerges that events are actually unfolding in Bulgaria. After slight puzzlement, I guessed that this might be a literary device to make English speakers (notoriously blind and cloth-eared to East European names) feel at home with the characters; and it does do so brilliantly.

Zdravka confirmed my hunch with this explanation: "I use Anglo/English names for the characters in the novel even though it is set in Bulgaria because I want to make the story more accessible to English-speaking readers. There is another reason, too. I wrote the initial part of the book in Germany where I met a guy called Johann Kole, a very interesting personality. This is how my character became John Cole. I have chosen Bulgarian names for my characters as well; for example, Ivan Georg. I finished the novel in Belgium, where my boss was called Sara. So the characters live in the book like ordinary people. I hope that by choosing names for my characters belonging to different national traditions the book I have written will speak to American readers about Bulgaria in a way that will inspire them to explore the rich and mystic Bulgarian culture and place it in the complex frame of European culture."

Having cleared that up, I invite you to share a wonderfully rich and complex story that touches on the very meaning of existence, which, as Zdravka hoped, has certainly prompted me at least into taking a much closer look into Bulgarian myths, legends and history—and will hopefully do the same for many other readers.

Nigel Suckling
July 2023
England

The little boy was looking for his voice.
I do not want it for speaking with;
I will make a ring of it
so that he may wear my silence
on his little finger.

—Federico Garcia Lorca,
"The Little Mute Boy"

Chapter One

I would like to introduce myself to the reading public before Wanga, the charlatan, takes the floor. Young and old in these parts believed Wanga was a blind prophetess who could predict the future. Predict the future, my foot! I am Sara Eutim, and they say I am a famous writer and researcher. Of course, things are much more complicated; they always are with me.

The old cars roared and rumbled along the narrow dirt road, sinking in puddles, stopping from time to time to let the engines cool down. There were no trees and no rocks on that mountain. Its slopes were barren, cold and steep. This place gave me the creeps. A couple of years ago, I had decided to make money from it. When I took a fancy to something, anything, I inevitably ended up making money. Not that I made efforts to get rich, no, I did not; maybe I was greedier than most people, or maybe I had a knack of turning everything I touched into a purse full of credit cards. I seemed to attract money. Everything I wrote made me wealthier. I was a very good journalist, and some critics wrote that I was the rare case where a good journalist proved to be a brilliant writer. I didn't care what the critics wrote about me. I simply felt like digging into the bizarre tales about the cheap quack Wanga. I wouldn't turn down the money that came my way, not by a long shot, but money had nothing to do with my visit here, to the back of beyond.

This time I was not a reporter, hunting for a riveting tale, and I was not a writer fascinated by a brilliant plot. I was Sara Eutim, the angry woman who had a personal motive to dig into the matter. I had always hated beating about the bush. To cut a long story short, I have to admit the name of my motive was Philip Mill, the reporter, the man who did not make me his wife.

Philip Mill was the only man in my whole life who had ditched me. I had had many lovers and I still have some. I believe I am a very pretty woman. He had asked me to marry him and I had said yes, agreeing to become Mrs. Philip Mill.

Then he published an article in the local newspaper, the *Dusk Daily*, a most unremarkable text dedicated to Bare Mountain. Two weeks after his story was published, Philip Mill told me his understanding of life had changed. He was a different man. He knew how wonderful I was, he said, how gentle, and he felt I'd soon meet another honest and handsome guy who'd love me. Philip still felt for me and adored me, but he had met someone, he said. He had met blind Wanga of Bare Mountain.

So now I was listening to the wheezing and roaring jalopies that crawled up to the top of the barren hill. I had my methods. I, Sara Eutim, was determined to stick to my decision, and I'd talk to Wanga no matter what Philip Mill would say. I studied thoroughly all scraps and pieces of information on Bare Mountain I could lay my hands on. Unfortunately, all materials I collected were two flimsy monographs on the superstitions rife in Dusk Gorge. I thoroughly studied all places mentioned in Philip's article, both important and unimportant, all of them in the capital of the region, the dusty gray town of Dusk.

There was a picture on the wall of my bedroom: five cherry trees all in full bloom, all their branches dry. It was a horrible picture—how was it possible, I asked, for dead branches to blossom? In the background, more cherry trees jutted out, ripe cherries hanging on the dry twigs. I carried this picture, and I hated it. It reminded me that Dusk Gorge was a dry tree for me, a place that gave the world poisonous fruit. Under the dry trees, somebody, maybe my mother, had printed out a short poem about a sick little girl. I liked the poem because I used to be that sick child, I had survived, and the pretty woman lived on.

He threw his dots to the wind. Why is the Tall Fellow so silly, mommy?
The Tall Fellow can destroy death.
And he must always hide.

Who was that Tall Fellow who could destroy death? I did not like that guy.

I read all the articles on the local myths and legends I could lay my hands on in the libraries of the region. All research papers boiled down to a handful of superstitious tales. The locals were afraid to climb Bare Mountain. If a man crawled to its peak, he immediately ran away from that place. Before the coward took to his heels, he left the stone or the pan he'd brought to the barren hill. An ancient legend had it that you had to choose an item from your kitchen, a frying pan or a cup, and leave it on the bare slope. Before you bid farewell to your household item, you whispered to it the name of the disease which made your life a misery. Within days, the pain went away for good. You took a stone from your meager garden and told the stone the name of the guy you hated. The poor bugger was in for trouble. You only had to leave that particular stone on Bare Mountain.

Of course, all the newspapers pointed out that it was silly of you to believe this pack of lies. Lengthy articles insisted that the old superstitions had to be eradicated. After all, Bare Mountain was just an ordinary hill.

Everything changed when Wanga settled there.

Even the well-known scholar Philip Mill who told me he didn't want me any longer, wrote an admirable essay dedicated to that con artist. In his opinion, she was a miraculous phenomenon. A man I paid generously—I won't mention his name—I always used care and discretion when dealing with reporters. To cut a long story short, the hack writer I'd hired wrote an article focused on the chinks in Wanga's armor: she was a cunning quack who came out of nowhere to spin yarns. The serviceable man's article explained that Wanga had built a small hut, using the stones, which despondent folks had brought to the top of Bare Mountain. Wanga used the pans and saucers the locals had dragged to the bare hill.

It was my ex-fiancé, Philip Mill, who told me Wanga was blind. At the end of his essay, Mr. Mill admitted he could not live without her. He was profoundly impressed by the interview she gave him in her hut.

Even before Wanga heard his footsteps she had said: *You will become my husband. You will be the death of me.* Philip Mill did quit his job. I talked to his boss, the editor-in-chief of the *Dusk Daily.* The man didn't know where Philip Mill had gone. Maybe he returned to Brussels, where he was born.

I didn't leave the matter at that. My motive had nothing to do with jealousy. I was curious. That was the reason I climbed Bare Mountain. I wanted to see the blind woman, and I wanted an answer to the question of why Philip Mill had given me the cold shoulder.

Mr. Mill met me at the foot of the steep hill. I could hardly recognize him. He had grown a disheveled beard, and I couldn't find a trace of the man I knew. I recalled the brilliant, self-confident journalist, wearing designer suits and hand-made shoes. The man I met in the wilderness told me bluntly, "She doesn't want to see you." Philip wore a pair of threadbare jeans and a baggy pullover. I had to admit he still looked very attractive.

"I don't want to talk to you," he said gruffly.

I simply went on climbing the precipitous and bare slope. There was no grass on it, no trees. Rocks and heaps of sand were all over the place. The dust was black, knee-deep, and unpleasantly hot. Thistles and anemic prickly plants sulked into the silence of the afternoon. I walked on, paying attention to Philip Mill.

"I'll set the dogs on you," he said.

It was true I was a woman of numerous foibles and weakness. One way or another, cowardice was not one of them.

"You set the dogs on me, and I'll shoot them dead," I answered.

Philip Mill didn't say anything. I saw him run towards the top of the hill. The dust hid him from my eyes. I had to admit he was an extremely handsome man. Three minutes later, a silhouette of a big mutt set upon me. I didn't see the dog, maybe it was the whisper of the thick dust that helped me discern a threatening presence, or maybe I simply heard the beast's shallow breathing. I shot at the silhouette, and an agonizing wail ripped the silence.

"I told you I'll shoot your dog, Philip," I shouted.

There was no answer. When the cloud of dust settled, I saw a woman, willowy and slender, outlined against the gray rocks of the hill.

"Wanga," I called out. She did not move or say anything. I ran to her, but the woman slowly turned around and gracefully, like a bird, climbed up the slope as she vanished out of sight. I stood, wondering if I had really seen anybody on that hill.

"You shouldn't have set your pooch on me," I muttered.

That was my first encounter with Wanga. I was not scared. The best policy was to bide my time.

After Philip Mill published his sensational essay about Wanga, crowds of people from the whole Dusk region thronged Bare Mountain three times a year: 20 April, that was Philip's birthday, 20 July, the day when I killed his dog on the mountain slope, and 20 November, Wanga's birthday.

I started writing my monograph on Wanga on 20 November. On that day, early in the morning, I put on an old sweater, a frazzled pair of jeans and my housekeeper's old boots. I hated the adjective *old* when it qualified my clothes. I had no old clothes. My autumn wardrobe was rich and expensive, all my shoes were hand-made, Italian or French, and I felt cheap in the ancient, frazzled coat I had bought from a second-hand shop. I didn't want to attract uninvited eyes, so I waited amid the caravan of boneshakers, all low-priced and rusty, that rumbled along the dirt road to Wanga's dilapidated stone hut. I drove an old ruin of a car I had rented in the town of Dusk. To be honest, I looked forward to seeing Wanga. I was curious. I hoped I could throw light on the mystery as to how she stole Philip Mill from me, not that I cared much. I had countless blessings, and I was sorry the woman was blind. She couldn't see how pretty I was.

I wanted to determine if the tales the tabloids wrote about her were at least partially true.

The editor-in-chief of the *Dusk Daily* had informed me that every year on 20 November Wanga emerged from her hut dressed in a white woolen garment. It didn't make any difference to her if a guy didn't have a penny to bless himself with. She would stare at the multitude, the editor-in-chief told me, her empty eyes sinking into the night, her tall, thin body trembling A tall man dressed in a long white shirt held her hand. The editor-in-chief of the *Dusk Daily* assured me Wanga's *husband* didn't talk to anybody. His face was handsome and attractive. Didn't I know how attractive it was? I had kissed it many times. The editor-in-chief made it a special point that the man in the long woolen shirt was Philip, his former brilliant reporter.

I was very curious to see Philip.

The dirt road ended in a gorge, from which a muddy and rapid stream gushed out. Rotten cars, some still exuding suffocating smoke, were parked along the steep sides of the ravine. The people, young and old, trudged up the hill. I followed a man and a woman, the man carrying a small sickly girl in his arms, the woman's shoulders drooping. I had jammed a cheap hat on my head, and I wore dark glasses although the light was fading. I looked shabby in my old clothes and brogues I had bought from the sleaziest second-hand shop I found after a thorough search in the poorest neighborhoods of Dusk. I was sure no one could recognize me, although I was a woman that often participated in glamorous TV shows and revealed my unorthodox views on gender equality.

The hill was steep. Tired feet stirred the dust, clouds of sand were in the air, the wind was stiff and sharp, and in the distance, wails of strange animals pierced the sullen, low sky. There was still a long way to go to the top of Bare Mountain. The fair-haired girl groaned in her father's arms, and her mother quickly offered her a bottle of water. In front of us other men and women, all glum, walked on in silence, their coats flapping in the wind. A huge heap of stones crowned the hill. If all I'd read in the articles was true, every stone was someone's misery, a tale of humiliation. Someone had furtively carried the ill-fated thing to the top, had thrown it behind his back and had run away as quickly as possible. There was another impressive heap, of rusty plates and pans, like skeletons of dangerous-looking animals, rotting in the moist thick air. Every plate was a sort of pain. Midway between the two mounds of despair and hate, a tumbledown hut blended with the crags and the sand. Its roof was flat, made of sandstone slabs.

People clustered around the stone piles, no one daring to cross a shallow furrow dug in the dust. The people, who had already reached the top waited, pressing each other, silent, fidgeting nervously. A narrow square space remained empty in front of the dilapidated hut. The newcomers behind our backs tried to push their way closer to the heap of dirty pans, but those before them refused to budge. We were a bitter throng. I didn't know what I had to expect. What was going to happen next? The eyes of the people around me waited, some glued to the stone hut, others watching intently the empty space in front of it.

It was cold, and in the distance, the wails of strange animals mingled with the persistent gurgle of the faraway stream in the gorge. No one paid attention to me. I studied the faces of men and women as I felt the dust rise and creep up my neck and face. A hush fell over the heaps of rusty stones. A thin figure emerged from the stone hut. I could swear I didn't hear any noise as she padded across the empty space to the furrow dug in the dust. A tall man dressed in a black shabby suit followed her.

I thought I had forgotten Philip Mill. I was sure I had met much more attractive men than him; after him, I had had lovers far more ardent than he had ever been. I believed Philip belonged to my past and I was confident I didn't care where he was or what did. When I saw him, holding that woman's hand, I hated myself. The way he looked at her! It was the worst defeat I had ever suffered. Philip Mill was the only man I cared about.

A girl in a dark coat crossed the furrow and took a step forward.

"Please, Wanga," she sobbed. "Make him come back to me."

"I cannot," the crackling voice of the woman rustled. "I can only see green dots going away with him. He will go away. The sooner you understand that the better."

"Will my son recover? Tell me, Wanga, please," a woman rushed to the slender figure that stared above the heads of the throng, above the winds and the sky. Wanga didn't answer. She walked past the multitude, her face dead, as if she was far away from the heap of stones and the black dust.

"Not your wife." Wanga pushed a face she had inadvertently touched. "Your house burned down a month ago. You set fire to it. You want your wife dead, but she'll outlive you."

A cry rent the silent, charged air.

"I didn't want to kill her," a man's voice rasped as the thin woman walked past him. Philip Mill supported her, his eyes on her face.

"Your daughter is … dangerous!" the prophetess breathed addressing the couple that had been walking in front of me all the way to the top of Bare Mountain. "Go home. Don't take her to Doctor Ivan Georg at Iztok

Clinic in Dusk. Don't." Then the prophetess shook. "Your daughter … this child … I can see her … she's dangerous, dangerous … her green dots …"

The mother sobbed, and the man, carrying the sickly child heaved a deep sigh. I stole a good look at the girl, a puny thing, fair hair, blue eyes, and no color in the cheeks.

"Will my daughter recuperate from her heart surgery, Wanga? Please, Wanga, please tell me!" a man elbowed his way towards the blind woman, but she turned her back on him, saying no word. The wind was blowing hard now, the dust was cold and Bare Mountain was an enormous heap of ice under my feet.

"Wanga, what can I do for my daughter?" an old woman called out.

"What must I do to save my mom?" a teenage boy shouted.

The blind woman did not listen to the shouts. She advanced past the man who held the sickly child, past the sobbing woman and suddenly she was in front of me. Philip Mill followed her, a silent shadow. The crowd parted, letting her pass, outstretched hands trying to touch her white shapeless dress. The bolder women whispered to Philip, "Give her this!" and thrust a faded T-shirt into his hands, but he would not take anything, and the absurd article of clothing fell onto the ground, stirring up the dust.

"When your mom left you," the blind woman's crackling voice echoed. "You thought you could hide behind the glasses from your aunt."

I had never told anyone my mother had run away from home. My father's sister, a lonely prudish lawyer, adopted me after Dad went out to buy groceries and never came back to our house in the town of Dusk. I called my aunt *Mom,* and I told no one, not even Philip Mill, that my parents had abandoned me like a foul-smelling box of junk food.

"You are wrong," I said.

"I know who you are," then the crackling voice softened. "You still keep her blouse, the only thing she has left you, in your closet."

That was true. I kept my mother's blouse. I had always hoped to meet her one day. She wouldn't be pretty the way she was when she left me. I knew what I'd do. In my dreams, she was old and frail. I was strong and famous. I would give her back her old blouse I had been keeping in my closet for years. That blouse knew all about my fears, about the boys

I was in love with, about the misery of loneliness I lived with. I didn't have parents. Maybe I loved Philip Mill just because he had abandoned me the way my mother had done. Maybe that was the reason I still kept his shirt in my closet. I told the shirt everything about my new lovers.

"You are wrong," I repeated.

"You still want him," she went on, ignoring my words. "Poor, poor …"

"Sara! You again!" Philip Mill shouted. "I don't want to see you. Stop dogging me."

"Don't flatter yourself," I said.

Suddenly the blind woman shouted, "Don't do that!"

The people listened.

"If you know me, you cannot calm down," I said. She failed to impress me. Someone must have told Philip about what sort of a woman my mom was. My aunt who had adopted me referred to my mother as "the lowly debauchee," an expression that terrified me when I was a little girl. I thought it was a horrible disease and I was convinced my mother had died in agony. Then I came to know that a life of debauchery could have positive aspects to it.

"You think there is no one strong enough to stop you," the blind woman said. "You are wrong."

"Go away!" Philip Mill said. I knew this tone of voice too well. It meant a lonely glass of whisky at midnight for me.

"Go to your brother," said the blind woman, her face cold as the dust on the road.

"I don't have a brother," I said.

"Your brother in Dusk …" she repeated. "He had a tumor in his head."

"I don't have a brother," I repeated.

"After the doctors removed the tumor, he speaks an old language. No, I'm wrong … it's not a language … He speaks about you."

Her face darkened.

The crowd was staring at me.

"Don't kill him. That fair-haired girl … what is she doing to your brother?" she breathed. Philip Mill caught her before she collapsed in the middle of the empty square of barren land.

It started raining. The first heavy raindrops hit the dust like horse's hooves. Bare Mountain was quickly turning into a mudslide. Some rushed to the bottom of the gorge where they had parked their cars. The two heaps, one of stones, the other of rotting pans seemed to float in the flood. The fearful Bare Mountain roared and creaked under the hammers of the torrential rain.

Philip Mill carried the charlatan to the shabby hut. A young woman took off her coat and rushed after the couple, shouting, "Wanga, please, take it."

I followed Philip Mill.

"Look here, she has to tell me more," I started.

He seemed to carry the blind woman with ease. It seemed she was as light as a handful of sand. Philip whistled sharply and a dog, as big as a cloud, pounced on me.

"Don't!" the crackling voice of the woman hit my ears. But it was too late. I hated barking dogs; however, I hated biting dogs even more. I took out my gun and shot. The dog yelped and gave out a high-pitched wail. After a short while, Bare Mountain was quiet again.

At that point, the blind quack did something I could find no explanation for. She waved her hands and out of thin air birds flew above her shabby shoulders. I saw that sickly fair-haired girl strolling all alone in the mist. Poor brat! One of the birds hit the muddy ground before me. I still remember the cold shiver that ran down my back. The black beak dug a deep round crater in the ground then, making no noise, the thing fluttered its wings and vanished in the rain.

It was cold and the rain had just stopped. Professor Andrew Gils looked at his patient, a middle-aged woman, a purple patch on her face as big as a box of matches. He had just told her she had a few more months to live. He knew her well. She sat there, gaunt and ashen faced, looking at the floor.

"I am ready to go," she had said. Then something in the room changed—was it the light that played on the walls, or perhaps the wind had stirred the curtain? It grew dark, although it was 1 PM. The doctor turned around and saw it—a flock of birds, their shadows so thick they seemed to devour the day. The birds were big. They fluttered their wings, but he could hear no noise. He smiled. Those ravens or were they blackbirds, hung in the air, obstructing the view. The professor was very tired, but then he felt happy for no apparent reason.

He turned to his patient. He rubbed his eyes as he stood up.

"What is it, Professor Gils?" the woman asked. She looked at him calmly. Nothing could frighten her.

"The spot on your face …" the doctor said.

She stared at him.

"Mrs. Robinson, the sore on your face is gone. It is impossible!"

Chapter Two

No one noticed anything wrong with the birds. The town of Dusk was not big, and in the autumn, it looked even smaller, the houses gray and sleepy under the thick clouds. The wind was stiff, the trees and the grass moaned and creaked with it, the people hurried to work or came back home, trying to escape from the cold as quickly as possible. No one seemed to notice the flock that hovered over the schoolyard. There's nothing extraordinary about these birds, Peter Stan, the teacher in the local high school, thought. He and his biology students were in the schoolyard collecting yellow maple leaves.

Ravens, though their wings look somehow formless. Too quiet, Mr. Stan said to himself, almost the color of asphalt.

Tony, the laziest student, in his biology class, said, "Mr. Stan, look!"

One of the birds had perched on a thin branch of the birch, and the teacher was just about to say, "It's just a raven, trying to take a nap in the autumn," but then he noticed something. The branch of the birch broke under the weight of the bird. It was not that big, but another, thicker branch bent to the ground under its black wings.

The flock hovered overhead as quiet as the shadow of a kite. Two ravens swooped down and landed on the ground. The asphalt cracked, and the two blackbirds sank into it. Their heads jutted out of it like a pair of strange mushrooms. The weird pair jumped out of the holes they'd dug and soared into the sky. The old teacher breathed, beads of perspiration glistening on his brow. The flock of grayish-black feathered creatures, as thick as a doormat, perched in the middle of the schoolyard, under the big lamp. The pavement gave away and the birds sank into the paving blocks. There was not a sound, not the slightest rustle as ravens pressed the stones, cracking them under their talons.

"I'll show them!" Tony shouted. Some of the boys and girls jumped.

Tony was already brandishing his satchel, shouting "Shoo!" The birds didn't seem to notice him. They pressed against each other, persistent, clumsy, their color gradually changing, becoming darker.

"Shoo!" Tony bawled as he ran to the hole in the middle of the schoolyard. The birds didn't seem to mind. Their black backs didn't budge; their wings fluttered, soundlessly as if the feathers were made of air. Tony hit at their heads with his satchel. One of the birds left the others and darted up to the streetlamp. For a split second, its body was motionless and the next instant the bird thudded on the pavement, its beak splitting the gray stone into pieces.

Two things happened instantaneously: the whole flock soared into the clouds, dozens of wings moving in unison, and for a moment the sky was black with wings. Tony screamed. His face was pale, his lips quivered. The wounded bird tried to crawl, stopped, its round head drooping.

"It will die," Tony whispered.

The flock came back and hovered above Mr. Stan's head. One of the ravens perched on Tony's shoulder. The boy bent down. Then he was down on his knees, his head pressed against the pavement.

"Tony … Hey, Tony, are you okay?" the old teacher asked. His student who a minute ago was screaming with pain was now smiling."

The boy was silent as the gray flock circled above his head.

"I'll take care of him," Tony said.

The bird he had hurt lay motionless on the stones. The hole it had dug was full of gray dust. No one knew where the dust had come from. The flock stayed in the air a minute more, then took to the sky, a black cloud of noiseless feathers as if the wings were wind.

Autumn came back to the schoolyard. The old teacher thought this might have been another of his dreams. He had strange dreams, and this was only natural for a person who had been teaching naughty boys and girls for forty years now. Sometimes he wished he was a writer, but he knew he was just an ordinary old man who would soon have to say goodbye to the classroom and his students.

The schoolyard was peaceful again the way it was in his dreams. They all ended in a sunny classroom with a class of smiling children, but … There was the big hole that the ravens had carved in the pavement of the schoolyard in the town of Dusk. There was a handful of dust that the injured bird had left in its wake.

The teacher bent and tried to collect it in his handkerchief.

His fingers burned.

She was a very good-looking woman; Professor Andrew Gils couldn't ignore that fact. What was her name? Bagd? Yes, she was Boya Bagd, the occupational therapist, the quiet one, so the professor was really surprised as she spoke to him in an urgent voice.

"Professor Gils, we simply must not reschedule this surgical operation. Please, do something! Ivan Georg is … he's dear to me."

Andrew Gils waited. Her hair was red like the dance of a dozen candle flames, and she had a worried look on her face.

"Could you, please operate on him?" Then she added nervously, almost inaudibly, "Please operate on him, Professor Gils! Ivan is … my boyfriend."

The pretty occupational therapist blushed scarlet.

Chapter Three

Ivan Georg thought he saw a sparrow in his room, but he wasn't really sure. He still had double vision after the brain surgery. Professor Andrew Gils had said the tumor in his brain was benign, but they were able to remove only seventy to eighty percent of it. Professor Gils had neutralized the remaining part of the tumor through Gamma Knife treatment. Two days ago, Ivan Georg learned to walk again after weeks of reeling and staggering. He loved the sun in the sky and the wind in the field. He was sure his name was Ivan, and he was twenty-five. They gave him pills that made him drowsy, and in his half-dream half-reality he saw many beautiful things: sunlit meadows, his flat on 3 Nopius Street with the big books on chemistry, neurology, psychiatry. He saw Boya, too. In his dreams, she often visited him in the clinic, a bottle of apple juice in hand. After his surgery, Ivan didn't look good. He could not close his left eye.

This is another of my dreams, he thought after he saw the bird on his bedside table, an odd, feathered thing, entirely black.

There was something wrong with it. The bird beat its wings against the wall; however, Ivan could hear no noise. This didn't come as a surprise; he had a complete loss of hearing in his left ear, and there were no sounds in his dreams. Very rarely, he could catch soothing words Boya had whispered to him. That black bird—was it a sparrow, a raven?—had just perched on the floor.

"Hey!" Ivan called out. The blackbird jumped jerkily onto the table where Ivan had left his lunch untouched and pecked at the glass tabletop.

Ivan's hand trembled; however, the feathered creature didn't appear to be scared of his jittery fingers. It flew to Ivan and perched on his head. I wish the dream never ended, Ivan thought. Now, he was convinced he was only dreaming. It was impossible for such a small raven to be so heavy. Its talons felt warm.

"Hey, what are you doing?" Ivan said as the heavy silent feathers touched his skin and the birdie climbed up his neck.

It gently pecked his head and the hard touch of its beak felt pleasant. Ivan Georg hoped Boya would come into his dream and the dark wings would go on hopping up and down on his neck. He hoped in vain. The nurse had left the door ajar; the bird flew out through the narrow opening, silent as Ivan's pillow. Ivan knew: no sparrow or raven could be that unobtrusive, and it was not a happy dream. Boya was not in it.

Behind the window, autumn was playing with the leaves of the trees, giving the clouds its cold glistening gold. The roofs were wet, the wind stumbled over the houses: a perfect day to think about Boya and a silent bird. Ivan Georg couldn't go for a walk because of the rain. He remembered something puzzling about his dream. He wasn't even sure it was a dream; everything in it had been so real.

A thin little girl, blonde hair, clear blue eyes, sat down by his side and put his hand on his forehead. Everything became so quiet, so serene and Ivan thought he was going to die. That little girl gave him peace. She was the sister he had wanted all his life. He had needed a sister to protect. He had reached his hand to her, then she was suddenly gone.

His good eye couldn't concentrate on printed texts, it leapt from line to line, and he could only try to remember old poems he had once read. He saw the places the poet told him about, and he tried to send letters to Boya in his mind, very cheerful letters, in which he promised her he would be all right. Very often he wrote to her how sorry he was he hadn't told her what she meant to him. He hoped she knew. She was so clever.

It was time for Ivan's speech therapy. He felt stronger than usual. His left hand had stopped trembling. "I am imagining things," he said to himself. He did notice something, a small heap of blackish feathers on the floor. Yes, feathers, looking very soft, warm and thin, but after Ivan lifted one of them, he froze in his tracks. The feather was as heavy as his pair of shoes. It's the brain surgery! he thought. Ivan remembered the bird he had seen in his room before he went to sleep. The memory of the soft gentle touch, the soothing warmth of the talons on his skin was still there. Now the feathers lay on the floor, a whole heap of them.

"That bird …" he tried to say aloud and failed.

He spattered, gurgled, hissed and coughed, unable to breathe. The nurse and Professor Andrew Gils rushed into his room.

"Ivan, what do you feel?" the Professor asked.

Ivan felt like answering he was okay, but instead of saying it, words in a bizarre, foreign language he didn't know erupted from his mouth.

"What?" the doctor asked, astonished. "What are you telling me?"

Ivan wanted to explain didn't understand a word of what he was babbling. He felt like speaking about the blackbird or the raven he had seen in his room, and he wanted to show the nurse the feathers he had found on the floor. He could not stop jabbering. The sounds kept pouring out of his mouth, cutting through the air like hailstones. He forbade himself to think about the bird and its feathers, and he thought he saw Boya. It was true she was a couple of years older than him, but that didn't matter, did it? He was so happy when one day he kissed her. Thinking about Boya, he stopped blabbering.

"Young man, tell me everything in plain English," the professor, always a polite, composed professional, said. "I like your native language, but I couldn't make heads or tails of what you were speaking about a minute ago."

"My native language is English, Professor Gils," Ivan answered.

"Then translate into English what you've just said," Professor Gils urged him.

"I don't understand a word of what I've just blurted out," Ivan said.

"Come off it, young man," the polite professor said, trying to smile. "I know what you've gone through. It has been hard on you."

"Professor Gils, look," the nurse said. "He can close his left eye. He's been unable to do that for weeks."

"Yes, he was sick," the professor said.

"Have you spoken like that before, Doctor Ivan Georg?" the nurse asked.

"No," Ivan said.

It was warm in the hospital room. The window gave a wonderful view to St. Nicholas Cathedral and to the autumn that offered its gold to the trees in the city. There was a book on Ivan Georg's bedside table, an intriguing maxim printed in yellow letters on the gray front cover: *Accept death as a door to a world you'll love.*

"Ivan, what's that nonsensical brochure on your bedside table?" the nurse asked.

Ivan Georg didn't have the energy to explain. "Boya Bagd," he breathed, feeling that the name of the woman he saw in his dreams made him sad.

The nurse smiled at him.

"I understand … Boya Bagd," she said. "A very pretty woman. What goes around comes around, Doctor Georg." The woman smiled again, glanced at the patient and asked, "And what's this thing in your hand?"

Ivan saw he was still holding the feathers of that strange bird. He opened his mouth to explain, but again gibberish in a language he didn't understand gushed from his mouth. He simply couldn't stop chattering.

"What?" The nurse stared at Ivan.

Ivan saw the little fair-haired girl that had drifted amid the chaos of his dreams the week before. He had thought … This time he was convinced he was going to die. *Accept death as a door to a world you'll love.*

Then the fair-haired girl was gone.

"Whose is this brochure here?" the nurse asked.

Ivan slept.

Chapter Four

"Interesting," Professor Gils said, looking at the young man. "You have never heard that language before, Doctor Georg?"

"I have never heard such *phrases,*" the young man said. "I was spewing out phrases uncontrollably after the Gamma Knife treatment, i.e., after you neutralized the tumor."

"Any particular event that might have triggered this outpouring of hissing rumble?" Professor Gils looked at his patient who stared vacantly at the wall. It was autumn, the air was pure gold, and a caravan of thick gray clouds crept in the sky.

"Perhaps a storm broke that day?" the Professor suggested. "Perhaps you had a bad headache? Or somebody told you something that provoked the outburst of unintelligible gibberish?" Professor Gils spoke quietly.

"It just happened," the young man said thoughtfully.

"Think," the Professor said. "You mentioned something about a bird. A bird was in your room. Did it frighten you?"

Ivan was twenty-six years old, a tall man. He wore glasses, and his legs were still not strong enough.

"I remember the bird," he said slowly. "How did it find its way into my hospital room? I had not opened the windows, and the door was closed all the time. That day, I was alone in the room. In the beginning, I thought I had been dreaming or … it could be the effect of the antidepressants the nurse had given me."

"What happened after you realized the bird was real?" Professor Gils insisted.

"You know, Professor, after the brain surgery, the left side of my face was paralyzed, I had double vision," Ivan began. "I thought the bird helped me somehow. That day I closed my left eye."

"The nurse told me that every night you left crumbs on the windowsill," the professor said sympathetically.

"I hoped the bird would come back," Ivan said.

"Did it?"

"Unfortunately, not," the young man sighed. "I wish it did."

"Why?"

There was a long silence. The wind hit the windowpanes and they sang. The office was very clean. Professor Gils was notorious for his maniacal cleanliness. His white coat shone, his glasses glittered, and his shoes sparkled, everything immaculately spotless, ironed and disinfected. His white, almost transparent hands rested in his lap.

"That day I felt happy for no reason at all, Professor," Ivan said. "I mean I felt healthy after I stopped prattling away in that … that language. It did me good."

"Fortunately, I recorded all your *gibberish*. I listened to it several times," Professor Gils fell silent, a flitting smile lighting up his thin sharp face. "Your endless blather made me … how I shall put it? My headache was gone."

"I bought a bird from the pet shop and let it fly in my room," Ivan said. "I lay in the same bed, and I used the same blanket. My mouth produced no sound."

"The mess of barking and chortling noises you produced seemed hardly bearable," Professor Gils smiled thinly. "My dog Spotty listened to it and I could hardly recognize him. He was so calm and gentle. So, I let my mother listen to the gibberish. *A blessed night,* she said."

It was so quiet one could hear a pin drop.

After a long silence the young man breathed, "I'd like to listen to the gibberish, Professor Gils."

"Your bad headaches could come back," Professor Gils said.

The voice was unmistakably Ivan's.

The jingle it produced was ear-splitting, a sharp dry cough, thinning into hysterical giggles. Every combination of sounds was a boiling cauldron of spite, a cascade of chuckles that turned into piercing wails. One word or was it a phrase?—seemed to edge its way to the surface above the din. Trun! Trun! Trun! Ivan's gibberish started with *Trun.* It swam amid the hurtling wasteland of hisses and hiccups. It cut through the havoc of speech that had no words in it. It was a single monolithic wheeze. Suddenly, a final, powerful Trun! spurted out of the recording machine.

"Ugly," the professor said after a minute.

"You are smiling, Professor," Ivan said.

"I thought about my mother," Gils said. "She's a strange woman … Ivan? Ivan!"

Ivan did not answer him. He was fast asleep, smiling, his breathing deep and regular. "Boya," he blurted out.

Who is Boya? Professor Gils thought. The pretty occupational therapist, the quiet one who visited Ivan in the intensive care unit? She hadn't come back. Poor Ivan. Professor Gils felt like adding something, but he forgot what he was about to say. He fell asleep, his white coat immaculate, his shoes spotless, a childish smile on his lips.

Somebody knocked at the door and a thin woman entered the office. She threw a glance at the sleeping professor, as she slowly walked to the young man, who had spoken the weird language. She produced a miniature syringe from her coat pocket and carefully pointed it at his wrist.

Ivan suddenly opened his eyes.

"Boya," he whispered, unbelieving. "I thought I was only dreaming …"

The woman thrust the syringe under her coat.

"I was looking for you, Ivan," she said.

Chapter Five

Peter Stan, the biology teacher, was in a cheery mood. The dull pain under his breastbone was gone. In the mornings, it had been so acute that he had to stay in bed, but now there was no trace of it. His fingers didn't tremble. Was he imagining things? There was another surprise; he looked at the newspaper and to his utter bewilderment, he could read without his glasses. Stunned, he touched his eyes. He was reading—not only the glaring headlines, not even the captions. He was reading the words in the footnotes, which only a week ago he read with the help of a magnifying glass. *I am imagining things!* He wished he could hear his wife's constant remarks on his wild imagination; they set his nerves on edge, it was true, but now that she was gone, he missed her.

"Impossible," she said when he tried to talk to her about his ideas on education. He believed that even the worst students, the bullies, would behave with dignity if you respected their opinion. His wife Margaret, a math professor, whose hobby was artificial intellects and artificial languages, used to say that the only way to influence bullies was to put a bullet through their heads. She was a cynic at times, and more often than not, she was an unrelenting opponent of his weaknesses. Peter Stan's mild temperament and his ability to yield to her arguments without hating her, transformed Margaret into his best friend, his judge, and into the woman he loved.

"You know what, Margaret," he spoke to her clothes which he left on the chair by his bed. "I can read the tiniest print in the newspaper. I know you won't believe me, but it's true." Then he went on telling her clothes that he missed her. "You won't believe me, Margaret, but it's true. I hate it when you are not at home. I hope you'll come back soon."

Peter Stan walked an hour and a half every day. A week ago, the teacher saw a thin little girl: fair hair, blue eyes. He had not seen this kid walking past their house before.

"Where is your mommy, child?" he asked.

The girl said nothing as she slowly backed away.

Strange, the teacher thought. Perhaps he should call the police? No. You don't want to become a nosy old man, Peter, do you?

Then he thought about his wife.

Poor Margaret. She was working on one of her crazy projects again. Quite secretive, the woman wouldn't tell him what exactly she was doing. A year ago, she quarreled with their son Thomas. Margaret didn't approve of Boya, their son's partner; however, Peter found nothing wrong with her. His wife had asked Thomas and his girlfriend to dinner. Peter couldn't quite get to the bottom of it. Margaret declared she found Boya doing something on her computer. That is far-fetched, honestly, was the old teacher's opinion. Margaret suspected everyone was after her experiments, especially her nosy opponents. She refused to tell Peter what she had said to poor Boya, their son's girlfriend.

The young woman never again set foot in their neighborhood, let alone their house. Mother and son fought, and Thomas, their quiet boy, screamed and raged, Thomas of all people who had never lied to them, never shouted abuse at anybody! Margaret remained silent, indomitable, tough. Peter had tried to reconcile them, he did.

"Tom," he had said, "Your mother didn't really mean what she said."

At that point Margaret said, "Your girlfriend is a thief, Thomas. I do mean every word of what I said. She uses you as a key to my project."

Thomas screamed that his mother saw ghosts. In his opinion, she was a mediocre scientist, a hypocrite and a liar. He added he didn't want to see her anymore.

Thomas vanished. Boya called, though. She informed Margaret that Thomas was admitted to Dusk County hospital with broken legs and a smashed shoulder blade. Boya was busy. She could not remain with him in that sleazy hole, so could renowned Professor Stan take care of her pampered son? The young woman had sold Thomas' computer, Thomas' car, and Thomas' bed because Thomas owed her money, and she felt she had to take it back from him. Peter and Margaret found their son in the county hospital, in the intensive care unit.

"Your son tried to commit suicide, Madam," the doctor, a gray-haired man, said. "His life has been hanging by a thread for weeks. A very beautiful girl was with him after the road accident. She wouldn't tell me her name. Yes, you are right, Madam. Your son gave her money. Yes, I know that for sure because he borrowed five hundred Euros from me and gave her everything, to the last cent. Madam, your son was ready to sell one of his kidneys; he needed money badly. No, Madam, I would not encourage anybody to sell his kidney or retina, or whatsoever. Of course not, Madam, do not worry."

Thomas saw his parents at the door of his hospital room and croaked, "Go away."

Margaret rushed to his bed. Thomas snarled, "Take one more step and I'll hit you."

Margaret went away to work on her projects in Dusk. In her laboratory, there were more video surveillance cameras than computers on the numerous tables. Peter's wife refused to come back home where every object, the air and the dust on the floor reminded her of Thomas. Even Peter reminded her of Thomas, so she could hardly stand him. "Peter and his aches and pains," Margaret muttered. "His son is just like him."

I can't lie to people, and he can't either, Peter Stan thought.

The pain in his chest was gone, the colic symptoms gave him no more trouble, and his breathing was even and powerful. I wish Margaret was at home with me now, he thought. I wish Thomas was here, too.

In the beginning, Peter couldn't believe his eyes. What he saw didn't make sense and couldn't be true. Down the lane, in the thick autumn rain, his wife Margaret walked, smiling and pretty, her hair no longer salt and pepper. She had dyed it light brown, and she looked young. She was talking to Thomas. Their son was smiling at her.

"I have a screw loose," the old teacher muttered.

The rain was heavy and persistent, the windows looked darker now, and Peter Stan thought his loneliness was a stone in his stomach.

"Peter!" his wife's eager voice swam through the clouds.

"Dad!" his son called out.

But weren't Thomas' legs broken? How come his boy recuperated so rapidly?

The teacher rubbed his eyes.

"How are you, old man?" his wife said. "Well, I must say you look good!"

A thought crossed Peter Stan's mind about the heavy blackbirds, the flock in the schoolyard and the huge hole in the asphalt. The pain in his chest had gone, and he could read the smallest print in Margaret's newspaper. For once, his wife and his son weren't fighting.

Too good to be true.

"I'm home," his son hugged him tightly.

"Thomas!" the teacher breathed. "I called you several times, Margaret," Peter Stan said, his eyes on her face. You didn't pick up the phone."

"Nothing seems to make you happy, Peter," she said.

Peter Stan looked up. He saw the little fair-haired, blue-eyed girl in the street in front of their house.

Chapter Six

If Wanga, the so-called soothsayer of Bare Mountain, imagined she had frightened me, I'd soon let her know she'd got the wrong end of the stick.

I remembered her long dress white against the black endless sky and I saw the women, their eyes riveted on blind Wanga. I called her charlatan. This word gave me satisfaction, yet her long white robe, her slim figure, so graceful and trim, haunted me. I couldn't forget the way Philip Mill looked at her. She wasn't pretty, wasn't even presentable, but I could not forget my mother's favorite saying: *Beauty is in the eye of the beholder.*

My mother had her moments of wisdom, I granted her that. She was smart with men. When she married her second or third husband, I remember having asked her, "You are not pretty. Why are those men running after you?" It was then she told me whose eye beauty cared about. She was very rich now, married to a man twenty-one years her junior, and when I last visited her, she said I was not most welcome to her house. Mother was afraid her new baby would succumb to my youthful charm. Every time I summoned up the image of my mother, I thought of scabies, a disease that caused severe itching and red spots on the skin. I didn't love her. I thought of Philip Mill and his prophetess. He was the only man who had jilted me, pining for a woman that was older and undoubtedly much less attractive than me. Every time I pronounced his name, I felt like going to bed with him. I tried hard to ignore the insulting rattle in his voice when he called my name. I invited men to my place and forgot them soon after they went out. I avenged myself on Philip by making other men suffer, and I made sure they suffered a lot.

I had read numerous articles on the myths and legends popular in the Dusk Gorge region, finding nothing of interest: bloodthirsty ghouls that snatched babies from their cradles, the usual evil spirits who punished the unfaithful husbands and wives. I didn't believe the unfaithful husbands should be punished. Divorce was a civilized method of breaking a man's heart and draining his bank accounts.

At some point, I stumbled upon a review article, "Samodivas: Truth or Mystification," and read that the Dusk region, a large and wild mountainous area in the western part of Bulgaria along the Struma River, was the Samodivas' homeland.

The Old Bulgarians, poor buggers all, assumed that in the beginning of the world, Samodivas were spirits that lived high up in the mountains. At a certain point, they settled in men's thoughts and conquered men's desires. The villagers saw a Samodiva rarely; she looked like an ordinary woman in a white robe, padding across a meadow. There are still villages in the Dusk region where old men fear a Samodiva could entice them into committing a sin. Some youths were convinced a Samodiva in your thoughts was a blessing. She either showed you the way towards the gold coins some fool had, or, above all, she could provide you with marital bliss.

The majority of the locals, however, were adamant that a Samodiva in your thoughts was a curse. She was believed to transform the guy whose thoughts she managed into a bloodthirsty pye-dog.

No one could seize a Samodiva, the article explained. Often, the evil Samodivas gathered together to dance in the moonlight or bathe in the streams. Bulgarians believed that if you could touch a Samodiva's white robe, she'd obey your orders. This contradicted the ancient legend, which had it that a Samodiva obeyed no one, yet she'd do everything for the man she was besotted with or *held very dear,* if you were in favor of linguistic purism.

The author of the article was Philip Mill.

I thought of the blind woman, and, in my mind, I saw my ex-fiancé. What if I stole the prophetess' white robe?

Wanga is a Samodiva. *Oh, give me a break,* I whispered to myself.

I could try my hand at pilfering her garment, and I'd do it just to spite the only guy I'd ever had a soft spot for.

I concentrated on the article. The long white robe, the slim figure, the stark mountain top, the heaps of stones and rusting pans came back to me in a flash.

Then I read a paragraph that sounded even more interesting.

It said that from time immemorial, there lived prophets or oracles who claimed they could actually *see* the Samodivas. The Samodivas had taken command of men's dreams, the fortune-tellers argued. Some seers were able to detect a Samodiva *hidden* amid men's desires. This sounded absurd to me. The author of the article, my ex-fiancé, elaborated on the so-called fortune telling phenomenon: the Samodiva led the man, whose mind she had chosen to inhabit, from event to event, from one village to another. In some historical sources, the Samodiva was referred to as man's fate.

Philip Mill's article focused on the myth of a mysterious man called the Tall Fellow. Years ago, the townsfolk in Dusk Gorge believed this man could defeat death. All other men were simple drivers because they drove their Samodivas from place to place. The Samodivas for their part goaded men's thoughts on as they led the poor fools to success and good fortune. In the end, death came. There were prophets who could tell a villager where his Samodiva wanted to go, i.e., where he had to take her.

Philip Mill contended that some soothsayers—he dubbed them seers, prophetesses, augurs, oracles indiscriminately—were so skilled they could drive the Samodiva out of a man's thoughts. After the Samodiva was expelled from her host's mind, the man was no longer her driver. He was free. Dozens of manuscripts told stories about men who got rid of their Samodiva, but then … from the frying pan into the fire! At this point, I squealed with laughter. The free man went roaming, pining away after his Samodiva, desperately looking for his ruler and tormentor. The free man wrote lovelorn poems, composed heart-felt tunes and became famous bards. At the end of the day, the pessimistic bard lay prostrate before the prophet asking him to please find his beloved Samodiva. Life made no sense without her. Alas, that was not possible. A Samodiva never returned to her driver.

Come off it!

I read on, learning that the village where the Samodivas gathered after they jilted their drivers was called Trun. A-ha, Trun! I knew that depressing place. It was situated on top of Bare Mountain, the highest hill in the Dusk Gorge region. Nowadays, notorious Wanga lived there, and people thronged her hut, tricked into believing she could predict the misfortunes that would strike one day or other. Predict, my foot! My handsome ex-fiancé, Mr. Mill, assumed Wanga was the last seer, a star much more talented than all the prophets of the past century rolled into one. He suggested the community benefit from her.

If you wanted to talk to Wanga, Philip argued, you had to pay a fee, and she'd solve all your problems. The municipality should build her a good solid house in the center of Dusk, and she'd be a respected citizen. The mayor could even provide her with a chapel if it would help her see better whatever she saw. Indeed, the Mayor of Dusk had written a letter to Wanga, offering her the best mansion in town.

On the following day, he received a letter written in black ink. It read:

Do not drive your car on the first Thursday of May.

I do not want the mansion.

The mayor drove his Opel on the first Thursday of May, and nothing happened. He parked his car and as he got out of it a truck hit him and broke his legs.

Oh, come on!

Philip Mill's article ended in a way that I did not like: *Samodivas feared and respected the Tall Fellow who some people called the Hidden One. They believed he or she could destroy death for good.*

Funny, isn't it? I thought. This time, Philip had gone too far. No one should discard death that lightly. The Tall Fellow … where had Philip dug this lie from? The Hidden One … interesting!

I remembered the crowd waiting for Wanga and I thought of the family with the sick child. Another memory came to mind: Wanga's voice and her cold fingers on my wrist. "Don't kill him. Don't kill your brother!"

I had to find out who my brother was, hadn't I? I should go to Wanga's place one more time. I'd talk to her even if this meant I had to strong-arm Philip Mill.

Wait a minute. Wanga predicted my future. Did this mean she had identified the Samodiva who governed my thoughts? Had Wanga seen me at a place where I could kill a man she thought was my brother? On the other hand, did Samodivas stay in every guy's thoughts, or were they squeamish and preferred bigwigs?

I knew what I'd do first thing in the morning. I'd sneak to Wanga's hut on Bare Mountain.

Chapter Seven

It had been a long day. The old teacher Peter Stan was tired. At the end of the lesson, the fifth one in a row that day, Tony said, "I'd like to give you the essay I wrote, sir. It is about the noiseless birds we saw."

"Yes?" the teacher asked.

"I want to find them," the boy said. "Please read the essay and you'll see what I mean." The kid blurted out, "I'll show you what the feathers have done."

"The feathers?" Peter Stan asked.

On his way home, the teacher stopped in the middle of a small square. The hole which the flock of silent birds had dug in the ground was full of dogs and cats. Drops of blood gleamed on some animals' backs and necks; ears and tails had been bitten off. The cats and dogs lay peacefully, huddled together in a brown hirsute heap. Peter saw an empty wheelchair. Among the cats and dogs, a small figure lay, a girl, sprawling at the bottom of the hole. A meager gray cat purred in the child's lap.

"Hey!" the teacher called out.

The child looked up.

"What are you doing?" Stan asked. "These animals … don't look clean."

The child kept mum.

"Do you want me to get you out of the hole?" Stan asked.

"It doesn't hurt," the child said. "It doesn't hurt if I stay in the hole."

"Who brought you here?"

"My mom," the child said.

Another wheelchair came into view. A small pale woman sat in it. She carefully eased the chair into the hole, her face calm, a smile quivering on her lips.

I have to bring Margaret here, the teacher thought. His wife complained of severe headaches. She'd lost weight. He shouldn't waste time. The rows of small houses, all of them white, looked beautiful and peaceful. A patch of red on the windowpane—that was the sunset in Dusk. Peter Stan loved the minutes of the serene sun in the window. Margaret would stop working and would listen to him. It was Peter who did the talking most of the time and didn't mind if Margaret wasn't listening. It was enough she smiled at him, her eyes absentminded, her fingers barely touching the bunch of wild violets he had bought her.

Peter Stan made his way to the flower shop. He took his time as he chose the violets his wife enjoyed so much, thinking about the bottle of wine they'd share.

"Peter!"

He turned around. "Margaret?"

She stood in front of the shop, her face taut.

The florist, an old lady Peter Stan knew well, hurried to them, a glass of water in hand.

"Please drink it, Professor Stan," she said.

Margaret took the glass and forgot to drink from it.

"Peter, I have to show you something," she said. "I could not stay at home," her voice broke.

Peter Stan was worried sick about his wife. She wouldn't complain; he knew his Margaret.

"Everything will be all right," he said.

But it was not all right. She didn't stop by the railway bridge and didn't touch the big poplar tree that cast its shadow on the path to their little white house. She didn't say anything as they entered their living room.

"Listen to this," Margaret said.

The walls of the room spewed gurgling, hissing, horrible sounds. Were these phrases of an unknown language, or was it a dying dog, gasping and choking on its own blood? Was it a tornado that tore open a burning home in which children screamed under the collapsing roof? What was that? Peter Stan's head burst with excruciating pain. His eyes hurt. He could not stand it.

"Margaret!" He grabbed his wife's hand and dragged her out of the hissing nightmare. Amid the whirlwind of crushing, deafening chaos, one word hit his ears. Trun! Trun! Trun!

"Are you okay?" he whispered when they were outside the roaring chaos. Trun! Trun! The walls wailed then everything was perfectly quiet.

"Margaret ..."

She looked at him puzzled, her fingers shaking in his hand.

"I hoped I'd run away," she said. "But it has found me again."

"Found you again?" he said, looking into her gray calm eyes. "You mean the pain?"

"Trun," she said.

"Trun?"

"I'd told you I was working on an artificial language, Peter," Margaret said. "This was a lie. One day I happened to ... I don't know. I recorded it ... No, one day my equipment went mad. Paper spewed from the computer printer. Trun. This word was printed on all the sheets. On that day, our son's girlfriend Boya Bagd, visited us ... after she was gone, the walls of my office started hissing. I recorded the awful sounds. It hurt, but I recorded them. How it hurt!"

"It will go," Peter Stan whispered. "It hurt, but it will go."

"It won't," Margaret said. "It has found me three times."

"Trun," Peter Stan said shuddering.

Then he saw a child in the street, that little girl, the fair-haired one he remembered well.

"Who is this child?" Margaret Stan asked. "I think I've seen her in the street all alone."

His wife looked exhausted and helpless. Peter could not imagine his life without her. He didn't want to live without her. The minute Peter thought she'd break down and cry, Margaret was alert, her eyes sharp, gleaming.

"You know what, Peter?" her sallow face was alive now. "I found a very interesting paragraph in an Old Bulgarian song. The word Trun was repeated eleven times in it."

His wife staggered as he held her against his chest. She's lost weight, Peter Stan thought.

"You are pretty," he said.

"That paragraph is intriguing," she continued.

Once upon a time, less than a century ago, there lived the Tall Fellow who had a small house in Dusk Gorge. He could kill your pain with Trun. This man was able to drive away death from the earth for good. You only have to look for him, shouting Trun! Trun! Death is very strong. This is the reason the Tall Fellow has to stay hidden all the time.

"It's just an old song," Peter Stan said.

"That little fair-haired girl is walking all alone past our house ..." Margaret said, her face pinched. "Look at her."

Chapter Eight

"Ivan, I'd like to show you something," Professor Gils said. Ivan was reading. He had to prepare a presentation in neurology.

"I didn't believe you were interested in the local newspapers," Ivan said. He felt ill at ease. The sick men and women in the clinic looked for him, queuing up to touch him. Professor Gils had given Ivan Georg an office in the hospital, where Ivan let the patients listen to what doctors, nurses, and patients called the *Healing Trun,* the ugly cacophony of the deafening gurgling sounds. Both the sick and the staff members felt much better after they heard the grunting and gasping cacophony. Ivan thought there must be a reason behind this. There must be an explanation why a patient with a brain tumor, to Professor Gils' utter astonishment, was, after six consecutive Healing Trun sessions, a healthy woman.

The news spread like wildfire. At night, when the professor dropped in to check on his patients, he found them whispering … Trun! Trun! Trun! Professor Gils had asked Ivan to inquire after words or phrases the patients had remembered from the Healing Trun. All without exception said they heard *Trun* repeated many times. None knew what this word meant.

"Ivan, I want you to see something," Professor Gils said as he gave the younger man a newspaper. "Read the article on the Samodivas."

"Samodivas? Professor, don't tell me you are interested in ghouls."

"I am not," Gils said.

It was a quiet, cold day, the park was deserted, and it was drizzling. Ivan wondered what the professor was up to. You could never tell what Gils was thinking about. The article was short. Suddenly, Ivan's heart skipped a beat. The author of the article was Boya Bagd. The girl Ivan could not forget.

The article stated that in the Old Bulgarian folk songs: *The Samodivas do not grow old. Disguised as slim, fair-haired women, they stalk men and cast a spell on their victims. Their magic eyes are able to bewitch and kill. These strange creatures hide under white robes and rarely come into view; the Old Bulgarian legends have it that the Samodivas resemble shallow streams of green specks. The Old Bulgarians called them green streaks or green shadows. Samodivas were believed to have danced around wells or mineral springs. The Dusk Gorge dwellers claimed that they could actually see Samodivas during the so-called Dirty Days, the period starting from 15 December and ending on 6 January. It was throughout the Dirty Days that the green streaks went looking for drivers and kidnapped young men.*

Ivan stopped reading. He remembered he was diagnosed with a brain tumor on 27 December; Professor Gils operated on him on 5 January.

The Samodivas gather together under gigantic, old trees which grow near rivers or lakes; they often stay in dark caves full of stagnant water or play near springs and wells. They spend the cold winter days in the mythical village of Trun.

"Trun!" Ivan exclaimed.

"The village of the Samodivas," Professor Gils said.

"Trun … I was ranting and raving about it … The Healing Trun! Professor Gils, are you sure the woman you diagnosed with a brain tumor … are you sure there are no traces of the tumor after she listened to the Healing Trun?"

"I am sure," the professor said.

"I talked to her," Ivan went on. "Now, she's scared to go home."

"That bird in your room you told me about, Ivan. I'd like to know more about it. First read the article to the end, please."

Common mortals, who have seen the dance of the Samodivas, describe it as a devilish flight of big, noiseless birds.

Ivan Georg paused, glancing at Professor Gils.

Samodivas have green eyes that are believed to connect our world to forbidden places outside it. These slim creatures are extremely dangerous. They bring ill luck to the man who meets them; they trigger lethal diseases, often without meaning to.

"I am thinking about the acoustic neuroma, your benign brain tumor," the Professor said.

Ivan read on. *Even today, in the Dusk Gorge region, old Gypsies avoid green-eyed women. The Old Bulgarians believed that a Samodiva would take care of the sick man she loved. The green streaks are believed to possess unnatural skills. They can combat and cure any disease.*

"This article is a waste of paper, Professor," Ivan said.

"Read it to the end," Professor Gils insisted. "Then I'll show you something."

The Samodivas spent cold winter days high in the mountains in shadowy, damp places, which many writers described as unclean, forbidden, and perilous. If a man passed through an area haunted by these vindictive creatures, he had to leave a pot, a pan, or a bowl under a tree there. If he failed to do this, death awaited him at home. The mountain on which the Samodiva village was built was bare and uninviting. No grass, no herbs, no trees grew on it. With time, the whole mountain was covered with old pans that rusted away under the rain. The power and beauty of the Samodivas attracted men. These evil spirits composed of green specks, their hair effervescing with green dots, had myriads of dark secrets.

Ivan smiled as he read. *The inscription on a memorial stone of the 13th century* AD *is of particular interest. It was discovered at excavation site 12 in the town of Dusk: If you know how to please a Samodiva … or … if by chance you make her happy … you and yours will be healthy until the end of time. If you make her angry, she'll take you to your death. Beware of dirt.*

A whole paragraph was dedicated to the Dirty Days. *Carry garlic in your pocket throughout the filthy days. Don't go out after sunset. Do not cross a street before dawn. The Samodivas are on the prowl to catch you. In their pockets, they carry your death. Women, hide a blackbird under your blouse, otherwise the green streaks will drown you in their Samodiva's milk.* Ivan finished reading and looked up.

"This article is the only document that mentions Trun, Ivan," Professor Gils said. "Samodivas are green dots that kill men. Tales of superstition still persist in Dusk Gorge. A legend has it that one of the Samodivas is Death, and it lives in the town of Dusk."

"And pigs will fly," Ivan said. "I'd like to have a taste of the Samodiva's milk."

"It's not a good idea," the professor said as he passed the younger man a newspaper clipping.

It was a short announcement, printed in the bottom left corner on page 11.

16 April 2020. Construction workers in Dusk, Western Bulgaria, stumble upon ancient ruins while working on the sewage system of the town. The ruins resemble a portal that leads to a small, circular room full of ancient ceramic containers, crude pans and simple earthenware pots. A team of archaeologists was sent to carry out extensive research into the site. The initial findings lead the scientists to date the ruins back to the early 13th century AD. On one of the walls, the team found three identical well-preserved frescos of a sharp, red-spiked thorn. The archaeologists called the site Trun Heathen Shrine, after the Old Bulgarian word trun, *meaning a thorn.*

"Pans again, and Trun Heathen Shrine," Ivan said. "I don't understand why this site of archaeological interest should hold interest for me."

Professor Gils' pale blue eyes gleamed.

"I thought you'd say so," he said. "There's more to that heathen shrine."

He gave Ivan another newspaper clipping.

The archaeological excavations at Trun Heathen Shrine in the town of Dusk, Dusk Gorge region, were suspended Thursday, 5 May. The two construction workers, who had stumbled across the heaps of crude ceramic containers, were taken ill shortly after they came back home. They complained of all the usual flu symptoms: high temperature and severe headaches. Their status aggravated progressively with time. The high temperature caused painful muscle stiffness. The team of archaeologists who took part in the excavations developed symptoms of severe limb paralysis. They were admitted to the local hospital where the doctors had conducted tests to diagnose the patients. No conclusion was reached, and the patients were transferred to the Iztok Clinic of Neurology.

"The Iztok Clinic? This is our clinic, isn't it, Professor Gils?" Ivan asked.

"Yes," Gils said. "They are my patients, Ivan, the two construction workers and the archaeologists."

Professor Gils' office was immaculately clean, and the violets in the flowerpots were in full bloom. Taking a step to the window, the professor said, "Ivan, I want you to let my patients listen to the Healing Trun you produced in your unintelligible language."

Gils waited.

Finally, Ivan spoke, "Why didn't you let them listen to the recordings yourself, Professor?"

"I did," Gils said. "It didn't work." He looked at Ivan, his golden-rimmed glasses shining briefly in the sun.

Ivan looked at him closely.

"Professor Gils, you told me you let your mother listen to the Healing Trun. She reacted positively to it, you said, but haven't seen her. You told me you felt happy after you heard the recordings. I was not by your side at that time."

The eyes of the men locked.

"Is there any special reason why you want me to be with the construction workers and the archaeologists while they'll be listening to Healing Trun?"

Professor Gils blushed.

"Yes," he said, looking Ivan in the eyes. Then he added, "Look, a little fair-haired girl's walking in the yard. I often see her in the hospital," his voice broke. "She looks kind of lonely."

Ivan Georg looked out the window. He saw the child and felt a tingle in his fingers. She was the same little girl he had seen in his chaotic dream after his brain surgery. Maybe it had not been a dream after all.

Chapter Nine

As usual in the morning, I was reading the news websites and thinking of Philip Mill. I had a dream about him last night. He smiled at me and that was all. I had noticed that things went wrong every time I dreamed about him, so I wondered what it might be now. Philip Mill and the blind woman from Bare Mountain. I had to talk to her and I would, even if I had to box Philip Mill's ears. I was a good fighter, and he knew that. A short article on duskdaily.com attracted my attention. What the hell, I said to myself, this can't be true.

They were digging in the center of Dusk again! The city authorities were renovating Gagarin Street, the hiding place of my childhood. I loved the narrow dark flat I grew up in. My mother used to instruct me to tidy up the living room because she was in a hurry to meet the next love of her life. I was alone at home, and I talked to the chest of drawers, imagining it was my uncle. I talked to the picture of a bearded man my mother claimed was her grandfather, a rich factory owner, who left her nothing in his will. I loved him for that, and I learned by heart long passages from the book of fairy tales, which he had given her, the only book we had at home. The man in the picture seemed interested to listen to my babbling. I missed that picture after my mother left the town of Dusk, and my aunt, a scientist, said the man in the picture was perhaps my father, but one could never be sure with mother.

I missed the narrow flat, although my aunt said it was no good. She sold it to a single mother who had a boy my age. My aunt bought a big apartment on the opposite side of the street, and in the evenings, I could see the window of my old room glitter. I wanted to be back there, with the chest of drawers and the picture of the bearded man, my only friend, who knew the fairy tales I told him day after day. My aunt refused to take the picture and the chest of drawers to the new apartment. She gave them to the single mom.

They were digging right there. The construction workers would demolish the old gray house, the one I loved, the room of my dark, quiet childhood. I wanted to buy that house, and I was sure I could restore it. Perhaps most of my friends would say I had a bee in my bonnet. So what? I loved the ramshackle building and I wanted to buy it.

I remember I slunk several times into the old house before my aunt discovered what I had done, and she forbade me to go there again.

"I want to see my uncle," I told my aunt, and she stared at me in a peculiar way.

"Your uncle?" she asked. "You have no uncle, Sara, and you know that."

I tried to explain to her all about the old chest of drawers I called my uncle, my mother's clothes stored in them, listening to my tales. My aunt didn't understand.

One day, I managed to climb to the top of the staircase where our old flat was and tried to open the door. It was locked. When I knocked on it, and a thin voice asked, "Who is it?"

I hoped this was the boy I had seen staring out of the window.

"It's me," I said. "Sara. We lived here before your mother bought the flat from us."

He didn't say anything.

"Can you open the door?" I asked him. "I'd like to see the picture of the bearded man and the chest of drawers, too."

The kid was silent for a long time, and I decided to go home. I was about to climb down the stairs when his trembling voice tickled my ears, "The door is locked. I don't have the key."

I liked the way he talked. My friends, the chest of drawers and the picture of the bearded man were silent all the time, and I had to imagine all the words they spoke to me. It was much better with this boy because I didn't have to think about the words he'd say. I was overjoyed. There were no children in this part of the town and there were no grownups even. This was an old one-end street, and most of the buildings in the area were warehouses.

"Do you want me to tell you a fairy tale?" I asked the boy.

"Yes! Yes!" he said behind the door, and I told him about Little Red Riding Hood.

He often interrupted me, asking, "Speak louder, I can't hear you" and I shouted at the top of my lungs, prattling away about the bad wolf, and even louder about Little Red Riding Hood's grandmother.

"Can you tell me another fairy tale?" the boy asked, and I was ready to tell him all the tales I knew, but it was growing dark, and I was cold.

"I'll come tomorrow," I said. "I live in the apartment opposite yours. I'll stay by the window, and you can see me there."

He couldn't see me that evening because Auntie declared I was to have a lesson in French. In the evening, she read to me Charles Perrault's story about a puss in boots. I didn't understand what she said in French, and I regretted that I hadn't asked what the boy's name was.

Now the construction workers were going to tear the house down.

On the following day, I went to the boy, and his mother was at home.

"Go away," she told me. "Andrew is ill. You can't see him now."

"But I am not ill, Mom," I heard the voice I liked so much. "She promised to tell me another fairy tale."

The woman slammed the door in my face. I ran back home, and I saw the boy at the window of the room in which I had grown up. He was waving at me. I waved back at him then the young woman, his mother, dragged him away.

After the French lesson was over, my aunt kissed me goodnight, and I told Andrew fairy tales in my mind. I knew he couldn't hear me, yet I mumbled on the tale about the seven dwarves. These were the happiest days in my life. I had a friend who waved at me from his window. The goodnight kisses my aunt gave me embarrassed me. Mother never kissed me goodnight.

"I find this child peculiar," the man my aunt had asked to dinner said. "She seems to hear voices."

"I don't hear voices," I said. "But I can see a green streak in your head, sir," I said.

"A green streak?" both auntie and the man said. "What do you mean?" the man asked, glancing sharply at me.

"Something like little green lamps inside your skull," I explained.

My mother had forbidden me to talk of what I saw in people's heads and ordered me to say *in their thoughts* instead. I told Mom that some people's heads kind of glowed. I saw green shimmering dots in their hair and told her the men's heads glittered. Mom was embarrassed and instructed me to keep mum. Unfortunately, the man my aunt had invited to dinner didn't seem to understand. I was sorry I told him about the green glowworms I saw in his thoughts.

"She has to see a psychiatrist," the man said. My aunt promised she'd think about it and after the man was gone, she asked me, "Sara, what is that green glow you speak about, my child?"

I hated her calling me "my child." I was not her child; mom told me once she hated her big sister. My aunt was "the brains" and my mother was nothing. I made up my mind not to mention anything about the shimmer I noticed in Mom's head from time to time.

"I was just joking, Aunt Mary," I said. "I didn't like the man and I wanted him to go away, that's all."

She didn't believe me.

"Can you see a green streak in my thoughts?" she asked.

"No," I said.

"And your mommy?" she asked. "Did you see that streak in her head?"

I was five or six at that time, and I was not a clever girl. How could a child be clever if she had only three friends: a chest of drawers, a picture of a bearded man and a boy she saw at the window in the flat opposite the street?

"Yes, Aunt Mary," I said. "Sometimes Mommy had a green streak in her hair."

On the following day, my aunt took me to a famous doctor. At that time, I didn't know what the word *psychiatrist* meant. I thought he was a clown who gave the kids candies, so I called him the *candy man.* He examined me and said I was a healthy, beautiful girl.

"Madam," the candy man turned to my aunt. "There is one more child who said he can see green dots in people's heads."

"Yes?" said my aunt.

"You might have seen this boy," the man went on. "His teacher brought him to me yesterday, and when she gave me the child's address, I thought it sounded familiar: Gagarin Street 36."

"Interesting," my aunt exclaimed. "Sara and I live at Gagarin Street 37." She looked at me. "Sara, this must be the boy who waves his hand at you from the window opposite ours. What's his name?"

"He is called Andrew," the doctor said.

I knew that.

"Andrew told me he saw green behind my forehead," the doctor went on. "Sara, can you see that green streak *behind my forehead* that your aunt told me you saw in your mommy's head?"

I stared at him. Yes, the green streak was there, bright like the tiny electric bulbs my mother had put on the Christmas tree, the only Christmas tree she had ever bought me. I loved her fiercely; I loved Mom, and I was so proud of the only Christmas tree in my life. I studied the man's face, and yes, I could see the green fireflies buried in his hair. I didn't tell him what I saw—I already knew better than that.

"I see nothing, sir," I lied.

Both the doctor and my aunt laughed.

"You are a healthy and pretty girl, Sara," he said and gave me more candies.

I liked the candies the man had given me, but more than that, I liked the thought that Andrew, too, had seen the green streak. Was the doctor blind, I asked myself, was my own aunt blind? Why couldn't they see the green dots? That was odd. The doctor gave me a little teddy bear and I forgot the green fireflies.

"I'd recommend that you leave the neighborhood, madam," the doctor said looking Aunt Mary in the eyes. "I'll be honest with you. A little girl, a very pretty one, too, lived with her parents in the apartment where you live now. Her father brought her to the hospital where I worked. The girl told me she saw small lamps in my head. She insisted there were green dots inside her father's head as well. I strongly recommended that the family should leave the neighborhood."

Aunt Mary thought for a while.

"I think I've met that family," she said. "I remember the girl. A little angel … Her father told me she was called Boya, and I thought, such an odd-sounding name. Perhaps this is the reason I remembered it."

"Yes," the doctor said, smiling. "That's the same girl, a very intelligent child."

Now they were about to pull the old house down.

I wouldn't let them. I'd go and talk to the mayor of Dusk and to the police chief. This house was at least three centuries old, gray and sad; if worse came to worse, I hoped I could talk the mayor into letting me buy it. I wanted my lonely and happy childhood back. I wanted to see that boy again. Andrew.

I thought of Philip Mill. He loved the old house. We went for long walks together and I noticed he loved to stop at its front door. Now it was locked; all the windows were shuttered. I wondered what attracted Philip so much to that place. "I'd love to buy it," he'd told me one Sunday morning.

Now Philip Mill lived with Wanga, and I was jealous of him.

A paragraph on the laptop display attracted my attention.

The three archaeologists who worked on the excavation in the town of Dusk, Dusk Gorge region, were admitted to hospital. They all complained of severe muscle pains. Their research activities were suspended, and the local parliament chaired by John Cole, the chief of Dusk police, issued a decree by virtue of which the pit dug out in the street was filled with stones.

This was strange. The chief of Dusk police had stumbled over something and was still shaking with fear. I knew that impressive physical specimen, John Cole, well enough. If my memory served me right, I had an affair with him in the past, or had I married him? I fell in love quite often and had admirers whose names eluded me. My mailbox was full of messages I didn't even bother to read. Men called me *bitch* behind my back; I had broken more hearts than I cared to remember, but men deserved that, didn't they? Philip Mill, my ex-fiancé, had left me for a whore in a long white robe, a Samodiva who could see the future. The future, my foot!

I cared about the house of my childhood. At times, I had a tingling sensation in my hands, and this happened only when Philip Mill stood near me. I felt the same when Wanga, the pearl of clairvoyance, caught hold of my hand and told me the idiotic thing about a brother I didn't have.

Why were the archaeologists admitted to the hospital? What was wrong with the pit? It had to be dangerous if the police chief filled it up with stones in no time.

The archaeologists erroneously believed they had come across one of the extremely rare Trun Heathen Shrines. They informed our reporter they found frescoes of red thorns on what appeared to be a door to a circular room full of crude, ceramic pans. In the Middle Ages, the heathens brought pans and pitchers to trun shrines, believing they'd get rid of diseases and spells cast on them by Samodivas.

I remembered Wanga's shack on Bare Mountain and the heaps of rusting frying pans. They looked ugly in the falling dusk. The memory gave me the creeps, so what. I didn't scare easily.

I asked John Cole out for coffee.

"No, Sara, dearest, you cannot buy that house," John Cole, the police chief, said after I asked him about the gray building of my childhood.

"Come to my place today at 9 PM.," I told him. "I have a bottle of Dusk wine. You know my wine is magnificent."

"I love you, Sara," John Cole groaned. "I'd do anything for you. I even married you years ago. But I can't let you buy that house."

"Why not?" I asked him.

"We are checking all buildings in this neighborhood now."

"What's wrong with the neighborhood?" I asked, thinking about the archaeologists in the hospital.

I thought of the picture on the wall in my bedroom: five trees, dry as dead eyes, juicy cherries hanging from the black branches. I carried this picture with me wherever I went. The police chief's face was a heap of autumn leaves in front of me.

"I don't know, Sara," he said slowly. "This neighborhood is no good."

Trun Heathen Shrine, the rusting pans on Bare Mountain; Trun and Wanga, the blind prophetess, and the police evacuating the place. Something was brewing there. I had to go to the local hospital and talk to at least one of the archaeologists.

"Are you sure you don't know why they are evacuating Trun Shrine?" I asked the police chief.

"Sara, have I ever lied to you?" he said. Then he hummed to himself.

Why is the Tall Fellow so silly, mommy? If the pain is too much for us, the Tall Fellow will destroy death—

John Cole stopped abruptly, and staring at me, said, "It's a beautiful song, Sara. I mean the one which is printed on your picture of the dry cherry trees." He smiled. "How come you found it, my pretty woman?"

"A psychiatrist gave it to me," I said. "He thought I was crazy and told me to learn the song about the Tall Fellow by heart. You look very much like this psychiatrist, John."

"You're off your rocker," he said.

John had never lied to me, of course. He couldn't. Any time somebody lied to me, there was that tingling sensation in my fingers. No, it was not that. I simply saw the green streak in his thoughts.

"Hey, Sara," he said just before I closed the café door behind me. "I have a souvenir for you. Here, take it." He gave me a small gray sharp-edged stone.

"What's that?" I said. I suspected the police chief was making fun of me.

"A stone from the archaeological excavation," he grinned. I did not like that.

"I'll throw it away," I said.

"Don't," the chief of Dusk police said. "Put it on your mantelpiece and keep it there. You'll see what will happen."

I put the stone on the mantelpiece by my favorite portrait of a woman who looked like my mother. I was sure I wouldn't know my mom if I met her one of these days. She might have died for all I knew. I kept another portrait of a woman on my mantelpiece, that of my aunt, the eminent scholar who had brought me up.

In the evening, the chief of Dusk police rang me up.

"How are things going, darling? Are you okay?" which was quite an extraordinary question. The chief of Dusk police telephoned me very rarely. I had a rule: if a man asked how I was feeling, I answered, "Not bad, but I've still got a headache." That allowed me enough room to excuse myself if I didn't like the man.

"Oh," he echoed, and this was a strange response. "Did you keep the stone I gave you?"

"It's on my mantelpiece, John," The man didn't have a screw loose, so why was he asking me absurd questions?

"Throw away the stone," he said quickly. "A friend of mine complained of severe headaches after I gave him a stone from the excavation. Throw yours far from your house, honey."

You are crazy, Chief, I thought, but said aloud, "I will."

"I love you, Sara," he said, but he was lying. "Throw that stone away, will you?"

"I love you, Chief," I whispered.

Chapter Ten

"Think of the archaeologists," Margaret warned her husband. "This article says they're unable to walk."

"I have nothing to lose," Peter Stan said. "I'll go."

It was raining and it was cold.

"I don't want you to go," she said.

Peter felt a surge of love for her. There she was, his Margaret. Margaret and Thomas, his son: that was all he had in the world.

"The analytical laboratory announced that all test results of the samples from the Trun Shrine excavation were within the normal reference values," he said. "No traces of radiation, no poisonous substances, no germs."

"Come back home early," Margaret said. "I'll wait for you in front of the Winter Fountain. Call me if something goes wrong."

Peter Stan was tempted to call her a dozen times during the day. He didn't do that. He hated to worry Margaret.

He asked himself why he had accepted to work on Trun Shrine, as the pit the bulldozers had dug came to be called by the townspeople. The excavation work was suspended, the gaping ditch was filled with earth. That was all the newspapers announced. When the police chief called the old teacher, Peter Stan was surprised.

"We left a passage to the circular room," John Cole said. "Come with me, Peter. I want you to see it. Do you remember what you told me about the birds, the noiseless, heavy ones that perched on the ground in the schoolyard and carved a hole into the asphalt?"

"When shall we go?" the old teacher had asked.

It was ten minutes to nine when the two men passed behind the yellow ropes that surrounded the last remaining traces of the tunnel to Trun Shrine. The earth was still wet, and Gagarin Street was gray in the pelting rain.

"I wouldn't like to put your life at risk," John Cole said. "I crept into that … place two days ago. I made up my mind to ask you for help."

Peter looked at him. His old friend's face was excited.

"I've brought flashlights, but you'll see they are no good."

"What do you mean?" Peter Stan asked.

"My flashlight didn't work," the police chief said. "Luckily, I had a box of matches in my pocket. It did the job."

John Cole was a big, strong man. He and Peter used to be roommates. They studied at the University of Sofia together. Peter had been in love with Margaret but was afraid of her sharp tongue. The truth was Margaret had chosen John Cole. She moved in with him and the two of them were married shortly after that. Peter Stan had to look for another roommate. He assumed it was only natural Margaret should choose John. He was handsome and his brown eyes smiled all the time. Peter was an excellent student, shy and quiet; he was not a leader and preferred reading Cicero to going to parties. Surely, Margaret thought he was boring. He was, he knew it.

Things didn't go too well between Margaret and John. Peter Stan still remembered that evening. It was snowing and it was cold in the flat Peter rented in the cheapest neighborhood in Sofia. There was no hot water in the building. As usual, he had tidied up his room. Peter was a tidy man; he cleaned for himself and for John when they shared the apartment. Everything should be in place, and this was how his life went on, no fun, no excitement, days and hours predictable like the endless row of dates in the calendar. Peter had read for hours and felt a little dizzy. He had just put away his book when somebody knocked at the door.

It was Margaret.

"Are you all right?" Peter Stan had asked.

She had not answered, had not even glanced at him.

"Would you like something to eat?" he asked her.

"Yes," she said.

She silently ate the sandwich he'd fixed for her.

"Can you give me some wine?" she asked.

Peter Stan had no wine and offered her water, but Margaret didn't want it. She sat at the table silent, reserved, and Peter wondered what he could do to cheer her up. She was a queer fish, Margaret was. She didn't seem to care about his admiration for her. He felt sick with worry.

"Will you marry me, Peter?" Margaret said without looking at him.

He stared, frightened.

He reached out his hand to touch her. Margaret cowered behind the table, and his immaculately clean room seemed to reel.

She did not say anything and didn't seem to care.

"I don't know," he said. She looked lost in his tidy room behind her empty glass. "I love you," he added, scared she might go away. "I'll marry you, Margaret," Peter Stan said.

He loved her.

Margaret never spoke about John Cole. She was a good mother to their son and a stubborn wife. She was a brilliant mathematician and was famous. Peter did not ask any questions. Something had broken between them that evening when he didn't have wine, or had it broken earlier when Margaret was John Cole's wife? She didn't tell him, and John Cole was still his best friend.

"Careful!" John's voice brought the teacher back to reality.

They stood in front of a big smooth slab of concrete.

"We have to push it away," John said. "Easy, no need to rush."

A narrow flight of stairs opened up before them after they shoved the slab away. The men shone their flashlights at the walls and started to climb down.

"This is the room with the pans. Watch your step," John said.

The room was circular and almost entirely full of primitive receptacles, crude stone and earthenware pieces that looked absurd, heaped up there, eight feet under the asphalt street and the sidewalks.

"What are these doing here?" Peter asked as he studied a clay jug.

"Don't touch anything," John warned him.

"Why?"

"Just don't."

Then Peter Stan saw a hole in the wall hidden behind the enormous heap of ancient pitchers and pans. To his surprise, John Cole crept into the narrow opening, holding the flashlight above his head.

"Follow me," John Cole said.

The opening gradually widened into a circular corridor then dipped sharply downwards. Peter Stan thought hard. Why had the police blocked that passage? Where was John leading him? He looked at the walls. They were gray and smooth. He strained his eyes as he tried to discern dents, rifts or cracks in the surface, and to his amazement, he saw none. The teacher touched the wall and quickly withdrew his hand. The stone felt warm! He touched the wall one more time, and his flashlight went dead. A split second later, John's flashlight also went out, and thick impenetrable darkness enveloped them.

"What's wrong with the flashlights?" Peter asked.

John Cole lit a candle and gave it to Peter. "My flashlight went dead here the day before yesterday," he said. "Let's go."

Peter Stan lifted the candle to the wall and could hardly believe what he saw.

"What is it?" John whispered.

"Look at this!"

In the flickering light of the candle, the wall was dimly red. There were miniature dents in it, like small niches, and a hole gaped at the bottom of the passage. The hole was not deep, a foot or so, and its walls appeared to be smooth.

"What is this?" Peter asked, putting his finger in one of the dents. His skin itched. The stone was as cold as ice.

"Let's go," John Cole urged, and Peter envied his courage. Margaret chose him, not me, he thought, and she had made the right choice. He didn't want to go further. The flame of his candle sputtered. He felt like running back home. The police had evacuated the neighborhood. He and John were crazy if they pushed forward into the darkness, the walls throwing heat at them, the dents colder than fresh snow.

"John," Peter said. "Let's go back, please."

But John Cole didn't hear him. His steps echoed in the blackness. He has nothing to lose, Peter thought. He has no family … Then, in the heat and darkness of the confined space, the teacher asked himself if

John was all there.

"I wonder what Margaret would do if she were here," John said as if he had read his friend's thoughts. "She's so impatient, isn't she?"

Peter Stan gave a start. Margaret impatient! She knew how to achieve what she wanted, she was rarely in a hurry and could wait forever. Perhaps John knew something about her that he, Peter Stan, her husband, didn't know. Margaret was a stubborn woman.

"She might tell us something about this place," John Cole went on. "This rotten Trun Shrine … and the Trun recordings she has made."

Peter Stan tried hard to turn around and shout, but he simply couldn't move. Margaret had told John about her recordings. This meant … this meant that she was seeing John again. This meant …

"I felt sick after I heard her Trun recordings. They call the thing *Killing Trun*. Margaret nearly fainted," John Cole went on. "She complained of a severe headache and vomited. I was slightly sick."

"When did you listen to her recordings?" Peter Stan asked, forgetting all about Trun Shrine, the walls that emitted heat, and the ice-cold dents in them. Margaret was seeing John, the Margaret he loved …

"A month ago," John said. "On me, the effect of Killing Trun, the wailing sounds, was hardly noticeable. She could not stand them, and Professor Andrew Gils was called for."

Margaret had told John about her work; she had not said a word about it to him, Peter, her husband. Was it possible she hadn't really broken from John Cole all these years? John Cole, his best friend … and Margaret. Peter Stan didn't want to lose her. He loved her rare smiles, her self-control, and her quiet voice gave him peace. He remembered another winter night, cold rain behind the window, he and Margaret sitting at the kitchen table.

"Give me some wine, please," she had said.

Again, like in a nightmare, he didn't have wine.

"I'm leaving you," Peter imagined her say. He thought of the evenings he'd talk to her old clothes. He was accustomed to the noise of her steps. He wanted her to be happy and dreaded the nights after she'd be gone.

"Margaret told me you were very sick after you heard the recordings, Peter," John Cole went on. "You were in pain. Now listen carefully. I was okay after I visited this place two days ago and I didn't feel sick after I heard Margaret's recordings. It could be dangerous for you here. You've read the articles on the archaeologists, haven't you? The same thing might happen to you. But I want to show you something. You can come with me, or you can go back. It's up to you."

The flame of Peter's candle flickered. John's face looked taut and worried in the dim light.

"You and Margaret …" Peter began, scared to look at his friend. "I mean you and Margaret … are often together."

"We've been working together all these years," John said. "The recordings she's been making are not … how shall I put it? She intercepted those noises by chance, and we've been wondering what they really meant. We couldn't make heads or tails of it until the day you and your students saw the silent birds."

Peter didn't care about the birds. He thought he never had wine when Margaret wanted it. She hadn't mentioned she'd been working with John Cole all these years. She didn't speak to Peter about her work, didn't even mention the awards she had won, or said a few words as if they meant nothing at all. He could understand; she didn't want him to feel inferior to her. Didn't she know he was proud of her brilliant mind? Or was he, Peter, a man who didn't deserve Margaret?

"I was afraid to bring your wife here," John said. "I thought she'd lose consciousness … or worse."

"I'll come with you," Peter said. He made up his mind. He'd see whatever John wanted to show him and he'd describe it to Margaret. He could do it.

"After you and the students found the strange birds, Margaret found the recordings in her computer. Killing Trun … how shall I put it? It … it is dangerous."

"Dangerous?" Peter repeated, holding up his candle.

"Margaret and I have listened to the so-called Healing Trun dozens of times, and she was fine. The birds appeared out of nowhere and then the screaming sounds made both Margaret and you very sick."

The two men reached the end of the corridor. There was an open door to a small, circular room on the left, and a door to a room on the right. John Cole reached out and touched the wall on the left side of the room.

"Ouch!" he thundered. "It burned my hand!"

Peter touched the wall too. It scorched his fingers.

The wall of the room on the right was freezing cold.

John Cole produced another candle from his coat pocket. Then Peter Stan caught a glimpse of something he did not expect to find there—a black bird laying on the floor. It was big and looked very much like the birds he had seen. The teacher reached out to stroke its feathers. John didn't warn him not to. The bird felt as warm as the wall. The minute Peter touched it he felt happy. He knew Margaret had not cheated on him. Her love for him was true. It was not like a fire, or like a burning torch, it was quiet and endless like a warm sky on a summer night. Her love was quiet and gentle. Peter knew Margaret would always be there for him, and he hated the days and months without her.

At first, Peter Stan had not noticed it. There was something on the freezing cold wall. It was a picture: of a slender woman, staring at the empty space in front of her. The teacher studied her thin face. She was blind. For a second her empty eyes met his. Peter Stan gave a start, panic racing through his veins.

"The room on the right is scary," he heard John say. "I can understand if you don't want to go in there. You may pass out. The place may kill you, but the thing I wanted to show you is there."

Peter listened, breathing heavily.

"It may kill me?" he repeated. "Did you describe that room to Margaret?"

"I did," said John Cole. "She said I was imagining things."

Peter Stan entered the murky room first. There were a couple of clay pans on the floor, and it was freezing cold inside. The blind woman's face came back to his thoughts.

"Look at this," John said as he pointed to the wall.

Then Peter saw little dents in the gray stone, like the ones he'd noticed in the corridor all freezing cold to the touch. In the center of the circle of dents, he caught sight of a basin full of red liquid.

"Is this blood?" Peter asked, his chin dropping. He staggered.

"Peter," John Cole said. "Hold on, Peter!"

"The pain," the old teacher groaned, writhing, blood pouring from his nose and trickling down to his lips.

John Cole grabbed his hands, lifted his head and quickly dragged his friend out of the room. He left Peter in the room on the floor, watching as the teacher thrashed, twisted and turned, blood gushing from his nose. The police chief waited. After a while, he touched Peter's forehead, clutched his shoulders, and shook him. Peter's body went into convulsions. John hesitated, pressed Peter's forehead again, took the motionless blackbird from the floor and put it on Peter's chest. Within seconds, Peter's nose stopped bleeding, his arms relaxed, his pulse slowed as color gradually returned to his face. John sat by his side, watching him closely, glancing at his watch, all the time keeping the candle close to Peter's mouth. Ten minutes passed. The teacher breathed evenly. Fifteen minutes passed. John took the bird away from Peter's chest and shook his friend's shoulders.

"What did you see there, Peter?" he asked, pronouncing the words slowly, his eyes intent on the sallow face.

Peter groaned as his fingers hit the stone floor. John lifted the bird again and put it on Peter's forehead. The teacher relaxed briefly then shrieked with pain. The bird was too heavy; Peter's skin was scarlet under it. John brushed the wings of the bird against his friend's cheek and when the teacher smiled and sighed, the police chief whispered in Peter's ear, "What did you see on the wall, Peter?"

The teacher smiled again, his lips twitched, his eyelids fluttered.

"The Deaf Crags," he said.

"The Deaf Crags?" John Cole asked, then laid the candle on the floor and rubbed his friend's forehead. Three minutes passed and he put the bird on Peter's legs.

"Stand up, Peter!" he said. "Stand up and walk!"

The teacher lay motionless on the floor.

The police chief pocketed the blackbird, lifted Peter onto his shoulders and quickly climbed up the narrow passage leading to the circular room with the jugs and pans. John was a powerfully built man, his steps were light and rhythmical, yet it seemed unnatural he could manage to keep up that rapid pace. He often stopped, laid the man he was carrying on the floor, propped the candle against the wall as he took the bird out of his pocket and pressed its wings against the teacher's chest.

An hour later, the two men were sitting in the police chief's car. John Cole's eyes gleamed as he muttered angry words under his breath. The blackbird had vanished. His pocket was full of fine gray dust. He smeared some of it on his friend's cheeks and said, "Wake up, Peter. We've come back home."

Peter Stan stretched, hitting his head against the back of his seat.

"The walls are so bright," the teacher muttered. "Is this a different room?"

"Peter, listen to me," the police chief looked sharply at his friend. "The Deaf Crags!"

"The Deaf Crags?" the teacher moaned. "What about them?"

It was dark, and the night was cool. There were no stars in the sky, and the light of the streetlamps was golden. It was warm in John Cole's car, and John knew why he felt so fresh and energetic after he had carried his friend all the way up the narrow passage. The gray dust felt heavy in his coat pocket.

"You said the *Deaf Crags* before you passed out in the room. There was a circle of dents on its floor," John said. "There were dents on its wall, too."

The teacher was silent for a long while.

"I remember," he said at last. "The dents on that wall reminded me of the holes in Deaf Crags Valley. Then a bomb exploded in my head."

John Cole drove his car through the empty town, saying nothing.

"I feel weak," the teacher said. "And I am happy. I couldn't tell you why."

They reached the marble fountain in the city park.

"A couple of days ago, I told Margaret that down there, in the room with the cold walls, someone had drawn a map of the hollows in Deaf Crags Valley," the police chief said. "She thought I was imagining things."

"Does Margaret know about the hollows?" Peter Stan blurted out, blood spurting out of his nose.

"Yes, she does. Easy, Peter," the police chief said. "Margaret loves you. She told me. I wanted her to come back to me. I thought she was tired of you, and I believed she made you look small. She said you were everything she cared for."

The police chief stopped his car at the gate of the city park.

"She told me she'd be waiting for you here," John Cole said. "Can you walk, Peter?"

The teacher didn't answer. He opened the door of the car and before he got out, the police chief said, "Peter, read carefully the essay that student of yours had written on the quiet birds."

Peter threw back his head and looked into the other man's eyes.

"Who told you about my student's essay, John?" he asked.

The night was quiet, and spring wind was whispering to the grass.

"Margaret told me," the police chief answered.

Peter Stan thought he must have imagined it. In the shadow of the trees, he saw a little girl, a fair-haired one, but it was impossible for a child that young to walk all alone in the thickening dusk. Old man, you are seeing ghosts, he said to himself.

At the back of his mind, like the cry of a dying bird, the face of a blind woman lurked. The memory of that woman made him freeze in his tracks.

Chapter Eleven

Transferred to the biggest room in Iztok Clinic an hour ago, they were waiting for the doctor's visit. The archaeologists were paralyzed from the waist down. All had a high fever. Two team members were delirious, unable to recognize their relatives. A small sharp-edged stone lay on a table near the window.

Professor Gils and Ivan Georg entered the room.

"Who left this stone here?" Ivan said, pointing at the table.

"It was Mr. Cole's idea," the Professor answered. "Mr. John Cole is the chief of police in the town of Dusk. He had explained to me he had taken this stone from the pagan shrine the construction workers discovered by chance."

Ivan took a step to the table and touched the stone. It felt cold, and his fingers tingled. Intense pain shot through his hands, taking hold of his shoulders and neck. Then it was gone.

"Acute pain?" Professor Gils asked. "My hand hurt after I touched this stone. Half an hour after I left the stone here, two of the men lost consciousness."

"Then why don't we take the stone away?"

After a long silence Gils said, "I kept this stone in my room, on my night table. I slept. I felt strong. I'll be honest with you, Ivan. I left this stone in your office yesterday while you were reading *Neurosurgery*. I was watching you closely. You were ok, so I left the stone in my mother's room. After three minutes her nose started to bleed."

"And you brought the stone to the archaeologists' room?"

"As I told you, it was Mr. Cole's idea."

Ivan grabbed the stone.

"Did Mr. Cole personally give you this stone?" he asked.

"He did."

"Did Mr. Cole have any complaints, pain, vomiting or loss of consciousness after he kept the stone?"

"None."

"That makes three of us: you, the police chief, and I," Ivan said thoughtfully. "We seem to be impervious to the influence of the stone."

"There's something more to it," Gils said. "Mr. Cole left the stone in an office where two detective sergeants worked on an armed robbery in Dusk. The two of them were admitted yesterday to Iztok Clinic. High blood pressure, splitting headache, partial paralysis of the limbs ..."

Ivan took the gray stone out of his pocket. Frost had covered its edges.

A huge inner rectangular yard stretched between the east and the west wings of Iztok Clinic. Lilacs and magnolias grew not far from the windows. Narrow sand alleys cut through the luxuriant grass. Beds of yellow, red, and orange flowers lined the path to the other building.

"What will happen if we drop the stone in your aquarium, Professor Gils?" Ivan suggested.

To him, the eel looked menacing. It lay on the bottom of the aquarium, motionless, unimpressed as the two men entered the office. Its long thin body twitched slightly after Ivan dropped the stone into the clear water; that was all.

"Tintin looked quite happy," Professor Gils remarked as he and Ivan headed for the biggest room in Iztok Clinic where the archaeologists were given specialized treatment.

"Professor Gils," Ivan said. "I have not spoken to you about an important fact so far," Ivan's voice cracked. The professor waited. "Professor, I can see green dots, dancing in your hair."

Gils winced.

"Green dots?" he said, watching Ivan closely.

"After the brain surgery I felt weak," Ivan began. "I thought it would go … It didn't. I can see little dots around your head. I don't know what to think of it all."

For a split second, a stunned expression flitted across Professor Gils' features.

"What?" Ivan asked.

"Have you seen those green dots around other peoples' heads?"

Ivan thought for a while then slowly shook his head. The expression in the professor's eyes made Ivan think something was wrong.

"What?" he asked.

The professor looked Ivan in the eyes. "I constantly see green lights in your hair and around your head, Ivan. I noticed it after your brain surgery, and I was scared."

Chapter Twelve

The professor plugged in the device. The whizzing sounds of Healing Trun filled the room. The recording resembled the maddening buzz of insects, sibilant noises in a nest of snakes, whirring sounds of slow-moving machinery, plaintive cries of dying kittens. Like the deliberate beat of a drum, the thrashing word *Trun* severed the cacophony of strident clamor. The deafening dissonance did not jar Ivan's ears, neither did it make him wish he were somewhere else. At the end, the low wail turned into an explosive, triumphant repetition, TRUN! TRUN! TRUN! which inexorably conquered the space. The walls reverberated with the powerful echo of these thundering thuds. The recording ended abruptly. Silence fell over the room.

"Try to walk," Gils said to one of the patients.

The archaeologist stood up. Reeling, he took a couple of steps forward. This can't be true. They were dying half an hour ago, Ivan thought. Something odd was happening, and he was a part of it. Maybe his tumor was the key to the mystery. At the end of the recording, Ivan felt happy. Professor Gils was smiling. So were the patients.

"What was the thing you made us listen to, Doctor?" asked one of the men, the youngest one of the group. "Howling wolves? Was that the Trun thing?"

"A new therapy," Gils answered.

"Doctor," the youngest of the group said. "Trun means thorn in Old Bulgarian. Several thorns were painted on the walls of the temple we discovered. I thought this might be useful to know."

"I've seen thorns carved on big boulders," another archaeologist, a short man, said, sitting up. "Enormous thorns they were. I checked. The locals call the place Deaf Crags. No one wanted to take me there. An old woman told me the stones there were no good. Her son fell ill after he sneaked to them."

"But the whining Trun thing made me feel much better," a big, muscular man said. "I'll have a thorn painted on the front door of my house. Anyway, I'm pretty sure the nurse was giving me the eye."

Professor Gils and Ivan left the room. On entering the professor's office, they stared.

Tintin's body floated on the surface of the water in the huge aquarium.

The eel no longer looked menacing. It was dead.

Chapter Thirteen

"Some more wine?" John asked me, the glitter in his eyes making me smell a rat.

He was smiling at me.

"You are very beautiful, Sara Eutim," he said. "I love you."

He didn't tell me anything I didn't know, and a very slight twitch of his eyebrows told me a different story.

"You know I do," he said.

"Yes," I said. A man who loved you didn't look at you the way a merchant would before he made up his mind to sell you, calculating to turn a profit. Love had nothing to do with profits, so I was on the alert. I always was with Mr. John Cole, the police chief.

"Are you okay, honey?" he asked, his voice genuinely sick with worry. He'd been asking that question for a while now, so I thought maybe I didn't look good, which was not the case—I had consulted the mirror in his reception room. Then why was he so keen on getting an answer from me? You never knew with John Cole.

"I don't feel all right," I lied. "Does it show?"

He didn't say anything. His eyes studied my face, the sharp glitter gone for a moment. But it was not a pleasure; I could print out that statement and sign it. John Cole's gaze had a peculiar severity to it that I found hard to stand. That particular look of his was a sign of trouble. I had asked John if I could visit Trun Shrine, which the police had sealed. I said I wanted to write a story about the place, a well-researched article that would help me gain recognition and perhaps win a prize.

"I will look for a connection between the shrine and the Samodivas," I said as I captured John's glinting eyes. His delicate nose twitched. This was an even worse sign. He did say he loved me, but the glint was there again, shrewd and careful.

"Philip Mill used to be your fiancé?" John Cole said, changing the subject.

"Yes," I replied.

"Philip Mill is Wanga's husband now," he said grinning widely, a thing that had often made me furious. Well, I'd lived long enough to learn that a woman should not show she got all huffy if a fool asked after her ex-fiancé.

"It was hard for me to get rid of Mr. Mill," I said. "He was domineering and wouldn't take no for an answer."

"How come he joined the lady charlatan?" Cole wanted to know.

I didn't bother to supply information on that intriguing topic, and this impressed my host.

"You don't care much about your ex-fiancés," the chief of Dusk police said. "To be honest with you, Sara, you've never struck me as being particularly sensitive."

"I love Philip Mill with all my heart," I said and that was the truth.

I had glued Philip's photo next to the picture of the five dead cherry trees.

"I can see that, it's all over your face," he grinned playfully, a thing I disliked. Then the police chief again sang that crazy song. *He threw his dots to the wind, and they don't protect him anymore. Why is the Tall Fellow so silly, mommy? The Tall Fellow must stay hidden …*

John Cole positively wasn't a singing talent. The Tall Fellow, my foot! John asked if there was something wrong, and I suspected a snake in the grass … I had made it a rule: if a man, no matter who he was, repeatedly asked me about something, I finally gave in and admitted that yes, I was trying to hide something from him.

"John," I began. "I'm dizzy. The smell of your wine makes me sick. I'm afraid I'm going to throw up."

"Oh," he said. "I'm so sorry. The clean air will do you good."

John was a caring and considerate man again, the sharp calculating glitter gone, but his face didn't love me. It was John Cole's everyday face, and its owner didn't want me to suffer. Why should I suffer in the first place? The weather was wonderful, crisp wind blew, the night was fresh, and the stars twinkled in the sky. The food was better than usual, and the wine was magnificent. If John wanted me to feel sick, who was I to trumpet my exuberant health?

His house was not very big. He lived alone and his housekeeper, a woman I had never seen, a creature with an interesting name, Boyna or Boya, kept the rooms brilliantly clean. I could see no speck of dust on the marble ornaments, on the collection of knick-knacks the man was so proud of. There were vases and gorgeous flowers in them. Everything in John Cole's house was magnificent, the brightly painted walls, the pictures of medieval knights and ladies, the peaceful landscapes, the green salad his housekeeper had procured and the wine which was so full-bodied that it made me feel dizzy. Everything was splendid. The carpet, rich and soft, felt like a warm path to eternal bliss, and I loved the small walnut table in the corner because it resembled the one my mother polished painstakingly to keep her magazines immaculately arranged on it. I looked at John Cole's walnut desk and I almost choked with amazement.

"What is it, honey?" he asked.

"What's that huge stone doing on your desk, John?" I asked.

I thought I saw the dark gleam come back to his eyes. The tiny twitch in the corner of his mouth was a bad sign, I knew.

"That stone?" he grinned again. "Oh, I like it. It's crude and powerful, don't you think?"

I didn't think it was powerful, I thought it was downright ugly, but I didn't say so.

The dark gleam was there, in John's eyes, very careful and observant. I didn't like to get in trouble. I didn't care about the big black stone on his walnut desk. Let it lie where it was, and that was all there was to it. When would I learn to keep my pretty mouth shut? A woman could babble as much as she pleased if she was sure the gentleman by her side was head over heels in love with her, which John Cole obviously was not.

"I feel sick," I said.

He took me to the porch, and I saw I had been wrong about the wind. It was not crisp; it was biting and cold. A woman hit by a wave of nausea should wait a couple of minutes before she asks important questions, so I did. I waited in the biting wind for John to take me back to his reception room. He didn't do that.

"I'll drive you home," he said. "Or do you think it would be better if I took you to hospital?"

To hospital? Was the man off his rocker?

"We all get headaches from time to time, John," I said mildly. "Please, take me home."

He looked at me, his sharp eyes all over my face, and I was sure he knew I was faking a headache.

"I'll take you home," he finally said.

It was in the car that I made up my mind it was time I asked him about Trun Heathen Shrine.

"Unfortunately, there is no shrine there," the police chief said. "I saw old ruins, nothing more than heaps of rubble, broken crockery, plus gas pipelines. The team of archaeologists inadvertently damaged the system. They were all poisoned, almost to death."

Pipelines, my foot, I thought.

"Can I visit the place?" I asked. "I'd love to see the pieces of broken crockery. A friend told me they were related to the Samodiva myth … the people in ancient times brought earthenware pans to the shrine when they wanted to get rid of an illness or fetched stones if they felt like escaping from a man they hated. I'll describe the place in an article, and who knows? Maybe I'll become famous," I said.

"You already are very famous," the police chief said. "A little bird told me you went and met Wanga the charlatan. Was it a very attractive man I know, somebody's ex-fiancé, you wanted to see? Sorry, Sara. The ancient folk songs focus on an interesting story. The natives of Dusk are still fascinated by it. They believe one of the Samodivas is Death. Maybe you'll try to find where Death hides?"

The wind was a minor inconvenience compared to the shock he gave me. I was itching to learn who had informed the police chief about my brief excursion to Bare Mountain. I could have asked John directly, of course, but I knew better than that.

"Somebody's ex-fiancé must have been too talkative," I ventured.

John's wide grin made me think it would have been much safer if I had not made any remark at all. If Mr. Cole grinned like that, he was not happy. I wished I were somewhere else.

"I don't feel well," I lied. Was it possible that the police chief had talked to the white-robed prophetess he labeled a charlatan? "I'd like to see the broken crockery, John. Will you take me there?" I asked.

He touched my hand, his face handsome as usual.

"No, honey, I love you too much to let you go there."

"Drive me to the hospital, please." I said.

"You look ok to me," Mr. Cole said as he stopped the car in front of my building. "Tomorrow, I'll come to check on you, Sara. Now I'll send a doctor to have a look at you. "Please, kiss me good night."

After my lips touched his cheek, he slipped a small bag in my hand.

"Put this on your forehead in case you develop a severe migraine headache," he said.

"What is this, John?" I asked.

"You'll be grateful to me," he smiled, got into his car, and blew me a kiss. The thing he'd given me was soft to the touch, and quite heavy.

I walked into my apartment.

The bag John Cole had given me was sealed. I slit the thing open and peeked inside it, then pushed my finger into what resembled fine gray dust.

Suddenly, I felt deliriously happy for no reason at all. I felt like singing and I loved the biting wind that pulled at the roofs. I held the small package in my hands, wondering why it was so wonderfully heavy, like a ton of gold, on my fingers.

I must have slept soundly that night for I had not heard the doctor ring the bell to check on me. In the morning, I saw the police chief standing in front of my building.

"I was worried about you, honey," he said. "The doctor said you were out, so I thought you were admitted to hospital." He looked at me quizzically. "Where did you spend the night, Sara Eutim?"

"I slept like a log," I said.

"Not typical of you, Sara," John Cole remarked. "The powder I gave you seemed to work, didn't it?"

I remembered the sudden rush of happiness last night.

"Can you give it back to me?" he asked. I knew he'd say something like that, and I was prepared. When I produced the package out of my bag, he said, "I'm sure you kept at least a third of the powder for your own use."

I had kept more than that.

"You've kept more than that," he said, looking me in the eyes.

"I didn't," I lied. "I don't need powder of any sort to sleep well."

"You went to Iztok Clinic," he said, his eyes searching my face. "The doctor said there was nothing wrong with you and then … then … Where did you go, Sara?"

Yes, last night I did visit Iztok Clinic.

We were talking in front of John's car. The sky was gray, and it looked like rain. My building was an expensive one, the neighborhood was an even more expensive one, so I hated it when a police chief spoke to me in an impolite tone of voice.

"I have to go," I said. "You know how much I enjoy your intelligent conversation, John, but I have to write that article about the Samodivas and Trun Heathen Shrine. I want to be very famous and rich. I'll have bodyguards who will not allow you to order me about the way you're trying to do now."

"I'll give you a lift," John Cole said. "Please get into my car."

He started the engine. "You visited the archaeologists in the hospital, the team that worked in Trun Shrine," he said sharply. "Last night you were not sick the way you pretended you were."

John, he didn't care much about me. Why was he so keen to find out what his ex was doing? I'd do my best not to satisfy his curiosity. The less John Cole knew, the less trouble he'd put me to.

"I was sick," I said.

"You were so sick you picked up the youngest archaeologist in the team and convinced Professor Gils to discharge him from hospital."

The police chief's eyes bored into mine. I was accustomed to men gawking at me like that, and I didn't mind John Cole's wrath.

"I asked you to let me go see the shrine, John," I pointed out. "You spun yarns about old gas pipelines," I said, beaming a smile at him.

John Cole was a careful driver. His Toyota purred as it danced its way amid the heavy morning traffic.

"The young archaeologist told me he and you were engaged to be married," the police chief snorted.

I loved it when John Cole went into one of his huffs. He looked younger when he was angry.

"Oh, did I get engaged to that young man?" I said innocently. "You wouldn't think I'd go that far."

The raindrops smashed against the windshield, and the wipers took good care of the Toyota in the driving rain.

"Your new fiancé told you about the dead birds they found among the ruins. He told you about the two rooms," John Cole said.

I was silent. I felt sorry for Jacob, the young archaeologist. He was such an innocent darling. Yes, he told me about the rooms, the first one as cold as snow, and the other hot as burning embers. I expected Jacob might lose his job, and he was a born scholar, thorough, ardent, and honest. I was pretty and I knew very well how to deal with ardent, honest, and thorough scholars, both young and old. I was a woman of substance who wanted to know the truth. I'd rather Jacob kept his mouth shut, and perhaps he could hold down his job.

"I wonder where the Samodivas hide," I said. "They surely prefer the cold room to the hot one."

"The unwise archaeologist who spoke to you about the shrine will be expelled from the Archaeological Association," the police chief said dryly.

The building of the *Dusk Daily* was not bad to look at. I had consulted the editor-in-chief of the popular newspaper for three years now.

"I have to go to work," I explained to the police chief. "As always, it was my pleasure talking to you."

John stopped the car, but before I opened the door, he said, "Sara, would you like to tell me more about what happened in Iztok Clinic last night?"

"Nothing happened in Iztok Clinic last night," I said.

"I'd try to search my memory for important details if I were in your shoes," John Cole said.

"Why should you?" One never knew with John Cole.

"You tell me," he said.

I watched the wipers struggling against the downpour. It was too warm in John's car. I had burst into sweat, and that made me a little uncomfortable.

"You must have done something impressive, otherwise Professor Gils wouldn't have asked me to arrange a meeting of minds between him and you. So, Sara, what did you do?"

John Cole's face looked genuinely intrigued. I enjoyed his twitchy mouth which was unable to keep quiet.

"I did something," I said, and that was the truth. "You can ask the famous professor about any colorful details, which I am sure you've already done."

John Cole was a handsome man, and I liked his strong arms. What I disliked was his broad grin. It meant I was in for a hard time.

There was a little thing I didn't tell John Cole about.

Last night, as I talked to the young archaeologist about Trun Shrine, two men in white coats entered the hospital room, and I suspected they were intent upon throwing me out of it.

"I have just visited my fiancé," I said, trying to soften the blow.

"I am Professor Andrew Gils," one of the men said. "It's a pleasure to meet you at Iztok Clinic, Miss Eutim."

I had never met that man before.

Then I noticed something that made me unable to catch my breath.

I was staring at green dots I had not seen since my childhood days. I thought of my aunt, and I remembered the candy man, the psychiatrist who had a green streak, a stream of tiny green flames in his hair, or should I say, inside his head, or *in his thoughts* as my aunt used to put it.

Professor Gils, or whoever he was, had a green streak in his hair as well.

I studied the younger man. There was something wrong with his left eye; he could not close it the way he should. I didn't care about his eye, though.

The back of my head hurt. This young man had the green streak, too. I saw green dots surrounding his head. At that moment, I thought I was out of my mind.

"You are sure there is nothing more to tell me?" the police chief asked, bringing me back to the pelting rain and the overcast sky.

"I am sure," I said, smiling at him.

Chapter Fourteen

Peter Stan was worried. His wife Margaret had just telephoned.

"I'll work late," she had said. "I'll hail a taxi, don't worry."

It was 9:20 PM. Margaret had not come back home. He dialed her number. She did not answer. His wife was the chairperson of the Trun Shrine Working Group. They tried to restore the shrine; at least that was what the *Dusk Daily* had written in its current issue. Peter tried not to think that John Cole, his best friend, was the co-chair of the group.

The teacher thought about his son. Tom had introduced his new girlfriend to his father, and Peter was glad his boy was trying to forget Boya, the woman who had ruined his life. Tom is a clever young man, Peter said to himself. Then his thoughts rushed back to Margaret, the working group and the two weird rooms, the dead bird, which John had found on the floor, and the pain he went through in the dark corridor. The journalist for the *Dusk Daily* mentioned nothing about the rooms. He only reported some archaeologists declared that the ruins were of no particular value, so the site should not be spoken enthusiastically about. Others, a much less numerous bunch, whose leader was Margaret, had published a memorandum.

After Peter Stan read it, he was seriously worried about his wife. Peter happened to be at home when Margaret drafted the message. In it, she wrote that the so-called Trun Heathen Shrine and the niches in Deaf Crags gorge were links of the same chain. A chain of death, Peter thought. She had described the steep passage that plunged under the asphalt square. A similar pit, a cube cut in a rocky outcrop at Deaf Crags, had puzzled scientists for years. Margaret had also written about the circular room full of crude pitchers and earthenware pans strewn on the floor of the passage under Gagarin Street. Peter was sorry he told her about it; his wife had also described the heaps of crude earthenware jugs and large baking dishes they had seen littering the narrow strip of land at the foot of Deaf Crags.

Peter thought. John Cole again … John had taken Margaret and Peter to Deaf Crags.

"It is a place that will stay at the back of your mind wherever you go," John Cole had said. It turned out he was right.

Deaf Crags were enormous and looked deceptively tranquil. The cliffs touched the sky, and there, under the ominous mountaintop which pierced the clouds, caves of irregular form punctuated the sheer rock face, black, imposing holes, threatening and fearful, gaped at the shallow valley below them. Margaret had whispered that they were bloodthirsty mouths big enough to swallow cities and men. The sinister, dark outlines of the holes and the steep red rocks underneath them appeared threatening. Peter still shivered at the memory of the murky, bottomless dips under the top of the enormous hill of hard red stone. These hollows were the eyes of a monster buried deep under the mountain, and Peter could feel the beast was not dead. It watched its unsuspecting victims, waiting silently to destroy them.

"The distance between the black holes is approximately one hundred feet," Margaret had said. "They form a belt below the summit."

"I wonder who carved them," Peter had added. "There is no path leading to any of them. And I can feel more than a hint of menace in the way the dark craters are glowering at me."

Margaret noticed it first: a crude, menacing sculpture of a bird, its wings of majestic black stone spread like a dark and stupendous cape. The beak, hard, strong, indomitable, seemed to have drilled the black holes, the tremendous talons had sunk into the red stone like the teeth of a beast of prey, and the whole mountain writhed in the relentless grip of the bird.

"How did you come to find this place?" Margaret asked as she turned to John Cole.

"I adore hiking in the Bulgarian mountains," John answered proudly. "It took me six years to catalog the so-called *unnatural sites* in Western Bulgaria. You still have not seen the most peculiar thing Deaf Crags are famous for, their eye. Follow me."

Margaret had jumped eagerly, thrilled, impatient like a little girl, full of admiration for the man who had cataloged that terrible place. She had never looked at Peter like that. Her eyes shone as she walked behind John, worshiping his steps, his genius, his litheness and daring spirit.

This was the unhappiest day in Peter Stan's life. He felt abandoned, useless, lost. Margaret had not even noticed he was not following them. John and his wife had climbed the hill where the enormous bird of black stone had perched. They looked tiny and insignificant next to its ominous shadow.

"Come over here, Pete," John Cole had called out. "Come and see the eye of the eagle."

Peter climbed reluctantly, almost crawling to the summit. Like a bolt out of the blue, it was suddenly there: he gasped, shocked and speechless. A perfect cube cut into the hard-red stone; a magnificent lake full of crystal-clear, transparent water glittered under the black talons of the stone bird. There was an enormous heap of earthenware pans, pots, and jugs on the brink of the artificial lake, and next to it stood another, even more enormous pile of stones, slabs and pebbles of all shapes and weights, and of different colors and hues.

"Maybe this is an altar or some other ritual place of an ancient Thracian tribe that lived in the valley," John Cole finally said. "Perhaps the big black holes below the summit were its burial ground."

"I think ... I think it is wonderful," Margaret had whispered, and on an impulse, she rushed to John Cole and kissed his cheek.

Yes, this was the worst day in Peter Stan's life.

He hated Deaf Crags.

He regretted that he had told Margaret about Trun Shrine in Dusk. He didn't want his wife to chair the working group in charge of deciphering the ancient ruins. He feared the biting sounds of the dreadful Trun recordings would hit Margaret once again. She was thin and physically weak, and he was worried about her. If only he could drag her away from this cheerless town of Dusk! He was sure he could find another place where she could be safe. If only he could convince her to give up the damned artificial language she'd been wasting her life on!

Peter Stan was a realist. He knew: Margaret would not give up her work. She would consult John Cole; she'd go again to Deaf Crags with the police chief. Maybe John would take her to Trun Shrine, to the two awful rooms. Peter feared Margaret would not survive the cold darkness in the endless passage. There might not be a bird for John Cole to put on her chest.

John Cole would touch Margaret's hand. Peter Stan could not stand the thought of it.

The heavy bird had saved Peter's life … Who had instructed John Cole to put the bird on Peter's chest? Who?

Peter Stan dialed Margaret's number one more time.

His wife did not pick up his call. It was 7:45 PM. He made up his mind to drive to the laboratory, and if he didn't find Margaret there, he'd look for her at the Town Hall. It was still early. He hated to wait.

Then it came to him: Tony's essay about the bird. Peter would read it now. Tony, the bully of the class, had taken the bird he had injured to his room. The feathered songster didn't sing at all; it dug a hole in the asphalt as it perched on it. The memory of the winged statue of black stone came back to the teacher; the pit that the flock of noiseless blackbirds plowed in the square, the ill child, the sharp talons of the bird at Deaf Cliffs.

The teacher went to his desk and read Tony's essay.

I called him Ben, the essay began. *He was not an ordinary bird. He was clumsy, and I knew the other birds hated him. I knew he didn't have friends and he was lonely.*

"Ben," I told him. "Cheer up. You are my friend. I'll be your friend no matter if you are plain and black and heavy like a ton of bricks."

"What is this damned bird doing in your room, Tony?!" Mom shouted.

She hated my cat and she poisoned it. She hated the tadpoles I'd brought home and she threw them in the dustbin. They died. I had a spider too, and I hid it from Mom in a jar. He was very strong, his legs were wiry, and his head was as soft as velvet. The spider was called James and he was my best friend. One day, I brought him to school and everybody screamed. I was the king of the school, and even Jason wanted to be my friend. I hate Jason, sir. He says I'm stupid. But I am not. A month ago, Mom found James, the spider, in that jar and shouted, "What's that damned thing doing in that jar?!" She suspected I'd feed him until he became big enough to bite her to death.

"He's not poisonous, Mom!" I tried to explain to her. "He's my best friend, his name is James."

She wouldn't listen and cautiously opened the lid. Then she poured water into the jar. James drowned. I saw his wiry legs kick the water and kick and kick, and his velvety head floated like a breadcrumb. I hated watching that. If Dad had been at home, James would have lived. Dad loved spiders; at least I hoped he did.

After James drowned, I was sick. Mom said she was ashamed of me.

"What's that bird doing here?!" she screamed again now, and I trembled with fear. She held a pail of water in her hand.

Then Mom smiled.

"Hi, birdie," she blurted out. "Are you hungry, birdie?"

I could hardly believe what I'd just heard.

"Give him something to eat," mom said.

I stared. She gave him breadcrumbs, but the bird would not eat. I knew it would not. I had given him bread, and grains of wheat and I had even given him my cheesecake. I knew Ben was not like the other birds. He ate nothing, and I was afraid he was going to die. Another thing happened, sir. Please do not think I am a liar, or that I have a screw loose.

Mom has a flowerpot with some white flowers in it. I hate flowers, sir, and I was glad Mom's flower was not doing well. She loved that flowerpot more than me. She watered it and cut the dry leaves. If Dad had not gone away, things would have been different. We might have played football, the two of us. But he was a sailor, my father was. He was a strong man, and he could beat ten bullies single-handedly. But Dad was a sailor and he sailed the seas, and Mom was crazy about her flowerpot. I put salt in it, sir, I put salt in it every evening, and every morning, too. And the flower wilted and withered, and Mom was unhappy.

That silly boy, the old teacher thought. He remembered: when Thomas, his son, was a little boy, Peter had bought him a dog. His son didn't like it. He didn't like the cat Peter had bought him. He didn't like the aquarium with the goldfish Margaret gave him for his ninth birthday. His son loved his mother's computer; he was crazy about all mechanical gadgets Margaret worked with. The pony Peter Stan had bought his son didn't make the boy happy. The little one hated riding it. Peter took care of their son. Margaret was the family's genius. His son knew that too. He loved the minute Margaret's car pulled up at the front gate of their house. Why isn't my son like Tony? the old teacher thought sadly.

I had poured so much salty water into the flowerpot that I was afraid Mom would notice. I collected plant lice and I set them free on the leaves of my mother's plant. She found them out and spent a fortune on some green smelly liquid that killed the poor old lice. This didn't help the flower. Its leaves were no good.

Don't call me a liar, sir. I remember that one day you told Jason I was not cruel, and I was not stupid. You said I was different. You said some children needed more time to express what they felt. I wouldn't lie to you.

I told you the bird didn't eat anything. Ben lay on the floor and I thought he was sick, but he wasn't. He flew to the withered flower. I was so happy: my Ben was strong and he simply didn't need food. He was a strange thing, my Ben was. Then I thought something was wrong. At first, I didn't know what it was. Then I knew. It was Mom's flower. It no longer looked dead. It was green and its blossoms were white as ice cream. New leaves sprouted as I watched the flowerpot. Ben, my bird, was looking at it.

Then the telephone rang. At last, Peter thought. It must be Margaret. Let it be Margaret.

A woman's voice Peter Stan didn't recognize buzzed in his ear.

"You don't know me," the voice said. "I am Boya Bagd, your son's girlfriend."

Peter Stan dropped the essay he was reading, He knew very well who Boya was: the woman who had abandoned his son while he was dying in the hospital.

"I know your son is doing fine," Boya said at the other end of the line. "And I know he still loves me. I have read all his emails and his letters."

This woman had taken his son's money and had run away.

"I'd like to tell you, sir, your son is a wonderful man. Please, tell him I miss him."

The old teacher didn't say anything.

"Please don't hang up!" the woman who had said she was Boya exclaimed. "I would like to talk to you, sir."

"How can I help you, Madame?" Peter Stan asked.

Boya's voice was melodious and light. He had forgotten how much he had enjoyed listening to it. Margaret had disliked the girl right from the start. Pure female jealousy, Peter had thought, dismissing the idea. He was not right, of course. Margaret was convinced Boya had tried to meddle with her computer and accused the young woman of trying to spy on her work.

"Sir, I work for the Trun Shrine Association."

Peter Stan gave a start. *Association?* Give me a break.

"I have to carry out an in-depth analysis of the birds, Mr. Stan." Peter kept silent as the woman went on. "We are aware of the fact that one of the birds was injured and a student you teach, Tony Jamison, took it, declaring he'd take care of it."

"Your information is correct," Peter Stan said.

"Tony Jamison's classmates informed me that he had written an essay on what exactly happened that day."

"Your information is correct," Peter Stan said.

"I'd like to read this essay," the women at the other end of the line said.

Peter Stan looked at the sheets of paper that had fallen onto the floor. He had not read the essay to the end.

Chapter Fifteen

Ivan was cooking his dinner when the doorbell rang. He didn't expect anybody. Was it Professor Gils? In the evening, the professor had telephoned, asking if Ivan would like to work as his assistant at Iztok Clinic. It couldn't be Professor Gils; the professor wouldn't drop in uninvited. He carefully planned his daily agenda and did not allow the slightest aberration from it. Perhaps Ivan's mother had rung the bell? Most improbable, she, a cardiologist, worked at St. Anna Hospital in the capital Sofia. Ivan had made her sick with worry. She was by his side when he was raving, and Professor Gils told him she had waited at the door of the operating room. Her hair had turned white within a fortnight.

I'm healthy, mother, he dreamed of telling her and was impatient to see her sweet eyes that had helped him struggle and live on.

"Coming!" Ivan shouted.

He opened the front door. Slim, light of foot, a beautiful woman he least expected to see stood in front of him, unsure what to do.

"Boya!" he breathed, panic rushing through him. His jeans were stained, his shirt was crumpled. His dinner was cooking, and a strong smell of burning food wafted in the air.

"Good evening, Ivan," the beautiful woman said.

He forgot his stained jeans. Her face told him everything was ok as it used to be. Or was it?

"My left eye ..." he blurted out. "You see, Boya ... I can't close it properly ... and after the operation my face ... I look bad."

"You look good, Ivan," she said. "You know I never lie to you."

Her smile gave him the feeling she cared. She did.

"The brain surgery was successful," he started. "Come in, Boya. I was cooking dinner … and … something happened to the mashed potatoes."

"I brought you some apple juice," she said. "I know you love it."

"Oh, yes, yes," Ivan said. "Please take a seat."

He stole a look at her, worried. He had not cleaned his room that perfectly, and she adored cleanliness. His books were all over the place, and she was as neat and tidy as Professor Gils. Ivan rarely dusted the television screen, and she would surely notice the thick layer of dust on the shelves.

"Your room is cozy as before," she said. "Let me see what that delicious stew is doing on the cooking stove."

"It's not a stew," Ivan groaned. "It's supposed to be mashed potatoes. Look, Boya, I …"

He stopped short. He saw them, the streak of green dots around her head.

"What?" the beautiful woman said. "You're staring at me."

"Nothing," he said quietly. "I just thought … I thought."

He fell silent, averting his eyes.

"What is it, Ivan?" she asked softly. "Have I grown older? You saw new wrinkles on my cheeks?"

"No, no!" he denied vehemently. "You are beautiful, Boya, and you know it. I know it. I can see it."

"Thank you," she smiled. "You can relax now. I'll go check what's happening to the mashed potatoes over there. It seems to me they are burning."

She handled the cooking stove, her fingers dashing to the objects with graceful lightness, her hair, dark brown, curly and thick, a whirlwind of happiness. The green dots glittered, swimming above her temples, minute flames, waltzing fireflies, and the air around him felt as if the apartment was on fire.

"What is it, Ivan?" Boya said as she turned around sharply.

"Nothing," he said.

She hates my face, a bitter thought crossed his mind and for a split second, he wished she were gone.

"I like the way you look," she said, her eyes agleam with delight. "And you are not as impatient as you used to be."

Ivan reached out his hand to touch her, but he could not bring himself to do it.

"Wait," Boya whispered. "Wait. I'll fix you something to eat."

She salvaged some of the mashed potatoes and gave him cheese she found in the fridge. Boya knew everything, it was she who found the best spot for every piece of furniture, she had chosen the chest of drawers, the shelves for his books. She had not visited him after his brain surgery.

"How's your mother doing?" she asked. "Is she as busy as before?"

"Busier," Ivan answered.

"She is a great woman," Boya said.

They ate quietly. He loved the way she collected the breadcrumbs, the glow of her clear skin a smile in the air, light like an afternoon breeze. He loved the softness of her hand and wanted the warmth of her body, but he could not bring himself to touch her. She knew everything about Ivan's mother, Dr. Mary Stevens.

When Ivan was twelve, his mother, 47 at that time, had said, "I want you to know something." He still remembered he had panicked. His mother's voice frightened him.

"I am not your natural mother," she had said.

She had always been by his side. She cooked meals for him and gave him medicines when he was ill. She had taught him to read and write even before he went to school.

"Your natural mother will come and take you home. You have to love her and be a good son to her."

He had swallowed hard as he tried hard to fight back a tear, but it had rolled down his cheek and he was ashamed of it.

Ivan had told Boya that story. She knew everything. His real mother was a much younger woman, soft spoken, calm blue eyes. She made pancakes and pancakes for months on end. Ivan's natural mother didn't speak much and often sent him to the local supermarket in Radomir, a small town with an ancient medieval church and a deserted park, where Ivan roamed. When the woman with the calm blue eyes stopped making pancakes, she sat in her chair for hours, her face expressionless. Ivan cooked leek soup for her. They rarely talked.

"Who is my father?" Ivan had asked her once.

"He's dead," the woman told him. "Go do your homework."

Ivan studied hard and read for hours.

"You don't seem to be clever," the woman said. "Is there something wrong with your memory? Other kids learn their lessons more quickly than you."

He had been hurt. Then a stranger started visiting their apartment, a monsieur with a mustache and a booming voice. One day he asked if Ivan had a girlfriend. Ivan said he hadn't.

"You're slow," the man laughed and winked. "Or perhaps you don't like girls?"

"I don't like them," Ivan said, and the man laughed again.

"Pack up your things," his mother had said, her blue eyes calm as usual. When his two suitcases were ready, she drove him to the railway station, bought a ticket for him, and when the train came, said, "Goodbye. Get off at the station in Dusk. Doctor Stevens will wait for you there."

Ivan had not said anything.

The woman selected a banknote and gave it to him. "Buy a sandwich."

Ivan took the money and didn't say thank you. At the railway station in Dusk, his mother waited for him. After he caught a glimpse of her green coat, he rushed like mad to her. She gave him a bear hug and kissed him, and her tears were on his cheeks. The cold and dusty station suddenly seemed so beautiful he could stay there with his mother all his life.

Boya knew all that.

"I went to look for you at Iztok Clinic, Ivan," she said. "I wanted to see you."

"Yes," he said quietly.

They ate in silence. Ivan wanted her so much that he was afraid to look at her. He could feel there was something wrong, and the cozy silence that used to hold them together before he fell ill, had vanished for good.

"Maybe you don't want me because you see something wrong with me?" she asked as she took his hand.

"No."

"You keep on looking at my hair. Is there something wrong with it … or with my face?"

The green dots, he thought. He should take her to the clinic. Would Gils see her green dots? Imagine Gils lied he had seen the green stream, floating above Ivan's head? Why should he? Gils had saved Ivan's life. Gils was there for his patient all through the long period of recuperation. But what if Gils had something else on his mind? An experiment? It was only Ivan who noticed green dots above Gils' head; nobody else in the clinic did. It was best to invite Boya to the clinic and introduce her to Gils.

Boya said, "I looked for you in the hospital twice, Ivan. I explained to the nurse on duty we were friends and I wanted to tell you something important. She informed me you spoke in a foreign language. The hissing and screeching sounds you produced were recorded and killed a tumor. The patient was cancer-free, she told me."

Ivan listened. The clinic was agog with curiosity. Doctors he didn't know said hi to him, others talked agitatedly in low voices after they saw him in the canteen. He had become a minor celebrity.

"Will you let me listen to these recordings, Ivan?" Boya asked.

He looked at her. Her face was serene and gentle, her eyes clear and luminous.

"Are you ill?" he asked.

"I don't know," she said.

"Come tomorrow to Iztok Clinic," he said.

She stood up, rushed to him and her mouth was on his cheek. She kissed him, kissed him warmly, hungrily, and everything was as it used to be when she chose his chest of drawers, the shelves for his books and his second-hand bed. She was the most wonderful girl Ivan knew.

"It's like before," she whispered.

"Yes," Ivan said. She was right. She always was. She was so pretty.

"I have to go," Boya said. "You are so kind. Thanks for the mashed potatoes and the cheese."

"Stay, please," Ivan said. She kissed him.

"See you tomorrow at the clinic," she said. "I'd like to meet your mother … no, not Dr. Stevens. Your real mother, the woman who used to make pancakes for you."

"Why?"

"She'll give me the recipe for her pancakes," Boya whispered. "I'll make pancakes for you, too."

No other woman had wanted to cook lunch for him. Boya was the most beautiful girl, the only one he wanted.

"I don't know where she is," he said.

"Don't you have her telephone number?" Boya asked and after Ivan shook his head, she went on impatiently. "Could you give me her email address, her postal address, anything?"

"She gave me some money, but it was not enough to buy a sandwich," Ivan said.

"Didn't you keep the money? Is it the only thing you have from your mom?"

"I gave it to a beggar," Ivan said. "Please stay."

"We'll find her, promise? Tomorrow," she whispered. "I'll stay tomorrow, and I'll make pancakes for you."

Her smiling eyes made the room bright and cheerful. The air was sweet to breathe with her by his side.

"Oh, I almost forgot," she said opening her purse. "I brought something for you."

Ivan was impatient. What might this be? Boya had an eye for tiny, beautiful knick-knacks. He kept them all—the little wooden zebras, the silver cups from which she had made him drink water, the brass tortoises, the glass cats …

"That's for you!" she said triumphantly, producing some sharp-edged, gray stone from her purse. "It's a good charm!"

Ivan watched it closely.

A good charm …

It was a stone that closely resembled the one which Ivan had dropped in Tintin's aquarium. It almost killed the team of archaeologists who had worked at Trun Shrine; the stone that had done in the eel.

"What?" Boya asked and smiled. "Don't you like my lucky charm?"

"I do," Ivan said.

The sharp edges of the thing were not pleasant to his eye. He reached out and touched the stone. Pain shot through him; his fingers tingled. His muscles were tense and hurt the way they did when he dropped the other sharp-edged stone in the aquarium of the eel.

"See you tomorrow at the clinic, let's say at 10 a.m.?" Boya said, smiling at him.

All pain was gone.

He fingered the stone, smiled back and said, "Let's say 2 PM."

More than ever before, the green dots over Boya's head looked like a cloud of magnificent fireflies.

Ivan looked out the window and saw the little fair-haired girl. He didn't know why he had grown to like her, perhaps because her shadowy silhouette looked like a veil of green dots.

Chapter Sixteen

I always felt ill at ease in hospitals; however, Iztok Clinic didn't look like a hospital at all. It was quiet and clean, no hurrying nurses were in sight, no doctors in white coats, and you didn't see patients either. I felt guilty, and guilt was a feeling that didn't sit well with me.

Jacob, the young archaeologist … he believed that he was engaged to me. I had to come to the clinic to let him know I was going to break off our engagement. This would break my heart too, that was what I was going to tell him. I wondered what men saw in me, intelligence, beauty, or perhaps sex and wildflowers. Did I inspire confidence? I had been engaged more times than I cared to remember; another engagement was a shadow of a kite in my backyard that would leave me quite unimpressed. Jacob, the young archaeologist, was an innocent soul, who didn't deserve the usual treatment I reserved for my fiancés. After I got engaged to a guy, I got bored very quickly and saying no word of warning to my beloved man, I collected all my belongings and deserted the battlefield. It was clean and easy, and when the stunned man called me, I explained he had not given me the tenderness and understanding I had longed for. That was not enough, of course. More often than not, the prospective husband felt insulted and demanded further explanations. Saying that I was in love with another man was the next step I made and that sealed the deal.

The innocent archaeologist didn't deserve that. I would simply tell him that we were incompatible and could not live under the same roof. I'd like to carve out a stellar career for myself, and that was a process which excluded married life, children, etc. I could always resort to the *I am in love with another man* approach if Jacob became difficult.

"Sara!" He jumped out of his bed, and I was afraid he'd fall on the floor. "I'm strong," he assured me, staggering worse than before. "Sara, I missed you! I missed you a lot."

He was tall and very thin as he stretched out his hands impatient to give me a kiss, his huge smile preposterous on his weak face. He had not shaved. I stared at him. This man reminded me of somebody I had seen before. I was sure of it: the thin fine nose, the dimple in his chin, the eyes, dark brown, gleaming.

"I haven't shaved," he muttered. "I dreamed about you. You are more beautiful than my dream, my Sara!"

I had made up my mind not to kiss him, but he gave me no time to react.

"I'm so happy you are here!" he whispered. "I treated the guys to coffee, and we celebrated our engagement. The doctors wouldn't allow us to drink anything else."

He seemed even younger than the night before when we got engaged.

"I told my friends about you," he said. "They want to see you. Here, I have something for you, Sara. I've kept it for you, my love. It's a nice candy bar."

Then I knew. Jacob the archaeologist reminded me of the candy man, the doctor my dear auntie had taken me to when I was a child.

Jacob's face was so pale and so happy I felt a stab of remorse. A woman suffers no remorse when she breaks her engagement: that was rule number one with me. A woman has to be independent; she feels no pity for men she plans to ditch. That was rule number two.

"I know why you're looking at me like that," the young archaeologist said. "Because I have no car and can't give you a lift home. But I am strong, honey. No car in the world can take you to a mountaintop, Sara, but I can carry you. Here, take the candy bar."

Take the candy bar ... the tasty almonds and chocolate.

Jacob Harvey looked so much like the candy man, the psychiatrist with the green dots in his hair who gave me candy bars: the dimple in his chin, the prominent cheekbones, the patient smile, the quiet kind eyes. It felt weird. I hated it when the past came back; its cold waves hit me hard as a ruler. I loathed the green dots in that psychiatrist's hair. It was one of the most disturbing memories of my childhood. This man, the archaeologist, looked so much like the shrink.

"We are …" I was determined to declare that we were incompatible, that I wanted a stellar career, but the warm sun in Jacob's eyes and his thin smiling face made me stop. That was a wrong thing to do, so I went on, "Jacob, we are …"

"I know! We are meant for each other," he said. "You've already told me this. I've been looking for you for so long."

Now, there were no monitors and no glass tubes attached to his body.

"Jacob … Jacob, I'd like to carve out a career and I think we are …"

"We'll carve it out together!" he said.

"I thought a lot about married life and …"

"So did I," he said. "I'd love us to have a big family, many children, fairy tales in the evening the way my father told us, my sisters and me. And my mother sang to us, you know."

"Jacob, I can't sing," I lied.

"Don't worry! You'll take on the fairy tales. You are a good storyteller, Sara. I know what I'm saying."

"Jacob …"

"Oh, it has almost slipped out of my mind … I was so sick, and I forgot to tell you. You asked me about Trun Shrine, remember, Sara?"

"Yes," I said, quite glad that he took a step back. I'd just let him kiss me and felt bad about it.

"I was going to die," he said. "And then Professor Gils and a younger doctor came up with an alternative therapy. A very unusual thing, so I thought we were doomed."

At that point, I wished I had delivered the monologue on incompatibility I had prepared well in advance. I didn't feel like wasting time on this buffoon. Yes, I was sorry for him. So what?

"Trun was the only word I could distinguish amid the cacophony: Trun! Trun! Trun!"

"What?" I said, suddenly intrigued.

"I told you it was a crazy thing, that therapy," Jacob grinned happily. "You wouldn't believe it, but it worked. I feel strong now. I can carry you to the top of Deaf Crags on my back."

"Where no car can climb," I said. "What about Trun?"

"I don't know," he said. "But we felt much better after those hissing sounds dissolved in the night. It was after the recording ended that I remembered the Old Bulgarian song about the Trun Chark. You've asked me to tell you about everything I've seen in the shrine. You wanted to know all I had heard about Trun."

He stopped talking. This time his dazzling smile made me angry.

"Oh, don't get scared, honey," he said interpreting my growing impatience as panic. In my view, this was a sure sign of his poor intellect. "It's just an old song no one remembers anymore," his voice thinned into a consolatory mutter. "I found it in the archives of Radomir Monastery not far from here." *The path from healing a man to murdering a man is shorter than a step. It takes a doctor to cure you and the same doctor to kill you,* he hummed softly to himself. "That's what the song says," The man paused, beamed a smile at me and blabbed on, "I love delving into the ancient Eastern Orthodox monastery repositories. They've accumulated great collections of Old Bulgarian manuscripts. You wouldn't believe how rich some of those moldy archives are! Well, I'll admit here and now that most items I've read are book-keeping notes, birth certificates, etc."

"What about that song … the song about Trun" I cut him short and that was the first time I had discovered the most annoying quality of the man I got engaged to over the weekend. He digressed.

"In an abandoned church, I discovered an architectural plan of Radomir Monastery a century and a half before it was actually built!"

"The song about Trun …" I nearly shouted, but he was extremely keen on telling me about Radomir Monastery first.

"I found the sketches of the frescoes a century before the foundations of the thing were laid! The Old Bulgarians were really remarkable."

His ravings about the unique frescoes, the secret hiding places, the gold crosses and icons had no end. If I interrupted him, he, full of beans, prattled on about the lives of saints he had studied, and quoted from memory long excerpts from ancient prayers. I listened gloomily, thinking I'd have been much better off if I had told him we were incompatible right from the start.

"The most remarkable thing I found in the monastery was the song about the Trun Chark," he said, and I was on full alert again. "Perhaps you know what chark means?" he went on impishly, and I had to make considerable efforts to keep my dark temper under control. I hated archaeologists who wasted my time. Don't ask questions, this became rule number one as far as conversation with my latest fiancé was concerned. Within a quarter of an hour, I intuitively stumbled upon the correct approach to this wayward intellectual.

"I don't know what *chark* means," I admitted.

"I thought so." He grinned. "It's an Old Bulgarian word which stands for *machine,* or a *complex apparatus.*"

"But Old Bulgarians had hardly any apparatuses let alone complex ones," I objected, forgetting momentarily rule number one I had imposed on discussions with the fervent archaeologist.

"That makes it all the more intriguing," he said triumphantly. "This song, if we believe the note scribbled in Greek that I found attached to it—mind you, the text of the song itself, is in Old Bulgarian! Well, the note in Greek says that this is a song dating from the twelfth century. *The path from healing a man to murdering a man is shorter than a step. It takes a doctor to cure you and the same doctor to kill you.* Remember?"

"No!" I exclaimed dramatically, hoping that saying no would spur the guy into getting to the point. I was wrong, alas! He went as far as expounding his views on the morphology and syntax of the Old Bulgarian language. Thank God, I didn't have a gun in my hand.

"The contents of the song might be of interest to you. I published a short article on this topic in *The Journal of Archaeology,* but no one seemed interested," he added gloomily, and this encouraged me to voice my indignation.

"No!"

"The song is unique, Sara," he heaved a deep sigh. "It is a very short one, though. It says that there is a *chark* in Trun, which can transform disease into excellent health. One has to bring a cup or any receptacle that can hold water, then simply throw the thing into the *chark.*"

I listened to him, but not that attentively.

"It rings a bell," I said. "I think I've read something about throwing cups and pans to get rid of your disease."

"Perhaps you've read my article in the *Dusk Daily,*" he said smiling.

"The one about Bare Mountain. I wrote it a week after I found the complete text of the Trun Chark song. In my opinion, this song is dedicated to the four steps towards truth."

Maybe he expected I'd break into rapturous applause, a move I failed to make.

"Sara, you told me you wanted to carve out a brilliant career for yourself," he said heatedly. "This song is the key to it!"

"Come off it, Jacob!" I said, finding it difficult to control the dark side of my nature.

"We found a heap of old pans and jugs in Trun Shrine in Dusk, Sara, a big heap of them," Jacob said. Then he took my hand in his and very slowly and clearly as if talking to a little and not particularly clever kid, asked, "Do you remember what else you read in that article?"

It was not necessary to try very hard. I took pride in my brilliant memory; it rose to the occasion one more time. I was not confident as to how my fiancé would accept the proof of my unerring intellect.

"I vaguely remember the article said something about throwing stones," I said. I knew from experience men wouldn't gladly stand clever women. So far, keeping my intellectual capacity under cover had been both the best escape route and the most rewarding policy for me.

"If someone in the Dusk region is ill, he or she takes a jug or a pan to the top of Bare Mountain," the archaeologist began. "The locals believe you recover your health after you leave the thing there. According to a proverb popular in Dusk Gorge, such a person is a dead tree, although cherries sparkle on the dead branches, and …"

Give me a break. Was he talking about the picture that hung in my bedroom: five dry trees heavy with ripe, juicy cherries?

"Oh," I said. He was still holding my hand. His fingers were warm, and I liked this, but carefully tried to loosen his grip.

"Your skin is healthy," he said. This was the first compliment of this kind I had ever received. I'd been told my skin was radiant, perfect, glowing, soft, flawless, or beautiful. "Sara, the song I've found is unique. It says—if someone gives you hell, you describe the jerk to a stone and throw the stone into the Trun Chark."

"And?" I asked, which proved to be a wrong way of responding to the archaeologist's enthusiasm.

"I have read everything one can possibly read about you in the newspapers and magazines, Sara. I've searched your name online a number of times and I think that you know very well what I'm speaking about."

I knew. I also knew that men could hardly stand clever women. I had had more affairs than I cared to reveal before the public eye.

"I can only conjecture that the Old Bulgarian song provides no proof as to the veracity of the information it hints at," I said rather formally, and my present fiancé's hand let go of my fingers.

At that moment, a beautiful young nurse entered the hospital room, cleared her throat, then, far too amiably, smiled at the patient, ignoring me altogether.

"Sir, I am afraid the young lady has to leave the ward. The doctor would like to speak to you in private."

I had to give credit to Jacob for his efforts not to smile fatuously at the extraordinarily pretty nurse. He nodded, then directed his attention back to me. I couldn't say I disliked that. I appreciated the fact that my new fiancé (though I was quite sure he'd be another short-lived item on my busy agenda) was truly fascinated to talk to me.

"The sick person threw the pan into the *chark* and went back home alive and kicking," he said. "I am that person, Sara."

He stood up, a weedy man, thin arms and thinner thighs all over the place under his pajamas. I couldn't help doubting that he could carry me on his back to the top of a moderately steep hill.

"I am strong!" he said rolling up his sleeve to show me his bulging muscles that didn't bulge at all.

He reminded me of a long-legged bird, a stork or a heron, that was on the verge of spreading its flimsy wings. The sunny summers in his eyes changed everything; they melted the ice under my skin.

"You don't think I'm strong," he said.

"No," I agreed. "But you look like a long-distance runner," this statement was part of a carefully deliberated strategy to never offend my fiancés. If he's fat, tell him he looks like a wrestler. If not, he's a long-distance runner—that was another important rule with respect to men who wanted to make you a decent wife. I doubted Jacob could be a runner at all. He was too lightweight to run; it would be easier for him to glide like a kite in the wind.

"Sara, I think I have to tell you something. It might be unimportant," he paused, and I was just about to interject another *No!* when he squeezed my hand gently and said, "Don't be afraid, it's nothing serious. I couldn't but notice it, you know."

I hated guys who beat about the bush. It would be more precise to say I despised guys who beat about the bush, but a bird in the hand was worth two in the bush, so I kept my irritability to myself. It paid.

"The doctors brought a big stone and left it in our room—a big room with three beds in it. We were there, the three of us that had worked in Trun Shrine. This stone almost killed my colleagues, you know. Everybody's noses bled, the guys puked all the time, and I thought they were going to cash in their chips. I know what you'll say, but it was not my imagination. I was all right. I felt no pain at all. All the rest were sick, and stabbing pain paralyzed Mr. Morrison, you remember him, the red-haired guy. Then they took that stone away and things changed for the better. I felt as strong as a lion … I always feel as strong as a lion; you can take my word for it."

I let him prattle on. I remembered that John Cole, the police chief, had given me a stone, a gray, sharp-edged one that I'd put on the mantelpiece. "Let this bring you good luck," he had said. Nobody had given me stones before; precious stones yes, but gray, ordinary stones? No, thank you. At the time, I thought John Cole had a screw loose.

The extraordinarily pretty nurse inserted her arrogant head into the room and, smiling sweetly, reminded me I had to leave without delay.

"There is something more to the song, Sara," Jacob said, his eyes as soft as breadcrumbs.

"No!?" I exclaimed, hoping my negative-interrogative approach would work again.

It did.

"Yes! The song tells you where you can find a quiet spot of love and happiness."

And pigs would fly, I thought as I blurted out, "Who built the *chark,* Jacob? Does your song mention something about this issue?"

It so transpired that the technique I resorted to was wrong. The archaeologist embarked on a long, convoluted lecture on Tangra, the Old Bulgarian supreme god, then concentrated on a cheerful crowd of

Thracian, Slavonic, Old Greek and Turkish gods and ghouls that left me none the wiser.

"So you don't know who built the thing," I concluded.

"No," he said sadly, more than ever resembling a stork hit by a torrential rain. The bright summers of his eyes sank deep into the flood. I kissed him on the cheek, feeling sorry for the long-legged bird that gave me warm winds in his words. I knew I'd abandon him. Don't fall in love with the man you are engaged to, Article 1 of my Law on Fiancés. Don't discover warm winds anywhere. You'll come to regret this later. All these were ground rules I'd laid down for myself. I'd never broken a rule so far.

"Please come tomorrow, Sara," Jacob said.

I had learned all there was to learn from this overenthusiastic scholar. It was about time I deserted the battlefield and sank into obscurity.

"Jacob, we are …" I had planned to say … *so different.* The guy deserved at least that. I suspected he had never had a lasting relationship with a girl, and I felt kind of—how shall I put it—I'd better not put it at all for if I did, I would break all the rules I had drawn up. "Goodbye, Jacob," I said.

"Don't say *goodbye,* honey," the archaeologist said. "Say *see you tomorrow!*"

"I'd like carve out a career for myself," I began.

"We'll carve it for you!" He was beaming at me. "Sara, dearest, I think I know one of these places."

"These places?" I started then, sensing I was on the wrong track, I corrected my mistake, "No!"

"I know where it is, Sara … the quiet spot of love and happiness. I can't wait to take you there. You'll see the Trun Chark at work."

"Perhaps you'll tell me about Deaf Crags?" I said, and I saw nothing but July afternoons and happy kites in his eyes.

"I searched your name, Sara. I read everything I could possibly find about you. You really are the woman I've hoped that I would find. Clever and beautiful, beautiful, beautiful …"

"Shut up, Jacob."

That was the most appropriate moment to tell him we were incompatible, but I missed it somehow.

"See you tomorrow, honey," he said, and before I could react, he kissed me. I kissed him back, breaking rule number five of my strict regulations on fiancés. What the hell!

I left the room smiling like a fool. The extraordinarily beautiful nurse I had come to dislike for no reason at all padded across the hall, smiled her charming smile I had no liking for, and announced in her measured, clear voice, "Professor Gils would like to talk to you, Ms. Eutim. It will take no more than a minute. Follow me, please."

Chapter Seventeen

The corridor was white and immaculately clean. At its end, a man in a white coat waited. He was tall, bespectacled and thin.

"Good morning, Sara Eutim," the man said.

I knew him right away, the famous man of science.

"Come in," he said, as he opened a door before me.

"Good morning, Professor Gils," I said.

His face was weak, very white, his blue eyes watchful behind the glasses, his lips thin. I saw them again, the green dots, floating around his head, and I tried not to pay attention to them, telling myself the greenish streak was nothing more than a scar. Let's leave it at that.

The room was big and very clean, the desk looked rather small, the chairs too ordinary.

"Please, take a seat, Ms. Eutim," the professor said, smiling at me.

I wondered why he welcomed me so warmly, scarlet patches aglow on his narrow cheeks.

"You wanted to see me," I said.

"Yes." Hhis pale eyes were on my face. "I wanted to talk to you," he paused, his cheeks pale again. "36 Gagarin Street. Do you remember the big house with the dark rooms, the narrow backyard and the street that was deserted most of the time?"

I looked at him. 36 Gagarin Street, my old house, the rooms with high ceilings, the chest of drawers I talked to and the picture of my uncle, or was it one of my mother's lovers that I'd told all my secrets to? My mother who didn't have time for me.

"I used to live in that neighborhood, Professor," I said. "37 Gagarin Street, a big house, spacious rooms, a piano, pictures on the walls, splendid garden that was transformed into a small park. Yes, Gagarin Street was deserted most of the time. That was the neighborhood of the warehouses."

"I am Andrew, the boy who lived in the apartment house opposite yours," he said. "The boy to whom you told your fairy tales."

"Andrew … So, you are Professor Andrew Gils," I said. "I wondered what had happened to that boy."

He smiled.

"Coffee, tea, mineral water?" he asked.

"I have to run," I said. "I'm already missing an appointment."

"I've read your books and I collect the articles you publish," he said. "I've wanted to talk to you all this time."

I didn't say anything. The man was not attractive, too weak, too thin, and too clean. I had read about him, too. Professor Gils was a brilliant neurosurgeon, among the best of his generation. Patients from all over Europe and Asia visited Iztok Clinic to be examined and treated by him. It was hard to believe that the sickly boy who hardly spoke a word grew into a world-famous scientist. I did not like him.

"Strange that the lonely girl who told fairy tales to a closed door would become such a beautiful, self-confident young woman," he said.

"Strange indeed," I agreed.

It was a pleasant autumn day. The sun shone, the leaves of the trees were yellow and red, and I didn't like them. I never liked autumn with its silence and unnecessary rains. It was quiet in the room.

"You see them, don't you, Sara Eutim?" the professor said softly. "You see the green dots inside my head."

I didn't say anything. He was calm, his tired eyes looking at me, his pale face closed.

"I see green dots around your head, Sara," he sighed. "Ever since I was a boy, I've looked for people with green dots around their heads. I found one man, the psychiatrist my mother took me to. Do you remember him? The guy who gave us candies."

"I called him the candy man."

"And I found you. Can you see them around my head, the green dots?"

If you see something that other people don't see, don't speak about it, especially if the thing in question is green dots around a renowned professor's head: that was a rule I established the minute I saw the tiny green flames, swimming around the famous guy's brow. Once you admitted what you saw, the next thing was to prove to a large board of psychiatrists that you were not mentally ill. This was an impossible thing to do.

"I see no green dots," I said.

"I think it is because we both lived in that neighborhood," the professor said. "36 Gagarin Street, 37 Gagarin Street … and now they are conducting an archaeological excavation there. You, Sara Eutim, got engaged to the archaeological team leader, a man they told me you hadn't known before."

"Professor Gils, it was an honor talking to you," I said.

"I happened to operate on a guy who lived in the same neighborhood, 35 Gagarin Street, Ms. Eutim," he said. "Perhaps you could spare a few more minutes. Would you like to meet him?"

"Unfortunately …" I started.

"Please, Sara," the professor asked, his voice young and quiet, bringing me back to the time when a little boy waved his hand to a little girl who lived in the apartment across the street. I knew the little boy was the only friend in the world the little girl had.

"Okay," I said.

The young man who entered the room was taller and more corpulent than the professor. His face was intelligent, a little distorted it was true, but open and attractive after a fashion. I could see the green dots in his hair, a thick swarm of green specks like a cloud of tiny glowworms on a warm summer evening. I made up my mind to accept them as another scar and attach no importance to their uncertain light. And yes, I was intrigued. I was a writer accustomed to summing up any situation no matter how difficult it was. Ms. Eutim was on the lookout for a good story. So, I knew of four persons that had the *green streak:*

1. The psychiatrist i.e., the candy man who had fought my *disease* when I was a child.

2. John Cole, the chief of Dusk police.

3. Andrew Gils, the famous neurosurgeon at Iztok Clinic.

4. The young man with the intelligent but not that attractive face, whose name I still didn't know.

For a split second, I noticed that Professor Gils and the young doctor exchanged glances.

"Yes," the young man said, and the professor nodded.

"Ms. Eutim, let me introduce you to Doctor Ivan Georg, a neurologist at Iztok Clinic," Professor Gils said.

"I am glad to meet you, Doctor Georg," I said.

Silence reigned in the spacious room. Doctor Georg fidgeted nervously, lowering his eyes as I looked at him. I could see a deep scar above his left ear.

"Welcome to Iztok Clinic, Ms. Eutim," he muttered. "I've read your novel about a little provincial town. I liked your book. I have forgotten the title. Forgive me."

They were there, and I could see them clearly, the crumbs of green light around Dr. Georg's head, so I did my best not to stare. I had a set of rules I went by: don't stare; don't show you are impressed; don't show you like something; don't show you dislike something. I had avoided trouble by applying these basic principles. Although my editors didn't envy me my happiness, I was a very happy woman.

"Ms. Eutim," said the professor who was the quiet boy from my childhood. "Can you sense something out of the ordinary in … in the room?"

He was watching me, and I didn't mind. I was used to being stared at.

"Should I?" I said as I gave him a quick once-over. Gils was pale, his eyes appeared shallow behind the glasses, and I could find no trace of the timid kid I used to tell fairy tales to. "I do not think you are the boy I used to tell about Cinderella, Professor," I added.

He smiled then most unexpectedly asked me, "Can you see a green halo around Dr. Georg's head or around mine?"

"Green halo?" I repeated. "I am sorry. I can see nothing, Professor."

"Not even small green specks?"

"Not even green specks," I said.

He smiled again.

"It was nice talking to you, Ms. Eutim. Perhaps we could get a cup of coffee one of these days?"

It was raining harder; the other doctor, the younger one with the exceptionally intelligent face, fidgeted uneasily, looking away.

"I have just got engaged to a clever man, Professor, so I don't expect I'd be having enough time to converse with you on topics of mutual interest."

"If one trusts the local newspapers, you've been engaged a number of times before," Professor Gils said.

I disliked the nettle sting in these words and the doctor who had uttered them.

"Professor Gils, Doctor Georg," I said, starting for the door. Before I could slam it shut behind me, the professor's voice sounded again, this time deep and hard.

"Ms. Eutim, I carried out a small, harmless experiment."

I didn't say anything.

"I slipped a stone in your pocket, a small gray one," Professor Gils said. "Can you give it back to me, please?"

There was a stone in my coat pocket, yes.

"It's a stone the archaeologists took from Trun Shrine. It caused severe headaches in the patients who touched it. Your fiancé might have told you about it. This stone remained for a while in his hospital room, nearly killing him and all his colleagues. You, Ms. Eutim, have not reacted to the stone. Neither have I, nor Dr. Georg. We were not sick when we touched it."

"I can sue you for attempting to ruin my health," I said evenly. "And I will positively sue you for endangering my fiancé's health by leaving dangerous materials in his room."

"It seems that the stones from Trun Shrine excavation have no influence on certain people, Ms. Eutim," Dr. Georg said quietly. "These stones cannot harm individuals who are able to discern a halo of green dots around other people's heads. The persons who can see the green dots have a halo of green flecks themselves … or so it seems."

"Isn't this fascinating?" I said. "A circle of light, a halo, like the one around the heads of the saints on Eastern Orthodox icons … you and Professor Gils may be holy saints or at least martyrs, Dr. Georg, but I can assure you I am not a saint."

"We established something else," Professor Gils said, looking me in the eyes. "The persons who used to live near Trun Shrine excavation … 35, 36, and 37 Gagarin Street have these green dots."

I was intrigued. There was a very good story behind that shrine, the halos of green light, and the stones that could make people give up the ghost. I'd rather like to lay my hands on such a stone!

"Your hypothesis sounds interesting, Professor Gils," I said. "But it is wrong. I do not see green halos around your heads."

That was a fat lie, of course.

Chapter Eighteen

Philip Mill waited, shivering under the lashing rain. It was cold in the freezing wind and the mountain looked desolate, brownish red, the top of it biting the low sky. He listened intently as he glanced at the narrow winding road. It was half past three in the afternoon. He had been waiting for an hour and a half now. The storm raged, but the man did not flinch. His thick woolen coat was wet, his fingers trembled as thunder rent the air, and the hill shook under his feet. Lightning flashed, yellow and poisonous across the sky, melting the black clouds, shredding them into bubbling patches of dark fire and raging water that hit the ridge.

"Hey!"

He gave a start.

"Where are you?" he asked as he looked around. "I can't see you."

"Philip!"

He saw her, a dark silhouette in the storm, dissolving into the powerful squall. A hand tapped him on the shoulder, and the woman was before him, her dark gray coat and hat gliding towards him with uncanny ease. He had not heard her steps, nor had he seen her slink past.

Philip hated it when she stalked him like that. He had the feeling she could sink into the gusts of the threshing wind.

"You are late, Boya," he said.

"Yes," she said as if it was the most usual thing in the world to make Philip wait for her in the storm, his clothes sopping-wet, his arms and legs numb and aching.

"Where's your car? I couldn't hear the noise of the engine," he muttered still uneasy about her unnatural ability to creep behind his back out of nowhere.

"You are hard of hearing," she said. "Do something about it or kiss me goodbye here and now."

Philip Mill didn't say anything, although he found that her words sounded rude and extremely irritating.

"She can't stand anybody but me," he said as he tried to dismiss the mocking overtones in the intonation of the woman who seemed unaffected by the cold. "And she trusts no one but me."

"Of course," the woman sneered.

"She wonders where I am," Philip said. "She already knows you've come here."

"I'm not afraid of a blind prophetess who hides in the wasteland," the woman said, brushing the water off her face.

"Do what you have to do and run for your life," Philip said. "Take my tip, Boya. Don't let her talk to you. Don't listen to what she says."

The woman's face was a blur in the shadow of her hood. The wind threw cold water into his eyes. Boya didn't seem to mind the downpour. She walked effortlessly as if the storm carried her forward.

"I'll call the police in two hours," Philip shouted at her, his voice a powerless grain of sand.

"Thank you," the woman in the dark coat said, turning her back on him. "Plenty of time for a task as simple as the one I have to fulfill."

"I've heard that the green streak around her head is as thick as glue," he yelled. "She'll know what you are coming for."

"That will not help her," the woman's words dissolved into the rain. Then she walked up the hill, the gale tearing at her, lightning flashing overhead, illuminating her agile silhouette.

Soon the mist was so thick Philip could not see her. He was forbidden to follow the woman, and he feared her anger. Yet he wanted to see what she was up to. He wanted to know. He sensed that one day soon Boya would come for *him*. Wanga had complained the green dots surrounding her were so dense they squeezed her skull like a vice. Philip was sorry for Wanga; he cared about her. He could feel *they* were already after him.

He didn't know who *they* were. The only person among them he knew was Boya. Philip guessed this mysterious group consisted of individuals who had those dots around, above, or inside their heads.

Chapter Nineteen

"How can you do this?" Philip had asked Wanga once. "How do you know what will happen to guys you've never seen?"

Wanga had not answered. Philip insisted although her face looked sad and pained.

"Please, Wanga, dearest, tell me. Tell me what will happen to me."

"The green dots ..." she had moaned. "I can see your green dots ... And I can see a small blue-eyed girl behind your back."

A tear rolled down her cheeks, her blind eyes empty, almost white.

"I don't have green dots," Philip had said. "But you tell me you can see them. You love me, don't you, Wanga? Tell me what will happen to me."

"The green dots lead men to various venues," Wanga had said, her voice low and cracked. "I don't see people. I see their green dots. I see the places where the green dots push men to go. The places the dots force us to visit are of minor importance ... the blue-eyed girl will be waiting at the end of the road. The past and the future are two sides of the equation that have the same value. Poor lonely kid ..."

"The blue-eyed girl. Who is she?" he breathed.

"You know her, Philip," she had said. Wanga's face was pale.

"I don't have green dots, Wanga," Philip had objected. "Does that mean I am a lesser man than those who have them?"

Wanga kept mum. Philip could not stand her silences; they were cold walls, closing in on him. Finally, she grabbed his hand, and her thin fingers squeezed his wrist.

"You are not *connected* to the machine," Wanga said.

"The machine? What machine?" Philip had asked, his eyes on her sallow face.

"You know," she breathed. "Don't try to lie to me. You can't."

"Tell me," he pleaded.

He threw his dots to the wind, and they don't protect him anymore. Why is the Tall Fellow so silly, mommy? The Tall Fellow will destroy death, son. And the Tall Fellow must stay hidden.... Wanga hummed.

"How do you mean, Wanga?" Philip asked, but Wanga said nothing as she put on her woolen blouse and left the big straw bed on which they slept.

"Then you cannot tell the future of ordinary guys like me?" he had said, feeling inexplicably sad.

"I can. It's easy if people with green dots are after them," she said so quietly he had to strain his ears to catch her words. "But you have them ... the little green flames, Philip." A thought crossed his mind. If Wanga could see these damned green flames, then she positively knew all about Boya.

He suspected Boya wanted Wanga out of the way, the blind woman who saw the green dots, collected stones that carried hate in their veins and gathered the pans of the sick and the weak. Philip wanted to see what Boya would do to the soothsayer of Bare Mountain.

Chapter Twenty

He followed the whisper of Boya's footsteps that vanished into the torrent. Strange how quickly and noiselessly Boya could run. The rain beat against Philip's head, and it was difficult to climb the steep path to the hut. He trudged through mud and puddles. A flash of lightning hit the stones which the sick had heaped at the door. The whole place swam in a pool of fire, the roof a towering black mass in front of him.

Philip informed Boya what Wanga had said about the green dots and the *machine;* a day after Boya received it, she came running to the wilderness. Was the *machine* what Boya wanted? No doubt it was of crucial importance—Boya had wasted no time. "You are not connected to the machine," Wanga had said to him.

Shivering under the pounding rain, Philip reached the hut, hesitated for a moment, and then opened the door. He was not supposed to do that. He was instructed to call the police after two hours. There was a narrow entrance hall adjacent to the bigger room Wanga had built. Philip tiptoed to the door Boya had left ajar and listened.

"You've come to kill me," Wanga was saying. "I'd be grateful to you if you do it. I wish I could stop seeing them all … the people with green fires in their minds."

"Tell me more about it," Boya said.

Philip saw two shadows—Boya's bending dangerously, and Wanga's thin and long.

"Green dots," Wanga said. "You won't kill me if you go on listening to what I say. You won't kill me even if you don't listen to me."

"You can't be so sure," there was a twang of threat in Boya's voice. It was deep and its cold edges gave Philip the creeps. "Have they learned to control the green dots? Tell me!"

Silence, strained and ominous, lingered in the air of the dimly lit room. Wanga used gas lamps for Philip's sake. He had wanted to install a small wind turbine, but Wanga had not accepted it. The place was neat and very clean. Wanga used some of the pans the strangers had brought to Bare Mountain, the most awful ones, he thought.

"Man's hatred is a river that will never run dry," Wanga told him one day. "But hatred is the violent shadow of love, Philip. A shadow can't hurt you, can it?"

Philip didn't think hatred was a shadow. In his view, it was boundless power that made one determined and strong. Hating was half the battle won. "Imagine hatred turning into a healing hand?" the blind woman had added that night, and it felt like she was losing her mind. Hatred didn't heal wounds. It inflicted wounds.

"Have they learned to control their green dots?" Boya repeated.

"I don't know," the blind thin woman said. "I can only see more people who have them. And that is so painful, so painful …"

"Why?"

"The suffering I see," Wanga breathed. The agony in her voice was pure and intense. Philip had come to respect that fragile woman, the *prophetess* who eased children's pain and gave hope to the hopeless, walking slowly among the desperate silhouettes, steeling herself not to break down and cry. Philip thought Boya was mad; but Boya had given him so much money for nothing. Now Philip was a rich man. He didn't have to work anymore. He simply had to stay with Wanga until Boya dealt with her. They'd pay him much more than he had already earned, but he came to love this strange, blind woman.

"The healing places are gone," Wanga added.

"You know about the healing places?" Boya said. "Who told you? How come you know they are gone?"

"They are not destroyed," Wanga said. "They can't make them work. I can see those who go there. They are terrified."

The dim light of the gas lamp flickered, and Boya's shadow danced on the wall. Philip stopped breathing. He peeked into the room and froze in his tracks. Boya held a syringe, the needle almost touching the pale skin of Wanga's arm. Then suddenly Boya's long-fingered hand withdrew the syringe.

"You know I've come to kill you. You might have lied to me."

For a minute, it was so quiet that Philip was afraid Wanga could hear his quick shallow breath rasping his lips. He pressed his hand to his mouth.

"I cannot lie," Wanga said. "I've tried to, but I bleed. I choke to death."

"Then … then … you are … a *New One!*" Boya gasped. Now she was facing Philip and he could see her face taut with concentration, unbelieving. She appeared to be shocked and … scared, yes, very scared, in the pale light of the gas lamp.

"You are lying to me, Wanga!" Boya's sharp voice was laced with animosity. "There are no New Ones. They've been wiped out."

"I don't know anything about the New Ones," Wanga spoke slowly, and Philip knew how tired she was. "If I don't tell the truth I choke on the air I breathe."

"Do I have green dots?" that cold twang crept into Boya's voice again, a menacing drawl Philip had come to abhor.

"You'll be the owner of a continent after we finish everything, Philip. You'll be someone great!" There had been that nasal twang in her voice, and he had not believed her. He had come to care about the blind woman. And there was something else that worried him. A little fair-haired girl had climbed close to Wanga's hut many times, always alone, like a sparrow, like a dying desert fox.

"I saw them long before you came here," Wanga said bringing Philip back to the rain and stormy wind. "Woman, the green dots are leading you to one of the healing places. They know your secrets."

Philip saw—Boya give a start as he tried to slip out of the narrow entrance hall. He thought he'd walked noiselessly as a mouse, but an angry, cutting voice hit him.

"Philip! You little pest! You've been eavesdropping, eh?"

His hair bristled. The words she pronounced were hollow and dead.

"I love Wanga!" he said.

"Liar!" Boya breathed, and that was worse than her snarls.

Chapter Twenty-One

Peter Stan was about to go to the backyard. It had rained yesterday, but now the sun was shining and the sky was blue. Life is beautiful, the teacher thought. The grass looked fresh, and his wild cherry trees looked quite strong. Grafting trees was his passion and Margaret often joked about the sharp knives he kept on a special shelf in the shed. His wife loved the trees he'd grafted and sometimes in the evening Margaret told him, "Let's go to your forest."

A couple of plum trees, an apricot, two cherry trees and a quince tree grew in his garden. "Their leaves make me feel peaceful," Margaret said. She was a peaceful woman. He compared her to the cherry tree, his favorite: thin stem, strong branches, white blossoms, a song on an early spring day. He wanted to kidnap Margaret from her laboratory, from that spacious room filled with equipment, from her futile experiments that took the color from her cheeks. We are no longer young, my love, he'd tell her. It's time we went for a long walk together. I'll tell you a fairy tale about an old man who finally believed happiness existed because his wife agreed to go to the cinema with him. It's a silly tale, Margaret, the teacher thought, but it's true. Happiness is a simple thing. Happiness is you.

"Margaret?" he said to the telephone. "You forgot something at home, eh. No? Then what is it?"

He listened on.

"What?"

Sometimes Margaret had strange ideas. If he asked a question, she said next to nothing.

"But why?" he asked all the same, forgetting the fairy tale about the old man who wanted to take his wife for a walk in the park.

"I can't possibly plaster the walls of your room so quickly. Can't I ask somebody to help me? Like my friend, the math teacher? But why not? Okay. I'll do it."

What had taken her? He'd learned not to speak about it, but it had stayed in his mind. Margaret wanted him to do some crazy thing, and he had to guess what the reason behind her whim was. Maybe another man would dismiss Margaret's eccentricities as minor signs of madness. Maybe another man wouldn't stand Margaret, but Peter Stan was accustomed to her oddities, her silent face and her short clear sentences.

This time it was a crazy thing indeed.

Margaret had asked him to peel the wallpaper in the small antechamber next to the sitting room in their house.

"Don't take notice of what you see on the walls after you peel the wallpaper, Peter. Scrape the images off. Scrape everything, every word, every picture! Then plaster the walls."

Another wild idea she didn't bother to explain. There was an urgency in her voice that bit him to the quick. Margaret had not spoken loudly. She never did. Yet it was there, the sense of sharp immediacy, of scorching necessity to get something done. She did not say, "Do this without delay." She had said, "Please, Peter. Don't call anyone to help you."

He was scared. Margaret had added something that made him realize how serious she was.

"Set fire to the room, if you don't have enough time to scrape the images off the walls."

He had found it impossible to stay calm.

"You mean set fire to our house?" he gasped.

For a moment, her voice died, and Peter thought something had gone wrong.

"Margaret!" he shouted. "Where are you? Margaret!"

"Please don't ask anything, Peter," she said.

"Is somebody coming to search our house?" he asked, but there was no answer, the line was dead.

One day, he found her listening to the rasping sounds that had made her head burst with pain a month ago.

"The noise will kill you!" he had said rushing to her computer and trying to wrench the cable out of the socket.

"Wait," she said, beaming a smile at him.

"Margaret, what are you doing?"

"I feel good," she said.

He listened to the hissing, hurtling cacophony for a while and suddenly the word *TRUN*, like an enormous whale, surfaced from the uproar! That awful harsh jingle had made her writhe with pain, depleting her vigor, rendering her speechless. This time the cutting, crashing reverberation of the hissing Trun made her smile blissfully. She's gone crazy, he thought.

"I'm not crazy, Peter," Margaret had said.

"It's killing you."

"You don't understand," she had said, grinning at him.

Peter Stan didn't understand. She was a silent little thing he cared about. And he trusted her. Then suddenly he was happy for no reason at all.

He peeled off the wallpaper from the wall that separated the small antechamber from the kitchen. The picture he saw left him breathless. It was a photograph of a naked corpse. The head was of a middle-aged woman, staring ahead of her, her eyes pale blue; the legs were thin and scraggly. Peter recognized the old trainers, worn, shabby and not quite clean. These trainers belonged to Tony, the boy whose mother had killed his cat and tadpoles. Tony had taken the wounded blackbird to his home and had written an essay about it. Half of the torso and the left arm were covered with thick black hairs; the other half of the chest had a breast with a dark, round nipple. Peter Stan's eyes were glued to the right hand. He noticed a gold ring on the ring finger. The ring resembled a small clam with a tiny ruby embedded in the soft glittering gold. He knew this ring. He had bought it for Margaret after she gave birth to their son.

Breathing hard, Peter peeled another piece of the wallpaper. About three inches above the floor level, he noticed a series of small photographs. The first one was of a blind woman, her pale blue eyes staring out of hollow eye sockets. Peter thought he knew who that woman was; he had read about the cottage that she had built on top of Bare Mountain. She was Wanga, the soothsayer.

His wife's picture was the second in the row. Margaret looked defiant, her high forehead serene, her face determined and beautiful. Then Peter recognized Tony's photograph. The kid's eyes conveyed an impression of indecision as if he couldn't answer a question the teacher had just asked. There were two more photographs: two bespectacled men Peter Stan didn't know. The face of the younger man looked peculiar: a long scar cut at the left corner of his mouth. Peter Stan had seen these men, or he had met them somewhere before. He could not remember.

The teacher studied the corpse. He noticed a series of numbers an inch under the ring he had bought for his wife. A second later, he discovered numbers printed above the blind woman's head, below the boy's shabby trainers and on the hirsute man's shoulder. What could they possibly mean? What would happen to Margaret on 22 June 2035? Was somebody planning to hurt her?

Scrape! He had to scrape off the picture of the hideous corpse from the wall. Peter ran to the sitting room, found his cellphone and took a dozen pictures of the wall. Then he started to work. Dust bit his eyes. He choked and coughed, but scraped on, rubbed and clawed at the wall. Who had drawn these pictures under the wallpaper? Margaret was involved in this, but how? He could not come up with any sensible explanation. Was Margaret to die on the 22nd of June? No! Don't be an idiot, Peter, he thought … just shut up and work.

He peeled off the wallpaper from the second wall. Words were printed on the plaster. A thought crossed Peter's mind—the person who had written them was mad. The handwriting was messy, spidery, the letters big and ugly. He read the passage near the ceiling: *THE NEW ONES speak the truth. Truth is their curse.*

Can you eat a poisonous mushroom and live on? Lies are poison for the New Ones. Truth is their grave. They are few. I know at least two of them.

He stumbled across something else, two specific dates—15.12.2033 and 22.06.2035—or had those sets of numbers a different meaning? Peter Stan hated what he was doing. What was going to happen to … Happen to whom? Was somebody going to die? Who were the New Ones? A thought crossed his mind that made him feel itchy all over.

"I cannot tell Mother that I care for her, Dad," his son Thomas had said. "A lie makes me sick to my stomach."

A minute later, Peter Stan discovered a dozen or so black-and-white photographs. The first was Tony's, his naughty student who had taken the blackbird home; the second picture was an empty square with a big question mark in it, and then the photograph of his old friend John Cole who seemed to wink at Peter. John Cole. But … the young woman in the next picture was … Boya Bagd!

Peter Stan looked out the window. He saw a fair-haired girl; the same one he had seen so many times before. She was alone again.

Margaret and Thomas had quarreled over Boya, the pretty blonde Thomas had fallen in love with. After the serious car accident Boya had jilted their son. And Margaret suspected Boya had tampered with her computer.

"My nose bleeds if I tell a lie," his son had said.

"Son, you put too much effort into telling a lie, that's the reason your nose bleeds."

The little fair-haired girl … That child was strange, very strange.

Truth is dangerous. Eliminate the New Ones, or they will eliminate you.

Peter scraped the words from the wall, his thoughts racing. Where was his son Thomas now? Has Margaret found out something about him? Who wanted to eliminate those who told the truth? Wouldn't it be wiser to take Margaret far from this house? He should talk her into leaving this town. He had to convince her … Come on, scrape old man, scrape. Two more walls … Maybe Margaret was imagining things. The strain she was under was too great to bear. No, he knew Margaret well. You set the room on fire, she had said. You set the house on fire.

The bell at the front door rang.

Tony's picture, then the empty square with a big question mark on it … Did Margaret know what these meant? Next to the big question mark, the photograph of his old friend John Cole, grinning. Peter took a picture of the wall and hid the cellphone in the breast pocket of his shirt.

The bell rang again. What does the big question mark stand for? Peter thought as he tried to scrape Tony's photograph off the wall.

Quick steps echoed in the corridor.

"Who is it?" Peter shouted. *If you haven't finished scraping the walls, set the house on fire.*

"Hey, Peter! Where are you, old man?"

This big, ringing voice … Peter Stan heaved a sigh of relief. It was his friend John Cole, the chief of Dusk police.

"Coming!" Peter shouted. The dust clogging his nose made him cough.

There are two more walls to scrape, he thought briefly. Another thought, a very silly one stirred in his mind. He hadn't read to the end Tony's essay about the bird. Burn the house if somebody comes while you are scraping the walls, Margaret had repeated. Peter looked at his friend, the police chief. The teacher had not scraped all the walls, but he wouldn't put his own house on fire.

"What's that big question mark doing on your wall?" asked John, the uninvited guest, as he slapped the teacher on the shoulder.

Chapter Twenty-Two

Doctor Ivan Georg liked the clinic and believed he was safe in his office. There were people queuing in front of his door, asking for help. In the morning, Professor Gils gave him a list of terminally ill patients, and Ivan let them listen to his harsh, babbling Trun. Rumors circulated in the country that a young doctor with an ugly scar on his face could cure the sick. No one knew for sure who that man was. Trains and cars packed with suffering people arrived in Dusk, there were jalopies parked down both sides of the streets, roads, alleys, boulevards; and everywhere around the clinic, men and women stared at the doctors, looking for the one with the scar. Ivan had grown a beard and put on his dark glasses every time he wanted to leave the clinic. It was difficult to live like that. The patients who had listened to Healing Trun, slowly, gradually started to feel better, people from the neighboring countries of Greece, Turkey, and Romania swarmed around the Clinic. Dr. Ivan Georg asked other doctors to use Healing Trun, but the results were not the same. No one in the clinic could explain what was happening, or how long this baffling phenomenon would last. The town teemed with impostors: men with scarred faces in white coats appeared in the streets, the sick thronged them, pleading for help, offering their last penny to charlatans.

I have to stop this, Ivan thought. We have to install loudspeakers in the biggest squares. We must let everybody listen to Healing Trun for free.

"This will be impossible," Professor Gils said after Ivan talked to him. "And it will not be the right thing to do."

"We have to try," Ivan insisted. "I have to stop this craze."

One day the loudspeakers wailed, blaring out the wheezing, biting sounds of Trun's unbearable stridency.

People streamed to the square, listening, some smiling, some laughing, still others weeping. The sharp sounds suddenly stopped, and the chief of Dusk police marched to the middle of the square.

"Go home," he said. "This horrible noise will kill you. No one has performed any examination of this volcano of ugly sounds!"

"Go away!" the crowd roared.

Cripples with crutches, men and women, their limbs shaking, a roaring multitude unable to walk crawled towards him, wretches with open wounds on their faces shouting, "Healing Trun! Healing Trun!"

"Trun can be a deadly poison!" the police chief shouted back.

A big man raised his crutch as he tried to hit the police chief on the head.

"Okay, then!" John Cole said. "Listen!"

The square shook and reverberated with the hissing, strident wails and yowls. A stunned wave of horror hit the throng. Screams of fright and dread rang out, piercing the sky. Growls, whimpers, horrible giggles rent the air, writhing bodies, squirming hands, trembling fingers, faces twisted out of shape with pain and agony, all mingled into a blind caravan of throbbing tortured shrieks. TRUN! TRUN! TRUN! The dark, ominous word pummeled young and old.

"Do you want more of that?" the chief of police roared.

Then suddenly silence reigned. The horrified shrieks died away. The mob squirmed on the ground, choking, moaning, whispering, coughing, whimpering.

"Stop it!" the police chief thundered, his voice a dead tree collapsing on the square. "Go home!"

A thin tall man with a big scar on his face rushed to John Cole.

"That was not Healing Trun!" the man with the scar shouted. "What you played was different."

"That's him!" gasped the woman who stood near the man with the scar on his face. "He's Ivan Georg!"

"The doctor!" a man yelled out. "The doctor!"

Behind a short plump woman, Ivan saw the little fair-haired girl. Blue eyes, pale, pinched face. He prayed for her.

Chapter Twenty-Three

Tony could not explain why he suddenly wanted to run out of the room. His heart raced as he looked for his blackbird.

"Ben, where are you?" the boy called out.

The blackbird usually waited for him perched on the floor. A week ago, its sharp claws had pierced the carpet and Tony dreaded his mother's anger, but nothing happened—his mother just smiled and said, "Don't you worry, Tony. It's nothing." The blackbird remained in Tony's room. It didn't eat or drink anything, its round shallow eyes watching Tony with a quiet glow the boy liked so much.

Ben was not in his usual place in the corner.

"Ben, where are you?" the boy whispered, looking around.

With the bird at home, his mother was a different woman. She didn't holler at Tony, didn't order him about the minute she set eyes on him.

"This is for you, son," she said once and gave him an apple. "I bought pears for you, too. You love pears, don't you?"

This had not happened before.

"You are dumb," she used to glower at him. "You'll be nobody. I think you don't deserve the bread I give you."

Tony didn't know what had transformed his mother into a gentle, caring woman. Deep in his heart, he felt things had changed after Ben perched on the floor in the kitchen while she was cooking dinner. His mom had said, "We can go to the zoo if you want, Tony."

She had not taken him to the zoo after his father went to buy bread and didn't come back home. Tony hoped against hope his father would bring him bread someday.

"The man's a liar," his mother said. "He stole my money. He sold everything he could lay hand on in my house and ran away on me."

That was what his mother used to say in the evening before Tony fell asleep.

"We don't have two pennies to rub together because of him. You can't study at a college. You are dumb and you won't find a job," his mother droned on. "Your father stole your money. He dug a grave and pushed you into it. Don't forget that!"

The blackbird was heavy, and its claws had dug an ugly hole in the living room. His mother would hit the roof, so Tony planned to hide in the garage or climb the oak tree in the backyard where she could not catch him. If worse came to worse, he'd run away from home. His mother saw the horrible hole in the carpet and grinned. At first, Tony feared she had gone crazy. Indeed, she cooked potato soup for him. She had not shouted. Ben, the blackbird, watched, his round, shallow eyes gleaming peacefully.

Now Tony could not find his friend. Where had Ben gone? The boy was frightened. His mother would come back late in the evening.

Then he saw the woman.

She stood in front of their house, tall and beautiful, smiling at Tony. Tony didn't smile back. The woman held a blackbird in her hands.

"That is my bird!" the boy said. "That is Ben. Give him back to me!"

"Easy, young man," the pretty woman said. Her smile was very sweet.

"That is Ben!" Tony said. "I want him back."

"I am Doctor Boya Bagd," the woman said in a pleasant, soft voice. "I am in charge of an investigation into the damage the flock of blackbirds did to the schoolyard of Isaac Newton Junior High School." Her hands had a firm grip on the bird's neck.

"Let him go!" Tony said.

"I have heard about you, young man," the woman said. "It's you who hit the bird. It's evident you've helped it to recuperate."

"Now Ben is strong," Tony said. "And I want him back."

It was warm, the sky was sullen and cloudy, and Tony was afraid it would rain. He knew Ben had lost some of his big feathers, but he had collected them all. Perhaps he was only imagining it, but the moment he touched their black, cold edges he felt his heart become as light as a happy speck of dust.

"Mom," he had said to his mother. "Take this and keep it."

She had laughed hard, and her laughter was not thin and sharp like the needle of a syringe. It was soft like the sea breeze that brought spring to their town.

"I know about the essay you wrote about the bird," the pretty woman said. "It is very interesting."

Then, Ben the blackbird uttered piercing, high-pitched sounds, cheeps of panic that Tony had never heard. TRUN! TRUN! TRUN! The sharp noise Ben produced frightened the boy. The woman hit the bird's head against the wall of the house. A desperate horror-stricken *Tru-n-n!* dissolved into the gray air.

"Let him go!" the boy yelled.

"I did nothing wrong," the woman said. "It is harmful to listen to shrill sounds. You'll get a splitting headache. Well, don't be afraid, I know what do."

Then Tony remembered something: the only person he had given his essay to was his teacher Mr. Peter Stan. "Who gave you the essay I wrote for Ben ... the bird?" Tony asked.

The woman smiled again as she took a step towards him.

"Who?" the boy said, looking her in the eyes.

"I like the way you've described the bird," she said. "You wrote it was your guardian angel."

Tony wished it had started to rain. It soon would, for the black clouds were waiting on the roof of the house.

"My guardian angel didn't help me," Tony said. "Ben did."

At this moment, Tony noticed a narrow, blue band on the woman's wrist. Two tiny lamps were gleaming on it.

"Do you have any of the bird's feathers?" the woman asked. "We have to examine everything, and I have to collect all of the feathers that the birds have lost."

Tony watched her face and didn't like it.

"I have no feathers," he lied. They were heavy and comfortable in his pocket. He'd hidden them there.

Tony reached out for Ben, but the woman did not let him touch the bird.

Something happened.

A whooshing sound rent the air; a momentary flash illuminated the woman's hands then Ben vanished. She stood empty-handed, calm, a thin smile on her magnificent face as a tiny, new lamp shone on her blue band. Now three tiny lamps were gleaming on the woman's wrist. A crisp wind blew; clouds clawed at the thick, black sky.

"What did you do to Ben?" Tony asked, his voice a festering wound.

The woman turned her back on the boy and calmly walked down the street. He balled his hands into fists, then dashed after. A second later, the boy gripped her hand. Trembling, he pointed to the tiny gleaming lamps on her wrist.

"You've killed two more birds like Ben!"

Chapter Twenty-Four

I followed Jacob, examining his thin neck. It was cold and cloudy; the air was damp as we followed the narrow path which ran senselessly through stones, briars, and thick nettles. Hills rose high up above other hills; trees, old, dark green, and wild were everywhere. Well, I didn't scare easily.

"Are you tired?" Jacob asked, looking at me over his shoulder.

I didn't answer.

"I love you, Sara," he said. It was the thirty-eighth time he had reiterated that. I wouldn't say his words annoyed me. What annoyed me was that the archaeologist walked too quickly, his spidery legs gliding forward with amazing dexterity. He often stopped to wait for me, his caring eyes on my face. I jogged every morning from six to nine in the morning, took long walks in the park and did simple keep-fit exercises at home, so I thought I had great power of endurance. My new fiancé proved my judgement very wrong. We'd been striding purposefully for three hours, clambering over rocks, pushing our way through the woods, scrambling up long hills. I felt like taking a nap.

"We're almost there," Jacob said. "Pull yourself together."

We walked an hour more. My feet ached, my arms hurt, and I could hardly breathe. There was no path in front of us. Thin, spiky branches jutted out all over the place, crags glowered at me, and the slope was steep like a hanging rope. Jacob tied me with his belt and pulled me upward. I tried to establish the direction we followed, looking for moss on the trunks of the trees, but moss was everywhere. Fortunately, the clouds went away, and the cold, blue sky pressed down on me, the freezing forest an infinity of wet leaves, bushes, shrubs, and scrubs.

"I love you, Sara," Jacob said. "Please close your eyes."

I could have killed him. Every square inch of me tingled; thorns, spikes and barbs were in my way, and I hated the idea of having to climb across another deep gorge, or crawl to the bottom of a foggy ravine.

"Open your eyes now!"

I looked and looked and could not believe what I saw. A huge statue of an enormous bird, all black, was in front of me, its powerful beak cutting the pale sky, its claws carving the top of a rock-strewn hill in the distance. A sheer crag stuck out of the black stone beneath the bird, firm and endless as its menacing face towered above me. Then I noticed several dark holes cut into the black stone. They appeared to be glaring at me, their blind, terrifying stare dead on my face. I had the impression the murky pits were immeasurably deep, and something dark and fearful breathed inside them.

Jacob took my hand and whispered, "Isn't the place magnificent? This is the Trun Chark."

"It's horrible!" I said. "The dead holes gape at me like graves."

"Don't look at the holes," Jacob advised me. "They are called Deaf Crags, and they are deaf: they devour the echo, and it feels as if you've lost your way in a large, dank cave. I'll show you the inscriptions," he grinned. "I love you, Sara."

This one got on my nerves. I was about to give him a piece of my mind, but his smiling face was very close to mine, and he kissed me before I had time to say another word.

"What inscriptions?" I asked, hating the idea of having to climb down into the shadowy holes.

"I'll show you. They're called the *steps to the chark*. Don't be afraid, honey. I wish you could see your own face!" He paused, grinning happily. "The Trun Chark is the pool," he added, holding my hand. "It's behind the monolithic black bird. You'll see it in a minute, a gigantic cube cut into the stone. It is full of a dark, sticky liquid. It's named *Samodiva's milk that feeds the Trun Chark.*"

"Samodiva's milk?" I repeated. "Is the Trun Chark a living thing that needs food?"

"An Old Bulgarian song says it is," he said. "The *chark* feeds on Samodiva's milk."

"But you've told me that *chark* means a *mechanism*."

"Yes, I did," he said. "And I'll show you the inscriptions chiselled into the stones. These inscriptions are the four steps to truth, or at least this is how I translate the text of the song. You'll see that the *chark* is much more than a mechanism. It … how shall I put it? It can feel."

A thought crossed my mind. This man had declared thirty-nine times he loved me. Now I feared he was out of his mind. Had he taken me to Deaf Crags to feed my bones into the *chark*?

"The song says that every letter cut into the stone stands for a man who lost his life as he tried to find out the truth about Trun," Jacob said, his face grave, and I thought I noticed a cruel glint in his eye. "Only the New Ones are not afraid of truth."

"The New Ones?" I said as I quickly removed myself from the edge of a cliff.

"You can touch the liquid in the cube, and you'll find out something about yourself," he said. "After I dipped my hand into the Samodiva's milk, the liquid remained perfectly calm, the waves died, and when I took my fingers out of the cube, the stones looked serene and inviting." The archaeologist smiled at no one in particular then added, "If a Samodiva touches the milk, the waves will rise and roar, the cliffs will hiss and claw, at least the song thinks so."

"The cliffs will hiss, my foot," I said. "I don't want to dip my hand into that liquid. It's dirty."

He looked at me sharply, shaking his head.

"What?" I asked, sensing something had gone wrong.

"The song …" he muttered.

"What about the song?" I asked.

"Nothing," he smiled again. "The song says the Samodivas refused to touch the *milk* in the *chark*. I've read in different newspapers you've been married once or twice, Sara," he suddenly changed the subject, and his next question almost made me jump. "Do you have children, Sara?"

"No, I don't," I said. His face was open and calm, his eyes were bright, and I thought I had imagined the cruel glint that I'd noticed a minute before. "Why do you ask?"

"Because the song says the Samodivas don't have children and would never agree to touch the water in the *chark*."

"Okay, Jacob," I said. "I am a Samodiva. I'll crush you like a nut, and you will explain to an earthenware pan that your chest hurts. Then you'll throw the pan into the *chark,* and you'll regain your health."

Jacob laughed, but his face looked sad.

"The song says the Samodivas are hope," he said. "When everything else has failed, a Samodiva can help. At least my translation of the Old Bulgarian song sounds like that."

"Why should a Samodiva help anybody?" I asked. What Jacob had just said sounded crazy to me.

"I don't know," he said. "The first part of the song does not say anything on this issue."

"Is there a second part?" I asked.

"The abbot of the monastery told me he'd seen the second part of the manuscript in the bottom drawer of the chest where I found the first part," Jacob explained. "I couldn't find the second part. It was gone. The abbot swore he saw it there a week ago—a loose piece of paper. He claimed he'd never destroy any old papers, although he supposed this scrap had no value whatsoever."

A stiff wind blew, the shrubs and bushes swayed back and forth, the sky hung overhead, infinite, threateningly calm as it touched the black head of the stone bird. I started climbing down the hill, resolutely turning my back to the gaping holes.

"Wait!" Jacob shouted. "Let me read the song to you. And I want you to see the inscriptions."

We sat on the ground, and he produced a crumpled sheet of paper from his breast pocket. It was so cold I could hardly stand the blasts of freezing air.

"I want to go home," I said.

"Don't tell me you walked hours in the freezing rain to come back home empty-handed," Jacob sad. "It is not like the Sara I am in love with." He waved the crumpled sheet of paper. "I translated the song before I knew the Deaf Crags existed. I didn't know where I should look for them, so I visited different villages in the Dusk region asking young and old if somebody had heard about ГЛУХИ СКАЛИ, i.e., *Deaf Crags*. I called round for a chat at seven senior citizen homes. No one could tell me where the Deaf Crags were. Yes, many people have heard fairy tales about the evil cliffs. Townspeople believed Samodivas still lived there, but …"

I was sick and tired of listening to his detailed accounts of the nursing homes he had intruded on or the dusty museums he'd poked his nose into.

"I am hungry, Jacob," I complained. "I am freezing. To cut a long story short, who told you how to find the damned Deaf Crags?"

"I placed advertisements in dozens of local newspapers," he said, looking at me sympathetically. "Weeks on end, no one answered the advertisements, until one day a man came to my place. He was a police officer, he said. He was the chief of Dusk police."

I pricked up my ears. *The chief of Dusk police?*

"What did he want with you?" I asked, thinking of John Cole, my ex-husband, who had brought a big. black stone to my house and inquired whether I felt sick. I had lied to him, of course. I thought about the bird statue of black stone as I looked at the black holes dug in the daunting face of the cliff.

"The police officer said I should drop the idea altogether. Those things were not my business, he pointed out. Of course, his words just whetted my appetite."

"I am very cold," I said.

"You want to know who helped me to find the Deaf Crags, don't you? It was an old man, a teacher who telephoned me after I'd given up hope," the archaeologist babbled on. "He too hinted I shouldn't meddle with the thing. The place is bad, he said. Peter Stan was a good man, yes. He warned me not to go to there."

Peter Stan. I didn't know the guy. How come he knew about Deaf Crags? I'd better check who he was. I unfolded the sheet of paper and slowly read the Old Bulgarian song:

If something hurts you, my little one,
Come to the Deaf Crags and throw a bowl into the chark.

If somebody hates you, my little one,
Give his name to a stone and throw the stone into the chark.
This bad man will pester you no more. The first pit is yours.

"Come with me," Jacob said and pulled me along a narrow steep path that zig-zagged steeply over the hill amid bushes and heaps of red chunks that had rolled down from the top of the hill. Suddenly, we were in front of the cube cut into the stone. It was deep and full of turbid liquid the colour of blue ink.

"And that's the Samodiva's milk? That mud?" I grunted.

"Look!" he said. At that moment I saw them: two huge heaps: one of stones, the other of deformed pans and jugs, in front of the weird stone bowl. I remembered where I had seen similar ugly piles: the stones and old plates nearby Wanga's hut looked peaceful compared to the stark, unsightly mass in front of the cube full to the brim with slush.

"Is this the Trun Chark?" I asked unbelieving.

"I think it is," Jacob said. "Read the second stanza of the song, and then I'll show you something else." At that moment, I hated his little voice that sounded thick with exultation. "We've reached the second platform that brings us a little closer to truth."

I perused the second stanza, detesting the crumpled sheet of paper, loathing the drizzling rain and above all hating my own idiocy. The second stanza read:

You are talented, alas. The chark cannot help you.
and cannot handle talent. Talent is torture.
If somebody hurts you, don't mention his name to a stone.
The stone won't help you. Samodivas cannot pierce your mind.
No one knows how talent came to be, but
talent made things go wrong.
Beware of talent. If you succeed in hiding your talent,
no one will hurt you. The second pit is yours.
Hide in it. You'll be safe there.

"This sounds crazy," I said, staring at the four deep holes in the face of the cliff. In my mind, they were the jaws of a wolf, his teeth on my throat.

"The second hole is the narrowest one," Jacob told me. "It looks pretty horrible, doesn't it? Well, it's quite comfortable up there. I'll take you to see the inscription carved into the rock."

"Can't you tell me what the inscription reads?" I said. "I believe you."

"You are talented, and you have to climb up there," he smiled again. "I love you, Sara."

"I'm not talented at all," I said firmly. "And I don't want to climb that hill. It is impossible to get to the second hole no matter what."

"You are a quick learner," Jacob said. *If you succeed in hiding your talent, no one will hurt you,* he read from the crumpled sheet of paper. "Please, Sara, dip your hand into the water. Please."

I stared at the opaque slush in the cube, and I didn't like it at all. The liquid wasn't a pleasant sight, thick and greasy like broth. I didn't feel like touching it, yet my nosiness was stronger than my common sense. I knew that curiosity had killed the cat and believed I could control the irresistible urge to come to the bottom of things. I scanned the dark holes carved into the cliff, peeked at the sky, which had become as gray as the "water" in the cube, and then I took a step back. I thought of the picture that hung above my bed: five dead trees, their branches dry and black, yet they all were heavy with wonderful red cherries.

"Come on," Jacob said. "The cube won't bite you," he rolled his sleeves and dipped his hands into the grayish liquid. It did not stir. Its dark surface remained perfectly calm. "It's not even cold, Sara! Come on."

I didn't budge. Then Jacob Harvey, the batty archaeologist, sang, *He threw his dots to the wind, and they don't protect him anymore. Why is the Tall Fellow so silly, mommy? If pain is everywhere, the Tall Fellow will beat death, son. The Tall fellow must stay hidden.* He sighed, "This is a splendid little song! I adore it, Sara, the song you've scribbled under the dead trees heavy with cherries in your picture!" Jacob smiled a fatuous smile.

I slid my hand into the water just for a second. Waves, muddy and thick, bigger than the surrounding cliffs, rose in the cube and crashed against my feet. The liquid wheezed and rasped, a distorted, booming thunder-like sound, an avalanche of explosions, *TRU-U-UN! TRU-U-UN! TRUN-N-N!* rent the gray air.

"What was that?" I gasped.

Jacob looked at me.

"How did you do that?" he whispered. "How the hell did you make the Samodiva's milk claw at you?" His eyes bored into mine. The hill was so quiet one could hear a feather drop. A couple of seconds ago, the mud was an ugly mini-volcano and now it slept passive, dark, dead.

"I think I know what the water hissed at us," Jacob said, his eyes a blue abyss. "Trun!"

"It didn't hiss," I objected.

He sat down on the cold stone in front of the cube and read aloud,

Samodivas are talented. They have hidden their talent
so well no one can discover it.
But they can't hide their ambition.
Talent is green. Green are the dots that reveal its presence.
The men's thoughts are the Samodivas' homes.
Only a Samodiva can see other Samodiva's green dots,
her green flames, her green streak.
Only the most important Samodiva can make the chark roar and sting.
The third hole is yours, my Samodivas. You'll be safe in it.
You are the Marked Ones.

The turbid, soup-like substance in the cube waited patiently, its surface smooth and still, a threatening presence in front of me. I dipped my hand into its lifeless serenity. Waves rose and broke against the cliffs, and fell, rolled, hurtled, and rumbled. *Trun!* They roared and snarled. *Trun!* I quickly withdrew my hand and the waves died, the shrill, growling sounds faded, the sky kept quiet, and I stood there watching Jacob.

"Who are you?" he breathed. "The cube reacts to you the way the song describes it. You are a Samodiva, Sara."

"Oh, no!" I said. "I don't care about loony myths the old wives keep alive, hoping to scare their grandchildren stiff."

Spruce trees, their needles dark green and sharp, combed the wind and injected poison into the clouds. The shrubs were dark green too, an endless maze of leaves and thorns as the bird of black stone jutted out amid the infinite weight of annoyance that made me stagger. I stole a look at Jacob. He immediately took me in his arms, whispering in my ear, "Sara, honey, calm down. It's nothing. Here, drink this." He produced a flask from his hip pocket.

I hoped he would offer me whiskey. But, no. It was pale, insipid tea. What was I doing here, drinking lukewarm tea, the damned holes gawking at me, the Samodiva's milk, the foulest liquid, a bowl of vile broth at my legs? Jacob kissed me, and I could live with that. The last straw about to break my back was his immense enthusiasm: the guy drank all the tasteless tea from his flat bottle, then sprinted to the cube, filled the bottle with dark mud, scurried back to me and patted me on the back.

"We'll examine this!" he cooed excitedly. "The pool doesn't respond when I touch its Samodiva's milk. It likes me and has a strong aversion to you. This means you are … you are magnificent, Sara. The song says it is once in two thousand years that a woman can make the lake sting. You did it."

"Are you sure you've translated the text correctly?" I asked. "You are an archaeologist, not an expert in Old Bulgarian."

"I wrote a poem for you in Old Bulgarian," he said. "I planned to give it to you as a wedding present. Do you want me to give it to you now?"

"I don't speak Old Bulgarian," I said. "This poem would be the most impractical wedding present I've ever got."

"I don't care what your ex-husbands have given you. I care about you. You can make the pool kick and thunder. This is a good sign." He smiled his face small under the enormous sour smile of the moon that lit a silver fire in the nest of my mounting anxiety. "I love you, Sara."

"I know," I said. I knew I'd commit an awful crime if I hurt this man. He was pure and gentle. Well. What if he is a good actor? a little thought poisoned my mind. I liked Jacob though. I wished I had met him many years before I started writing scientific articles. His dark eyes were the color of the path that led to places I loved.

"You are the most beautiful woman I've ever seen," he said. I doubted there had been other women before me in his life. "I had a colleague, an archaeologist from Greece," Jacob went on. "I took her here, to the Deaf Crags," his eyes were sad. This Greek archaeologist must have broken his heart. "I had translated the song and had just found the Trun Chark when Ekaterini and I visited Deaf Crags. She loved the place. It was summer and it was warm. She swam in the stone cube, but the water didn't jump." Our eyes met. "She didn't make the water roar and explode, and she said I was a fool."

I touched his face with the tip of my fingers. Yes, I liked this man. He was the thinnest of all the guys I'd met, but I saw spring winds in his smile, and I found the places I wanted to visit in his quiet gaze.

"Read the song to me to the end, Jacob, will you?" I said as I kissed him on the lips. I liked his tanned skin.

"I think the last two stanzas sound crazy," Jacob said. "I have no idea what role the number three plays in the song. I'll give you a copy of the text in Old Bulgarian. You may speak to Professor Margaret Stan about it. The woman is a world expert on artificial languages and Old Bulgarian manuscripts. I discussed my translation with her. There are major aspects on which we disagree. We argued over subtle details. I still think she is wrong."

I took the crumpled page from his hand and read:

The fourth hole is for the New Ones!

If a man is a New One and tells a lie, he cannot breathe. He bleeds to death.

Fraud, deceptions, and schemes rule the world.

The path between murder and healing is but a step long.

There is a path to happier places. New Ones, you will be safe

if you hide in the fourth hole. If not, woe to you!

Jacob muttered … There is a path to happier places. "Professor Margaret Stan thinks my translation of this particular sentence is wrong. She argues it means … *Frauds, deceptions and schemes rule the world, and you, New Ones, are the path to happier places.*"

"It seems to me the professor you speak about is wrong," I said. "Frauds make the world go around and the most sophisticated embezzlement is the path to the happiest place under the sun. Men incapable of telling a lie! Give me a break!"

The New Ones didn't interest me in the slightest.

"How can one be sure the New Ones are humans?" Jacob asked.

"No man is so dim-witted as to speak the truth if it kills him," I remarked. "The anonymous poet must have made a joke, or your translation is all muddled up."

"It is not," my latest fiancé insisted. "Professor Margaret Stan thinks my translation is quite accurate. She congratulated me on my ability to preserve the beauty of a language that no one speaks today and said she'd give me an A if I were her student."

"What's the name of the Abbot who gave you the first half of the song?" I asked, changing the subject. I'd hate it if Jacob started telling me the padre spoke Old Greek, Aramaic, plus the language of the Thracians. Jacob didn't answer my question, and I suddenly itched to learn a thing I wasn't particularly interested in. "So, what's the Abbot's name?" I insisted, looking the thin archaeologist in the eye.

"Why should you want to know it?" Jacob said.

"Perhaps I'll check if what you've told me is true," I said, feeling the icy air in my bones.

"His name is Dimo, and he preaches at the Parish Church in Dusk. Unfortunately, I could not find the second half of the song."

I knew the Parish Church in Dusk very well: my second wedding took place in it, and I happened to know the priest. His name *was* Dimo. Jacob was not lying to me.

"Okay," I said. "Let's read the last stanza you've translated."

"The fifth, i.e., the last stanza I've translated does not make sense at all," Jacob began. "I thought I had not understood the meaning of the words. Here is my translation. Read it, please. Then I'll give you the translation Professor Stan has made. It is important that you see the two of them."

"Why?" I asked suspiciously.

"You'll understand after you read the translations. And we can make a little experiment if you agree."

"Are you trying to use me as a guinea pig?" I asked indignantly.

"The song doesn't explicitly say who is able to force the Samodiva's milk to kick and bark," my fiancé said. "However, what you did proves that my translation is correct. One might say the black monument on Deaf Crags, the statue of the bird, is of crucial importance. I think the song drops a hint that it is a monument to Death. Listen now," Jacob began to read slowly.

The green dots make it possible for every human being to live long, long, long.

The green dots will help men to remain disease-free. Trun!

Human beings will not pay in any type of money. They'll pay in their talent.

Talent is money!

Never forget the Lonely One who finds everybody!

The Lonely One is stronger than talent and is always by herself.

You'll see no cats, no dogs, and no children at her place.
The Tall Fellow can destroy the Lonely One.
Only the Tall Fellow can do it! Trun!
The black statue of the bird belongs to Loneliness.

I stared. The wilderness around me appeared dark blue. I could be sure of nothing anymore.

"This is the oddest poem I've ever read," I said. "Did you translate this part of the song, or was it Professor Stan?"

"I did," Jacob said. "And I don't know why the anonymous poet uses the number two in this stanza. In other stanzas the number three is used. Why? Professor Stan's version has it that if for some reason the Samodivas perish, the world is doomed. The Talented Ones are cruel because they are vulnerable. The suffering they have to endure makes them weak."

"Can I see Professor Stan's translation?" I asked.

Jacob fidgeted; his narrow face too small for his uneasy smile.

"You have to see the inscriptions carved under the four holes first," he said.

Chapter Twenty-Five

Professor Gils rubbed his eyes. The blue-eyed, fair-haired girl was running in the street towards him; a couple of seconds later she was gone. Strange, he thought. He had just received a message that sent his thoughts racing. An exclamation mark glowed red on the computer screen, and the alarm bleeped as he read: *This message will be automatically deleted in 19 minutes.*

Professor Gils saved the document in a separate folder, copied the electronic address from which the message had been sent, then carefully read its contents.

FOOD: something that people and animals eat (or plants absorb?) to keep alive. Food brings about change. Food is instrumental in causing the transition from living matter to nonliving matter and vice versa. NOTA BENE: the influence of food on triads (i.e., the trios) has not been researched; some adventurers resort to possibilities the triads offer, expecting to have great fun or hoping to make headlines in the mass media releases. However, cases have been recorded when adventurers were caught in the world of old age after absorbing alcohol; we are unable to release these patients from the trap they have jumped into of their own accord. The path of death leads them nowhere.

Triads? Trios? What is this, Professor Gils thought. Who sent me this message? Who knows my email address? This was his secure line address he used within the system of Iztok Clinic solely for the purposes of the Healing Trun investigation. Four people knew it: 1. Doctor Ivan Georg; 2. John Cole, the police chief; 3. Sara Eutim, the young journalist, the little girl who told him fairy tales when he was the loneliest boy in the world—she was the woman he had been in love with all these years; 4. Professor Margaret Stan, the scientist famous for her research in the field of artificial languages and who worked on a code she believed was the key to unraveling the mystery of Healing Trun.

Professor Gils thought about the little fair-haired child with a blue ribbon in her hair: he saw her yesterday in the clinic. She looked so much like the girl who had told him fairy tales in his childhood. He had to find out who that little girl in the hospital was. Triads or trios, a group of three people, or things, he thought again. What should this mean?

Gils went on reading.

We have been part of a failed project. Our efforts have been futile. All living organisms absorb death the second they are born or more precisely after they see the light of day. At a certain point, the concentration of death in an organism reaches the required level and the respective living entity dies. What really happens is a transition from one age slot to another. Thus, death is the only path leading from one age niche to the next one—childhood, adulthood, old age—the three different locations in the world of a triad or trio. Death is one of us. Death has green dots like every one of us. The living creatures are unwilling to die. We have proof: in case the rational beings on this planet suffer from disease, they collect earthenware pans, crude receptacles of nonliving matter, to describe their aches and pains to, then bring the pans, jugs, etc., to the Transformers we have built for them.

We believe the rational beings on this planet are aware that the prevailing part of death is hatred. Hatred is loneliness. We have noticed that human beings shout the name of the person they detest at a stone and then bring this stone to a Transformer we have built. They try hard to get rid of malevolence; perhaps they realize that hatred increases the concentration of death in their system. These individuals have no knowledge of death. Death is not the end of their existence. We are the end. We love them. We love truth more than we admire death. Some of us believe death can be destroyed. One of us is the Tall Fellow, an entity that refused to enjoy the security the green dots provide. He has learned to feel pain like any human being, and he learned to stay hidden too.

Professor Gils blinked. He poured some fresh water into his glass, drank it, and read on.

We do not know how many of our Transformers are still operational. Our strategists still believe that at least two of them have not ceased functioning.

Our project has passed through four stages that reflect the development of the rational beings:

1. The Ordinary Ones: male and female individuals who will not suffer from diseases and will not hate anybody because they bring the bad pans and bad stones to our Transformers;

2. The Talented Ones: rare rational beings that achieve extremely high results, although we have not taught them how to achieve perfection in the spheres they have chosen to excel in. It remains an inexplicable fact for us how talent came to be. (The emergence of the Talented Ones was the first warning sign of the breakdown). Talent is unmanageable and unpredictable. We cannot live in a Talented One's thoughts.

Therefore, we planned to destroy the Talented Ones.

3. The Marked Ones: extremely intelligent rational beings. We use them to drive us from one destination to another. We have assumed that a Marked One is able to intercept us as we stay hiding in the thoughts of another human being. The Marked Ones perceive us as a thin green halo or a circle of tiny green dots. At a certain point, the Marked Ones may be able to find out who we are. The humans can break the code of the Transformers. So far, they have succeeded once in triggering the mechanism thus generating a new Marked One. This occurred after a young man underwent brain surgery, and the result was he was able to see us, a faculty he had not possessed before the surgical intervention. The fact that he broke the transformer's code was a highly alarming sign.

We believe that the humans achieved this transformation by pure chance and are unable to repeat it. They do not understand the meaning of the recordings and use the code the patient had inadvertently cracked only to cure other sick men. They are unaware that these vibrations can transform the whole planet. If they learn to transform the Ordinary Ones they call humans (these liars, murderers, thieves, con-men, sadists call themselves human!), they will be deadly dangerous. In their world, truth is weak. They still do not know what a Marked One can do! We must never let them know. It may be wise to eliminate all the Marked Ones, thus abolishing the root of evil; the Marked Ones are the most intelligent and truly analytical rational beings among the humans.

What is talent? It is the unpredictable ability to transform loneliness into inimitable works of Art! Beethoven, sick and impoverished, composed his most magnificent music when he was dying; another musician Mozart composed his unsurpassed Requiem when he was on his deathbed. Conclusion: we can transform disease into good health, hate into peace. This is cheap to do.

We cannot transform pain and loneliness into magnificent music, into poems or short stories. The Talented Ones can do this, and we do not know what mechanism they use to achieve these inexplicable results. We have been living on this planet much longer than the humans have. They are a product of our making, and they are able to do things we cannot even dream of. The absurdity of it!

If we exterminate the Talented Ones, we will never learn how they create art. We will lose the incomparable pleasure of music and poetry we cannot produce ourselves. By killing them all, we will make it impossible for the New Ones to come into being. We will have to leave the planet and abandon the experiment. Of course, there is always the possibility of imprisoning all the Marked Ones (it will cost practically nothing), but our experience so far has proved that prison humiliates the Talented Ones as well as the Marked Ones, but it does not break them. Examples, Giordano Bruno, Galileo Galilei, Socrates, Confucius (to name a few).

We have observed that in the vicinity if our Transformers, especially the ones installed underground, very often Marked Babies were born. Most of them died very young. This leads us to the conclusion that we have to destroy the underground Transformers, or crush talent, thus abolishing music, literature, painting which we would not like to do. The mixture of truths and downright lies humans call science makes us raw with laughter! One wonders how they create Art. We cannot generate music or write poems. Yes, we can arrange sounds in a certain order, and we can string together a sequence of words, but this is not a poem. We can describe a phenomenon in the most accurate manner, but this is not a novel.

They imagine Death is a big ugly man holding a scythe in his hand. This is ludicrous, a big man! We are small and so careful.

A mistake in our experiment probably introduced talent into our existence: talent, an unstable element that every human being has in his genes. We have inadvertently created talent and it may be the path to our extinction or … survival. Talent is stronger than any plans, more powerful than fear. Alas, it is impossible for us to inhabit the Talented Ones or even stay temporarily in their thoughts. We have to constantly observe how talent functions. Men carry us; they are both our vehicles and our drivers. There is nothing more pleasant than to be carried by a Marked One—you live in the poems he has read; you dissolve in the music he listens to. Humans call us Samodivas and this name is enormous fun....

Doctor Gils took off his glasses. He took a deep breath. Who had sent him this email? An ambitious science-fiction writer? How come a writer found his classified email address?

It was raining again, and dusk was falling behind the windowpanes.

Was Ivan Georg transformed into a Marked One after his brain surgery? Did Ivan send him this email? Or was it Sara? Sara, the woman he had not forgotten all these years. Professor Gils thought of the persons who knew his classified email address. He could talk to Ivan Georg right away. John Cole, the chief of Dusk police, a difficult man. Of course, Gils respected Professor Margaret Stan, the renowned scientist. She had asked Gils to meet with her. She had made a series of experiments, the professor said on the phone, and she had obtained a sequence of sibilant sounds, a combination repeated a number of times. The word TRUN! TRUN! TRUN! exploded at regular intervals like bomb blasts. She had let some of her friends listen to the cascade of jarring noises she called the Trun series. The participants in her experiments complained of splitting headaches, tremor of extremities, twitching eyelids, and short-lived facial paralysis. She said her nose had bled. Gils looked forward to meeting Professor Margaret Stan. He planned to compare Ivan's Healing Trun with Professor Margaret Stan's Killing Trun recordings.

The triads ... was there a grain of truth behind this concept? What is the meaning of a trio he asked himself but found no answer.

A fierce wind blew and raindrops hit the sand paths in the hospital yard. Gils thought of his meeting with Sara. She had quickly agreed to see him, and he was intrigued. He had stumbled on gossipy newspaper articles focused on her divorces, but this was of no consequence, was it? All his life, the professor had been attracted to extraordinary persons and Sara ... Sara was the beautiful fairy tale of his childhood, his happiest summer afternoon; Sara was the smile he needed to keep warm on a rainy day. He had seen the green dots around her head. Then she was a Marked One, a Samodiva? Oh, stop it, Gils thought. Sara is the girl who told you tales, the only friend you had. And she's turned into a very pretty woman. He hoped she still liked him. Somehow, he knew she didn't. Come on, Gils, he thought angrily. You are the best neurosurgeon in the country. She is famous and stunning. She is the most beautiful woman you know. He shook his head as he read on, the rain pirouetting across the window, the air dark and impatient.

Stage Four in the development of the humans is of vital importance. This is the territory of the New Ones. If they tell a lie, their skin cracks, bleeds, and they die. Initially, our experiment consisted of three phases: Ordinary Ones, Marked Ones, and New Ones, their trailblazer, the One who found everybody and was always alone, leading the way.

The Project was plagued with glitches, and a major failure occurred. Talent, an inexplicable phenomenon, was rampant in the world. Even among the Ordinary Ones, who our Transformers could work with, processing hate into benevolence and cancer into health, babies were born who could not lie. These were rare cases, of course.

Our experiment has come to a standstill. We think the reasons are:

1. Now, the Ordinary Ones do not go to our Transformers. Hate and envy poison them. They suffer from deathly diseases and their funny science is incapable of helping them. Therefore, we resorted to the Blackbirds. This project was a catastrophe. Clumsy and ungainly, the birds failed to fulfill the task assigned to them. Since the day the flock of blackbirds was launched, the saying, The bird of happiness does not perch twice on your shoulder, spread quickly and widely. The bottom line was that the bird was too heavy and broke the man's shoulder blade.

2. The Talented Ones aroused envy in their colleagues and rivals. Envy is the shadow of endeavor. Envy destroys both the envious person and the target of their envy. The Talented Ones rapidly reach the threshold of envy their system can support, so most of them die young. Few can disguise their talent by donning the mask of simplicity. Talent is a mystery we must solve.

Professor Gils thought hard. Talent is a mystery we must solve. Who were the shadowy we? Were they related to the triads or trios?

3. Marked Ones, or those who can detect our presence. They can see us as green dots or perhaps as tiny green flames. They successfully hide their knowledge from the world. The result is we suffer a colossal loss.

4. We have intercepted messages that lead us to believe that some New Ones may be in existence. They are practically innocuous; anybody can exterminate them by coercing them to tell a lie. Are the New Ones the future of humankind?

5. Who is the One that finds everybody? A detective? Does not death find kings and beggars alike?

After talent saw the light of day due to the serious mistake in the experiment, things took a turn for the worse. Talent triggered a wave of envy that our Transformers could not process. We need to repair the Transformers, and we need carriers to take us to them. The Marked Ones can do that for us. On the other hand, we thrive on talent. Talent proves to be the best environment for our development. The Marked Ones are evil, but they can take us to the places and situations we desperately want to reach.

The screen went blank. Professor Gils pounded on the keyboard, but the computer did not respond. Beads of perspiration shone on the professor's forehead. The rain thudded against the windows as the screen flashed, flickered, and was alive again. The message the Professor had read had vanished. I've saved a copy, he thought. I'll retrieve it now. He had saved the file as *anonymous message*. He checked the folder. The file was not there. He checked it one more time. There was no *anonymous message* in the folders of his laptop.

Somebody knocked at the door. Even before Gils could respond, the door burst open, and Ivan Georg rushed into the room.

"Professor Gils, did you send me this e-mail message?" he asked, waving a sheet of paper in his hand.

Gils took a deep breath, "Ivan, I've sent you no emails for days."

"You know my classified email address," Ivan objected. "No one else does."

"As a matter of fact, I, too, received an email message, Ivan," Professor Gils said. "It was anonymous and very strange. Its focus was four types of human beings who participated in a controlled experiment."

"Let me see it," Ivan said.

"I can't show it to you," the Professor said. "It was automatically deleted and I couldn't read it to the end."

"The message must have been quite long," Ivan paused glancing at the sheet of paper in his hand. "Look at the one I've got," he said. "I printed it out for you."

You are the first artificially generated Marked One, the text read. *And you will be the first one they will kill. You are the key to the experiment aimed at producing Samodivas. If you lose the key, the experiment fails. This is why they will eliminate you.*

The pouring rain drowned out the swishing, menacing howls of the wind.

"I didn't send you this email," Professor Gils said.

"Who did, then? You are the only one who knows my classified email address," Ivan repeated as he looked the professor in the eye.

Chapter Twenty-Six

"Let me go," Boya breathed. "You know what, Philip Mill? You've tied me with a rope. It means you're digging your own grave."

"Boya, I had to do it," the tall man said, staring at his shoes. "I'll let you go the minute we get to your car."

The rain beat against windowpane, the trees buffeted by the wind moaned and shook as the flickering light of the candle jumped and threw a warped shadow on the wall.

"I know the exact minute of my death, Boya," a small voice, as thin as a splinter sank into the flame of the candle. "I will not die today."

"You cannot be so sure," Boya said. "Your life is in my hands. The next time, Philip won't be around and I'll decide when you'll die."

"Let her go, Philip, please," the blind woman said, her words a handful of timid raindrops.

"If he lets me go, I'll kill you," the young woman said, her voice a freezing winter night.

"I don't know where, but I do know when I will die," the blind woman said. "And I know the person who will kill me."

Boya laughed. "Then why waste time?" she said sharply. "Tell me the day, I'll come to your place and I'll do the job." She paused, thinking. "Wanga, I have a better idea. You can come somewhere near my place, so I wouldn't have to plod across your ugly Bare Mountain."

"It is not you who will kill me, Boya," said Wanga, thin and tall, a dry, brittle twig.

Philip pushed Boya to the door.

"Fool!" she said dryly. "Hey, Wanga, if it's not going to be me, then who will kill you? Tell me. I'd like to buy that guy a drink."

It was quiet, the candle burned, the flames pirouetting like exquisite ballerinas in the air.

"Philip Mill," the blind woman breathed.

"What!" The big man jumped.

"Wrong answer. This sissy wouldn't kill a cockroach," Boya said. The shadows the flames cast looked like Chinese hieroglyphs as they leapt onto her face in rapid succession. It was a thin and beautiful face, not one of a killer, yet Boya had come to the prophetess' house to kill.

"Wanga," Philip began. "You've told me you can see only the green dots, not the men. No green dots swim around my head. You've repeated this time and again. How come you know that I will kill you?"

It was so quiet that Wanga's shallow breathing echoed like a series of shots. The pile of old empty pans in the room loomed threateningly white in the corner, and close by the low bed, dark, sharp-edged stones were stacked in a heap.

"Those are the stones that the tormented souls throw here, aren't they?" Boya said. "And these pans heavy with agony … I wouldn't say the furnishing is to my taste. You seem to enjoy hate and disease, Wanga."

"Let her go," the blind woman said.

Philip Mill produced a knife from his pocket, cut the rope around Boya's neck and untied her hands.

"The dots around her … they are so numerous, the prophetess said. "So many … and she can control them."

Boya took a step towards the blind woman, bent forward, and said, "Why do you think I can control the dots, Wanga?"

The pale blind woman leaned against the wall as she lifted her hand over the burning flame of the candle. "I cannot lie to you," she said. "But I will not tell you. Pain helps me to keep silent."

The flame seared the skin of her fingers and a smell of charred flesh wafted in the air. Boya pushed the prophetess' hand away from the candle.

"You said I would kill you, Wanga," Philip said, peeking into her blind eyes. "You know how much you mean to me. I'd never ever harm you. I'd die for you."

"Stop sniveling," Boya cut him short. "How come you know Philip will kill you? He has no green dots, and he is a weak man, boring and dull."

Wanga shook as Philip held her close to him.

"Wanga, you know very well that you and I can see the green dots," Boya hissed. "You say you can see them in the future and in the past. I think this is impossible. But you cannot lie. There must be a key to this puzzle. What is it, Wanga? I am confident that you cannot see Philip in the future or in the past. There are no green dots around him. He is a Mr. Nobody; therefore, he must be invisible for you."

"Leave her alone!" Philip said evenly. "Or I'll kill you!"

"Oh, the lover is angry at last," Boya mocked. "Wanga, tell me!"

The flame of the candle shot to the ceiling, the rain and the window fought on their fierce battle, and the wind was a motherless child.

"Everyone ..." Wanga's voice thinned into a sob. "Everyone has green dots. There is no exception to the rule. *I know who you are, woman.*"

Wanga's pale face turned crimson.

"Water!" Philip shouted. "She's sick!"

Boya watched Wanga's contorted face. "You say everyone has green dots. But this is not true, Wanga," Boya shook her head as she squeezed the frail shoulders.

The blind woman breathed deeply, the purple color slowly leaving her cheeks as her face turned back to its normal ashen pallor.

"Does that mean that even this mediocrity here" Boya pointed to Philip, "That even he has green dots, and the ruffians whose intelligence verges on asinine stupidity?"

Wanga didn't answer. She breathed evenly.

"You are a New One, aren't you? You cannot lie," Boya pushed on. "You tried to lie to me about the green dots. And you choked near to death."

"Everybody, every human being has them," Wanga said. Her hands didn't tremble.

"Then you tried to lie to me about something else," Boya snarled. "You said you knew a lot about me."

"I will not tell you anything," the thin woman said.

"You will."

Boya clutched at the thin wrist of the woman, pushing it towards the flame of the candle. The smell of burning flesh filled the room.

Philip lunged forward. The blind prophetess' thin wrist jerked away from the flames as Boya fell onto the ground, shrieking with pain.

"Wanga," Philip whispered as he bent low over the unseeing eyes. "You will be safe with me."

"I will not tell you more, Philip," she touched his face. Her fingertips traced a path down the soft oval of his cheekbones, paused at his lips, and caressed his chin. "You should have guessed."

Both Philip Mill and Boya, who had scrambled to her feet, followed the slow, hesitant movement of Wanga's head. It seemed her blind eyes were trying to concentrate on the heap of sharp-edged stones.

"Guessed what?" Philip asked, his breath sharp.

"You tried to make me believe you were somebody else, Philip," Wanga said. "You care about me. I thought … I thought that maybe you and I … but I saw them. I saw where your green dots led you. And I refused to believe them."

He took her hand. Wanga pulled it away. The flame of the candle had dug a gaping wound in her flesh.

"It was staring me in the eye. I refused to believe. I thought you loved me," she said, her words dry autumn leaves on fire.

"Philip tricked you into believing he was in love with you," Boya jeered. "You are an old blind fool."

"I am an old blind fool," she said her face expressionless, a piece of dead wood in a cold fireplace.

"Wanga!" Philip said. "I'd die for you."

"You'll kill me," she said softly.

"Wanga, my dearest," he whispered. "My dearest! You make me feel like a child, a man, and an old man at the same time. I cannot live without you."

She did not say anything.

Chapter Twenty-Seven

Professor Gils' spacious office was immaculately clean. The inner yard of Iztok Clinic glistened silvery and peaceful in the incessant October rain.

"Professor Gils, Doctor Ivan Georg, thank you for inviting me here," Professor Margaret Stan said.

She was a tall woman. Her graying hair was short; her dark gaze paused on Professor Gils' face then caught Ivan's eye.

"I listened to Healing Trun you provided for me, Doctor Georg. Thank you. The headache I had had for months was gone. I studied how often the word *Trun,* or shall I call it *the piercing combination of sounds,* appeared in your Healing Trun." She paused. "For months, I had been listening to Killing Trun, the malware recording of wails an anonymous 'guardian angel' had sent me. Blood spurted from my nose, and I could not stretch my legs. The word *Trun* was clearly audible, so I analyzed its occurrence in the recording that made me sick, comparing it to the number of times it was used in its Healing Trun counterpart. The machines intercepted three peaks in Killing Trun. No such peaks were present in its Healing twin."

"What you tell us is interesting," Professor Gils said. "Maybe we should attract other scientists to study the two recordings."

Professor Margaret Stan looked up and said slowly, "It is technically impossible to make this comparison one more time."

Doctor Ivan Georg studied her face. It looked beautiful, the skin pale, regular features, hardly visible wrinkles around the eyes and the mouth, a dimple in the chin, high smooth forehead, and the eyes! They were dark, a slow quiet fire burning deep inside them. He had the feeling the woman could read his thoughts, and the sound of her voice, deep and composed, calmed him down.

"Why should a simple comparison be impossible?" Professor Gils asked.

"The emails I received made it clear the recordings would be destroyed if I contacted other scientists," the woman said, her eyes on Gils' face.

"You contacted us," Professor Gils pointed out.

"To be honest, I didn't trust you," Margaret Stan said. "I'd like to thank Doctor Ivan Georg. I have wrongly assumed he wouldn't send me his Healing Trun, and suspected that all stories about its therapeutic potential were downright lies. However, I listened to Healing Trun and my headache was gone. My left knee that has given me trouble for years hurts no more. So I asked to see both of you."

"A week ago, I didn't know that Killing Trun would cause internal hemorrhages and paralysis," Professor Gils said. "When I saw you had signed the report on this phenomenon, I was worried." He paused; his head bent low. "After my mother listened to the recordings you provided for us, Professor Stan, I believe every word of what you'd written. Her nose bled, after a minute into Killing Trun, she had double vision, and felt totally disoriented. She screamed and said excruciating pain swept through her bones. She was dying. If I had not switched off the recording device, her heart might have exploded."

After a moment of hesitation, Ivan asked, "Professor Gils, what was your response to Professor Margaret Stan's Killing Trun?"

A stunned silence fell over the room. The air seemed to thicken. It was 4 PM.

"Killing Trun had no effect on me," Gils said slowly. "At the beginning, I developed a mild headache. That was practically all."

The young doctor wrote something down on a sheet of paper, and stealing a glance at the woman, asked, "Professor Stan, who sent you the recordings that would lead to death?"

Margaret Stan's eyes flashed sharply, but the words she pronounced sounded measured and calm.

"A fortnight ago, I came back from the laboratory and found a file I had not seen on my computer before. Somebody must have planted in there, among my documents. It was an audio file TRUN.wav. I suspected it was spyware, or a document containing a computer virus. So, I deleted it."

Her eyes gleamed dangerously.

"What happened later?" Professor Gils asked as he offered her a bottle of mineral water.

"On the following day, TRUN.wav was again among my documents. This time, I asked myself who had had access to my files," she paused. "I already had a pretty clear idea who had planted this file in my computer."

"Who was that?"

"I wouldn't give you her name unless I was absolutely sure," Professor Stan said. "At that particular time, my son's girlfriend Boya Bagd was on a short visit to the place where I live. I found her in my study twice. The first time she said she liked my flowers. I had deleted TRUN.wav and I installed a micro camera in one of the flowerpots. I checked the video recording. Boya Bagd was working on my computer. After she was gone, I checked what she had done. The file TRUN.wav was there. I opened it. The hissing and howling sounds hit me, and my nose bled. I panicked, crept to the computer, and deleted the file. Then I realized how illogically I had acted. I lost the file. I lost something extremely dangerous that I should have kept." Professor Margaret Stan thought for a while. "I'd like to tell you something else, gentlemen. I saw a little child in the street, a girl, a fair-haired one. My husband tells me he has seen her in our neighborhood many times. She was alone. An hour after the girl was gone, a neighbor died, that is what I had noticed."

Ivan thought about the little girl he had seen in his chaotic dream but said nothing. A scary thought crossed his mind.

"What if someone decides to use Killing Trun to make the whole town an obedient mass of sufferers?" Ivan said. "Killing Trun can keep the whole country under control. Anyone who owns it can transform the earth into a hostel for terminally sick patients."

Professor Stan's raised her hand.

"Yes," she said. "I thought of the only person who could have left the harmful file on my computer: Boya Bagd. Killing Trun *was* in her hands, and she could do whatever she pleased with it. Why should she give it to me? I deleted it, and when on the following day Boya Bagd came again to see my son, I was very curious what I'd find in my computer."

"What did you find?" Professor Gils asked, his eyes intensely blue behind his glasses. His hands looked unusually white; the skin of his palms almost translucent in the light of the strong neon lamps. "Was it the dangerous file?"

"Yes, the file was there, in my computer. I did not open it, I was afraid of the pain, but in the evening, when Boya Bagd was gone, I listened to the recording. My nose bled, and the headache, much worse than before, was back. I was unable to crawl to the computer to switch it off. Within three minutes that appeared as long as three centuries, the screeching, slurping and howling sounds ceased, and I lay in a pool of my own blood on the floor. I wondered how I could analyze the recording I had. Frightened to listen to the destructive sounds, I decided to resort to remote control trials. Complex devices recorded the frequency with which the word Trun surfaced in the biting screams. The recorders registered other stable combinations of sounds that surged up throughout the recordings. *Three* stable combinations were repeated fairly regularly, if we trust the analysis the computers performed."

"Three stable combinations?" Gils said. "Professor Stan, do you have any idea what they might be related to?"

Margaret Stan hesitated, or perhaps the corners of her mouth twitched slightly. Professor Gils was certain she knew something she kept to herself.

"Professor Stan," he ventured. "Did you analyze Healing Trun, the recording that made the pain go away, the one Doctor Ivan Georg provided for you?"

The eyes of the two men were on Margaret Stan. Professor Gils did not believe she would answer his question. Her expression was cold and distant. To his surprise, her response was direct and straightforward.

"I did analyze Ivan Georg's Healing Trun. "Apart from the word Trun, there were no other stable combinations of sounds in it."

It was beginning to drizzle, the sky was no longer gray, and the clouds, luminous nests of moonbeams, seemed to gleam.

"Tell us more about the combinations of sounds in Killing Trun, please," Professor Gils said. He already knew: if Professor Stan wanted to tell you something, she would, even if you did not want to hear a word of it. If she was determined to be silent, no question in the world, no matter how subtly phrased, would make her speak.

"Yes, I analyzed the repetitions," she said. "And I came to certain conclusions that astonished me. There were three stable combinations of sounds in Killing Trun. I did tests on mice. The first stable combination killed baby mice, the second one destroyed only adult mice, and the third one exterminated all old mice. I stumbled on a triad-based pattern."

"Have you discovered a similar triad pattern somewhere else?" Doctor Ivan Georg asked.

At sixty, Margaret was still an attractive woman. Professor Gils thought her face made one think of a peaceful autumn afternoon, but her eyes … Dark, persistent fire burned in them. He shuddered.

"You may not believe me," the woman with the dangerous eyes said. "I found this *triad* or *trio* pattern in an Old Bulgarian song."

"Could you tell us more about the trio model?" Gils asked.

She looked at Ivan Georg then she dropped her gaze.

"I have a vague idea about it," she said. "I might be wrong."

That, in Professor Gils' view, could mean one thing. Margaret Stan had reached a certain point in her analysis and could go no further. The woman was either scared or up in a creek. He had read her articles on artificial intellect. She was a person who did not scare easily. Margaret Stan had listened to Killing Trun twice and had come to in a pool of her own blood. It must be the second option: she found no way out and needed their help.

"A fortnight after I started my experiments with Killing Trun, the screeching sounds hit me again," Margaret Stan began. "That day, I received an unexpected SMS. It read, *Take care, Boya Bagd.*"

"Your son's ex-fiancée, Boya Bagd?" Professor Gils asked.

"Yes, the young woman who had planted Killing Trun in my computer."

A sudden silence fell over the room and in it Ivan Georg's voice sounded uncertain. "I have to share with you a fact I have kept to myself so far." So far, the young doctor had listened silently to what they were saying. "Professor Stan," Ivan went on. "I have a girlfriend and her name is Boya Bagd. I am not sure if she is the same young woman who was your son's fiancée. This is her photograph. Please have a look at it."

He handed Margaret Stan his mobile phone.

The young woman was very beautiful, dark-green eyes, red hair, perfect complexion. Professor Gils liked her smiling face. He had glanced at it then studied Professor Stan's face. Something happened deep inside her dark eyes. They flashed—or had he imagined they did?

"Yes," Margaret Stan said firmly. "The woman in the photograph is Boya Bagd, my son's ex-fiancée."

Ivan Georg kept mum.

"Boya Bagd," Gils said thoughtfully. "Maybe we should contact John Cole, the police chief. He is my friend."

"I wouldn't do that," Margaret Stan objected. "I know that man well. He's been my close acquaintance for years."

"And you don't trust him?" Professor Gils ventured, avoiding her eyes.

"I don't," she said.

Ivan did not seem to hear anything. Poor Ivan, Gils thought, he really cares about that girl. It was getting dark, dusk settled in the corners of the spacious office. Maybe it was a good idea to turn on the lights. In the darkness, Gils saw the pale green specks of the shimmering halo around Ivan's head. He wondered if Ivan could see the green dots surrounding his own thinning hair. Ivan and I are lonely men, Gils thought. Sara Eutim, the beautiful journalist, who had visited the clinic, his only childhood friend ... He had seen the thick circle of green radiance around her head and shoulders. She had denied that she saw his and Ivan's green specks of fire, and Gils suspected she wasn't telling the truth.

Why was she lying? Ivan had put her to the test: the stone that killed Tintin the eel and caused hemorrhages and paralysis in other patients, had no influence on her. Ivan had slipped it into Sara Eutim's coat pocket. The individuals, all loners, who had these green dots were immune to the destructive effect the stones from Trun Shrine exerted on other people. Sara Eutim, the glamour queen, had been married a number of times. She lived alone, too, and had those damned green seeds of lonesomeness in her magnificent hair. These dots eliminated the power of Killing Trun, or did they really? Gils studied Ivan's face.

Ivan agreed to listen to Professor Margaret Stan's recording of the deathly Trun. Would he feel pain? Would the hissing sounds paralyze his limbs? Was it right to ask the young man to endure a new cycle of torture? The complex brain surgery he had undergone, the suffering, his plain face, the story of his girlfriend's photograph, Boya Bagd, who turned out to be the ex-fiancée of Professor Stan's son.

"A simple experiment can help us to determine what our next step should be," Ivan Georg said. "I am ready to listen to the recording Professor Margaret Stan sent us. We'll check if I'll be adversely affected by Killing Trun. I am sure that Professor Gils will turn off the recording device if my life is endangered."

"It might be extremely harmful to you," Gils said.

"You'll be around, Professor Stan," Ivan said slowly. He drank a glass of mineral water, and glancing at Margaret Stan, asked, "How long had you been listening to the excruciating noise before you felt sick?"

"I felt crushed right away. The splitting headache broke me the minute I switched on the computer."

"Then you have to leave the room," Professor Gils suggested. "You can wait in Ivan Georg's office on the fifth floor."

Professor Margaret Stan did something that made Professor Gils jump.

"Ivan, are you sure Gils is your friend?" she asked.

Professor Gils' face turned red.

"He saved my life," Ivan had said.

"He saved your life before you were famous, before you generated Healing Trun," Professor Stan pointed out. "I'll stay here," she declared. "I'll switch off the computer if the recording gets too dangerous for Ivan. I do not trust you, Gils."

"You will bleed to death, Professor Stan," Gils said evenly.

Ivan remembered the email he had received. *You will be the first one they will kill.* Professor Gils was the only person who knew Ivan's classified email address.

"I'll stay here," Margaret declared. "I'd like to see how Killing Trun will affect Gils."

It was much easier than everybody expected. The hissing and squawking sounds crashed through the dusk in the room, hit the walls, boomed, and squashed Margaret Stan. Ivan Georg felt absolutely nothing. Trun! Trun! The air pulsed, shuddered, leapt, and Ivan compared the roaring sounds to giant raindrops splashing against the roof of his house. Trun was a million horses galloping on the windowpane, but their hooves could not reach him. Ivan ran to the computer and turned it off. Poor Margaret, he thought. Her face was sallow and droplets of blood oozed from her nose. Ivan was sorry for Margaret. The Trun poison had not affected Gils. What if … Ivan thought. No, this was out of the question … might be too dangerous. But … they should put his idea to test. They had to!

"Could I make a suggestion?" Ivan heard himself say. "The screeching Trun sounds I produced turned out to have positive effect on patients. The Killing Trun that Professor Stan has provided us with results in paralysis or death. I asked myself what would happen if we listened to both Healing and Killing Trun, sounding simultaneously. Would this combination have an impact on us?"

For a long time, no one said anything. Finally, Margaret Stan spoke, "Let us try and see what will happen."

Her face looked pinched.

Gils took a step to the window and, heaving a sigh, patted Ivan on the shoulder. "Killing Trun had no effect on me. Let us see what the mixture of Healing and Killing Trun will do," he said. "If someone among us feels sick, the other two will immediately turn off the computer."

"What if they don't turn it off?" Margaret Stan said.

"Professor Stan, I'd like to assure you that …" Gils began.

"You treated the members of the archaeological team," Margaret Stan said. "They were all dying."

Gils was the only person who knew my classified email address, Ivan thought. *You will be the first one they will kill.* He shuddered.

Gils produced a heavy iron bar with which he secured the door of his laboratory in the evening.

"I'll smash the computer if something goes wrong," he said.

"I am ready," Ivan said. "I will start Healing Trun in 15 seconds."

"I am ready," Professor Margaret Stan said calmly. "I will start Killing Trun."

"I am ready," Professor Gils said as he gripped the iron bar.

They sat in complete silence. Suddenly hissing, shrieking, wailing explosions tore into the air, bawling and deafening cacophony, unbearable reverberation and clanks burst with ear-splitting throbs in the room. TRUN! *TRU-UN!* The word beat like the heart of a hungry, voracious monster over the thundering, blood-curdling noise. Ivan reached out his hand to turn off the computer, Margaret Stan shook, and Gils raised the iron bar. Then the deafening screams and howls died down, a heavy silence lingered in the air. The calm before the storm … then music, heavenly and beautiful, echoed through the window. The tune flowed, peaceful and sweet, magnificent and slow, like Beethoven's *Für Elise,* soft like a mother's kiss. The melody was so gentle that Gils dropped the bar, Margaret Stan closed her eyes and thought of the green meadows above Dusk, the small town where she was born. She was again a little girl, and the sun was her brother. She remembered her lifelong dream of becoming a scientist, she thought about her father, a tall, strong man who showed her twigs and leaves of different shrubs and said, "Trees are cleverer than us, my little one. They do not fight. They are quiet and help the earth survive. We destroy it. The stronger we grow, the weaker our world becomes."

"Mom says the world is a wonderful place," Margaret had said. "God loves us and He loves the world."

Her father had looked at her, the smile dying on his lips, his eyes sad and solemn. "God begins where knowledge ends, my pretty girl," he said. "We, human beings, are weak. We have invented God to help us in our plight. At the back of our minds, we knew that only God we keep in our hearts could give us a hand."

"You don't know!" Margaret had said quietly.

"Don't cry," her father said. "When you find yourself in times of trouble, you have to know that the way out is inside you. The path to freedom exists, Margaret. You only have to look carefully at the world and you will find the open door. The daring rescue is inside you."

The music sounds so soft and glorious, Gils thought. Like a river that had no end and no shore, a river that flowed into his heart, carrying away all his anxieties. You will find the shore, young man, and it will be your home. You have a map that shows you to the right place, and the map is your blood. The electronic calculator is your God, the only one you believe in, but you should believe in your blood instead. It can sense the right direction. Professor Andrew Gils did not believe in instinctive choices. He disliked premonitions and hated superstitions with all his heart. A successful day was the day when science took a step forward. His task was to fight ignorance. He did not believe his blood knew the answer to difficult questions and was very open about his profound distrust of soothsayers and astrologers. Andrew Gils did not believe that some hissing and squealing sounds could destroy malignant tumors, but this had happened. *You will find the shore, young man. The music! This magnificent music was everything Doctor Gils did not believe in.*

Ivan had waited for this music for a long time. Ever since he was a little boy, he had wanted a friend, someone he could trust. You should learn to love yourself. You are your own best friend. If you respect yourself, everybody else will. You have to concentrate on the power your own mind has, and all the other people will notice and admire it. Hesitation is the product of your fears. You have already cured many men of degenerative diseases. Help mankind endure. It is worth living in this world. Maybe you will find a woman with a heart of gold. You do not believe it now. But it is in you, the glory. What was that? Ivan thought. He had a naturally suspicious mind and catchphrases of any sort put him off. It was different now. The music was everything he had been dreaming of.

The sounds died away, and it was peaceful and quiet in the room. Light rain wove nets of hope in the air, and the soft whispering touch of the raindrops was a tune of harmony and joy.

"This melody brought my father back to me," Margaret Stan said. "How beautiful it was. I heard the word Trun. It sounded like the promise of spring."

"I saw a river that had no shore and no end," Gils said. "But I knew I was its shore. It was beautiful. I thought Trun was inside me."

"I forgot about the howling sounds," Ivan said. "I thought Trun was my best friend."

Professor Margaret Stan's face turned suddenly pale. She glanced at the two men sitting opposite her.

"Gentlemen," she said firmly. "I think I am seeing ghosts." She took a deep breath and said something that made Professor Gilds and Ivan exchange a look. "Gentlemen, I can see green dots around your heads. Either I am going crazy or I'm struggling through a nervous fit."

At that moment, Professor Gils saw green shimmering flames: they were bright and they swam around Professor Margaret Stan's forehead.

"Ivan," Professor Gils said hesitantly. "Can you see it around her head … the intense halo of green specks?"

"Yes … the green streak," Ivan said." The dots in Professor Stan's hair are much thicker than the ones surrounding your head."

Professor Margaret watched two men carefully.

"Doctor Ivan Georg, I can see green dots around your head and around that of Professor Gils. *The stronger we grow, the weaker becomes the world,*" Margaret went on. "That is what my father told me when I was seven years old." Her intelligent eyes studied Gil's face.

Ivan's voice shattered the awkward silence, "Professor Stan, I wonder if Killing Trun will have a traumatic effect on you now that you have the dots."

They performed the experiment with Killing Trun again. *TRUN! TRUN!* wailing and screeching, screaming and shrieking sounds rent the silence in the room. Professor Margaret Stan's nose did not bleed. She felt no pain.

"I am a bit weak and dizzy, that is all," she said.

Boya read the essay one more time. Something in it was wrong, a detail, a minor inconsistency worried her. The boy had written he gave the blackbird breadcrumbs to eat. A blackbird eating crumbs? This was absurd! Then she saw a child, a fair-haired girl.

"Can you tell me the way to the park, Miss?" the child asked her.

Boya did not like the girl. Skinny little runt, Boya thought, and why is the little one all alone? "I don't know," she answered. "Go away."

The child did not say anything. Her eyes, sharp and biting, met Boya's. The woman shivered. An evil little monkey, she thought as the girl walked slowly away.

Chapter Twenty-Eight

"Listen, Sara, I'd like you to meet a very interesting person … She … she is very intelligent, she's exceptional, and I'd be very happy if you can spare half an hour. Please speak to her," Jacob's voice, thrilled and exhilarated, frolicked in my mobile telephone.

I did not like enthusiastic voices, especially ones that belonged to my fiancés as they described another woman's accomplishments. He's like the rest of them, I thought sourly, remembering Jacob's beaming face two hours ago. Then he told me I was the most ravishing, beautiful woman in the world and so on. It was evident he had discovered another ravishing female individual who, in addition to her other accomplishments, was extremely intelligent, which I was not, alas.

"Unfortunately, today I am exceptionally busy," I started to say. "Sorry, maybe some other time…"

"Don't say this," said Jacob's voice through my mobile telephone, a dreadfully expensive gadget, his fervent voice a pool of happiness in it. "She's unique. She gave me the second part of that song."

"Which song?" I asked although I remembered clearly: The Old Bulgarian song and the Trun Chark; the barefaced lie about how you describe your pains and aches to a saucepan then throw the thing into the *chark*. Not only do you become as vigorous as an Olympic weightlifting medalist, but you also get rid of your worries and nagging suspicions.

"Don't tell me you don't remember," my telephone protested energetically. "It's the song about the *chark*."

"Yes, the *chark*," I agreed.

After a week of heavy rain, the weather was good at last. It was true the sun was as big as my fist and the clouds tried hard to drown it in their gray beards, but the sky made its best efforts to remain radiantly blue.

"I have the second part of the Trun Chark song!" Jacob's voice pirouetted on my nerves. I was on the point of turning off my mobile when I changed my mind. "And she would very much like to meet you."

Was I imagining it or did he really sound very happy because he had met another woman, younger and more attractive than me? No, I was not imagining things. I knew it. The little idiot had fallen in love, and his telephone turned a somersault in midair, so what, Sara Eutim? Your fiancé deserts you again. This seems to happen too often in your life: first Philip Mill, now Jacob, the archaeologist enamored with another woman. Sara Eutim, you know love is a tawdry tale invented to produce tears in dimwitted housewives' eyes. You are not dimwitted at all, my girl. Isn't it funny that you are jealous of a man who is thinner than his own shirt?

"You can't imagine how beautiful the second part sounds, how unbelievable! I must read it to you right now. Where are you, honey?"

I did not answer.

"Where are you?" Jacob's mobile telephone bleated impatiently. "She would like to see you. She says it's urgent!"

I was in Paradise Café, but I thought it would be unwise to reveal my whereabouts.

"You are in Paradise Café!" he said eagerly. "I can see you sitting at the table by the window."

"Who is she?" I asked. I caught the sneaking notes of admiration for the mysterious she that his phone transferred from his voice to my ears.

"You cannot start imagining what the second part of the song says! I already have a bold hypothesis about the Samodivas you are infatuated with, my ingenious girl."

I was the ingenious girl, and *she* was the girl he admired.

"Leave the song alone," I said not too politely. "Tell me why she wants to see me."

"Her name is Boya Bagd, and she's a historian knowledgeable about Old Bulgarian songs. Miss Bagd informed me she had visited Dusk monastery and had found the second part of the song, which Priest Dimo left in that drawer … do you remember, I told you everything about it."

"I don't think I have heard or read about a historian Boya Bagd," I cut him short. "And I'm not interested in whatever she might wish to enlighten me on."

"But, Sara, she hinted it was about an essay a boy had written about the birds, do you remember … the ones as heavy as iron balls. The feathered songsters dug a hole into the town square after they perched on it."

Yes, I had read an article in the *Dusk Daily* about a flock of heavyweight ravens that punched a crater in the schoolyard as their claws touched the asphalt. I had heard nothing about them ever since. To be honest, I hated the enthusiasm Jacob showed for that very interesting Boya Bagd. I was convinced I had forgotten all about jealousy the minute I turned thirteen. Well, I was wrong.

"I love birds, Jacob," I admitted. "Unfortunately, I have more important issues to concentrate on. No matter how much I appreciate the opportunity to study the information your friend Boya Bagd might wish to share, I am in no position to see her today."

"Hey, Sara," Jacob's voice on my telephone went sour. "Are you ok? Why are you saying these things?"

I looked up and saw Jacob and a stunning redhead behind the crystal-clear windowpane of Paradise Café. A tiny detail I'd noticed made me hide behind the table in the dark corner at the back of the café. I saw green shimmering dots swarming around the belle's head and felt no overwhelming desire to speak to her. The information she had on the second part of the Trun Chark song wasn't my cup of tea. At the back of my mind, I kept counting the persons with green dots buried in their hair—Professor Gils, the boy I used to tell fairy tales to; Ivan Georg, the young doctor who had produced the Healing Trun nonsense (which became the talk of the town); and now that spectacular woman. Far too many individuals were sporting green dots, I thought. Give me a break.

Someone tapped me on the shoulder as I walked slowly to the table I had chosen in Paradise Café. There was no need to turn around. I knew who stood behind my back, that beauty queen. Jacob was waiting at the front door of the angelic drinking establishment.

"I've already seen them," the gorgeous woman declared. "There's no point in trying to hide from me."

"I have not had the pleasure of knowing your name," I said. "I'd like to inform you that I can discuss neither the Trun Chark nor the awe-inspiring blackbirds with you, Madame."

Her complexion was impeccable, her eyes dark blue, deep, and calm. I couldn't but admire the powerful determination in her stare and immediately knew she would not let me go.

"I can see your green dots," the woman said. "Why waste time? I am sure you can see mine."

Jacob, my sweet fiancé, came up and began to talk, "Honey, I'm itching to show you the second part of the Trun Chark song. You can't imagine …" before I had time to find my tongue, he planted a kiss on my forehead, then another on my lips, and yet another on the top of my head. He did not even bother to glance at the smashing redhead, and suddenly her unique complexion was of no consequence. "She has the only copy of the song and answered the advertisement I placed in a number of newspapers … She is a member of the scientific team that examines the blackbirds. You remember them?"

"Mr. Harvey, could you please go to the shop at the corner and make a copy of the Trun Chark song for Ms. Eutim?" asked the young woman with the stunning legs. Her smile was so warm it could easily melt the North Pole, but Jacob Harvey the archaeologist did not notice it. What a jealous little woman I was. I was positive I stumbled on a surge of enthusiasm in Jacob's voice the minute he started speaking about the pretty doll face. Oh, come off it. "Mr. Harvey, a cup of coffee will be waiting for you after you come back. I will take care of that."

Jacob lingered at the table, but the redhead pushed him not too gently to the door. At that moment, I was sorry for her. She didn't know Jacob! The man did not even look at the shop she had pointed at. He eased himself into the soft chair.

"Look at this," he said his voice bubbling with impatience. *They are inside you. Your doubts and hopes are the land they live on, your courage is the food they eat. They are your happiness. They are your pain too. Your thoughts are their home. Your dreams are the fun they have. What is it that no one can escape from? Is it love? Everybody goes there; you will go there too. Everybody meets it; you will meet it too: it is in your bones and it is in your mind. Your grandmother met it; your mother will meet it. Your child will meet it. When, oh when will you meet it? How do you know? They go to your children, the Samodivas do.*

"I will stand no nonsense, Jacob," I said. From the corner of my eye, I saw pretty Boya fidget nervously.

"This is the second part of the Trun Chark song!" Jacob exclaimed. "Can't you see? They live inside us, within our thoughts."

I hated it. My fiancé sat by my side leaving me unable to make sense of his curious elation.

"Who are they?" I asked a short clear question, hoping to get a short clear answer. Alas, I knew Jacob Harvey too well.

"The Samodivas, of course!" he exclaimed. "Your thoughts are their home, and your dreams are the fun they have. They live inside us."

"You mean they are worms?" the redhead said, an edge of sarcasm slashing her clear voice.

He did not even look at her. How could I suspect foul play on Jacob's part? What is wrong with you, Sara Eutim? You were *jealous,* weren't you?

"This is a unique song! Just imagine! They are wraith-like dots that inhabit our thoughts. How stupid we are!" Jacob went on ranting and raving at me. "We look for extraterrestrial civilizations on faraway planets, and we see no further than our noses! They are blooming inside us. They are a civilization that thrives on our subconscious mind!"

"Oh, come off it," the beauty said and yawned.

I yawned too.

Then I noticed the redhead's mouth twitch. She could not stand Jacob Harvey! This time, for once, I could sympathize with her. Jacob was capable of driving anybody crazy, even me, and I was a very patient and easy-going woman. Then I noticed a shadow of worry flit over the woman's face. Worry? Why? That was interesting. The woman was upset; I could see that clearly.

Did Jacob say something that upset her? What was it?

"So you think that the Samodivas are creatures inside us?" I said watching the pretty woman. "Is that it, Jacob? You think they are a *civilization* inhabiting our thoughts?" My words failed to impress the *belle.* Her worries vanished; she beamed at me, friendly and radiant, too friendly, and much too radiant to my taste.

"This hypothesis borders on psychotic disorder," observed the incredible redhead as she smiled at me. I did not like her smile. It made me think of the ditch the bulldozers had dug in the street where the house of my childhood still stood. It was an empty house the municipal authorities had planned to demolish. That was what her smile was, a heap of old bricks and ruined walls.

"It sounds farfetched, yes" Jacob said. "But we visited Deaf Crags and you saw the pool, Sara. We made the waves roar, so I just wondered . . ."

"I am glad you visited that place, Ms. Eutim," the glamour girl turned to me. "I went there last week. A friend told me the water hissed and churned after you dipped your pinkie in it. This is intriguing to say the least."

"Who told you about Deaf Crags, Boya? How come you found it?" Jacob looked as innocent as a little boy. I could feel his admiration for that brave and brilliant lady Boya Bagd. Brave and brilliant, my foot!

"I work for the team that studies the strange blackbirds," she answered, beaming a smile at him. "So, I traveled to Deaf Crags."

Jacob, to give him his due, remained thoroughly unmoved by her sweet carol.

"Boya, did you actually put your hand into the water?" Jacob's eyes settled on her face, failing to notice how stunning it looked. "I mean, you dipped your hand into the liquid, and it roared and howled, is that right?" he pressed.

"Yes and . . . no," Boya said. "I heard the water hiss after I touched it. It was very unnerving indeed."

A nagging suspicion lingered in my mind: the woman was lying. "Did it hurt?" I asked. "Did your fingers tingle when you touched the dark water, or shall we call it the *Samodiva's milk?*"

"Yes and no," she said. I was confident she was at a loss what to do next.

"And that boy's essay," Jacob began. "Perhaps you could give it to Sara . . . I mean to Ms. Eutim. It's a very perplexing essay, and I have to admit I was sorry for that boy."

Another shadow flitted across the redhead's angelic face; for a split second, it crumpled and fell. Something kept bothering her, and I was curious what it was.

"Mr. Harvey," the beauty queen smiled at Jacob gently, he bristled, and I thought I hated her. A minute later, I knew why—she flirted with my man. I thought I did not care about Jacob. Yes, he was sweet and sincere, an honest guy altogether, so what? Most of the guys who loved me were sweet, sincere, and honest. Jealousy was not a part of my robust constitution. What had gone wrong then? I was in a jealous rage, and this was funny, honestly. "Mr. Harvey, would you be so kind to read to Ms. Eutim this very interesting excerpt from the essay? Please read slowly and loudly."

Her eyes melted with gratitude as Mr. Harvey started reading, blushing furiously.

She killed my bird and I thought I was going to die. That bird was all I had ever had—my brother, my friend, my father, and the good voice that lulled me to sleep every night. I saw my blackbird turn into black dust in her hands. Something deep inside me shouted, 'Don't give up life, bird. Struggle! Live! I'll be there for you.' I thought my heart would burst. The woman took the black dust my bird had turned into, and my heart stopped beating. I thought I was dead.

I was confused.

"Did you kill his bird?" I asked, carefully watching the beauty.

"Yes," she said. Then she turned to Jacob, her gorgeous face unsmiling for once. I had to admit that even though her lips made me think of a poisonous toadstool, she looked very beautiful. Jacob must have established this fact too. "Mr. Harvey, please go and buy us a bottle of wine. Don't come back soon. I need to talk to Ms. Eutim in private," the woman said.

To my utter surprise, Jacob scrambled to his feet and made for the door.

I smelled a rat. How come Jacob became so tractable?

"Jacob, wait," I called out. "Please tell me why you agreed to go away? Did she pay you to?"

His face glowed red. "Yes," he said. "And I accepted the money to buy you a wedding ring."

"Mr. Harvey, either give me back the money or run to buy us something good to drink," said the redhead. "Take your time. I need to talk to Ms. Eutim."

She did not know Jacob: at some point he would throw the money onto the table, totally outraged by her insolence. It turned out I did not know Jacob either. He produced no money as he looked at me. At long last the thin tall man said, "You didn't read to her the most interesting part of the boy's essay, Boya. I refuse to go buy anything to drink before you read the essay to the end."

I enjoyed the sun that was playing hide-and-seek with the leaves of the trees. The beauty's pinched face, especially her pursed lips were fun to watch. She was a woman I felt comfortable with; I could deal with any rebellious human being, a man, a woman, a baby, or an old grouch.

"I am listening," I said, looking the woman in the eyes. Her face looked narrower and I loved it: a face of a beautiful woman who was mad at me.

"You'd better start reading," Jacob said. He could be fun at times; I'd grant him that.

The sun, the fat yellow caterpillar in the sky, crawled on towards midday. It felt cozy and pleasantly warm. The belle's voice crawled too, using a reluctant reading technique typical of a pampered girlfriend. I did not have a soft spot for girlfriends, pampered or not.

The bird was my friend. It gave me a home, peace and quiet, but it had no life in it. It had no death in it either, the redheaded explosion read, chewing off sounds, biting into the words and spitting them out crushed into a monotonous croon. *My friend Ben had never been alive and that is why he turned into dust. He simply could not die and I could not bury him. He didn't have what we all have—one's death.*

I did not think that the essay was good. A bird had turned to dust. So what? I stood up. It was about time I left that pleasant café for, in my opinion, the beautiful woman had nothing important to enrich my mind with.

"Can't you see?" Jacob jumped enthusiastically from his chair. "It is very funny, isn't it … what we all have … what we are all entitled to is death!"

"Will you be quiet, Jacob, please?" the dazzling woman said as she reached out her hand, her fingers perching on Jacob's elbow. He instantly calmed down and I disliked that. After the redhead's dainty fingers flew away from his elbow, Jacob blurted out, "Can't you see? Just think—the Trun Chark song says: *Everybody has it, you have it too!* The boy writes in his essay that the bird, his friend, did not have the right we all have: to die! Death is simply a part of us."

"Shut up, Jacob," I said.

Boya Bagd, the famous researcher in love with metal birds as heavy as anchors, smiled at Jacob.

"Mr. Harvey, you are a remarkable thinker," she paused, her smile outshining the sun. "The hypothesis you formulated is truly amazing. All the time, we lug death around like a suitcase."

I laughed, "Can't we throw Death's suitcase in the mud and live forever?"

Even Jacob laughed, his thin face a ray of sun looking for me. After everybody calmed down, he said, "What if the Samodivas in our thoughts are paths leading to death? What if death is a Samodiva, just one of the many wraith-like green specks?"

The waiter brought us wine.

"I think your idea is brilliant," Boya Bagd said a smile flickering across her face. The woman's syrupy sweetness got on my nerves.

"Jacob, my dearest," I stood up and kissed his forehead. "I feel much safer if you are close to me. Could you please bring me my sunglasses from the car?"

"Death has an important role to play in all Samodiva-related issues," Jacob muttered as he started for the car. "Death and Deaf Crags … What if the black holes in the cliffs are doors to death? Or are they pitfall traps?"

It was so quiet one could hear the tablecloth rustle. Boya Bagd and I were alone at the table. The redheaded perfection looked up at me and said, "I can see green dots in your hair, Ms. Eutim."

I did not say anything.

"As chairperson of the Trun Shrine Association I am legally obliged to talk to all persons who have green dots in their hair. Ms. Eutim, I am sure you can see that I too have green dots."

"I cannot see anything in your hair, blue or green, Ms. Bagd," I said. "I am not interested in the Trun Shrine Association."

"I have checked our records," the glamour girl went on. "I checked every single entry very carefully. You are not one of us. But you can see the dots around my head."

The redhead's lips quivered, I liked that and peacefully kept mum.

"Who are you?" she asked. "And why are you so very interested in Wanga, the crazy soothsayer?"

The sun waltzed the breeze around on the walls of the building opposite the café. Shadows touched the street and the pavement seemed to dance.

"You have to find out who I am," I said. She fidgeted and perhaps was about to say something unpleasant. "You'd better find out who I am before it is too late," I added.

Chapter Twenty-Nine

Peter Stan did nothing the way he should have done. Put the house on fire, Margaret had told him. If anybody comes to my room, even if he is your best friend, put the house on fire. No one must see the pictures. No one! Who had drawn those pictures? Peter had asked. His wife had not answered his question. The Municipality Council had provided Margaret with this house, and the mayor gave her a scientific achievement certificate. When had Margaret discovered the pictures? Or had she drawn them herself? Why should Peter hide them from John Cole, the police chief? The teacher did not have time to look for a box of matches. Where was his lighter? Peter did not want to set the house on fire. He loved his home.

Even before he could say anything, John Cole was in the room staring at the pictures.

"Plastering the walls of your house, Stan, eh?" the police chief said. "Are you trying to hide something from me?"

"Yes," Peter said, his voice bubbling with worry. "Please wait. Let me take you to the kitchen, or to ..." It was too late. John Cole stood by the wall, staring. He studied the walls that Peter had scraped clean, touching the dented surface as he bent down to examine the pictures. Stan watched. He saw the police chief's expression change, his profile a slab of stone, his eyes sharp and shrewd.

"Who told you to scrape the pictures off the walls, Peter?" the chief of Dusk police asked. "Was it Margaret?"

John Cole's manner, cold and distant, frightened the teacher. What had happened to this man? What was Peter Stan supposed to do? Something had gone wrong. What was it? Set the room on fire, Margaret had said. Destroy it. Now John squinted at him as he pressed his hands against the walls Peter had scraped.

"When did Margaret tell you to destroy the images?" John Cole asked. "Tell me, Peter. It was Margaret and I that made the pictures on the wall, so you can be frank with me."

"You?" Peter muttered under his breath. This was impossible. Peter Stan had been living in this town, in the house, since the very first day the Municipality Council provided it for his wife.

"When did you and Margaret ... draw these pictures?" the teacher asked, his voice a river that had run dry. "I mean ... Margaret cannot paint. And I never go anywhere." Peter was so angry he was unable to stop babbling.

"The International Science Teachers Association awarded you the prestigious Einstein Prize in September half a year ago, Peter," the police chief said. "And you were invited to Austria, Vienna, to get it. How long did you stay in Vienna?"

Peter Stan tried to remember. "Twenty-one days," he said.

"Didn't it cross your mind that one doesn't stay twenty days after one gets his prize? The Nobel laureates stay in Stockholm five days."

"I did not deserve that prize. They gave it to me so I would be kicked out of my house," Peter had the feeling that the floor shook under his feet.

"I arranged everything, my friend," John Cole said. "I wanted you to go somewhere for a week or two. I needed time to work in this room. And, Peter, I am convinced you deserve the Einstein prize."

"You needed time to work in my house with Margaret, my wife?" Peter Stan muttered, a layer of fog thick before his eyes. Then why had Margaret said *Set the room on fire if somebody comes. If you cannot scrape the pictures off the walls, set the house on fire.* Was John Cole a friend? "You arranged for me to get it?"

The midday sun was weak and Peter Stan felt sick in its pale light.

"Yes," John Cole said.

Peter Stan had been so proud of that prize. He had worked hard, he loved his job; he thought the children he taught deserved his efforts, and his love. He had tried to make them believe in the power of thinking. When he held the miniature sculpture he thought that yes, his colleagues in the association were aware of what he had achieved: he had prepared young adults able to work with dignity. It turned out this was not true. John Cole had simply managed to get rid of his friend for a couple of weeks. Peter, you old fool!

"Why did Margaret order you to destroy the pictures?" John Cole asked.

"She didn't order me," the teacher said.

"Then why did you damage them?"

Peter Stan got angry.

"Margaret doesn't give me orders," he said. "She doesn't even know what I'm doing."

He saw something on Cole's face—a smirk, or was it only a tiny twitch?

"So, it is not Margaret?" John Cole breathed. "I don't believe it. It's not like her. She is very secretive, and that was the reason, my friend, why I couldn't live with her. She hasn't told you anything, Peter, because if she had …"

"I want her to be happy," the teacher said.

"A woman cannot be happy if she experiments on brain death," the chief of police said, his sharp eyes on Peter.

The teacher looked up.

"To be precise, your wife experiments with the exact date and time when a person dies. I was sure you didn't know, my friend. I am afraid you are in the dark, as always."

Peter kept silent. A gusty wind combed the leaves of the elms in the yard. This spring was too cold and too gloomy. Peter wished he had set fire to the house he loved so much.

"She told you nothing. If she had, you would have destroyed this picture first." He pointed to Margaret's picture; then his index finger touched the date 22.06.2035.

"The date that used to be under your wife's picture was 22.06.2020. Peter, try to remember what happened on 22 June 2020, a month or so ago. Think hard, my friend."

Peter Stan knew exactly what had happened. Margaret had a splitting headache. The memory of that rainy day still haunted Peter: Margaret's sallow face, the anguish. She lay in bed, whispering *The horror, the horror.* Margaret never complained, but on that day, 22 June 2020, she had told Peter Stan *Today I will die.*

"I don't remember what happened on that particular day," the teacher said.

"Oh, you *do*," the chief of Dusk police insisted. "She told me she had screamed with pain. You were by her side. She told you she was going to die. What she had not told you was that she knew the exact hour and minute when she was supposed to meet her maker. Has she mentioned 6:17 PM to you?"

Peter thought hard. The labyrinth of memories devoured him. He was groping blindly his way forward, struggled on and remembered.

"Wait until 6:17 PM, Peter," she had said. "Then we'll see."

"What will we see, Margaret?" Peter had asked.

"If I'll make it."

He had watched the clock, having no idea why 6:17 PM was so important. Nothing happened. Margaret slept, her breathing shallow and tormented. He had sat by her side.

"Your wife believes she can change the time when one is expected to die," the chief of Dusk police said. "As I told you, my friend, she is trying to find out how the mechanism of dying works and wants to control it."

Peter thought hard.

"Why didn't you stop her, John?" the teacher rolled his hand into a ball. "You gave me a prize instead, an award I do not deserve. Why are these pictures so important? How can a simple layer of paint play any significant role?"

John Cole smiled, and the teacher noticed a wicked gleam in the dark blue steel of his eyes. He had known John Cole for years. His steady glance meant trouble.

"You asked for it, Peter," the police chief said. "I'll give you the answer." John Cole leaned forward as he scrutinized the picture of the corpse on the wall. His fingers slalomed down the outspread hand and stopped on the ring—a gold ring resembling a small clam with a tiny ruby embedded in the soft glittering gold. "You bought Margaret the ring after she gave birth to your son. Is that true?"

"Did she speak about it to you?" Peter Stan mouthed.

"She tells me many things, my friend. Bring me a glass of water and I'll show you what this paint can do."

There was an abyss exuding black panic in John Cole's words, yet the teacher wanted to know. The police chief opened the fridge, took out a bottle of mineral water and filled one big glass. Then he studied the wall again, his attention focused on Margaret's picture.

"22 June 2035, no way!" John Cole muttered as he poured some droplets of water on the palm of his right hand, then pressed it against Margaret's face. Nothing happened, and Peter Stan breathed a sigh of relief. John Cole sighed too. He poured more water onto his hand and pressed it harder against Margaret's forehead painted on the wall.

Hissing, screeching noises like a million barking dogs hit the teacher. Neighing horses, agonizing babies, deep, gusty sighs of a dying fish enveloped Peter Stan, then shrieks, and a deafening TRUN! TRUN! burst in his head, crushed his brain, destroyed his thoughts, severed his nerves, and scorched his eyes. Blood poured from his nose. Trun! This word had tried to kill Margaret.

I have to live on. I have to survive the attack. I have to tell Margaret, he thought, then everything was black, the world was blood and thrashing pain.

John Cole bent down over the picture of the naked torso and smeared some water on the thin legs of the boy. Very quickly, the police chief raised his wet fingers and smeared water on the pinched face of a thin, blind woman.

"Come on, Wanga," he said slowly.

The hissing sounds were the same; the air in the room rang, shrilled, and creaked. The ceiling reeled, the floor kicked and spat. John Cole put his hand on the blind woman's pallid face and pushed the wall hard. TRUN! The blind eyes thundered and roared, the air growled, and the walls shook … Trun! Trun! Trun! A shadow of a smile touched Peter Stan's lips. Trun! The teacher sat up, the smile on his face big as a sunrise. Trun! Peter scrambled to his feet.

"Do you understand the role the paint on the wall in Margaret's room plays?" asked the police chief. "Your wife is a clever woman, no, she is a genius. She found out the murdering combination after we came back from Deaf Crags. Something happened to her. She did not want to see me anymore."

"After we came back from Deaf Crags …" Peter wheezed. "… she was sick. She thought she was going to die."

Peter Stan looked through the window. Dusk was falling, and the familiar silhouettes of the elm trees dissolved in the night. Peter did not know how long he had been out of this world. What had John Cole done while the teacher lay groaning on the floor?

"I saved your life one more time, my friend," John Cole said. "Now tell me why Margaret wanted you to destroy the pictures."

Peter Stan did not know. Margaret makes no mistakes, he thought. She was probably aware of something, a small detail the chief of Dusk police had overlooked, otherwise he wouldn't have demonstrated the power of that coat of Trun paint. Did John Cole say Margaret had discovered a mechanism by means of which she could control death? John Cole knew how to make the Trun paint kill a man; he knew how to ease the excruciating pain and drive it away, but he couldn't do something his wife Margaret could.

Was Margaret able to control *death?* Could she postpone it or summon it?

"You don't know," John Cole said." She's always kept you far from the important events and ideas in her life."

It was getting dark and the moon, inquisitive like a skylark, peeked behind a big gray cloud.

"I love her," Peter Stan said sadly. "I have been far from the important events in her life. I could not help her when she needed me most."

"Stop sniveling, old man," John Cole said. "Now I'll tell you something for the sake of our friendship. You don't know who used to live in this house before you and Margaret moved in, do you?"

"Why is that so interesting?" the teacher asked. He was tired, he had a bad headache, and was worried about Margaret.

John Cole scraped off the plaster under the windowsill, and beneath it, on the right-hand side, the teacher saw a small red square. On the left, a little blue square gleamed, just another daub of bright cheerful paint. The police chief pressed the red square. A ball of flames burst out of the wall. Peter Stan flinched, and immediately John Cole pressed the blue square.

"Do you remember the ice-cold stone in the tunnel to Trun Shrine?" John whispered, his breath on Peter's cheeks. "Think about the singeing stones on the floor of the room with the old earthenware pans and jugs."

Peter remembered: the huge heap of stones that had burned his fingers. Then the freezing cold touch of the tunnel was on his skin again.

"Sara Eutim, the writer, lived in this house, which Margaret wanted you to set on fire," John Cole said. "Sara Eutim installed the blue and red square mechanism. If you are as clever as I believe you are, you'll come to the conclusion that Sara Eutim, too, knew about Trun Shrine. Perhaps she had also tried to learn something about the process that keeps death under control."

A thought crossed Peter's mind.

"How come you know about all these things, John?" he asked.

"I have to know what potential troublemakers are up to, and Margaret is the toughest one among them. I've followed all conversations and jokes she and you have enjoyed in this room. I knew what you two did in your bedroom. I also knew everything about Sara Eutim's boyfriends. This house has been under observation since the first day the mayor awarded it to Ms. Eutim. And Sara Eutim was the first one who had written about the Samodivas."

"Then why don't you know anything about the mechanism controlling death, the one Margaret allegedly found out?" Peter Stan asked defiantly.

"There are ways to make her tell me," the chief of Dusk police said. A dark smile on his face.

"John, I hope that the pictures I've destroyed will damage the red and blue square device," the teacher felt he should have spoken nothing at all.

"I don't like this, my friend," the police chief declared. "I'll take you to a place that you'll recognize. I am afraid you'll have to listen to the Trun story again. By the way, the word *Samodiva* in Old Bulgarian means *one who determines by herself how long she will live.*"

John Cole poured a few droplets of water on his hand and again pressed it against Margaret's face painted on the wall.

"Her intelligent face can kill you," John Cole said.

Peter Stan was thirsty. "You mean ... that Margaret is a Samodiva?" the teacher breathed. "You're telling me she succeeded in postponing her own death?"

"Peter, you are a knowledgeable man," the chief of Dusk police said. "It's a pity you love Margaret so much. I'll have to do this," he added as his hand pressed Margaret's ring with the twinkling ruby. "By the way, my old friend, who is that little girl in the street, the fair-haired one?"

The teacher looked out the window and saw her: the same cute, lonely child.

John Cole's countenance hardened. His eyes glinted—dangerous, cold eyes.

"I can see she's arrogant," the chief of Dusk police muttered under his breath.

"Whom are you talking about?" the old teacher asked, but his friend did not answer.

The hissing sounds rent the air, the room shrieked, the window bawled, TRUN! TRUN! hit the books on the shelves, slapped the newspapers on the coffee table and shook the bowl of delicious apples on the writing desk. Peter Stan fell on the floor. His nose bled. Dizzy with pain, he thought he noticed something strange. First, John Cole studied Tony's portrait on the wall, then his eyes dwelt on the empty square with the big question mark in it, and finally his fingers touched his own picture—the black-and-white portrait of John Cole, the chief of Dusk police.

Chapter Thirty

One never knew with John Cole, at least I did not. He had asked me to try his red wine. We sat at the imposing mahogany table in his house, and as I waited for his miraculous glass of Chardonnay, he said, "I'll introduce you to a remarkable scientist."

Wasn't that a surprise! A host should not foist strangers upon his guests, remarkable scientists or not.

"I don't feel like meeting anybody important," I declared.

John Cole's sitting room, a place I knew too well, hadn't changed a bit. The easy chairs were enormous. He had made love to me in every single one of them. The windows were enormous too, the curtains were drawn—a fact that amazed me. John Cole loved the sun and enjoyed walking in the open. There were two coffee tables and not a single book in sight. The three bouquets of red and white artificial roses were still in their expensive vases in the corners where I had left them. John did not like vases or flowers. I distrusted men who kept artificial roses at home. Quite apart from the artificial flora, I couldn't but notice an interesting detail that made me very suspicious of the man: I could see green dots, a thick stream of them, above his forehead, in his coarse, auburn hair that some women might describe as sexy. I disliked the green dots.

"The conversation will be very interesting," he grinned, and I hated him. "She has a story to tell you ... about the Samodivas."

I want neither your honey nor your poison. I read this sentence in an article on the wicked avengers, the Samodivas. These words revealed what I felt for John Cole. No farmer wanted Samodiva's honey, the chicken-livered soul! The muttonhead gave up heaven because his teeth chattered with fear. I was not scared of poison; I believed each of us produced enough of it to destroy a continent.

"You'll be surprised to learn how much she knows. By the way, the great scientist thinks … well, she is quite sure that you, Sara, have generated Killing Trun."

"I did what?" I didn't burst into laughter, although the man's announcement was funny enough.

"The crowds that waited in the squares, the blaring loudspeakers, the crushing cacophony of scraping, shushing and squeaking shrieks. Young and old groaning with horror, sick children prostrate on the sidewalks. Trun mowing the town with the scythe of Death …" John Cole's voice trailed off. Then he looked at me. "Yes, this scientist believes that you have produced the sounds that kill."

"Let us assume the scientist is right," I reasoned. "Well, if I had a killing machine like this, would I live in this provincial town, trying to eke out a living? Death's owner wouldn't put up with it, John."

He looked at me, his eyes inquisitive and quite unpleasant.

"It is strange," the man said evenly. "She, too, used exactly the same phrase, *death's owner.*"

I was not interested in death. What worried me was the watchful expression on John's rugged face. It was evident he did not intend to let me enjoy his fabulous wine.

"Before she comes …"

"Is the mysterious scientist beautiful?" I said, amused.

He grinned and said casually, "I cannot see your green dots now. Isn't that amazing?"

I agreed it was. Then the athletic man said something that sounded inappropriate to me. "Sara, I was looking for your fiancé. Do you have any idea where he might be?"

"Why is my fiancé so important to you?"

"Perhaps you have already broken your engagement?"

I looked through the window. John Cole's backyard did not look attractive at all. The grass was messy and unkempt, thorns and spiky shrubs jutted out, and I could see thick nettles in the shadow of the wall, encircling the property. This man positively was not fond of flowerbeds. Police chief or not, I wouldn't let him invade my privacy.

"Your handsome fiancé knows something and was willing to hazard a guess, so you made up your mind to silence him," the police chief conjectured.

What was John driving at? Very interesting …

"Jacob Harvey is an adult, so I take no responsibility for his actions," I pointed out.

"You have learned to hide your green dots, Sara," John Cole returned to his much-loved topic. "Well, my dear, I had a little chat with Wanga the prophetess of Bare Mountain. She told me something about you."

Now oddball Wanga! I didn't appreciate John Cole's passion for beating about the bush. However, I was comfortable with men who beat about them. I smiled at John Cole, which seemed to spur him on to grin at me. His beaming face was an eyesore. Why did I dislike this man? The thought that we were a couple a year ago made me sick.

"Wanga the soothsayer told me she saw green dots in your magnificent hair, Sara. This happened when you visited her place. She told me she was frightened, no, she said she panicked after she talked to you."

"Didn't she tell you she saw something else?" I asked him. "The woman is blind. How could she see anything?"

The man's face swam in sugary syrup of condescension.

"She also said you planned to kill your brother, and if you did, the whole town would be destroyed."

"How dramatic! Please don't overlook a significant detail, John. I do not have a brother. Take my tip, treasure. You'd better not take seriously the pack of lies the woman tries to foist off on you."

"She's incapable of telling lies," the chief of Dusk police said. "She bleeds if she does."

"And I am the Queen of Spain," I said.

"I talked to Professor Gils and to young doctor Georg," John's statement left me unimpressed. "Professor Gils claimed he saw green dots around your head, Sara. I, too, can see people's tiny green flames. I saw them above Professor Gils' head and in the young doctor's hair. I am alarmed that today I cannot see any green dots in your hair, Sara."

Somebody knocked at the door, and a slim, or should I say, scrawny woman entered the room. She had perfect complexion, her unblinking dark eyes sparkled, and her clothes looked expensive.

"Professor Margaret Stan this is Sara Eutim, the famous writer and Samodiva researcher. Sara, I'm honored to introduce you to Professor Margaret Stan, the scientist who discovered the pictures on the walls of the living room in the house where you, dear Sara, used to live before Professor Stan moved in."

"How do you do, Professor Stan," I smiled at the woman as I saw something that surprised me—a streak of thick green dots enveloped her high forehead.

"I have read about your impressive achievements, Ms. Eutim," Margaret Stan, the scientist, said her eyes all over the place. I had the feeling she was reading my thoughts, but of course that was impossible. Then I thought of the green dot people I knew: 1. John Cole, the chief of Dusk police; 2. Professor Gils at Iztok Clinic; 3. the man with the scarred face; 4. young doctor Ivan Georg who had produced Healing Trun; and 5. Wanga, the crazy charlatan.

I had placed advertisements in a number of local newspapers, offering great opportunities for people with *green halos,* whatever this meant. No one turned up.

If my memory served me correctly, I remembered I had already seen Margaret Stan, the scientist. She visited me in my apartment with a purse and 1500 Euros in it, asking if by chance the thing was mine. I was positive that at the time I saw her she didn't have any tiny green flames. This could mean one thing: the woman had somehow *learned* how to acquire the dots.

"I have met Ms. Eutim, John," the scientist said. "I found some money in my house and I thought it belonged to the previous tenant. I asked who that tenant was and so I found Ms. Sara Eutim."

"But the money didn't belong to me," I said as I looked through the window.

"I checked at the Town Hall and Mr. John Cole helped me," the professor with the perfect complexion said her intelligent dark eyes quite impertinent. I lazily thought that the chief of Dusk police was never in love with me. He needed information and an engagement ring was the shortest path to it. So far, I had been astute enough not to trust my fiancés.

"I thought about you, too," I told the scientist. "I asked myself why you bothered to show up. You left no stone unturned to find me, and I could not believe your desire to help was genuine. This short episode sounded out of tune with the whole symphony. You simply checked on me."

The sun pierced the clouds and the patch of luxuriant thistles in John Cole's backyard smiled at me. The old trees were awake, strong and green, and the broken bench was a thing I disliked. John Cole had kissed me as we sat together in the warm July dusk. John Cole had green dots, and John Cole had asked me to become his wife; he was in need of information that I could provide. I had provided him with a gorgeous love life instead.

"It turned out you were the first and only tenant of the house, Ms. Eutim," the intelligent professor said, her dark eyes watchful.

"I investigated into the team that had built your house, Sara," John Cole chimed in. "The chief architect met his death even before the house was ready. The head of the construction team died shortly after him; the workers all died in a road accident not far from the house. It seemed death stalked behind every corner of your mansion."

Unfortunately, the sun quickly sank into the clouds, and John Cole's backyard was a maze of shadows wallowing in the pearly mist. I was sure the bench had forgotten me.

"I found nothing wrong with the house," I said. "I even wanted to purchase the place as you very well remember, John. You explained to me it was public property and there were serious legal issues related to the process of acquisition. You gave the house to Professor Margaret Stan, and after she moved in, the legal problems vanished into thin air. Professor Margaret Stan bought the place. All this looked downright decent and transparent."

"You also wanted to buy the dilapidated building in Dusk and the grounds where the archaeological excavation took place, Sara," John Cole took the floor again.

"And of course, I was confronted by problems which I couldn't cure," I said. "The excavation was suspended, and the property was sold to somebody else, to Professor Margaret Stan of all great scientists."

"You seem to know much about Professor Margaret Stan," John Cole remarked.

I did not think it was my duty to concentrate on this topic, so I simply enjoyed the quiet atmosphere in the room. Soft drizzle flirted with the rough grass in the backyard, and I loved the light unobtrusive fingers of the dusk on the windowpane.

"Professor Stan had pounding headaches in your house," John Cole said, tilting his handsome face up to me. His rugged features failed to fascinate me, and his words didn't charm the pants off me. "Professor Stan suspected something in the house was out of order and she was right, of course. The Professor discovered the pictures."

Perhaps I should have exclaimed, "What are you talking about?" but I did not.

The chief of Dusk police went on, "Professor Margaret Stan found her photograph on the wall and tried to wash it away. She wet the photograph, and it started hissing and gurgling. The Professor instantly developed a severe headache."

I kept silent.

"The headache returned every day," Professor Margaret Stan said. "It found me everywhere I went. When the archaeological excavation in Dusk began, and Doctor Ivan Georg somehow produced Healing Trun, the headache was gone. It came back only when I wet the pictures on the walls in the living room."

I liked Professor Margaret Stan's high forehead. What I disliked were the green dots surrounding it. They all glowed like nothing I had seen so far. How had the professor acquired her green halo? That was a challenging question.

"I am really sorry about your headache problem, Professor Stan, but I am not the person who can solve it," I said. "The house was given to you by the Town Council, and its most influential member is Mr. John Cole, the chief of Dusk police. I see a possibility here: maybe the police chief painted the pictures on the wall for you, Professor."

"All information I have collected so far leads me to the conclusion that you are involved in the generation of the so-called Killing Trun that causes violent headaches, paralysis and death."

My ex-fiancé's words amused me.

"In other words, you think I generate death," I said at last.

"Or you can somehow control death," Professor Stan said.

"Or I am Death," I said, and my interlocutors exchanged glances. "It's a possibility, and you should think twice before asking me hard questions. This is equivalent to digging your own graves."

The professor's green dots glowed like a dead fish's bones.

"You are the only survivor of the members of the construction team that built your house, Ms. Eutim," Professor Stan pointed out.

"You survived the house as well, Professor Stan," I said. "Maybe you painted the pictures on the wall. I am impressed with the way you discovered how to initiate Killing Trun. Who can prove you really suffered from headaches? It is your word and you have no other proof."

John Cole's eyes dwelt on my face. Then he studied Professor Stan's expression. I studied it too: a smile that made me freeze in my tracks. Well, I tended to exaggerate my fears. Actually, I feared no one.

"There is a way I can find out who's who," the chief of Dusk police said. "It is wonderful both of you are with me in this room, ladies." He grinned. It was a habit of his I loathed.

"By the way, Professor Stan," the chief of Dusk police said casually—another habit of his I loathed. "Professor Stan, can you see green dots around my head?"

I noticed again that thin, twitchy-lipped smile on the woman's face. She kept silent.

"Do you, or don't you?" the chief of Dusk police insisted.

"I do not," Professor Stan said calmly, and I admired her cold blood. I had reason to believe the renowned scientist lied to the police chief. She did it with style.

"I can see green dots in your hair, Professor Stan," John Cole declared. "You didn't have them the last time I saw you. I'd appreciate it if you tell me how you acquired them."

The woman was quite attractive.

"I don't know what you are talking about," the professor said.

"There is a way to find out," John Cole said as he gave me a friendly wink. Friendly, my foot!

At that moment, *TRUN! TRUN!* exploded in the room, the air

rippled and swelled, deafening sounds punched the walls, the ceiling screamed *TRU-U-N!* The floor jumped and screeched. Chaos of biting sounds split my ears. *TRUN!* Professor Stan waited unperturbed, at peace with the ugly dissonance and the horrendous noise that rent the house asunder. The police chief stood, a granite statue amid a raging storm. I wailed and I tossed, I turned and writhed; finally, I fell onto the shabby carpet that covered the marble floor. It was evident neither John Cole nor the housekeeper had bothered to sweep it properly. I hated littered floors, but the specks of dust on the carpet helped me put on a good show. I was the star and I played my part in a superb manner. I hit my nose with my thumb and it bled.

Then the hissing Trun madness stopped. Silence reigned, and I wished I had thrown up on the shabby carpet. It was the same as I remembered it since the time John Cole and I made love on it.

"Stop it!" the chief of Dusk police thundered. "That's enough, Sara!"

I pressed my fists against my forehead. I hoped against hope my face was pale enough.

"It was Healing Trun you listened to, Sara."

At that moment, a plump middle-aged woman entered the room. I knew who she was: the housekeeper.

"This Trun thing made me feel strong, sir," the woman said.

Professor Margaret Stan and the police chief stared at me as I tossed and turned on the tattered carpet I remembered so well.

"Sara, where is your fiancé?" John Cole barked. "Jacob Harvey said something you did not like and he vanished into thin air. You were afraid of him."

"John, if I can control death as Professor Stan suggests, it would be easy for me to bump off my new fiancé," I said, as tranquil as a sunrise in May. "It was a pleasure speaking to you, Professor Stan. Do not forget you met me, i.e., your death. Miraculously, you are still alive and kicking. Next time the outcome might be different." I opened the door and went out.

I met a small fair-haired girl not far from the front door of Mr. John Cole's house. The child smiled sweetly at me.

Chapter Thirty-One

A black cloud covered John Cole's house. An impenetrable shadow swooped down, crushing tress and benches in the backyard. A flock of enormous blackbirds, their noiseless wings fluttering, took the sky by storm. The birds perched on the roof. Some of the tiles screeched. The roof beams bent and broke. The ceiling clanged as it caved in.

"The blackbirds!" John Cole's housekeeper exclaimed. "They've come at last, sir. Now my back will hurt no more!"

John Cole smiled as he stared at the black feathers that filled the space behind the window. The thick shadow crept towards him, flooded the whole room, devouring the tiny patches of light that still fought the darkness of the quiet wings.

"It hurts!" the housekeeper screamed, doubled over, writhing, her face sallow and sick.

Professor Margaret Stan thought a razor had split her head and carved a blazing chasm of pain in her brain. She fell onto the floor, pressing her fists against her head. This is the end, she thought.

John Cole's body shook, his spinal column disintegrated as blind, hungry, icy pain took hold of his entire chest. My lungs, he thought. My lungs will burst. This is the end.

Suddenly the shadow disappeared, the air rang, the ceiling rattled and the old crystal chandelier came crashing to the floor. Thump! The noiseless flock dissolved into the dark sky, the wings evaporated in the thin air, the slashing Trun turmoil faded away as the three squirming bodies on the floor twisted and turned no more. Shards of crystal glittered in the pools of light, the lamps shone brightly, the TV screen lit up as the small radio on the table clicked and screeched, advertising a new miraculous brand of soap.

A black minivan pulled up by the front door of John Cole's house. A young red-haired woman got out of it, a man followed her, his lips tightly drawn. They did not talk. The man stood by the window and peeked into the room. The redhead dashed forward, crossed the yard, and sank into the house. A panel of the fence slid sideways. The man returned to the minivan, started the engine, steered the car towards the backyard and stopped by the back door. He got out and quickly entered the house. A couple of seconds later, he came out bent under the weight of a limp body. Professor Stan was too heavy for him. The woman with the stunning red hair sprinted to him, clutched at Professor Stan's legs, then they thrust the body into the van.

"Is she dead?" the man whispered.

"If she's dead you'll die too," the woman snapped.

She ran into the house again. The man followed her. A minute later, they shoved John Cole's body into the van. Suddenly, the chief of Dusk police sat up, reached out his hand and his fingers squeezed the woman's throat.

"Why, Boya?" the police chief wheezed.

The woman's fist plummeted, crashing against John Cole's forehead. The chief of Dusk police flinched as a rivulet of blood oozed from the corner of his mouth. The woman's fist plunged down, crashing into Professor Stan's forehead.

"You shouldn't do that," the man muttered. The woman didn't bother to look at him.

She returned to the room. John Cole's housekeeper lay prostrate on the floor, moaning. The redhead bent down and delivered a sharp blow to her mouth. Then Boya calmly walked out of the room, smoothing her magnificent hair as she passed by the mirror in the hall.

"You took too long," the man complained after she got into the car. "They'll catch us."

She smoothed her hair again and applied lipstick on her full, soft lips.

"Boya!" the man grunted.

"If the birds don't kill you, I will, Philip. I'll do it right away if you don't shut up," the woman said, a dangerous sparkle digging a trench in her beautiful eyes.

Chapter Thirty-Two

Bare Mountain glistened in the sun, a huge mass of stone eaten by winds and storms, scorched by the sun, gnawed and beaten by torrential rains. Its harsh beauty gave me a whisper of happiness. I admired the threatening splendor of the crags, towering over the winding road that suddenly ended in front of a heap of stones, sharp-edged and dark. I knew they were stories of hatred, so thick and tangible I could feel their suffocating weight on my shoulders. Then I saw the heaps of earthenware pots and pans, bigger than I remembered them. I thought of the dangerous diseases, of the blind soothsayer, her white robe a pool of light in the center of the awe-struck women, men, and children. I saw the trembling figures of the sick, their arms outstretched, their eyes glued to Wanga's pale face. I disliked the thought of having to talk to her; but more than her dead eyes, I hated her dogs. Why didn't they bark? The mutts whined and I could feel the stones and the clouds wanted me to die. Wanga's beasts could have felt something dangerous approaching.

"You again!" the impenetrable darkness said. Of course it was Philip Mill.

"Yes," I said.

His hair had turned gray at the temples, he looked much older, but so attractive that my heart sank. He was the only man I cared about.

"She cannot talk to you," Philip declared.

"She'll have to," I said as I tried to pass by him.

He grabbed my shoulders and shook me. It was not necessary to speak; a revolver is more convincing than any argument I could think of. I had a good gun and was ready to use it.

"I'll shoot you in the knee," I told him in a matter-of-fact tone. "Say another word, and I'll shoot the mongrels."

Handsome Philip took a step back. It was evident he was not a courageous guy. He wanted his knees safe and his two pooches alive and howling.

Then I saw her: she stood at the door, the candlelight slaloming down her exquisite shoulders, her long blond hair a dazzling halo. The halo of her green dots looked so magnificent that for a moment I hated myself for being here, at the back of beyond, in the nest of the menacing cliffs, staring at Wanga and not admiring her. I remembered the haggard faces of the sick turning to see her. I hated myself even more.

"This time they've gone," she said, her blind eyes empty. "I cannot see them."

I thought I could feel the waves of panic washing over her.

"What is it, Wanga?" Philip Mill ran to his fiancée. At that moment, I envied her. He had never talked to me like that when we were a couple. "What can't you see, Wanga, dear? Tell me!"

The moments of blessed silence when the wind was dead were so rare in Bare Mountain that I treasured them beyond compare. The cliffs seemed to murmur, the first drops of rain hit the heaps of malicious stones and earthenware jugs. The whole mountain held its breath.

"Now I can see them!" She whispered the horror in her voice so tangible I could feel its throbs. "I can see the green dots. They are everywhere. They are devouring her!"

"Wanga! Dearest!" Philip Mill pleaded as he rubbed her thin, long fingers. The candlelight touched her face, and I was suddenly anxious for her as she shivered in the cold.

Wanga let go of his hand and took a step to me. "You can hide them!" her whisper flickered like a minuscule flame in the air. "They are everywhere. Millions of them! Who are you?"

"Are you speaking about the green dots, dearest?" Philip Mill said, his frightened eyes on my face. Wanga kept mum. "Sara, why have you come?" He stared defiantly at me. "Go away. Don't torture her!"

Wanga stretched out her hands, groping for things only her blind eyes could see. Finally, she caught hold of my hand.

"I want to tell you something, but I'm scared. I am sure I am right. You can hide your green dots and you can make them appear again. I think I know who you are. Why don't you take me with you?" her voice was calm as she bent down and grabbed one of the jugs. "Will my disease be like this one?" she whispered. Her words dissolved in the motionless dusk, and her eyes were smiling when she breathed, "I've been waiting for you so long."

The moon hid behind the clouds as I stepped inside the charlatan's cabin.

"There is no running away from you," Wanga said.

Philip watched.

"Who is she, Wanga?"

The blind woman didn't say anything.

Her shack was nothing special, a wide room, low ceiling, a narrow window and two small beds: a detail I preferred to interpret as a good sign. At least they didn't spend the night in one bed.

"You are ... empty ... empty like the end," the woman said slowly. "Only emptiness can make the green dots disappear."

"No, Wanga, I've known her for years," Philip Mill, the brilliant journalist, said.

Wanga didn't pay attention to his babbling. Well, I had a task to fulfill here.

"I'd like to ask you something about my fiancé Jacob Harvey, Wanga," I said. "Can you read his future for me?"

"I'll tell emptiness nothing," the charlatan's lips formed an obstinate line. "You are not interested in Jacob Harvey," she paused, her voice unafraid. "You want to know everything about a woman who has learned to capture green dots. Now she can control the dots. You are afraid of her."

The blind woman's thin fingers looked for support in the air.

"You showed poor judgment, Wanga. I'm not empty and I am afraid of no one."

"I cannot lie," she whispered. "I'll bleed to death if I do."

"Then you are a New One?" Philip Mill asked, stunned.

Philip speaks about the New Ones? Give me a break! How come he knows? I thought hard. Who told him a woman incapable of lying was a New One? Let me see.

To my surprise, I saw earthenware jugs and stones in the two corners of the shack. Another surprise: a little crudely carved statue of a thorn, its spiked point glittering and sharp, stood next to the door. I remembered that the Old Bulgarian word for thorn was *trun*, the word that could heal you. Heal you, my foot!

"Has the other woman discovered a way to control *emptiness?*" I asked.

"No!" Wanga answered. Her nose started bleeding profusely.

"You're lying," I said.

Her blood ran down her cheeks, dripping onto her white dress. So far, I had not noticed her dress was so immaculately white.

"I'm not lying," she gasped as she tilted her head back. "I don't know.

"Then you are an incredibly precious tool!" I cried out. "I ask a question. You must answer it no matter if you know the correct answer or not. If you start bleeding, I'll know you've given me a false response or you simply don't know."

"Go away!" Philip Mill barked as he pushed me towards the door. His long, beautiful forefinger pressed a small black button in the wall.

TRUN! TRUN! filled the air, spurting out from tiny cracks in the wall.

"I am sorry I told you that you are a precious tool, Wanga," I said. "The truth is you are a very primitive one."

Trun whispered the cracks in the walls, and her nose stopped bleeding.

She turned to me. Her face so pale it frightened me.

"They are everywhere, your green dots," she whispered. "Hers are also everywhere. She is a talented one, and this makes it very difficult for her. You can crush her like a nut."

I saw a blackbird on the small bedside table. Was it one of the clumsy creatures that had dug a hole in the town square?

"If you prevail over life," she whispered, her eyes boring into mine, "the birds of prey birds will exterminate men."

My ex-fiancé, the attractive Philip Mill, spoke as he got hold of my wrist. "A minute ago, Wanga said you were empty like the end … and her nose didn't bleed. The end of what? Or are you Death?"

I did not feel like talking to him. He had walked away on me and chosen this skeleton, the blind eyes, the sinister heaps of pots and stones.

"How did the other woman obtain her green dots?" I asked. "You said she didn't have them."

The charlatan's ashen face did not change; not a shadow of fright or hesitation disturbed her features.

"You can ask that woman yourself," she said.

"I don't feel like chatting with Professor Margaret Stan," I said.

Then Wanga touched my shoulders. Her fingers were as light as gossamer, her hands were white wet mist that sent rivulets of cold sweat on my skin. "I want to tell you something. I want to tell your green dots something very important," she gasped. Her voice hardened as her gossamer fingers traced the outlines of my face, flitting from my forehead to my chin, her fingertips warm like flames of a burning candle. "Don't kill your brother. He is grass and birds. Kill him, and you will be no more. Children will be no more. He is life …" she struggled to stand up, her breath a path to a place you wouldn't like to visit. Quickly, like a thief, Philip Mill kissed her hand, then mumbled, "Let me help you, Wanga. Dearest!"

I could learn nothing more here, so I turned my back on the enamored couple and made for the door of the hut. A hand gripped my shoulder.

"Who sends you here?" the ex-journalist asked.

I felt like snickering in his face. The man was beside himself, so he failed to cheer up his dearest Wanga. I did snicker at him.

"A minute ago, you reached the conclusion that I was the incarnation of Death, Philip. Do you think somebody can order Death about? I'm sorry for your pretty little soothsayer."

"I'll crush you like a nut!" he thundered.

"Try me, Phil" I said smiling. "You'd better tell me who informed you about the New Ones. It was not Wanga. You seem to know too much, honey. Sweet, knowledgeable boys like you don't get lucky at the end of the day."

He looked me in the eye as he snarled, "The person who told me about the New Ones can play your little green dots game. I don't care about you."

"I'm glad to hear that," I said, patting his cheek. "You are the only one who does not care about Death."

I let him freeze in his tracks as I concentrated my attention on the wonderful crags. Most of them looked like warships, sailing stormy waters. I was the fierce storm. My fast, second-hand car waited for me on the narrow winding road. For a while, I watched my attractive ex-fiancé sinking into the darkness.

Chapter Thirty-Three

As the night wore on, it grew colder and the cliffs of Bare Mountain rendered invisible by the dusk towered above the dirt road, the gorge wrapped up in the endless blanket of the sky. A minivan drove around the large heap of stones. After a while, the all-terrain vehicle pulled up behind the hut, and a slim woman jumped out of it. Her long, red hair gleamed in the moonlight, her lithe body swathed in darkness as she entered the rickety building. Silence fell over the heaps of earthenware jugs, a thick, black cloud descended over the hut, brushing its tiled roof.

The redhead emerged from the door, dragging behind her a tall, thin woman dressed in a white robe

"He jilted you, Wanga," the red-haired woman said. "Now you are a dry leaf in the wind. He's run away and he's a coward."

The woman in the white dress didn't say anything.

"Tell me my future," the redhead said.

The black cloud swooped down and perched on the roof of the hut. The tumbledown construction shook and creaked, the walls gave in, the beams broke and bricks crashed against the barren stones of the mountaintop. A few blackbirds shot away from the cloud and vanished in the night.

"I can see the green dots around your head," Wanga said at last. "I can see them even when you will be no more."

"You cannot lie," the redhead said slowly as she pushed the blind woman towards the minivan. "How come you can see my green dots after I'll *be no more?* Does that mean that I'll die and somebody else will inherit them?"

"Your green dots will run away from you."

The night was quiet and Wanga's words sounded like gunshots. They stung the red-haired beauty and she recoiled.

"You said … *and you will be no more*. What does that mean?" the young woman persisted. The black cloud throbbed, wobbled, pulsated, quiet like dust, noiseless, its shape constantly breaking, transforming the darkness into a ball of stalking shadows.

"You should know what it means when the green dots abandon you," the prophetess whispered. "Philip Mill must have told you."

"You tell me!" the woman said. "Now!"

The black cloud perched on the rock by the ruins of the hut. It had a thousand noiselessly stretching wings, it had beaks and tails, and the moment the black claws touched the earth, the stone split, gave in and the birds carved a deep round pit in the rough surface.

"Death! Green dots are death," the prophetess breathed. "You will lose yours. Why did you bring the birds here?"

"Maybe I've learned to control the green dots. Maybe I can make them disappear like that Stan woman."

"Who told you about her?" Wanga asked, her blind eyes glued to the black throbbing cloud. "Why did you set the killers free?" She paused, breathed shallowly then said, "Does Philip Mill know about the woman who can control the green dots?"

"He knows everything. He pretended he loved you. Philip's very good at winkling out secrets, Wanga."

"Poor Samodivas! Poor green, green Samodivas!" the blind woman whispered.

TRUN! TRUN! filled the air, the mountain lurched, rocked, rumbled, the crags quaked and squalled, the dark heaps of stones and pans rang. TRUN! Wanga collapsed, tried to stand up and failed.

"Deaf Crags! Death lurks behind the heap of stones," she whispered. "Samodivas are waiting!!"

She lay on the cold stones, her face falling apart, her fingers twitching, thin and colorless. The young woman collapsed by her side, blood pouring from her nose. TRUN! … TRUN! … the mountain growled, the cloud of blackbirds soaring away, as dark and quiet as a murky apparition, sucking hope and courage dry. *Trunnn …* the night murmured and finally silence reigned on the top of Bare Mountain.

The minivan, a weird beast of prey, skulked in the shadows, prowling, treacherous and savage.

A tall, strong man emerged from the darkness: Philip Mill.

He carefully lifted the blind woman, touched her cheeks with his fingertips, and kissed her. He carried her to the minivan and carefully let her lie on the gurney inside. Then he returned, shouldered the redhead, and started for the minivan.

"Pain is an unpleasant experience," he said under his breath. "I hope it hurts a lot!"

The clouds captured the sky. The moon, a pool of yellow fear, gleamed for a second and was gone.

"I heard what you said. You'll pay for it," the redhead suddenly hissed then the immense weight of the sky killed all sounds.

The minivan soon disappeared, climbing down the narrow dirt road. The tall, attractive man was behind the steering wheel.

Chapter Thirty-Four

"Professor Gils, thank you for coming to have a chat with me," I said.

The man wore an expensive gray suit, no tie, expensive shoes, and his vintage Rolex Submariner was of the highest quality. As a rule, I didn't like guys who wore vintage Rolex Submariner watches. I knew three or four guys who did, all of them sour and suffering from an inferiority complex. That was the reason I mistrusted the eminent professor. As a rule, men like him tried hard to compensate for their lack of confidence by being at the very top of their profession. I disliked them. They all were boring. Another important detail: I disapproved of scientists in gray suits. Professor Gils' face was quite colorless, and his brilliant blue eyes were interested in me. We were chatting in Primrose Café, drinking hot chocolate.

"I still remember the fairy tales about the Happy Prince you told me two hundred years ago," he said.

I remembered the story I had invented during the endless hours as I waited for my mother. She never came home on time. It was an absurd tale, and now it still sent rivulets of loneliness in my veins. My mother used to tell me, *I leave you with the Happy Prince. He'll be here for you, and if you are angry, or hungry, or afraid of something, just call out, Happy Prince, please come keep me company. He'll arrive in a minute.* Very often, I called out Happy Prince, Happy Prince! He never came, but I invented him and I thought the dust in the corner was my Happy Prince.

"Where have all your green dots gone?" Professor Gils asked, openly staring at me. He looked surprised or perhaps a little frightened. Why should he be? A lifetime ago, he was the boy I told fairy tales, making up stories and improbable, happy endings to cheer him up. How could I tell him my happy prince was a dark corner that could not speak?

"You look beautiful without your green dots," he said, but I could feel there was something else he longed to tell me.

"What is it?" I asked. "Perhaps you need to know more about me."

He smiled, his eyes misty blue behind his first-quality glasses.

"I've read your article on the Dirty Days or Pagan Days," the professor said. "You argue that these are the days when evil spirits break loose from our minds, and no one can find them. Legend has it that they rally in their Trun dwellings where they devise fiendish plans of revenge. You believe the Samodivas are evil spirits that can vanish only during the Dirty Days."

I was right to suspect that the man in the gray suit was no good. Professor Gils gradually twisted his smile into a wry grimace.

"Your article says the Dirty Days start on 15 December and end on 6 January," he went on. "Today is Sunday, 5 January," his eyes settled on my face, blue and uncomfortably clear. "The Samodivas vanish into thin air during the Dirty Days. Now I can see your green dots have disappeared, Ms. Eutim."

I beamed at him. "Perhaps your eyes are not as good as they used to be," I said, a good-natured expression on my face, or at least I hoped so.

He stared, amazed.

"Now I can see them," the professor heaved a sigh. He reached out his hand and his pale long fingers brushed my cheek. His skin was as cold as frozen chicken legs. "They've come back, your green dots. So, he's right!"

Snowflakes whirled in the air, giving it a white, pleasing weight.

"Who is right?" I wanted to know.

"John Cole, the chief of Dusk police," the professor said. "Mr. Cole tells me you are a very special person because you can control the green dots. You can make them disappear and come back as you wish." He paused, his eyes again good and warm. "I knew you were a very special girl long time ago. You shared my loneliness, but my mother was afraid of you. People who lived near our house scared her. Some hi-tech device or perhaps radioactive waste was buried in the ground near the warehouses, she said. The children born in the neighborhood died very young. Those who survived were … peculiar. They talked to people that were not there—like you did. The kids in the neighborhood had green dots in their hair."

"You have green dots, too," I said.

"Unlike you, I cannot make them vanish," he pointed out. "You were my friend from time immemorial," Gils went on. "Teach me to control my green dots, and I will let you know something you'd be truly interested in."

I could have asked him what this thing was, I might have pleaded with him to tell me, but I hated asking men in gray suits to do things for me. They might draw a wrong conclusion I was itching to extract precious information from their clenched teeth. Therefore, I had no questions for the luminary in the field of medical science and silently enjoyed the pirouettes the snowflakes turned in the air. This year, the Dirty Days were gloomy and distastefully cold. It rained a lot or it snowed and rained again. When I was a little girl, I thought the days were dirty because I stepped on dirty snow and my shoes looked never clean enough. I believed I was the guilty party; I had soiled the best days of the year.

"Sara, I hoped you wanted to talk to me," the man said. "Honestly, I could not flatter myself that you felt like spending the entire afternoon just shooting the breeze with an old friend. John Cole informed me you were impressed by Professor Margaret Stan's green dots. We both know she didn't have any of these and found a way to obtain them."

Professor Gils was a clever man. This was exactly the reason why I wanted to talk to him, but if you revealed the goal you wanted to attain to a man in an expensive suit, you wouldn't live long enough to reach it.

"I wouldn't say this topic is interesting enough," I said. "I wanted to ask you something else. How did your colleague, Doctor Georg, produce Healing Trun? This is my first question, and question number two is how come your wonderful friend, the chief of Dusk police, produced Killing Trun which nearly murdered young and old?"

I expected no answer. All I wanted was to divert Gils' attention from the topic that was of real interest to me: that obstinate Professor Stan, and the way she got her green dots. If she had learned how to obtain them, she would soon learn how to make use of their energy: to murder or heal, I was sure of that. *The path between murder and healing is but a step long.* That was what my fiancé Jacob quoted as he translated the song of the Trun Chark. On the other hand, I had read a religious hymn titled "God Can Find a Cure for Any Disease."

"The key to the mystery is very simple," clear-eyed Gils said. "Professor Stan listened to Killing Trun and Healing Trun that sounded simultaneously. I mean both Healing Trun and its murderous twin were on at the same time. After the noise died, she got the green dots, and stunned us all." Professor Gils spoke confidently, his sonorous voice reverberating in the cozy quiet cafe. "If the green dots are Samodivas as you suggest in your article, we can control them with the two types of Trun-barking symphonies, don't you think?"

I was the overall winner, in other words, I had accomplished my objective. I knew how the shrewd professor had laid her hands on the green dots. It was unnecessary to waste more time in this eatery, chatting to a bespectacled doctor utterly unable to negotiate with me. Was he lying? Probably. I was sorry for him. I saw the thin pale boy of my memories who listened to my fairy tales about the Happy Prince. This boy used to be the only friend I had. I truly believed that his pale face at the window in the building opposite ours was that of the happy prince I had wanted to meet all my life.

"And what will you tell me about *Samodiva's milk?*" he said just when I was about to stand up and go.

"Samodiva's milk?" I muttered. I hadn't told anybody about the Samodiva's milk. "I don't know what you are talking about."

"Your fiancé Jacob does," Gils said. "He has just published an article, 'Samodiva's Milk,' dedicated to you. It tells a story about a small lake and only a very special Samodiva can make this lake churn." He paused, his eyes smiling at me. "There is one more thing. It appears that your fiancé took a sample of the liquid he'd dubbed the Samodiva's milk, then submitted it to Professor Margaret Stan. Jacob Harvey adds he discovered an interesting aspect to the stones he took from both Trun Shrine and the Samodiva's milk area. When Mr. Harvey heated the Samodiva's milk, the stones he had put on the table in his living room became scorching hot."

Jacob published an article and took a sample of the Trun Chark liquid. Give me a break! Jacob had been pouring honey in my ear and made a pledge he would be true *till death did us part.* Meanwhile, he wrote controversial articles on the Samodiva's milk behind my back. Perhaps he published other pieces of writing in *The Legal History Series of Myths and Old Bulgarian Folklore.*

"By the way, where is your talented fiancé, Jacob Harvey?" Professor Gils asked. "The chief of Dusk police was worried about him. Mr. Harvey didn't answer his phone. *She can control both her green dots and her men,* John Cole says about you. His words saddened me. I was late for the most important meeting in my life. Jacob met you before I did."

At that point, I thought I liked this man in spite of his gray suite and the thick streak of green dots above his forehead.

"Jacob must have said something that made the chief of Dusk police highly distrustful of you, Sara," Professor Gils said. "John Cole thinks Jacob has mentioned something you wanted to keep on the hush-hush. What was it, Sara?"

Gils' face loved me, or more precisely, the man doted on the memory of me. He had not forgotten my fairy tales. Perhaps they had stayed in his life as a lonely sparkling light the way they had stayed with me. The Dirty Days! Snowflakes whirled behind the windowpane and I thought of Jacob who had vanished without a trace. It was true he had not answered his phone. Was I worried? No. I knew where Jacob was, at my holiday villa in Dusk Gorge, the wildest place in Bulgaria.

"I am sure I know who informed the chief of Dusk police about Jacob's activities, Professor Gils," I said as I remembered our pleasant chat—Jacob, the self-confident redhead (was her name Boya?) and I.

"John Cole thinks you might have ... eliminated Jacob Harvey," the professor said.

I liked the pirouettes of the snowflakes and admired the evil winds of the Dirty Days. Throughout this period of time, the Samodivas were on the prowl at night and hid in the gorge in the morning. At least that was what I had read in *Old Bulgarian Myths and Legends.* The ethereal ladies drank Samodiva's milk, and no man alive could resist them.

"Mr. Cole has the right to think whatever he pleases," I said.

"What did Jacob say that kept John Cole on the edge of his seat?"

"I don't know," I said.

"I suppose you don't know who sent me an email dedicated to the different stages in the progress of the *experiment:* the Ordinary Ones, the Talented Ones, the Marked Ones, etc.? And those stunning lines on talent …"

"Talent is the ability to do things that no one has taught us to do?" I said looking into his eyes that loved me behind his glasses. "Yes, Andrew, I sent this email to you. I wanted to protect you." I saw Professor Gils give a start, his pale face turning to paper. I loved his face. I always had. "You were the only friend I had, Andrew."

"Did you send Doctor Ivan Georg an email informing him he would be the first to get killed?"

"I did," I said and I was very sorry I had to torture this good honest man, Andrew Gils.

"But why?" he whispered. "Is it because he inadvertently discovered an important code?"

It was evident Professor Gils had not forgotten the most important part, the core of the message.

"Who are you, Sara?" the man whispered, his fingers touching mine.

I did not answer. He said he had read all my books, so he should know. The Dirty Days, the vile Pagan Days, squeezed an icy knot around the town. I was not scared of icy knots. I was afraid to lose this man. I wanted to have a friend, not a fiancé, not a lover, not an admirer. I wanted somebody I could tell fairy tales to.

"I still love you, Sara."

"This is a wrong thing to say it," I whispered.

Then suddenly his voice grew weaker as he said, "What do you hope to achieve by controlling the green dots?"

That was a very wrong thing to ask. He ruined the magic I had believed in. I had no friend. I would never have a friend, and the fairy tales I'd think up at sunset would go to no one.

"Teach me how to control the green dots," he whispered his voice so thin it dissolved in the quiet twilight of the warm café. I could hardly hear what else he said.

"Eliminate someone and you'll learn everything you want to know," I said as I left a 50-euro note on the table. At that moment, I felt empty like a river that had run dry.

"I don't want to *eliminate* anyone," Professor Gils said. "By the way, Sara, the article Jacob wrote … It seems very peculiar that the translation of an Old Bulgarian song about Trun Chark he provided was different from …"

I stood still itching to know what he'd say next. The professor was looking at me, a smile as big as the winter sky on his lips.

"You were telling me something about the differences between two translations of an Old Bulgarian song," I ventured.

"Professor Margaret Stan's translation reveals an interesting peculiarity. She has stumbled upon an Old Bulgarian word in the text, ТРОИЦА, i.e., *trinity* or *trio,* which your fiancé failed to translate correctly. She thinks that every human being is a trio, a combination of three people: a child, an adult person, and an old one."

His fingers touched my hand.

"I am afraid Professor Margaret Stan's interpretation is quite inaccurate," I said as I carefully removed his fingers from my hand.

He stopped smiling.

"You are wrong, Sara," he said.

I stood still one more time.

Chapter Thirty-Five

Peter Stan did not worry about his wife. She would be late again. It had happened so often he had got accustomed to her absences. Then he thought about the pictures on the walls in their living room. The teacher found John Cole's behavior difficult to explain. Peter had not scraped off all the images. Why had Margaret asked him to destroy them? What did she mean? His thoughts flitted like startled fish. He could feel danger closing in on all sides …

Where am I? he thought. Stones and crags were all over the place, and the sky was gray above him. Was it snowing? He was freezing. Why was it so cold? What he saw made him choke on his own tongue. Lying prostrate on the rock-strewn ground, his wife Margaret groaned, her voice a tortured sigh, her face so white it appeared blue.

"Margaret!" he breathed, struggling to scramble to his feet. His blood exploded within his exhausted veins as the stones wobbled under him.

"Margaret!"

He knew where he was. Four gaping dark holes dug in the black crag stared at him. A gigantic blackbird of dark stone had perched on the hill, crushing its top under its colossal weight. The teacher had seen this bird before. Its empty eyes held the valley in their impenetrable blankness. He could see another statue, sharp edges, cutting surfaces, black shadows. It slowly came back to him. It was a plant, its barbs tearing the sky into segments of menacing twilight. That was an enormous thorn of black stone! Now Peter Stan was sure where they had taken him. Deaf Crags!

"Margaret!" he shouted. No, he was too weak to shout. He could not even speak.

Peter saw a thin figure, lying perfectly still; the white patch of the face a gleam of silver against the clouds dark as the threatening eyes of the bird. The white garment of the woman was in stark contrast to the peaceful dance of the snowflakes. Peter Stan strained his eyes and what he saw sent tingles down his spine. A tiny rivulet of blood trickled down the woman's cheek. Her eyes were open, and there was no color in them. Peter knew who the stranger was; he had seen her photograph in newspapers and magazines and her face was painted on the wall of his wife's room. Wanga, the prophetess of Bare Mountain! Her chest rose and fell. She was breathing. Or was he wrong? Peter thought he noticed his wife's lips twitch. He crawled towards her, slowly and laboriously, his body a big throbbing wound.

"Well, well, well," a voice exclaimed. "Isn't this a surprise? Let us see who this strong old man is!"

Peter was sure he had heard this voice, but he could not relate it to a face he knew. It was a sonorous young woman's voice. His aching head was so heavy it hit something hard as it crashed against the stones. He looked up. It was the woman, elegant and very pretty, who wanted to read his student's essay about the blackbird. A century ago, she used to be his son's girlfriend.

"Boya ..." the teacher moaned.

He was not sure if it was a stone, an iron bar, or the pretty woman's fist that hit him. Who took me here, he thought. It must have been John Cole. John and that pretty woman, then darkness deleted his thoughts.

Chapter Thirty-Six

Today, she had not cleaned her room.

I wonder if she's all right, Andrew Gils thought. His mother was a peculiar woman, never complained, and he suspected she suffered in silence. One never knew with Constance Gils. She was a woman of few words and stayed in her room most of the time, she had no friends, and her favorite pastime seemed to be walking in the forest for hours on end no matter if it rained, snowed or the day was scorching hot.

Andrew's father died when Andrew was two. Constance Gils kept one of his photographs: a thin, fair-haired man in a thick forest.

"Your father loved trees. Birches were his favorite," that was all Constance had said on this issue. She had planted eleven birch trees in their backyard, and Andrew, a ten-year old boy, remembered how his mother gathered seeds and put them in a box full of sand. Thirty little birches sprouted in the box. Eleven survived.

The birch trees in their backyard used to be Andrew's father, or so Andrew thought. He had often seen his mother press her forehead against a birch. They didn't have neighbors, and Andrew grew accustomed to her long silences. He believed his mother's silence was his home. The only thing he did not understand was why his mother did not let him talk to the little girl who told him fairy tales back then, in the shabby block of flats.

"We'll leave this apartment," his mother said one day. "I don't want her near us."

"But why?" he had whimpered.

His mother kept silent for a month as she pedantically gathered all their things, packaged his shoes, his old shirts, his picture books.

"This girl is the only friend I have," Andrew had insisted. "I want to stay here, in my room, because I can see her face in the house opposite ours. I am very happy, Mother."

"There's something wrong with her," his mother had said. "I can feel it."

Mother and son left the apartment and bought a house in a nearby village.

The building was small, a hut, in a huge meadow. It was then that his mother planted the birches.

Andrew didn't like the new house; he was scared of the big backyard every time he woke after midnight, whimpering. He missed the fairy tales the girl told him. It was so astonishing to meet Sara Eutim after all these years, and yes, she looked more beautiful than ever. He could not take his eyes off her, but ... As always, a *but* swam in his thoughts, a shadow that made his heart sink.

Sara could control her green dots. "Eliminate somebody and you'll learn to control yours," she had said, and her voice was narrow and cold as a blade. "Something's wrong with that girl," his mother had said, and his mother was rarely wrong. The quiet small woman saw things no one noticed, and she could sense danger the other people were unable to spot. She was a queer fish, his mother was.

She sold the house with the backyard and the eleven birches in it. She sold her golden rings, her car, and her collection of exquisite Chinese teacups. She had done the impossible: she paid for his education, and she was proud of him.

"Professor Andrew Gils," she repeated in the cold dusk, her happy voice waltzing with the clouds. "Professor Andrew Gils, my son." He had the feeling these words were her treasure and hope. Her happy voice had forgotten the eleven birches in that endless backyard.

Professor Andrew Gils enjoyed coming back home. His mother and her silences waited for him.

It was a cold winter day. Snowflakes somersaulted in the air, and the wind howled in the empty streets. As always, his mother didn't complain. She had started drawing odd pictures of forests, and bright patches of light among the trees, mysterious silhouettes darting across the thick underbrush.

"What are these?" Andrew had asked, and his mother answered, "Just friends." The sun was her friend, too. She said she was happy and quickly added as if the idea had just crossed her mind that it was time he married a pretty woman. His mother had never spoken of that before. Andrew thought how happy he could be if only Sara … pretty Sara Eutim would come to see his collections of stones. No one knew about Andrew's passion for rough ordinary stones he happened to glimpse at as he walked in the rain. Stones were codes that launched the great cycle of a planet's development. Stones were symmetry and destruction of patterns at the same time. Their resilient beauty reminded him of Sara, the woman he had loved all these years.

Sara Eutim had a fiancé.

Professor Gils had cut his forefinger in the morning. Sara Eutim was another open wound that would not heal. Sara Eutim could make her green dots disappear and come back. His forefinger pulsed and itched. Should he ask Sara Eutim to dinner? She had told him she loved snow.

"Andrew!" he heard his mother call. "Please come here."

He opened the door and saw his mother sitting in her favorite armchair. This time, she had drawn a black sun, and the forest under it was red: the trees, tall and massive, touched the black sun, their leaves blue under the black rays, pouring down onto the earth.

"I have a bad headache. Nothing helps."

His mother never complained. Was her headache *that* bad?

"Why didn't you listen to Healing Trun?" he asked.

"I tried," she said. "It didn't seem to work."

Andrew ran to his room and brought his laptop. He had saved Healing Trun and he listened at times. No one knew if the weird sounds had any side effects; however, after a minute of TRUN! TRUN! he felt so vigorous and cheerful he was ready to fall in love with the world. He had saved the other Trun, its killing twin, which caused paralysis, just in case someone attacked him. Gils needed protection, and if pain was his partner, he could win any battle. He could … if only pain and death were his allies.

"Quick!" his mother whispered, beads of perspiration glistening on her forehead. She was struggling for breath.

Andrew pushed the button and the grating, rasping, avalanche of TRUN! TRUN! struck the walls of the room. TRUN! TRUN! Agonizing pain split his skull. TRUN! TRUN! His blood seethed with thousands of shrieks of agony. TRUN! The walls disintegrated and everything in his eyes burst. The world was the black sun in his mother's picture. Had he selected the wrong file? Did he switch on Killing Trun? How could he! This was impossible! He caught a glimpse of his mother's face. What was happening to it? The wrinkles on the forehead grew deeper, her haggard cheeks lost color, her face aged rapidly before his terrified eyes, furrows, dark and livid, ravaged her neck, a dreadful net of deep lines cut into her skin, her hands withered. His mother was dying!

Exhausted, utterly powerless, hardly able to breathe, Andrew tried hard to concentrate. He clenched his fists, gasped for breath, gritted his teeth and started punching on his laptop. Did he do it? Was he able to stop the murderous flood of sounds?

Suddenly silence fell upon the scene. This could mean one thing: Andrew had managed to suppress the lethal Trun. He darted a glance at his mother's face and froze in his tracks. Her morbid complexion, her trembling hands, the wrinkles, the deep and harsh lines that had appeared around her eyes and mouth terrified him. She looked so old he feared she would disintegrate. What had he done! He groped for his laptop, his eyes searching, aching, itching, and exploding with pain as he clicked on the Healing Trun file. Hissing and moaning wails, strident, shrill, and deafening, spurted out of the microphones. TRUN! TRUN! crept, leapt, hit, clashed and beat against the walls. The bliss he felt. The gratitude he was still alive, the ecstasy the powerful sounds gave him! Blood rushed through his numb legs, warmth and peace caressed his freezing bones. Fears left him, his strength came back and he suddenly felt like singing.

Something was happening to his mother's face. The wrinkles, big as open sores, disappeared, the lines that had severed the skin around her mouth and eyes were vanishing as if some invisible magic wand was deleting them. Her neck, which a minute ago resembled a scaly slough of a snake, was now smooth and pink and looked healthier than ever before.

What was happening to his mother? She had a pink glow to her face, her cheeks gleamed, smooth and soft, blushing, young and beautiful. Andrew rubbed his forehead. Was he imagining things? He stared at his hands as he remembered he'd cut his finger in the morning. The itching wound was gone. His skin was hard and healthy. His mother was smiling at him. Her eyes sparkled, her face beamed with happiness, and she looked so young he was speechless. TRUN! TRUN! The air roared and screeched, gurgled and coughed, and his breath, his blood found bliss and harmony. Now Andrew Gils knew joy felt like a summer day. His mother grinned happily at him. Sara Eutim, loving and wonderful, was on his mind.

Suddenly the Trun sounds died. There was complete silence, but it was warm and inviting. Mother and son exchanged glances.

"How handsome you look!" Constance Gils whispered, looking at her son unbelieving. "You are just like your father, just like him!"

"You look younger! Much younger … honestly, Mom," Andrew muttered. This was true. Constance Gils did look younger. No wrinkles, no lines, no brown dots or freckles marred the perfection of her face.

"I was dying," she said. "Now I think I have another thirty years to live." She looked at her son. "And you've never been so handsome before. What did you do, Andrew?"

He grinned. His mother never flattered him. She spoke what she thought was true.

"I don't know," he said.

Had he blundered by switching on Killing Trun? He nearly died. His mother had shriveled before his eyes, she had one foot in the grave. She was about to breathe her last. Then he managed to switch on the avalanche of Healing Trun. His mother was still smiling at him, her dear face kind and beautiful.

"Andrew, go buy me some chocolate," she said. "I can't believe what had just happened."

He was about to tell her chocolate was no good to eat; his mother had not eaten chocolate for eleven years, but he changed his mind.

"Come back quickly," she said.

Andrew Gils was happy as he went out in the street. His mother had chosen the house and he had paid for it. It was a big Victorian mansion;

twenty-one birches grew in the backyard behind it, but they were not like the magnificent eleven trees of his childhood. It was snowing heavily, snowflakes falling slowly, gracefully, melting on his cheeks. When he was a little boy, he used to stick out his tongue and catch their icy secrets. The silly kid thought that eating snowflakes would take him to the big cloud, the father of all snow and rain in the world. At this moment, although he liked to think of himself as a man for all seasons, he was sure he simply loved winter.

Then Andrew Gils saw it, a white minivan parked at the end of their backyard. This came as a surprise. Their house was far from the town, and they had no neighbors. This was his mother's choice. She loved peace and quiet and enjoyed the sight of her birches before sunset. Nosy busybodies spoiled her evenings, she said. What was that minivan doing here, in the freezing wind? There were no other tire marks or footsteps in the snow. He noticed a man's face behind the steering wheel.

As he approached, the door opened and a woman got out of the minivan.

"Good afternoon, Professor Gils," the woman dressed in elegant black coat said. She had red hair, a good figure and a beautiful voice.

"Oh … uh … Boya…," he recollected seeing her at the clinic. "Good afternoon, Ms. Bagd," he said. A perfect occupational therapist she was, he knew for sure.

The longer he looked at her, the more uncomfortable he felt. Something had gone wrong. What was it?

"I am very glad to see you, Professor Gils," she said. "I was waiting for you."

Andrew Gils remembered. Boya Bagd, the occupational therapist, worked at Iztok clinic at the time Ivan Georg had brain surgery. She was careful, considerate, one of the best in her trade. Andrew suddenly knew what it was that made him feel uneasy. Boya Bagd used to have green dots in her hair. Now her green dots were gone!

Could she control the green dots the way Sara Eutim could? "You have to eliminate somebody to learn how to control them," Sara Eutim had said.

"Where are the green dots?" he whispered.

Then Andrew thought the snow turned black. For a split second, he saw the black sun in his mother's picture, but this was not a black sun.

It was a flock of black birds. Their wings fluttered and made no noise. Wings and beaks hovered above his head. This goes against nature. A thought crossed his mind then a splitting headache exploded in his skull. TRUN! TRUN! the air shrieked. The snow burst and the quiet alley exploded in his eyes.

"Boya, help me!" Andrew breathed as he collapsed on the snow. Something happened. "You again?" Gils mouthed. He imagined he saw a little fair-haired girl. Her blue eyes rested on his face, and he knew he was dying.

"I will help you," the red-haired woman said, her face twisting into a grimace. She clutched Andrew's feet and dragged him towards the white minivan.

Chapter Thirty-Seven

Ivan didn't expect Boya would pop in for a visit and when he saw her at his apartment entrance door, he didn't know what to say. He felt so happy that he could not stop smiling at her.

"You know what … I didn't believe I'd see you again. You look beautiful … as always. No, you look more beautiful than always. Please come in."

Her blue eyes gleamed, and a weak smile touched her face.

"You have not changed, Ivan," she said.

He thought she was a woman worth living for, his woman. He forgot the words she had said when she left him. Her steps as she walked away still haunted him. It was snowing outside, and the wind whistled like a happy child. For a second, he believed he saw that little fair-haired girl playing happily in the snow. The whole neighborhood seemed friendly, and Ivan didn't know what to do with his happiness.

"I …" he wanted to say, "I still love you," but was not strong enough to do it.

Ivan was glad that the carpet was clean, and no speck of dust spoiled the perfection of the marble floor.

"Please take a seat," he muttered, not knowing what else to say. "I could fix you a sandwich, but I have only some tomatoes here," he admitted.

"You know, Ivan," she paused looking at him her, smile brighter, closing in on him. "I care about you. I am I truly and deeply …" She paused, a shadow thickening in her eyes. "I've had sex with many men. I forgot them the minute they were gone. I should have killed you. I should have killed you back then, at the hospital, after the operation … But …"

"Boya!" His mouth felt dry. Hesitantly, he reached out his hands and touched her quiet, sad face.

"I thought you saw me," she said. "I was going to inject poison into your system. In fact, I got that job at Iztok Clinic to be able to eliminate you. You were in my hands," the red-haired woman choked on her own voice as her eyes searched his. "I love you. I couldn't do it. You suffered so much."

"Who are you?" Ivan breathed. "Boya, my dearest …"

"If I had killed you, you wouldn't have blurted out the horrible Trun curse!"

Then Ivan noticed them: the green dots in her magnificent thick hair. He was sure these soft emerald lights were not there when he first saw her, slim and vulnerable, at his front door.

"You've got the green dots," he said.

"You have green dots, too. Do they bother you?" the second she stopped talking, the soft green lights disappeared.

Ivan took a breath hardly able to believe what he'd just seen.

"I cannot do that," he said. "I can't make the green dots go away. They follow me everywhere."

"Or you follow them," the pretty woman said. "I will teach you how to make them go, Ivan. It's easy."

"But why should I learn to do this?" he heard himself whispering as he touched her white, soft hand.

It was snowing so hard he thought the air was as thick as water.

"You will learn to kill pain," she said. "You'll become impervious to suffering," her eyes studied his face, or perhaps waited for him to say something important. Ivan kept silent. "I'll teach you, but you teach me how to produce the Trun curse."

Her eyes, a minute ago quiet and loving, now glowed, hard as blades. It was a different person that sat in his armchair, watching him.

"I don't know," he said. "I have no idea how it happened. I was shouting and was unable to stop. Nor did I realize I was spluttering and wailing."

"You must have felt something … a bad taste in your mouth or a surge of elation," she spoke calmly, the metallic glint in her eyes stabbing him. "You'd better be open with me now, Ivan," then her voice softened and sounded like a warm summer night and a song he had forgotten.

"It was just after surgery," he said thoughtfully. "First, the flock of the heavy blackbirds came from nowhere … and that bird appeared in my room."

"A blackbird? Did you touch it?" her breath was about to burst as her voice swooped down on Ivan.

"I touched the bird," he said. "No. It was gone. I thought I was only dreaming, but no, I found a feather."

She looked puzzled.

"You should have died. Every person who repeated Healing Trun died. You didn't. Was it that bird that saved your life?" her face was again sweet and angelic. "They'll force you to pass medical tests. They'll have to discover how you came up with the Trun thing. Then they will kill you."

"Who are you? Who are they?" Ivan asked. "Why should they kill me?"

"You solved the riddle of death," she said. "It's a pity you'll carry the secret to your grave. They will ruin the recordings, and everything will soon be forgotten. The story of the sick men you've cured will pass into legend. But Ivan! I love you."

He looked into her eyes. They wanted him to be happy.

"I love you," he said.

"I know," she whispered as she took him by the hand. Her skin was soft and he loved it. He loved her magnificent hair. Suddenly her green dots were gone again.

"They disappeared," he said slowly. "What does that mean?"

"It means you think about somebody's death," Boya said. "It means you want him dead."

Ivan wanted to kiss her blue eyes, but … what had she just said?

"So, when you think of killing someone your green dots disappear?" he asked, shivering.

"You won't understand. I can save your life. Come with me. I'll show you … a little flock of blackbirds."

"Blackbirds?" He looked at the snow behind the windowsill, the deserted street, the empty sidewalk. Then he saw a minivan, a white one, like a cat, purring on the thick blanket of snow. He looked at Boya. The metallic glint in her eyes was gone. She was the girl he cared about. She was his girl.

"Come. Let me show you the blackbirds," she said. "Look, look, they've come."

Strange, Ivan thought. The birds were not there a minute ago. They had perched not far from the minivan, and the snow had sunk under their weight.

"Let's go," Ivan said, touching her hand.

She smiled at him.

The wind buffeted their bodies, pushing them back to the house. The flock didn't move as Ivan and Boya approached the black wings. The minivan, white as a statue of ice, waited, a huge, mechanized snowdrift.

TRUN! TRUN! the air exploded, blasting, hissing, shushing, deafening.

"Easy, my friends," Ivan said smiling at the storm of murderous noise. The gust of wind prevented him from seeing Boya's face clearly, so he thought it must have been his imagination. Her face looked pale and frightened. Her eyes were horrified.

"Don't you feel pain?" she mouthed.

"No," Ivan said. "Why?"

Yes, what he saw in her eyes was unmistakably horror.

"It doesn't even make you sick," she said, snowflakes dead on her lips.

"No," Ivan answered. "These are the blackbirds, remember, the ones that help."

"These are the ones that kill," she barked. "But they can't kill you."

"What is it, Boya? Boya, dearest ... I ..."

He wanted to say he still loved her. Her fist shot up. She hit him on the forehead with a small black handgun. Ivan's legs collapsed under him.

"Ivan," the stunning young woman whispered. She leaned down, although the wind hurled a handful of snow in her face.

"I won't let them kill you." She hesitated for a second then kissed his cheek.

"A little fair-haired girl …" Ivan muttered. "Her eyes are sad." The dreamy ballet of the snowflakes stole his weary sigh.

Boya clutched his shoulders, her fingers dug into his blue overcoat and she dragged him to the white minivan.

Chapter Thirty-Eight

"You are late again," my fiancé said as he kissed me, his admiring eyes two lakes of happiness on his face. "Sara, I waited for you, but she said it was useless. She thought you'd give me the slip. She said you'd kicked all your boyfriends out of your life and was sure you had no friends."

"And who's that Miss Know-all?" I asked, although I guessed the answer straight away: a blue-eyed, attractive young woman, her green dots—an infestation of green plant lice—sparkling in her hair.

"Boya Bagd," he said. "I don't think she likes you, Sara. She said you were one of the meanies."

"The meanies?" I grinned. "And who are these bad, bad guys?"

Jacob didn't grin back at me. His face was a slab of granite or another material, colder and more rigid. This was strange indeed. I had not seen this man that serious.

"Boya said that you were one of those crazy Samodivas that inhabit us."

"Samodivas? Come off it, Jacob. The Samodivas are a figment of man's imagination, mythological creatures, hateful shadows etc."

"She told me you left all your boyfriends in the lurch, and I am afraid I was about to believe her," the young archaeologist said his eyes sad. He looked like a frightened child. "You don't have children, do you Sara?"

"No, I don't have children, I've already told you" I said. "Why are children so important now?"

His blue eyes lit up, not a shadow of doubt in them.

"The mean ones didn't have children she said," he said slowly. "So, you suspected they could be Samodivas."

The afternoon sun was bright patches of light on the narrow street in front of my little house where I had taken Jacob. I rightfully wondered how come blue-eyed Boya found him.

"In the middle ages they said the women who couldn't have children were witches," I said. "I can have children, but I don't want to. So far, I have not met an adoring father for them."

"You met me!" he whispered, his face breaking into a grin. "Isn't it time we worked towards this end?" the man said vaguely as he planted a kiss on my lips.

"I'll think about it," I promised.

"By the way I don't care if you cannot have children," Jacob said a smile of gold on his face. "We can always adopt a child and you'll love him."

"Shut up," I said.

He was the kindest man I had ever met. I loved him. We made love and I liked it. He was an ordinary weak guy. Wasn't I crazy, indeed? Yes, I was.

"Do you know what else she asked me?" he said, his face open like a favorite book on the page where the protagonist kissed the principal female character, asking her to become his wife.

"I am not particularly keen on learning what Boya asked you," I said.

"Well," he sighed. "It's kind of creepy ... she asked me: *As an archaeologist, you should know that human societies and practically all religions denounced suicide as an act against God. Christians believe that committing suicide is a sinful act of blasphemy. Have you thought about the reason why?*"

I looked at him.

"And what did you tell her?" I asked.

He stared at the setting sun that made his face golden, a thoughtful, thin face I liked for no reason at all.

"A penny for your thoughts," I whispered. I wanted to kiss him. He seemed so vulnerable, so childlike I felt like a mother to him. Well, not exactly like a mother.

"I think," he said, his face still golden with the last sun-rays of the day. "I think that maybe by committing suicide man becomes stronger than death. Man is not afraid and this makes him more powerful than nonexistence. In a way, man becomes master of death because—"

"Master of death?" I exclaimed. "This can never be."

He stared.

"I said something that made you angry," he said. "What was it? Tell me."

"How come you know what makes me angry? Maybe I'm just curious."

Jacob avoided my gaze. I was intrigued; so far, I believed no one could guess if I was furious or happy, even His Excellency John Cole, the chief of Dusk police. He used to hold my face in his hands. I'd love to know what you are thinking about right now, that was what he said so often that I came to hate him for it. Now the young archaeologist knew I was angry.

"The first time we argued and you left in a huff," he started, "was when I said something stupid about a civilization that existed in human beings, in every one of us. Boya laughed her head off, I remember that well, and you ..." Jacob's voice trailed off.

His silence dissolved in the sunset and got on my nerves.

"What about me?" I urged him. A wrong move, of course. Jacob shut up like a clam. The best solution to his silences was to leave him alone. I did, and it worked.

"That Old Bulgarian song I told you about, the one I translated into English ... do you remember? It sounds crazy. You remember what the song says about talent. *Samodivas cannot penetrate you, Talented Ones.* What if ... talent is death? Only one Samodiva, the one called Death, can live within the Talented Ones. So you can buy talent *by causing death ...*"

I listened to him. The best policy was to let him talk as long as he turned blue around the mouth.

"I said something about the Samodiva civilization and you got angry. Your eyes looked like knives," Jacob muttered. "Your eyes turned dead again when I said something stupid like *When man kills himself, he becomes the master of death.* You had poison in your eyes," his voice broke down. "I was scared of you, Sara."

Jacob was a remarkable man able to discover a poisonous gleam in your eye. I wondered how he did it. No one before him could, even John Cole, the police chief. Wasn't that intriguing?

It was almost dark and Jacob's white skin glowed like a cobweb of moonlight.

"What is it, my love?" my fiancé asked, looking concerned or perhaps scared. "Did I say something wrong again?"

"Yes, you did."

"What was it?" He looked astonished.

I thought about it. Soon twilight would be everywhere, in his beautiful eyes too. And I loved this man, stupid me.

"The *Journal of Ethnography* published your article on the Dirty Days and Samodiva's milk, Jacob. A very long and, let me be honest, a shallow piece of writing. You argue the Samodivas are *green dots* that ruin man's reasoning skills. Ludicrously, you conclude that Samodiva's milk is death."

"I didn't write this article," Jacob said.

"Didn't you?" I said as I handed him the spring issue of *Journal of Ethnography Legal History Series, Myths and Old Bulgarian Folklore.* Jacob Harvey, PhD, was the author's name under the article titled 'Samodivas and Other Proto-Bulgarian Legends,' pages 330–371.

"I have not written this article," Jacob repeated. "But I do think that the Samodivas are related to death. In the first draft of my translation of the Trun Chark song, I wrote that the Samodivas are *green death.*"

I glanced at him. His face looked innocent enough.

"Sara, your eyes are dead," he whispered. "Did I say something wrong?"

"You are a very clever young man who wrote an article," I told him. "And now you are lying to me you have not written it."

"I have not written it," he insisted. "May I read it, please?"

"Professor Gils from Iztok Clinic thinks the article says something important. He tried to contact you."

"Boya had given the professor my telephone number, and I explained to the man that I had not written the article. Sara, the only person who knew about the Samodiva's milk, and the only person who could make this milk churn was you. I don't mean to insult you, Sara, but I think the only person who could write this article is you."

He was right. I did write that article but had no reason to confess my unforgivable sin. I had my motives, of course.

"Your eyes, Sara," my fiancé exclaimed. "The poison has come back."

I didn't like his remark about my eyes, and his way of mumbling jarred on my ears.

"See you tomorrow, Jacob."

"Don't go," he said, but I didn't feel like wasting more time.

I wanted to go home as soon as possible.

A large black cloud crawled on the sky.

I got into my car, and Jacob, thin and tall, jutting out in the field like a dry thorn, made my heart skip a beat. I loved this simple man, and this was the worst thing that ever happened to me.

As I drove my powerful sports car along the narrow winding road, I was aware I was wrong. Not a dense cloud had obscured the sky; it was a flock of birds as black as ink. They were silent in the twilight. I saw a white minibus speeding past me. It was very strange the small vehicle stopped in front of my villa. I pulled over to the side of the road and watched. The hideous blackbirds perched on the sidewalk, and the stones sank under the weight of their feathers. A stunning redhead got out of the minibus, Boya Bagd, an inquisitive damsel in distress. I didn't wait to see more of it.

"You are an intelligent boy," his mother had said, and Tony could hardly believe his ears. He got an excellent grade on a math test, and she added he'd be a great man. Tony smiled. He felt so proud of his mother, of his room he loved so much, of the town he lived in. He was on his way back home, on a cold Monday afternoon. It was about time he attended biology classes. His favorite teacher, Peter Stan, had said Tony had a knack for getting on with animals. Tony had not noticed that.

Then suddenly he saw them, the silent blackbirds. They were a thick mass, a blur, a noiseless swirl of wings and beaks, hushed protuberance of seething and pulsating shapes. At the beginning he felt happy. He'd have another favorite bird, or perhaps ten favorite blackbirds! TRUN! TRUN! The swishing, screaming, biting sounds exploded in his head. The birds were quiet, their wings fluttering; their eyes pulsing. Tony's heart was about to burst. His nose bled, his teeth chattered and ached and burst.

Then he saw a white minivan, pulling over in front of him, and then, in a flash, a red-haired woman getting out of the vehicle. Tony knew her. She had stolen Ben, his bird, and had killed it.

"Go away," he breathed.

He could see nothing else.

The woman gripped his arms and dragged him to the minivan.

Chapter Thirty-Nine

The wind cut through the treetops that hissed and creaked in the freezing gusts, the sharp leaves of the frost-covered grass cut the glinting air, the crags looked gray, dark, enormous, and the four gaping holes, like dead eyes of a corpse, were fixed on the narrow patch of land where about a dozen people lay huddled together, their hands tied behind their backs. The frozen soil was black, and bumpy, the narrow patch of land was surrounded by jutting cliffs and interminable wasteland of bulging boulders, some like venomous lizards, others resembling petrified snakes that were forced to lie still as penalty of disobedience.

The men and women kept silent.

A dark cube carved in the stone, its depth full of turbid liquid, glared at the low sky, motionless like a sheet of heavily rusted corrugated iron. The liquid in the cube appeared to be harder than the crags.

"You can untie them now," a man's deep voice echoed. A slim red-haired woman, too beautiful to be true in the wilderness of broken stones and contorted trees, ran towards the pile of human bodies.

"Untie Margaret first," the man said. "Professor Margaret Stan."

"Boya," Professor Margaret Stan said. The attractive woman gave a start. "You are still afraid of me."

The redhead said nothing.

"John Cole," Margaret Stan said. "From the very beginning, I suspected you were behind it all. And I wonder where the other two are."

"What are you speaking about, Margaret?" the man's deep voice asked. "I don't understand."

"Oh, you do," Professor Margaret Stan said. "I speak of the Holy Trinity or perhaps you prefer the term *trio?*"

"Professor Stan, the Trinity or the trio, if it sounds more polite to you, is a hallucination and no, I am not a religious man, although I hold Christianity in considerable respect. Are you ready, Boya? I would like all of you to be comfortable while we discuss an issue of utmost importance." John Cole, the chief of Dusk police said as he stood in front of the group. "Well," he went on. "I hope you all can see the green dots each one of the others has. Perhaps you are interested to know why I've gathered you all here."

Silence reigned as the charming redhead bent over the prostrate figures and untied their hands.

"Welcome to Deaf Crags, ladies and gentlemen," John Cole began.

"The green dots you possess are impressive indeed. It will be useful to say a few words about each one of you members of this illustrious assembly, so I begin in no particular order. Number one: Professor Andrew Gils, a brilliant neurosurgeon, the man who performed brain tumor surgery as a result of which Doctor Ivan Georg, number two on our list, produced what came to be referred to as Healing Trun. I asked myself, did Professor Gils make something special, something extraordinary that brought about the outburst of the hissing Trun chaos?"

John Cole continued, "Number three on my list is this captivating lady, Boya Bagd. She was engaged to Peter Stan's son, and the teacher Peter Stan is my best friend. I am also aware of the fact that Doctor Ivan Georg, the star who produced Healing Trun, was, and I suppose still is, deeply in love with charming Boya. Number four of our guests of honor to Deaf Crags is Jacob Harvey, a talented archaeologist, a man who, alas, has no green dots like the famous representatives of science and culture present here. Why is he with us then?" the police chief's matter-of-fact voice trailed off. "Or perhaps Jacob has green dots too?"

A man sat up, rubbed his hands and said, "I am Jacob Harvey. You know me, Father Dimo, don't you? You gave me the original lyrics to the Trun Chark song. Do you remember me?"

All eyes were on the archaeologist's dark silhouette. As thin as a lath, he stood up and took a step to the chief of Dusk police.

"I am number five on our list, and my name is John Cole," the police chief said.

"Father Dimo, the copy of the lyrics you gave me was printed in a meticulously clean hand in Old Bulgarian."

John Cole shook his head, his voice firm as he said, "I gave you the lyrics to the chark, an Old Bulgarian song, but I am not Father Dimo, I am the chief of Dusk police."

The archaeologist tried to say something, failed, then finally gasped, "Why did you lie to me that you were a priest?"

"I wanted to find out something about you, Jacob," John Cole said.

"I wanted you to see this song, and I wanted someone else to see it as well. I had in mind number six on the list of our VIPs, Professor Margaret Stan. She is an old flame of mine, a fussy eminent scientist, so I hoped the lyrics to the Trun Chark song would lead her to a discovery, and so they did. Number seven is her loyal husband, the teacher Peter Stan, my best friend as I've said. Number eight is Philip Mill, the only man who ditched the magnificent woman over there I deeply admire, Ms. Sara Eutim, a famous writer, decision-maker, and scholar. She was, by the way, my fiancée and then my wife some years ago; Sara is number nine on my list, a remarkable woman indeed. Number ten is Tony, the boy who captured one of the blackbirds and kept it in his room. The essay Tony wrote on the bird left my old friend Peter Stan guessing about … well, Peter himself will tell us if he smelled a rat in the boy's essay."

"I didn't smell anything," the teacher said gruffly.

"Why aren't we surprised? You are a particularly credulous person, Peter. I don't use the word *gullible,* mind you. Neither do I resort to the adjective *thoughtless,* although I should. I don't believe you, Peter." The chief of Dusk police gritted his teeth.

"And now the most special among us, number eleven on my list of celebrities, Wanga, the blind woman believed to be a soothsayer capable of *seeing* or, shall I say, *intercepting* the green dots that people of all walks of life possess. Let me make a point here: Wanga was the reason why Philip Mill, this otherwise respectable man, broke his engagement to

Sara Eutim, the eminent writer, and moved in with Wanga in her rickety hut on Bare Mountain. Wanga is a queer fish. She collects broken pans and believes they can neutralize many dreadful diseases men suffer from. Is she a quack, hoarding heaps of stones, or a woman deeply convinced these stones can remove hatred that poisons ordinary folks? Wanga has an exceptional ability to predict one's future. She can also speak in detail about events that happened to one in the past."

The chief of Dusk police carefully studied each face in turn.

"Wanga, I am terribly sorry we had to drag you here, but now is the time to reveal why your presence among us is vitally important." John Cole cleared his throat as he glanced at Professor Margaret Stan.

"The total number of people on our list is eleven. Some of them have green dots, others claim they don't. Yet Wanga the prophetess claims that everybody has them. The focus of our discussion is the green dots."

John Cole paced in front of the ten shadows lost amid jutting rocks and trees. His words rang in the frozen air, hit the statue of the blackbird, towering above the frozen valley, its fierce dark eyes noticing everything, hating everything, and spilling venom over the gaping holes in the crags.

"But why am I here, Mr. Cole?" I don't know you, and I don't have a problem with the green dots you speak about," Jacob Harvey, the archaeologist, said, as he looked at the black statue.

For a while, the chief of Dusk police was silent, a wry smile flitting over his lips.

"You must know why, young man," he said. "Or I have overestimated your basic reasoning skills."

The young man's cheeks turned blood red.

"Shall I gather the lyrics to the Trun Chark song you gave me were a fake?" the archaeologist asked.

"No, they are authentic. Mr. Harvey, aren't you tempted to find out why I took pains to provide you with the lyrics, pretending I was an old priest?"

The archaeologist clenched his hand into a fist but said nothing.

"In the first place, Mr. Harvey, you made a bizarre statement that amazed both Ms. Boya Bagd and my ex-wife, the distinguished writer Sara Eutim. Boya provided me with a written report on your statements," John Cole studied the young man's angry expression.

"Mr. Harvey, you said something that spurred Ms. Sara Eutim into action. She did something and you were unavailable for a long while. Do you remember what you told her, Mr. Harvey?"

"Why should you drag me into your mess, John?" Sara Eutim said, her voice a frozen sea. John Cole left her question hanging in the air, concentrating on the archaeologist instead.

"Jacob Harvey, can you remember what it was that shook your beloved Sara?"

The archaeologist puckered his lips. "Sara, I said something about a civilization that lived in our thoughts," he spoke loudly and clearly. "I assumed those strange creatures might be the Samodivas we read about in the Trun Chark song and in numerous Old Bulgarian folktales. But what I said was a joke."

"A joke that put your fiancée Ms. Eutim in great trouble, young man," the police chief glanced sharply at the archaeologist then he seemed to speak to the cold stones, although the intended addressee stood in front of him.

"Mr. Harvey, I gave you the authentic lyrics to the Old Bulgarian Trun Chark song because I wanted to see if your translation of the piece would differ from the one my friend Professor Margaret Stan had made," he said as he uttered the words with utmost care.

"Your translation, Mr. Harvey, was somewhat different from Professor Stan's. And *somewhat* is a word that fails to describe the abyss that separates what you've seen in the song and the meaning that Margaret has managed to extract from it."

John Cole observed the archaeologist clench his fists, and deliberately, brazenly, studied the faces surrounding him.

"I'd like to emphasize the fact that while the young archaeologist concentrates on interpreting the meaning of the *holes* at Deaf Crags and on certain types of humans, Professor Stan focuses her attention on the number *three*. She even uses the word *triad*, which came as a surprise to me, a rather unpleasant one, I grant her that."

No one said a word as the police chief turned to Sara Eutim, "My dear, I was glad that after you broke our engagement you found a new boyfriend, this brilliant archaeologist here. Well, it turned out he was not so brilliant after all. He'd prattle on about a civilization that does not prosper on a faraway planet; those creatures have the nerve to inhabit our own thoughts, our human subconscious, instead. Well, Peter, what do you think of this *civilization?*"

The old teacher said nothing.

"I've always thought my old friend Peter Stan is a simple, that is to say not an exceptionally clever, man," the chief of Dusk police went on. "Kindhearted, yes, by all means: the combination of a heart of gold and lack of acute intelligence is a disastrous one, especially in my good friend's case. So, I asked myself a question again: is it necessary to bring Mr. Peter Stan to Deaf Crags at all? If he stayed at home, and his darling Margaret vanished without a trace, he'd raise hell as a result of which Peter is with us now." The police chief laughed under his breath.

"I admit Margaret is another cup of tea. I wouldn't say she is incredibly clever. No, she is not. She is a hard-working scientist; she toils and moils like a slave, like an office drudge, like a mole, and was not inclined to reveal to me what she'd been working on. I could garner extremely scanty evidence of what Margaret was doing. I concluded I had to approach her in a different way, so I asked her to become my wife. One can follow one's wife everywhere without raising her suspicions, can't one? Sorry, Peter, these are the tricks of the trade."

"I'll kill you," the teacher said quietly. He didn't even glare at the police chief.

"Margaret did not want me, old man," John Cole said. "I could not find out how Margaret interpreted the meaning of triad. I did not know what exactly she had extracted from the Old Bulgarian Trun Chark song."

"Is that why you tasked this woman, Boya Bagd—your fiancée number three, a short-lived one, I checked—to use my son as a peephole into my work?" Professor Margaret Stan asked.

"Yes, your assumption is correct, she used your son," said the chief of Dusk police.

"I should have guessed," Ivan Georg, the scar-faced young doctor said quietly. "I came up with Healing Trun, and she had to find out how I did it."

"No," a calm, resolute voice soared in the air and died in the wind. "This is not true, Ivan," Boya Bagd said.

"You can take her word for it, Doctor Georg." The chief of Dusk police said.

"Several months ago, you received an email that warned: *You will be the first one they'll kill.* I sent you this email, not Sara Eutim as she had claimed. It was Boya Bagd who had to perform the crucial task of eliminating you. You are still alive and kicking, Doctor Georg, and you have to know one thing: Boya Bagd botches up a task only when she refuses to execute it. The question is, who wanted you dead and why?"

A fierce wind swept through the narrow valley. The crags skulked behind the trees like beasts of prey and the four holes in the slope scowled at the wasteland of stones, ravines, and deep shadows.

"You must not overlook a little-known yet quite revealing fact," the police chief went on. "Wanga, the blind prophetess I truly admire, had pleaded with Sara Eutim, *Don't kill your brother!* An intriguing piece of information, don't you think so?"

"It is Mr. Philip Mill the Fair who reports on meaningless jabber to you, isn't it?" Sara Eutim chimed in.

"This is a clever girl," John Cole said, smiling at her.

"I don't have a brother," Sara Eutim said.

"I'm sure you don't," the chief of Dusk police agreed. "I checked on you, Sara. One thing worries me: so far, Wanga has never made a mistake. It seems she is friends with the green dots, and so far, they haven't misled her."

Something happened. First, the wind died and small stones crumbled to dust. Suddenly TRUN! TRUN! TRUN! rent Deaf Crags Valley. The air thundered, grunted, and throbbed, spreading a chaos of ugly piercing sounds.

One man among the group wailed, his screeching voice a desperate nest of pain amid the Trun avalanche of deafening blare.

"Peter! Dearest!" the tall, thin woman shouted. "Stop it, John. He's dying!"

But the murderous Trun did not stop its vicious attack. Another scream, shattered, squashed, agonizing, dissolved into the cacophony of lethal sounds.

A dark-haired very attractive man, Philip Mill, squirmed and writhed in agony.

A thin piercing wail rent the sky, hit the crags, filling the four dark holes with darkness and rancor. Sara Eutim had howled. Harsh heartbreaking groans made the air twist and split. Sounds erupted from the nearest dark hole in the steep face of the mountain. All heads turned to its glaring depth.

"Now we know who is who," Professor Margaret Stan breathed. The screeching, stuttering Trun sounds died. "I know for sure who has green dots and who has not," the tall thin woman sounded unperturbed, distant, and cold. "I never go anywhere without Killing Trun. There are two facts that invite suspicion," she went on. "In the first place, why did the eminent writer Sara Eutim howl with pain? I think she shouldn't put on this artistic show for us. Second, why didn't Mr. Harvey, the archaeologist, writhe in agony? Why didn't this boy, here" she pointed at Tony who sat peacefully on the cold stones. "Why didn't this kid groan with pain? Both Tony and young Jacob, the archaeologist, should be squirming in agony. As you can see they are impervious to Trun torture like the rest of us. But we have green dots, and they claim they don't have them."

All eyes followed Margaret Stan. The wind cut through the forest and the trees bent to the frozen ground.

"Why did you take us here, John?" Professor Margaret Stan asked.

"You should have guessed, my dear," The chief of Dusk police said. "It's obvious you haven't, so I'll make my best to offer you a reasonable answer."

Professor Margaret's face remained impenetrable. It said nothing to the group of men and women who sat on the freezing-cold stones.

"What is it, Margaret?" Peter Stan asked as he touched his wife's hand.

The thin, tall woman kept mum.

"Professor Andrew Gils maintains that while he operated on the most important member of our group, Dr. Ivan Georg, he did nothing to put his life in danger," the chief of Dusk police went on. "Doctor Georg produced the so-called Healing Trun, and now he *claims* he knows nothing about the way he did it."

"You should have paid closer attention to somebody on your list, police officer Cole," Peter Stan, the old teacher, said. "She's hiding behind your back—Boya Bagd, the woman who stole my student's essay on the blackbirds from me. She used to be my son's fiancée. She didn't scream when Margaret produced Killing Trun. What is the role Boya Bagd plays in this nightmare?"

The red-haired woman stood unafraid of the stiff wind, aloft and motionless, ignoring the teacher.

"I didn't know you were engaged to another man before me," Ivan Georg said, his face an open wound in the cold. "You and I ..." his voice trailed off. "I noticed it too, Boya. You didn't scream after Professor Margaret Stan started Killing Trun. I know what it means. You can hide your green dots and you can control them."

"And the one who can control the green dots can control death too?" Professor Margaret Stan said, every word a sharp edge.

"No," a strained voice rose and dropped almost right away. "If one can hide one's green dots, one is in the past and in the future at the same time," Wanga, the blind soothsayer, spoke slowly, leaning on Philip Mill's hand.

"The poor woman," Peter Stan said. "It is a crime to keep her here."

"What she says is true," Margaret Stan nodded to her husband. "I have come to a similar conclusion. John and Peter, both of you saw the pictures on the walls in my room. I didn't tell you why I wanted to destroy these pictures."

"Tell us," the chief of Dusk police said.

"There were three photographs on the wall," Margaret Stan began. "The first one was Tony's, the boy who captured the blackbird and took it home. Tony didn't scream after he heard Killing Trun. His essay on that blackbird was exceptionally interesting; especially the part about the peace and comfort the bird gave the boy and his mom as it drove away pain and hate." Margaret went on, carefully choosing her words. "The third photograph on the wall was yours, John. You were not the reason why I wanted to delete these photos. I wanted to remove them all, and the reason was the second picture in the series. I am sure you remember it."

"The second picture, Margaret!" Peter Stan, the old teacher, said. "There was no picture at all. I remember that clearly. Somebody had scrawled a question mark on the wall."

"Yes, it was a question mark, and I'm sure John Cole knows what it means."

"This is a puzzling statement, Margaret. I dare say it makes no sense to me," the police chief declared.

"I doubt it," Professor Margaret Stan said. "I'd like to inform you, John, that now I think I know who the person behind that question mark is. However, you are looking for something else. You are not after that question mark. What you are after, John Cole, or should I say … Tony?"

The chief of Dusk police winced, his handsome features hardening.

"We are freezing, John!" Peter Stan, the teacher, thundered.

"I'm sure Ms. Sara Eutim can alleviate your plight," the chief of Dusk police said, smiling a wry smile. "She knows how to do it. Would you care to make us warm, Sara?"

"I don't understand what you mean, Mr. Cole," the attractive writer said, her expression amused and challenging at the same time.

"Put your hand in the water over there," John Cole pointed at the irregular cube dug in the rock. The cloudy liquid looked harder than the crags, its surface black and immobile like a square in a dead village.

"Put your hand in the water, Sara," the chief of Dusk police repeated his voice a cold whisper. "Or I'll throw you in this tarn myself."

"It's not a tarn, it's the Trun Chark!" shouted Jacob Harvey angrily, as the archaeologist jumped to his feet. "Leave her alone, Mr. Cole. I wonder … Who told you what would happen if she … if someone special touched the water in the Trun Chark?"

"I know what will happen if *someone* called Sara Eutim does," the chief of Dusk police barked.

The valley seemed stunned into eerie silence as the four dark holes drilled into the mountain face gaped open like mouths of monstrous predators.

"I'll stick my hand into the black mud of the tarn, if you, Mr. Cole, introduce us to the person you are hiding from us," Sara Eutim spoke calmly her words a chain, keeping all hostages in a precarious hug of fear. "I could hear the young man shriek with pain while I was screaming with pain, and you were not, Mr. Cole."

The chief of Dusk police shuddered as she looked him in the eye.

"I heard him, too" a whisper as quiet as a shadow of a flying sparrow escaped from the soothsayer. "And you," the blind woman said, her trembling hands pointing at Sara Eutim.

"You howled like a pack of wolves, but I saw your green dots. You were not in pain."

Her blind eyes were closed doors on her weak face. "I can feel his pain!" the blind woman breathed.

A gusty wind cut through the valley, hugged and pushed stunted trees, broke branches, shoved pebbles and dead leaves, hurling hard snow against the menacing statue of the bird that watched the frozen hill. Its colossal wings jutted out like gallows in the cold air.

"Okay, then," John Cole said. "Philip and Boya, you know where you left the man. Bring him here."

Boya, agile like a savage, untamed creature, unafraid of the blustery wind, stood up, not bothering to register the stares that followed her. Philip Mill, tall and strong, kissed the blind woman on the forehead and said, "I'm not your servant, Mr. Cole. You cannot order me around. I don't trust you, and I won't leave Wanga in your hands."

"As far as I know, Wanga has mentioned a number of times that you will kill her," the chief of Dusk police said flatly.

"How come you know about this?" Philip Mill said, panting. "I wrote nothing about it in my reports."

"I know everything, my friend," John Cole said. "*Everything.* Write that down somewhere and read it twice a day. Go bring the man you left to die in the freezing cold. Now! Then perhaps charming Sara would be as good as her word. She can do something to make us feel comfortable. I hope she'll agree to do a thing or two to the *mud,* as she chose to call the water in the cube."

The smile on John Cole's face was not an inviting sight.

"Yes, I can see it clearly now," the blind woman said, her words dead oak leaves on the stones. "Philip will take me to death."

"No!" the journalist whispered.

"Death is in the air," the blind woman mouthed.

"No, it is not," the chief of Dusk police said. "Mill, bring the suffering man here."

The journalist was about to say something but changed his mind and remained silent. He turned around abruptly and disappeared into the snowdrifts. Then slowly, like caterpillars, two shadows trudged down the hill, staggering towards the cube carved into the rock. A tall man stumbled and almost fell. Boya Bagd came up to him and gave him a push to make him walk faster. Philip Mill gripped his arm.

"You'll be okay," he said.

Both Peter and Margaret Stan rushed to the reeling man.

"Son!" the old teacher lisped. "Who did this to you?"

The man's face was covered with dust and mud. His cheeks were severely bruised, spattered with blood. His eyelids were blue and swollen, horrible.

"Thomas," Professor Margaret said.

The turbid liquid in the cube looked dead. The wind whipped up its surface and ran away quickly as if it had hit a heap of dry bones.

"Thomas," Professor Margaret whispered.

Boya pushed the tall man, her beautiful face expressionless.

"It is the Tall Fellow Boya works for," Thomas Stan hissed. "In her opinion, he drives away death and kills pain. This is a lie!" The newcomer spat blood. "The Tall Fellow and Boya hate me," he gasped.

"Why?" Margaret Stan asked looking her son in the eyes. "I've read something about him, a short poem. Do you know him?"

"If I'd known him, I'd have broken his neck," was the answer her son gave her.

Chapter Forty

"My friend Peter Stan told me something about his son," the chief of Dusk police began slowly. "As usual, I didn't attach any importance to his words. Peter was saying, *My boy Thomas cannot tell a lie, the poor guy. I asked him if his girlfriend Boya had ditched him. Thomas said he didn't love her anymore; this was a lie. His nose bled.* I hold Peter Stan in high esteem, although he really is easy to fool. An important detail came to my mind: Wanga, the honorable clairvoyant, is incapable of lying to anybody; if she happens to be economical with the truth, her nose bleeds. An interesting coincidence, I said to myself, and it was the reason I attracted Boya Bagd to work for me."

"She had worked for you before I met her," Thomas, his bloodstained face an eyesore, growled.

"Don't say another word," Margaret Stan warned her son.

"So, Miss Bagd, you became my son's girlfriend to be able to spy on him? I, the old fool believed you!" the teacher said.

"Yes, that's right," the slim redhead said.

"Then, quite accidentally, you became Ivan Georg's *girlfriend* after he *generated* Healing Trun," Professor Margaret Stan pressed on. "Boya, you have green dots, too. I can see them."

"My dots look as intensely green as yours, Margaret," Boya Bagd retorted.

"John, my son doesn't have green dots. Why did you bring him here?" Peter Stan said. "Why did you beat him?"

"I didn't. He told me a lie and almost bled to death," the police chief answered. "I saved your son's life, Peter."

"And what was the lie he told you?" the teacher asked.

Cole's answer threw further confusion and anxiety into the puzzle.

"For now, I'll only say he spoke about death and the Tall Fellow."

"I am cold," Tony, the boy, whimpered. "I want to go home."

"Sara Eutim can help us," the police chief said, pointing at the ominous cube of thick slush-like liquid.

"I cannot do anything," the beautiful woman objected. It seemed she was unaffected by the cold wind and the dark clouds, plowing black furrows in the festering sky.

"You are being economical with the truth, Sara. So, I will have to make an experiment," the police chief purred. "Each one of you will have to touch the liquid in the stone cube."

"Why?" Professor Gils said. He'd been silent so far, and all eyes were on him.

"You'll see," John Cole answered. "Professor Andrew Gils, you have the honor to be the first one. This will not be dangerous for you."

The professor, his glasses coated with rime, walked slowly to the cube. He bent down, dipped his finger in the slush and rapidly extracted it. Nothing happened. The cube did not react.

"Well?" the chief of Dusk police asked.

Professor Gils did not look up, just stood still, a thin bespectacled man, an unimportant detail in a bleak landscape.

"Boya, it's your turn," the chief of Dusk police ordered.

The dazzlingly pretty woman did not bother to say anything or acknowledge anybody's presence. Impervious to the cold, she calmly walked to the cube and thrust her fist into the liquid. Her face was the epitome of self-assurance, a lovely condescending face. Suddenly the water hissed and leapt to the clouds, the wind dropped, the stones glowed yellowish red. Green dots, thick like a swarm of bees, plunged into her hair and floated above her.

"Trun!" she shouted. The echo hurled her piercing screech to the sky. The muddy liquid in the cube did not budge, but the stones that held it in place became much warmer.

"Like the hot stone walls in the tunnel you took me to, John," the old teacher whispered. "The archaeological excavation on Gagarin Street, the red-hot thorn, the heaps of stones and broken pans …"

Boya Bagd kept her fist in the motionless, threateningly dark mud. It stretched, stock-still like the body of a dead flatworm.

"Try again, Boya" the chief of Dusk police ordered.

The woman thrust her hands into the cube, but the liquid did not respond, its motionless surface black like midnight. The stones were freezing cold again, and again the wind roared heavy with snow and tiny pieces of sharp-edged ice.

"Doctor Georg, it's your turn," the chief of Dusk police said.

Boya walked toward the man with the swollen eyelids and bloodstained face.

"Thomas, you lied to me. I know everything about your mother," she said, and the man flinched. "You are aware lies mean death to you."

"I love you," he said under his breath.

"You've never been smart, Thomas" she said.

Ivan Georg, his face pinched and drawn, walked to the cube, reached out his hand and let it sink into the opaque mud. Nothing happened: no ripples ran through the dark mass, no hissing sounds rent the air, and no Trun shrieks tore the gray ballet of the clouds.

Jacob Harvey, the archaeologist, was the next to disturb the silence and torpor of the cube. The liquid in it remained inert, its depths stalking its invisible prey, treacherous glue-like mass, refusing to register the archaeologist's attempt to stir it into life. John Cole dipped his right hand in the liquid. It remained as silent as the four gaping holes leveled at the valley like muzzles of loaded guns. Professor Margaret Stan left the stone cube oblivious of her presence. The old teacher's fingers shook as he pulled his hand out of the gruel-like mud.

"Cold," he muttered. "Like those slabs in the tunnel under Gagarin Street. John, why are we here?"

The police chief glanced at Philip Mill who held the blind woman in his arms. "It's your turn, Mill. Go to the cube. A stab of pain will shoot through your arm, but you won't cash in your chips."

The liquid remained indifferent to Mill's hand, and the man returned to the blind woman, intent on protecting her from the fierce wind.

"You command us to *sprint to the swimming pool* in strict alphabetical order," said Sara Eutim the famous writer, as she took a step toward the dark, stone cube. "You are not a superior officer, don't forget it, Mr. Cole."

She didn't hesitate, thrust her hands into the gray sludge and waited. Nothing happened. The wind went on whistling, and the blackbird, an unpleasant excrescence of dark stone, towered over the valley, the bottomless wells of its savage eyes searing a path of rancor in the air.

"The liquid roared when you touched it a month ago!" exclaimed Jacob Harvey, the archaeologist. "It was jolted awake and it recoiled from your touch. It thundered. Why is the cube silent now?"

John Cole's face resembled an abandoned house, a face like a coffin that kept death under the lid.

"Can you control the movement of the *chark*'s water, Sara?" he asked. The lovely writer kept silent. "You were quick to demonstrate your ability to your fiancé. Why was that handsome archaeologist so important to you?"

Sara Eutim said nothing.

"Why?" the police chief pressed.

"We have known each other for a long time, John," Sara Eutim said. "Now I believe I've known you much longer than that." The expression on her face revealed nothing. "I have in mind a certain question mark which I am sure you wanted to erase."

"It's your turn," the police chief said as he nodded to Thomas Stan, the thin tall man who sat on the ground, frozen droplets of blood glittering like rubies on his pallid skin.

Thomas Stan failed to make any impression on the gray slush in the cube. Then Tony, the kid who had taken care of the wounded blackbird, stuck his hand into the mixture of sand, melted ice and black dust, and waited. The cube was as silent as an empty mousetrap. Wanga was too weak to walk to the cube. Philip Mill carried her, his feet sinking knee-deep into the snow. He supported her as her fingers stirred the dark liquid. Hardly audible sounds escaped from the slush, the wind momentarily died, and a narrow patch of blue-white sky shone above the stark silhouette of the mountain slope pitted by the four murky holes.

"Come here!" the blind woman whispered. "Come here, Trun."

The stones glowed. Then the wind blew again, the winter returned and blazed a silver trail of frost around the cube.

"I'm cold," Tony groaned.

"She's freezing," Philip Mill said, holding Wanga close to his chest.

John Cole rushed to the cube, dipped his right hand into the liquid, thick and dark like pitch. The stones became scorching hot, the dark holes spewed brown smoke, the cliffs rang, but the liquid was dead and flat in its stone trap. A stream of tiny green beads shone on the edge of the cube and vanished in a flash. No sounds of Trun severed the air, the ice that had tied the valley in its icy knot turned into a dozen rivulets, which dug and raked the ground as green creeping plants sprouted from the crevices in the rocks. The clouds broke, the sky climbed to its proper place, postcard blue for a couple of seconds, the wind came back, warm and balmy, impatient to ease the pain and dispel fears. The four dark holes growled and tolled, the sun shone, and it was warm. The green plants that shot and budded among the stones were as hard as slashing spikes.

"Who are you, John Cole?" Professor Margaret Stan asked.

The chief of Dusk police drew his hand out of the dark liquid. The mountain devoured the wild streams, the black stone of the statue crushed the whirlwinds, and silence, beautiful and fragile like a toddler's smile, enveloped the cube.

"You tell me the truth about your son, Margaret Stan," the chief of Dusk police barked. "And perhaps I'll let you know who I am."

Chapter Forty-One

They all sat on the warm stones, Philip Mill holding Wanga's hand, Margaret Stan whispering something to her husband Peter who looked small and worn out, their son Thomas kept silent, his bloodstained face in a mess, his eyes riveted on Boya Bagd. Jacob Harvey, the archaeologist, sat down next to Sara Eutim and rested his head on her shoulder. Professor Andrew Gils watched Sara. He looked lost and vulnerable, absurd in his overcoat immaculately neat in spite of the storm. Tony was no longer cold. The kid had taken off his coat and sat so close to his teacher that their shadows were one formless black splotch. Ivan Georg leaned over the cube and studied the slush in it.

"I have not betrayed you, Ivan," Boya Bagd said. "I want you to know this."

"Your betrayal is of no consequence now," the police chief remarked. "You aborted your mission, Boya, and I'll pay you for it. I wanted you to bring them all here, in the shadow of Deaf Crags to face the Trun Chark."

He stood close to the *chark,* orange and golden thorns at his feet, bottomless blue sky above his head, the wind a gentle touch on the face and hands. They had taken off their hats and coats. The piercing eyes of the blackbird watched them and hated them.

"You cannot hurt me, Cole," the red-haired belle said.

"About a year ago," John Cole began, totally ignoring her. "Numerous scholarly articles on Samodivas, the mystic creatures of Bulgarian folk songs and fairy tales, were published in the regional magazines coming out in Dusk District. Four respected scholars authored groundbreaking pieces: Mr. Philip Mill, a journalist I hold in high esteem. He gave up his star career and moved in with Wanga, her hut on Bare Mountain becoming their safe haven. Boya Bagd, my professional associate, is another renowned scholar. I also read a series of intriguing monographs by Sara Eutim. A short essay, quite controversial and radical, by Mr. Jacob Harvey, attracted public attention. These four authors are with us now. In her article 'Samodivas in Bulgarian Folklore,' Boya Bagd argues that the mythical creatures possess iridescent *green caps,* a symbol of their power. Any man can control a Samodiva if only he captures her green cap. Most of you have green dots, swarming around your heads. Wanga," the police chief turned to the blind woman. "You told Philip Mill that a man who has green dots is in fact a Samodiva's *driver;* i.e., he takes the Samodiva to places where she wants to go. Is that correct?"

"It is," Wanga's small voice was a short-lived spark in the air. "Philip has betrayed me. You pay him, and he tells you everything we talk about."

"No!" the tall journalist said. "This is a lie."

"Philip would do anything for money," Sara Eutim remarked.

"Wanga, how come you are able to *see* events that will take place in the future?"

John Cole said. "And how come you can tell what happened in the past to persons you don't know?"

"Past and future do not exist," the prophetess spoke slowly, with difficulty. "I see the green dots in the child and the green dots in the old man, and I see the green dots of the man I am talking to now."

"It's not clear!" the chief of Dusk police interrupted her. "If you, Wanga, can see someone's green dots, or shall I say their green cap, do you think you can control them? The legend goes that you can control a Samodiva if you steal her green cap."

"Death takes everybody's green dots away," the blind woman said. "And every time I can see death approaching ..." she turned around to face Sara Eutim and Professor Margaret Stan but said nothing more.

John Cole looked at Sara Eutim as he said, "Mr. Mill wrote an article on the Dirty Days, the period 15 December–6 January. He asserts that the locals of the Dusk Region believed that throughout the Dirty Days men should not leave their homes because the evil spirits of Samodivas would kill anybody in the open. On 5 January, Doctor Ivan Georg was operated on. On 6 January, the last of the Dirty Days, he produced Healing Trun that cured terminally ill patients. Doctor Georg recuperated completely after the operation with the exception, well, of his face. I asked him how he came to generate the utterly maddening Trun mayhem, and he said he didn't know," the chief of Dusk police waited, a forced smile on his face. "I'm sure there is something you have not spoken of to anyone so far, Doctor Georg?"

"No," was the doctor's answer.

"As you wish," John Cole said. "The truth will out, Doctor Georg," John Cole glanced at Boya Bagd. "In her article, 'Samodiva Myths in Dusk Region,' my collaborator Ms. Bagd focuses on the notorious saying: *A Samodiva is a healer and a murderer.* In this framework, please note that it was Professor Margaret Stan who produced Killing Trun."

"Boya Bagd must have planted the deadly Trun in my computer," Professor Margaret said. "I believe you. Mr. Cole provided her with it and then she *befriended* my son Thomas."

"I'd take this with a pinch of salt," the chief of Dusk police said. "So, we have Healing Trun and Killing Trun; on the other hand, Ms. Boya Bagd points out that a Samodiva cures you of a deadly disease or kills you if she so chooses. A very interesting remark, isn't it?"

"I don't want to know anything related to Trun," Thomas Stan said.

"What you want or don't want is hardly of any consequence," the chief of Dusk police pointed out.

"Then why did you order your henchman Boya Bagd to poke around in my apartment?" Thomas Stan's red-rimmed eyes gleamed. "It was a miracle I survived the car accident she was involved in. Boya and that arrogant man," Thomas Stan pointed to Philip Mill. "If I am of no consequence, why did they drag me here, Cole?"

"If you haven't already guessed, you are not worth my while," the police chief cleared his throat. "One aspect I am particularly interested in..."

"Idiot," Thomas Stan gritted his teeth.

John Cole took no notice of him. His eyes flitted from face to face. The police chief was a big man with a dimple in his meticulously shaved chin. "The green dots phenomenon, or as Ms. Sara Eutim puts it, the *Samodiva case* of the fabled creatures neglected and forgotten for centuries, spurred up keen interest. I think it is more than sheer coincidence that scientists concentrated on that narrow topic. Then the odd blackbirds came out of nowhere," the police chief went on. "It was Tony, that boy over here, who injured one of them. The most distinctive feature of these mute, feathered songsters is their enormous weight. They perched on the asphalt in the schoolyard in Dusk and dug a deep hole in it. Now, I'd like to draw your attention to the four black holes above our heads. Peter Stan, my good old friend, saw the cavity the birds carved in the schoolyard. Peter, could you tell us more about it?"

"First, you've never been my friend, Mr. Cole," the teacher said. "Second, the crater-like cavities here in Deaf Crags resemble the hole the blackbirds dug in the schoolyard."

"You are my friend, Peter. You told me that sick animals seemed to be attracted to that hole. The blackbirds made no noise, you said, and this seems hardly possible, bearing in mind their weight. What leaps to mind is that these birds do not belong to our region, or should I say, to our world. Where do they belong? Who sent them to us?"

The chief of Dusk police stole a glance at the enormous blackbird on the mountaintop that loomed dark and foreboding over the stone cube.

"I can see the little sick fair-haired girl who visited me with her parents," Wanga's voice stirred the deaf air. "I know you," the blind woman went on. "You are that little girl. Don't kill your brother! Don't, or he will take you to a place that will be the end of you."

All eyes were on the blind woman.

"What do you mean, Wanga?" John Cole breathed. "Who is that girl?"

Philip Mill whispered in Wanga's ear. "Are you in pain, my dearest? Forget about that girl."

"Her parents brought her to me a couple of months ago, remember? She is that girl. Philip. You used to love her. You loved that woman … It is strange. Her green dots lead nowhere … I wonder … I wonder who that woman is. I don't know."

"I am totally confused," Jacob Harvey, the archaeologist said. "How come a human being is a little fair-haired girl and a woman at one and the same time?" He addressed his question to no one in particular.

"Judging by the way the clairvoyant speaks, this enigmatic lady is quite undisciplined."

Philip Mill, handsome in spite of his shabby coat and clumpy shoes, spoke first, "Wanga speaks about Sara Eutim. The famous Samodiva writer visited our hut with many other unfortunate souls. I heard Wanga tell her, *no,* shout to her, *Don't kill your brother!* I saw the ill, fair-haired girl."

"Sara Eutim is your ex-fiancée, Philip, isn't she?" the chief of Dusk police cut in.

"Yes. Now she means nothing to me," Philip Mill said. "I am worried about Wanga. She's ill, very ill."

"Wanga said she could see Sara the woman and Sara the child at the same time," Professor Andrew Gils said. He rarely spoke and as always, his words commanded attention. "I remember Ms. Eutim as a little fair-haired girl who told me fairy tales. She was the only childhood friend I had, a friend who had green dots in her hair and lived in the house opposite ours on Gagarin Street."

"Were you engaged to this man as well, Sara!" Jacob the archaeologist muttered, staring at his boots. "So, both Sara and Professor Gils lived in houses on Gagarin Street," he went on. "They both have green dots. Trun Shrine our team discovered was underneath a square near Gagarin Street as well," the archaeologist cleared his throat, his eyes on Sara Eutim. "Whoever you are, Sara, I love you!" He took a deep breath as he unexpectedly turned to face the tall, thin woman, sitting by Peter Stan. "Professor Stan, I still disagree with your views on the translation of the Old Bulgarian song of the Trun Chark. However, an idea has just crossed my mind."

"Yes?" Professor Margaret Stan said.

"The lyrics to the Old Bulgarian song were given to me by a man who said he was Priest Dimo," the archaeologist went on. "A very gentle soft-spoken man ... now it transpires this soft-spoken man is Mr. Cole, the chief of Dusk police. I think that the chief of Dusk police had carefully planned his steps," the archaeologist swallowed hard as he turned to Professor Stan. "Professor Margaret Stan discovered a rhythmical repetition of the number *three* in the song: three ordinary people, three who are talented, and three Samodivas ... I, too, noticed this persistent recurrence of the number three, but I thought it had a function and purpose: to impart a particular musical quality to the verse."

"What are you driving at, young man?" Peter Stan asked.

The sun shone in a clear blue sky, a boat of gold above their heads. The winter blizzard struck no more, no ice weighed the rocks down and the gray slush waited in its stone prison as quiet as a new coffin.

"The Trun Chark song says there are different types of human beings on our planet," Professor Margaret Stan began. "The Ordinary Ones shout the name of the disease they suffer from into a pan, carry the pan to the Trun Chark and miraculously recuperate. Likewise, they shout the name of the person they hate at a stone, throw the stone at the *chark,* as a result of which they are no longer dogged by ill fortune. A Bulgarian proverb is relevant here: *The evil eye sleeps only if you cover it with a stone.*"

Professor Stan glanced at the police chief. "Now, at Deaf Crags, two heaps are in front of the Trun Chark: one of pans, the other of stones. Similar heaps of pans and stones were found—and Jacob Harvey can confirm that what I say is true—in the underground Trun Shrine on Gagarin Street." Professor Stan went on, her eyes fastened on the famous writer. "In her in-depth article on the green-dots phenomenon, Ms. Eutim describes two piles, one of pans, the other of stones, in front of Wanga's hut. A minor detail in the song caught my eye: the phrase *Ordinary Ones* is invariably followed by the number three."

"So, you mean, Professor Stan, that the locations you've just enumerated are some sort of devices, transforming pain into good health and hatred into good fortune?" Professor Gils asked, his eyes finally interested behind the thick glasses.

"I admit a similar thought crossed my mind," Margaret Stan said thoughtfully. "Another type of human being described in the Trun Chark song are the Talented Ones. Trun Shrine cannot cure them, and they cannot get rid of hatred by shouting at a stone the name of the person who has mistreated them." Margaret Stan smiled wanly. "The Talented Ones do not need shrines or *charks* to ease the pain they go through. A talented person is able to transform pain into a superb *Ode to Joy* as Beethoven did, sick and miserable though he was. The number three appeared in the song every time the phrase *Talented Ones* was used."

"Excellent, Margaret," the chief of Dusk police said. "But I still don't understand what you are driving at."

"We'll get there, Mr. Cole," Margaret Stan said. "The Trun Chark song says that the Marked Ones are human beings who, like most of us present here, have green dots. Again, the phrase Marked Ones is always followed by the number three. In the article by Philip Mill, 'The Green-Eyed Samodivas,' I stumbled upon a sentence that I found particularly confusing. Mr. Mill quotes one of Wanga's oracular messages: *Samodivas are our last chance.* I asked myself: Why does Wanga say so?"

"Samodivas are paths to places we cannot reach," the blind woman said, her voice fading as it touched the crags.

Margaret Stan's smile was small, almost no smile at all. "Suppose the Samodivas of the folklore *are* the green dots enveloping our heads," she said. "Only the Marked Ones of all human beings can see these green dots. I assume the Samodivas are a road to an important place. Wanga can *see* this *road* and so she's able to *predict* the future."

"I didn't have green dots," Ivan Georg, very quiet so far, objected. "I got them after my brain surgery. It was after the serious surgical intervention that I became able to see the persons with green dots, i.e., the Marked Ones."

John Cole, his hands balled into fists, watched him closely.

"I didn't have green dots either," Professor Margaret Stan said. "I obtained them after I listened to Healing and Killing Trun that sounded simultaneously. It was a painful experience. I was and still am able to see other people's green dots. With green dots around my head, Killing Trun does not affect me. In my little experiment, I used Killing Trun. Some among us, who had declared they didn't have green dots, did not shout with pain. This leads me to believe that they too are in possession of the green halo. These persons are: Jacob Harvey, the archaeologist, and Tony, the boy who discovered the heavy, quiet blackbirds." Professor Stan paused, squinting at the imposing statue of the blackbird, cleared her throat, and went on, "On the other hand, Ms. Eutim shouted in pain, although I could clearly see *her* green dots. Did she feign sickness and suffering? By the way, her dots have miraculously disappeared."

Sara Eutim waited calmly as heads turned to the archaeologist and to Tony, the kid.

"Margaret," the teacher scrambled to his feet. "The series of pictures on the wall you wanted me to erase! The ones in your room, you know them. The first one was Tony's portrait. The second was an empty frame with a question mark in it. The third one was John Cole's photo. Margaret, what if Jacob Harvey's portrait is to take the place of the question mark. Tony, Jacob Harvey, John Cole .... But what could connect them? They don't have anything in common."

"John Cole must tell us about it," Margaret Stan said stonily.

John Cole kept silent, the veins on his forehead protruding and blue like a fresh bruise.

"The Trun Chark song describes a fourth category of human beings, the New Ones, as individuals incapable of lying," Professor Margaret Stan spoke firmly and slowly. "Without exception, the number three always follows the phrase *New Ones*. If a New One lies to anybody, he or she bleeds to death. I believe there are two New Ones among us now," the Professor said. "My son Thomas is one of them. I think Boya, his ex-girlfriend, has discovered this fact. It is not difficult to establish that Thomas cannot lie to anybody. My son has no green dots and is now, in my view, of special interest. When Wanga, the clairvoyant, tells a lie, she bleeds just like my son does. But she herself has green dots and can see the green dots in children, adults and people advanced in years."

The holes carved in rock stared at the thick shady forest. Immutable and savage, they exuded cold air, and the gigantic statue of the blackbird seemed to shudder against the deaf infinity of the sky. The two heaps, the bigger one of old pans, the smaller of stones, towered like ruins of an ancient fortress.

"Then I thought *why?* Why is the number three repeated so often in the Trun Chark song?" Professor Stan spoke softly and slowly. "There had to be some reason behind this. I thought about the Christian doctrine of the Holy Trinity, the Father, the Son, and the Holy Spirit. And, I quote, God said: *Let us make man in our image, in our likeness.* What if each human being is a trio, a trinity of three persons of different ages: a child, an adult, and an old person?" Professor Margaret Stan's words sounded as even as the surface of an operating table. "Then I thought, perhaps a man's triad, or trio is an entity consisting of a child, an adult, and an old man, each one capable of existing at one and the same time i.e., in parallel with and independently of the other two. If this is true, the choices a human being faces are practically unlimited."

"This sounds highly improbable," John Cole said.

"Then why has Ms. Sara Eutim left this series of pictures on the wall of the house I bought from her? Why didn't she remove the empty frame and the big question mark in the middle of it?" Professor Margaret Stan ignored Sara Eutim's expressionless face, its beauty a mountain of ice, the eyes as cold as windswept ridges.

"I am fond of photographs," Sara Eutim said firmly. "Of question marks too." She slowly walked to the stone cube and dipped her pinkie into the turbid liquid. The slush turned blue, then black, then rippled, jumped and was flat again. "The Samodiva's milk churns only when a Samodiva touches it," she said. "This is the most famous line of a famous Old Bulgarian song." Sara's smile fled to the horizon that was as black as the odd substance in the cube. The heap of old pans chimed, the pile of stones tolled as she added, "You saw that the Samodiva's milk hissed and glowed only after three people touched it: the chief of Dusk police, this secretive lady Boya Bagd and me. It's a wicked little riddle I offer you, and it is up to you to arrive at the right conclusion."

"Perhaps Ms. Eutim's goal is to attract our attention to the so-called Samodivas in order to divert it away from something much more important," Professor Margaret Stan said. "Like, for example, the Trun Chark song. Let us study its last stanza. *You, who find everyone, are always alone. No children, no cats, and no dogs live in your house. You are feared and revered, but you must go on alone, or you will be no more.* End of quote. A very interesting detail here," Professor Margaret Stan's voice dropped, or was it the light breeze that gave her words a twist? "The pronoun *you* in the last stanza is always followed by the number *two*. Jacob Harvey has also translated the Trun Chark song and he will tell you that in this case the use of the number two has nothing to do with the rhythm or the structure of the sentences."

"This is correct," the archaeologist said. "I cannot explain why in this case the number two is used. The stanza is about somebody that finds everyone but is always alone. In the other stanzas, three is the number regularly repeated after the phrases *Ordinary Ones, Marked Ones, Talented Ones,* and *New Ones.*"

"And who is always alone, although he finds everyone else?" Peter Stan asked. "I can't imagine who this may be, a sleuth, a usurer or what?"

The blackbird, its enormous wings spread like dark thunderclouds, its eyes dead under the deep stalking sky, stared, spurning everything and everybody in sight.

"It's a fairy tale my mother told me, and it gave me the fright of my life," Tony, leaning on his old teacher's arm, said hesitantly. "I know who this one is. He finds everyone. I could not sleep at night and I hated this tale. I was scared he was after me. I saw his hands, clutching at my throat. He is Death. Everybody hates him …" The boy swallowed hard. "It is the only tale mom told me. I know what death is like. This stone blackbird over there is not like my Ben. Ben loved me. This one hates me."

"Deaf Crags is Death's home," Boya Bagd said.

"The One who catches everybody and is always empty-handed," Thomas, Margaret Stan's son, spoke briefly as he rubbed his bloodstained chin. "Boya, you once told me a tale, too. It was about a path that found every living soul, yet it was always deserted. A horrible tale … I knew it was the path of death."

Peter Stan hobbled across the patch of land to his son, but the young man turned his back on him.

"Somebody dug four deep holes in the black rock of Deaf Crags. Somebody dug a shaft and built Trun Shrine underneath Gagarin Street," the chief of Dusk police said, his eyes lingering on Boya Bagd. "The Trun Chark song is about four groups of human beings: the Ordinary Ones, the Talented Ones, and the Marked Ones who have green dots swarming around their heads. It happens that both Sara Eutim and Professor Andrew Gils lived in houses on Gagarin Street near Trun Shrine," the chief of Dusk police licked his dry lips. "Then the songs tell us about the New Ones who cannot lie." He cleared his throat and almost spat the words out. "The one who finds everybody … does he have green dots?"

"Every man or woman has green dots. I can see them," Wanga, the blind woman, breathed. "I have seen these greenish flames since I was two years old."

"There is a clear connection between the green dots and Killing Trun," Professor Margaret Stan began thoughtfully. "The individuals who have green dots—for the time being, I am not inclined to believe that every human being has green dots as Wanga said …”

"Wanga will die if she lies to anyone," Philip Mill said emphatically. "She cannot lie."

"In this case, I have in mind only the individuals in possession of green dots I have met," Professor Margaret Stan said. "They seem to convincingly survive Killing Trun and are practically unaffected by its shrieking sounds." Professor Stan studied Boya Bagd's magnificent face. "I had acquired green dots, and Killing Trun did not harm me. So, I had an idea to compare the characteristics of Healing Trun and its killing counterpart." Professor Margaret Stan's eyes glowed, firm and sharp. "And I think, Mr. Cole, that I know why you gathered us all here."

"I'm intensely curious to know more about this, Margaret," the chief of Dusk police retorted. "Maybe I was a fool to give up on you. I should have eloped with you under my friend Peter's nose."

The teacher balled his hands into fists.

"It's okay, Peter," Margaret Stan said to her husband as she softly pressed his temples with her fingertips. "It's okay, *mon vieux.*"

"You used to call me *mon vieux,* Margaret," John Cole said. "I taught you to."

"This remark is in bad taste and is irrelevant to our discussion," Professor Margaret Stan said. "As I mentioned, I have compared the characteristic features of Healing and Killing Trun, and I stumbled on a striking difference between them. In Healing Trun, the sound waves outline four apparent peaks of equal height. In Killing Trun, the number of the peaks is not four. There are *five* peaks. The last one of them that I dubbed the apex is of great magnitude."

Silence fell over the group of people who watched as Professor Margaret Stan sat down by her husband.

"Then this fifth peak, the apex, in Killing Trun is the factor that causes death?" Jacob Harvey's voice sounded deep and eager as it dissolved in the shadow of the blackbird's outstretched wings.

Chapter Forty-Two

The sun, bright like a red-hot coin in the deep blue pocket of the sky, shone on their faces, their shadows creeping smudges on the rocks. Silence hung over the turbid liquid in the stone cube, making it look darker.

"I cannot understand," a strong voice rose, startling the boy. The old teacher patted him on the shoulder, and Tony relaxed. The journalist Philip Mill paused as he took the blind prophetess by the hand. "Wanga, you said something that sounded strange to me. It was *Everybody has green dots.* Perhaps you made a mistake."

"Every human being has green dots," Wanga said.

"Then why, Wanga, you can see them, and I cannot? Why can John Cole see the dots, and other guys cannot?" Philip Mill asked, defiantly staring at the police chief.

"Mr. Mill, why do you think Sir Isaac Newton was a genius and his gardener was not?" Sara Eutim remarked.

"I can see them in everyone," the blind woman said. "Very rarely do I encounter a human being devoid of green dots. He a sad man and she is a miserable woman."

"No!" the police chief objected. "This is impossible."

"It is possible," Wanga said. "There is someone among us who has lost her green dots."

"Among us?" John Cole exclaimed. "And who is that?"

For a while, Wanga was silent, her chin resting in her cupped hand. "She will let you know, if she wants to," the blind woman said finally.

Professor Margaret Stan met John Cole's eyes first. Sara Eutim's beautiful face was an impenetrable night, and in the middle of the group, Boya Bagd sat, red-haired, slim and mysterious like murky liquid in the stone cube.

"There is a way to find out," the police chief said as he turned to the archaeologist. "You wrote an article, 'Samodiva culture: an attempt at finding traces of an ancient civilization.' It was published in *Archaeology*, Volume XXI, 2020."

The archaeologist said nothing.

"Mr. Harvey, your colleagues thought that your article was a joke, and perhaps it was intended to be one," the chief of Dusk police went on. "The publication date of Volume XXI was 1 April 2020; however, the tone of your research paper was serious and humorless. You argue that Samodivas are an advanced civilization. They inhabit human beings, the human subconscious mind to be precise, and thrive on men's dreams. You believe that the Samodivas are perceived as a series or a streak of green dots, and you give details of your interview with Wanga to the readers. She, in your opinion, can see these green dots."

The archaeologist shifted uncomfortably from one foot to another.

"Sara Eutim asked if it was you who wrote the article, and you answered in the negative." John Cole said. "Why did you lie to her, Mr. Harvey?"

The archaeologist shrugged his shoulders. "The publication of my essay stirred up serious unrest," he said. "Considering the fact you tried to pass as Priest Dimo and you foisted the 'Old Bulgarian' Trun Chark song on me, I think that what I've written sounds idiotic."

"But the Trun Chark exists, doesn't it?" the police chief said. "There are four holes in the mountain face. The Trun Chark song is authentic. On the other hand, you are right. Most of what you have written sounds idiotic, Mr. Harvey."

"I don't have green dots and you, Mr. Cole, dragged me here against my will," the young archaeologist pointed out calmly. "I think I am quite valuable to your cause whatever it might be. You needed me and you captured me."

"You have green dots, Mr. Harvey," Professor Andrew Gils pronounced the words with care, yet they had the effect of bullets ricocheting off the crags. "When Professor Stan let us listen to Killing Trun, you did not suffer. I think you are trying to mislead us one more time. Why don't you tell us more about your pioneering research on Samodiva culture?"

Crisp wind rippled the dark liquid in the cube. The four gaping holes exuded cold humid vapor that soared to the sky and sank into its blue infinity. The archaeologist jumped to his feet.

"Wanga!" he said, his voice going up. "You told me *they live in us,* didn't you? You told me they use us as drivers. We, the human beings, drive *them* where *they* want to go. And you see them as green dots."

The blind woman's face looked thinner, a yellowish, transparent plastic cup.

"Leave her alone. She's sick!" Philip Mill shouted.

"I'm not sick," the woman's weak voice cut him short. "I will tell you the truth."

"You think you know the truth?" Sara Eutim said.

The liquid in the cube simmered, welled up, sizzled, hissed, and the vapors spewing out of the four holes turned into formless gray clouds.

"I know the truth," Wanga said. "I remember you and I know who you are," her voice broke. She stiffened. "Don't kill your brother," she breathed. "It will be the end of you."

Sara Eutim frowned, "Aren't you sick and tired of reiterating this nonsense?" she asked.

"The fair-haired girl looks so much like you, the sweet little thing," the seer said.

Sara Eutim shrugged, an ironic smile flickering across her lips. Wanga turned her blind eyes to face her. "I can see them," she gasped. "I can feel them ... They are after our pain and hate." The veins on her forehead throbbed, her cheeks were red and her chin quivered. "That is why I collect the pans that conceal disease and pain. I collect stones poisoned by malice. I try to attract *them* and trick *them* into leaving the poor souls alone ... I cannot stand it when men suffer," her words broke into shards of agony. "I cannot stand it when children writhe in pain."

Peter Stan, the old teacher, squirmed uncomfortably as he spoke, "Trun Shrine you took me to, John ... remember? The archaeological excavation on Gagarin Street, the shaft with the two chambers ... the old earthenware pans and the stones ..." Blood dripped from the tiny, cracked sores at the corners of Peter Stan's mouth. "Is Trun Shrine a place that captures disease and hate? Is the shrine meant to attract *them,* whoever they are, the ones who thrive on evil?"

The chief of Dusk police opened his mouth to say something, but the archaeologist Jacob Harvey spoke first, "The places where the Samodivas spend the winter are dark nooks near lakes, and blackbirds guard them."

"What was this, Jacob?" Professor Margaret Stan asked.

"It's a line from an Old Bulgarian song," the archaeologist answered. "The song describes the Samodivas' path to their home near Trun Chark. Death drinks Samodiva's milk for the first time in December, and after that the Dirty Days begin."

"15 December–6 January," Professor Margaret Stan echoed.

"Let me repeat that on 5 January, Ivan was operated on," the immaculately clean Professor Andrew Gils said. "On 6 January, he produced Healing Trun," Gils paused, cleaned a speck of dust from his sleeve and added slowly, "And it is 6 January today, the last of the Dirty Days."

It was quiet when Ivan Georg, his eyes closed, said, "Maybe Wanga tried to build her own Trun shrine to ease the sufferers' pain."

The liquid in the stone cube looked as thick as asphalt. It was motionless, black, and silent like a predator on the prowl. The four glowering holes were silent, too. The blackbird's dark wings seemed to reel against the bitter depth of the sky.

"Jacob Harvey," the chief of Dusk police began as he came up to the archaeologist. "Why did you lie to Sara Eutim that you had not written the article on the Samodiva civilization? You maintain the Samodivas do not live on a distant planet. You argue they inhabit the thoughts of human beings."

"It was a joke," the archaeologist declared. He shook his head, spread his arms and blurted out, "The Old Bulgarian song you gave me, Mr. Cole, says that at Trun Chark, only a *very special* Samodiva can make the Samodiva's milk churn. I took somebody to Trun Chark and she made the water churn. She did it."

Chapter Forty-Three

"The series of three pictures on the wall in my room was a trap," Professor Margaret Stan said. "The first was Tony's picture and Tony is one of my husband's students. I had scrawled a big question mark in the middle of the blank frame, and now I know the man behind the question mark—the young archaeologist Jacob Harvey. Number 3 was John Cole's portrait. Now I know what connects these three human beings."

The chief of Dusk police laughed, Jacob Harvey shrugged and Tony, startled, glanced at his teacher.

"Let me start with Tony," Professor Margaret Stan went on. "Tony writes an essay on the mute *feathered songsters*. An important detail: his bird Ben *does not eat anything,* no crumbs, no bread, no wheat grains. Ben seems to *kill his mother's pain and make her anger fade.*"

"But she destroyed him!" the boy cried out as he pointed at the thin blonde woman. "She is evil. I kept some of Ben's iron feathers and I still keep them. My mom loves me. She does not shout at me and threw out that man …"

Professor Andrew Gils raised his arm. "We have proved that a feather produces the same effect as the flock of heavy and clumsy birds," he said. "A little boy can carry a feather on him like a talisman." He turned to the police chief. "The following is also true: a slab or a pebble, no matter how big, from Trun Shrine had the same lethal effect on the team members," he paused as he glanced at Boya Bagd. "You destroyed the birds that fought and cured killer diseases, Ms. Bagd. This could only mean one thing: you cater for pain and death fused as a single entity, and I can see that you work for John Cole."

"Mr. Cole could elaborate on your thought-provoking hypothesis," Boya Bagd said with a smile. "I am sure he will oblige."

"I know Boya!" Ivan Georg said, his face darkening with anger. "Boya is a wonderful person, an experienced researcher, a gentle and caring soul."

Margaret Stan's son fidgeted, his eyelids swollen, smudges of mud on his forehead.

"I know her, too," Thomas said dryly, a crust of dried blood on his cheeks and neck. "She is a mean liar."

"Boya Bagd planted Killing Trun in my computer. Now I hope she'd be so kind to explain why she fulfilled this task," Professor Margaret Stan said.

"I hate repeating myself," the beauty responded unperturbed. "Mr. John Cole has all the answers. I am under orders and I do what I am told."

The chief of Dusk police looked her full in the face. "I am positive you conceal something from us, Boya," he said. "And I am sure that your secret has to do with the period of time when Doctor Ivan Georg produced Healing Trun. In my view, Doctor Ivan Georg also conceals something from us all."

"You captured and dragged us all here," Peter Stan interrupted him. "I've known you for years, John. I am sure you will profit from our plight."

"Important facts are still a mystery to me," the chief of Dusk police began. "The trap of Healing Trun … My dearest friend Margaret, who used to be my wife for a very short time—an industrious scientific drudge, I grant her that, maybe not too intelligent, aren't you, Margaret?—perhaps she already knows. Then Sara Eutim, the brilliant writer and man-eater, my fiancée for a couple of weeks, and Jacob Harvey's fiancée at present— she positively knows. My associate Boya Bagd, a reticent lady, Thomas Stan's ex, and as her report goes, Ivan Georg's girlfriend today; even she might have guessed why I gathered you all on 6 January, the last of the Dirty Days, at Trun Chark, the place where the Samodivas spend the gloomy winter months. Another insignificant detail, Doctor Ivan Georg underwent brain surgery on 6 January, Boya Bagd strongly insisting the team should by no means postpone the surgical intervention. Am I right, Professor Gils?"

The quiet, clean man in an immaculately ironed dark-blue shirt nodded his head. "Now that you ask me, I remember clearly. Yes. Ms. Bagd was adamant that we could not reschedule this surgical case. She personally asked me to operate on Dr. Georg. I remember she said Ivan was her boyfriend."

Boya Bagd, beautiful beyond description, said, "Yes, Ivan is my best friend."

"In January this year," Professor Margaret Stan began, her cutting voice as dark as the liquid in the stone cube. "In January, Boya Bagd was engaged to be married to my son Thomas."

The silence lasted for about a couple of minutes. Then John Cole's voice whizzed with the force of a gunshot. "Three remarkable women Margaret Stan, Sara Eutim, and Boya Bagd have one thing in common. They all have green dots." The chief of Dusk police took a step towards Jacob Harvey. "So, young man, you've stumbled on a number of legends in the Dusk region. If we cut all superfluous details, everything boils down to a simple fact: one of the Samodivas is Death." John Cole cleared his throat and almost whispered to Ivan Georg, "Doctor Georg, at the time I sent the scary email to you and Professor Andrew Gils, I still hoped I wouldn't have to drag you all here, to Trun Chark."

"The email said I'd be the first one to get killed," Dr. Ivan Georg said. "I am waiting for your explanation, Mr. Cole."

"You'll have it after you tell me what happened in your hospital room and you produced Healing Trun, Dr. Georg."

"I have nothing to tell you," Ivan Georg said.

"Then you'll wait a long time for my explanation," the police chief declared. "And ..."

"I suppose you are right that I am not too clever, Mr. Cole," Professor Margaret Stan said. "I was speaking about a triad i.e., a trio of persons who might be the key to solving the mystery as to why we are kept prisoners here. Along this line of thinking, the question, does Mr. Cole intend to eliminate us? is a logical one. I think he does, but this won't be too sensible of him."

No one said anything; the black mud in the stone cube seemed to watch, patient like a murderer's steps.

Margaret Stan went on, "In my view, Tony, the first one who saw the blackbirds, is number one in our trinity or shall I call it the *Trio of Death,* John?" the police chief waited. "Who hides behind that big question mark in the blank picture frame on the wall of my room?" she added as she met Jacob Harvey's gaze. "Mr. Harvey gave me the original Old Bulgarian Trun Chark song dedicated to the four black holes in the mountain face. It transpires Mr. Harvey has procured the manuscript of the song lyrics from Priest Dimo." Margaret paused, a mocking smile on her face. "The priest is John Cole, the chief of Dusk police. Jacob Harvey translates the song with admirable precision; however, he fails to notice the repetition of the number *three* in the first four stanzas, and the numerous times the number *two* surfaces in the *last, fifth stanza.* I don't believe that a serious researcher would overlook these important details."

Margaret Stan was not smiling when she said, "It was Jacob Harvey who first wrote about the Samodiva civilization." She squared her shoulders and spoke evenly, her voice a cold abandoned house. "In Mr. Harvey's opinion, the Samodiva civilization inhabits human beings. The archaeologist admitted he had taken Sara Eutim to the Trun Chark and had made her touch the liquid, i.e., the Samodiva's milk. Why did he do that? My assumption is he attempted to check on her, but why? An intriguing tidbit of news about the young archaeologist is the article he published in the anthology *Rites and Lies: The Samodiva Myth.* The piece highlights a legend highly popular in the Dusk region. The natives of Dusk still believe that the most important and beautiful Samodiva is Death. It's not clear if this detail means anything at all."

"Your words scare me," the chief of Dusk police remarked. "I remember that every time you say *It's not clear,* you have a few tricks up your sleeve."

The mountains in the distance were covered with snow, while the patch of flat land surrounding the stone cube basked in the glorious sun. The sky above the wind-swept slopes was overcast, ominous; not a cloud marred the azure tranquility of its depth above the dark holes, the four festering sores of the *chark.*

"You should be frightened, Mr. Cole," Professor Margaret Stan said. "You dragged us, men and women having green dots, to the Trun Chark. You dropped Doctor Ivan Georg an email, asserting that *creatures* in possession of *green halos* were Samodivas. Jacob Harvey mulls over the idea that the most beautiful Samodiva is Death. Who is Jacob Harvey, I asked myself. Who peeks behind the question mark in my room?"

"Samodivas are our last chance," the blind seer whispered. She didn't say anything more, just sat there, her head on Philip Mill's shoulder, her unseeing eyes on the indifferent faraway blue of the sky.

"Why should the critters with green dots be our last chance?" the teacher Peter Stan asked. "This makes no sense. The Samodiva myths are pure fiction. The women with green dots among us are real."

Philip Mill smiled. Sara Eutim chuckled.

"You ask weird questions, Professor Stan," Ivan Georg said. He spoke like a man who saw something no one else could see. "Professor Gils read to me something I cannot forget. It was an excerpt from ancient Dusk myths. I quote: *Samodivas' green eyes are a door to another world.* Before my brain surgery, I thought I was going to die. Boya Bagd came to see me as I lay dying. She brought me a book I've never read. The one thing I remember about it is the sentence on its front cover printed in big yellow letters: *Accept death as a door to a world you'll love.*"

He kept silent for a while, looking at Boya, as if there was no one else at Trun Chark.

"It might mean that if one of the Samodivas is Death, then she is that door. And maybe the Samodiva as death is the last chance to visit that world."

"I brought you that book, Ivan," Boya Bagd said. "I wanted you to calm down."

"You worked for John Cole," the teacher Peter Stan remarked. "Coincidences do not exist as far as John Cole is concerned. He ordered you to bring the book, didn't he?"

"No," Boya said calmly as the black statue above their heads.

Professor Andrew Gils raised his hand again, the pale skin of his wrist an absurd detail amid the wasteland of snow.

"Ivan, do you mean that death is the bridge, or shall I call it the mechanism, which transfers men from our world to *the other one they'll love?*" Professor Andrew Gils' voice was loaded with sarcasm. "I do not believe in life after death, and I do not believe in reincarnation. We make efforts to combat and eradicate diseases. This is what we do."

A gust of scorching hot wind blew then suddenly the wind died down.

"Excellent!" John Cole said, a polite smile on his lips, as he applauded the immaculately neat professor.

"Wait a minute, Mr. Cole," Margaret Stan said. "There may be more to what Ivan Georg has just said," she paused, approaching the police chief who stood at the very edge of the stone cube, his shadow a crawling insect on the dark surface of the liquid. "You tricked my husband into going down to Trun Shrine and nearly killed him," she went on. "Your crony Boya Bagd spread Killing Trun and nearly killed my son Thomas. Now she is Ivan Georg's girlfriend. It is highly probable she did something to him which resulted in the emergence of Healing Trun." Margaret paused as her eyes studied the redhead's face. "It appears that the men Boya Bagd falls in love with rush headlong towards their untimely demise. Mr. Cole, you elaborated on the four types of human beings who live on the earth. You also admitted you sent Dr. Georg and Professor Gils the threatening emails. You raised the alarm about the Samodiva civilization."

It was so quiet one could hear a pin drop; however, there were no pins at Trun Chark. The dark Samodiva's milk was asleep in its stone cradle, and the sky was frighteningly clear.

Margaret Stan went on, "Mr. Cole, you are itching to tell us something essential about this civilization. Even a not too clever person like me couldn't but take notice of the Herculean tasks you'd performed so far. You went to great lengths to focus our attention on the entities sporting green dots."

Peter Stan and his son Thomas exchanged glances. Sara Eutim looked relaxed, balanced, her expression beaming benevolence. Doctor Ivan Georg watched Boya with dark concentration, Professor Andrew Gils cleared his throat, but Ivan Georg ignored him.

"The team of archaeologists drew up a report," Professor Gils said. "I read it carefully. All the team members were admitted to Iztok Clinic after they examined the earthenware objects in the shaft on Gagarin Street. Trun Shrine dates back to the thirteenth century." He turned to the chief of Dusk police. "Mr. Cole, shall we assume that the Samodiva civilization existed in the thirteenth century CE? And the Samodivas seemed to build that shrine because they were anxious to collect pain, hatred, and malice for reasons I cannot grasp."

"They thrive on pain and malice," Philip Mill said as he gently touched Wanga's hand. "There is enormous power behind wars and murders, boundless energy behind envy, lust for money and possession. Someone collects this perpetually fresh momentum to use it to a specific deadly end," he went on, measuring his words with caution. "We lie and cheat. We betray our friends and kill one another. I've been working for John Cole for two years now and I feel intimidated but not discouraged."

The mud in the stone cube seemed to recoil from its walls.

"I refuse to believe that an evil civilization exists intent on coercing the human race into killing, stealing and cheating," Peter Stan said.

Suddenly, a stiff wind rose and cut through the closed valley.

"You are wrong," Professor Andrew Gils said. "Ivan showed me the email he'd received. It said: *You'd be the first one they will kill.* Ivan produced Healing Trun. Patients recovered from terminal diseases after they listened to the Healing series of sounds. Thousands got rid of excruciating pain. Ivan defeated agony and anguish."

The blackbird seemed to shudder as the four black holes exuded whitish vapor which crept towards the bare crest of the hill.

"Boya, why did you destroy the blackbirds?" Ivan asked. "Obviously, they were mechanical devices. The boy said they ate nothing, drank no water, but they eased or killed the pain altogether. You captured them. What sort of a man do you work for, Boya?"

The beautiful woman smiled at him.

"Are you a murderer, Boya?" Ivan whispered. "You work for John Cole, and he admitted he'd sent me that email. Why should Mr. Cole expose you, his spy? A compromised agent is cheaper than the knife his boss will pay for to stab him with."

No one was prepared for what happened. Sara Eutim, the famous and pretty writer, stood up. Slowly, gracefully, she walked to Tony and when she spoke, her voice was a little girl's gentle whisper, asking her big brother to give her a hand with her homework, "Tony, could you please show me your left arm?"

"Why is this necessary?" John Cole asked sharply, but the boy, radiant, was already rolling up his shirt sleeve.

A big scarlet scar came into view, garishly red, carved into his white even skin.

"This is for you, Tony," Sara said as her full lips slowly, softly kissed the ugly scar. The smile on the boy's face was broad and happy as sunset.

"Thank you," he mouthed then hesitantly, haltingly, his big dirty hand stroked her hair. "You … you are so pretty," he muttered.

Sara Eutim walked away from the boy and gracefully like a bird tiptoed to the archaeologist. She did not ask him anything. Her fingers ran up his left hand, unbuttoned the sleeve of his flannel shirt and rolled it up. A horrible scarlet scar stretched from the elbow to the shoulder, a purple furrow that cut the white skin, destroying the blond hairs. Again, Sara's lips touched the scar and, light like fireflies, climbed up to Jacob's shoulder.

"I love you," Jacob breathed.

"I love you too," Sara Eutim said.

Professor Andrew Gils stared at his feet, a red mist of embarrassment clouding his cheeks. Sara Eutim ignored that insignificant detail. She took a couple of tiny, butterfly-like steps towards the chief of Dusk police. Saying nothing, she stood a breath away from him, and he cautiously as if his life depended on it, rolled up his sleeve. An appalling purple scar crawled up his left elbow, thick and ugly like a caterpillar. Sara Eutim studied it.

"Won't you kiss my unsightly scar, too?" John Cole asked, his smile an open wound on his face.

Sara Eutim said nothing. Gracefully, with utmost care, her fingertips touching the ugly damaged skin, she said, "I remember this scar. I was a little girl when I saw green dots in a doctor's hair. The doctor was a psychiatrist. He had an ugly scar like yours. My aunt took me to him because she thought I had a screw loose. That doctor treated me to a candy bar, and it was very delicious …"

"The candy man!" Professor Gils said. He rose to his feet, ran to the chief of Dusk police and stared at his elbow. "I remember this scar, too," he said. "I've seen it in my nightmares ever since my childhood."

John Cole said nothing as he beamed a smile at the well-groomed professor. Taking his time, he rummaged in his pocket and produced two bars of chocolate. He grinned as he patted Professor Andrew Gils on the shoulder.

"This is for you, Professor," he said, handing Gils a bar of chocolate. "The second one is for my beloved ex-fiancée Sara."

"I'm glad to see my beloved candy man," dazzling Sara Eutim said as she glanced at Professor Andrew Gils. He had an air of authority, the mist of humiliation putting an edge on his words.

"Mr. Cole, first you passed for priest Dimo," Professor Andrew Gils began, his short sentence gruff and scathing. "As Priest Dimo, you gave Jacob Harvey the 'Old Bulgarian' song about the alleged Samodiva civilization, whatever this means. Then it turns out you were the psychiatrist who consulted Sara Eutim and me, two little children who had *green dots*. These two kids happened to live near a venue which— again, like a bolt out of the blue—turns out to be an ancient shrine. All this could mean one thing. You had been following closely both Sara Eutim and me since the day we were born with *green halos*." Professor Gils looked the police chief in the eye. "I think the Samodiva civilization is a long-term project you manage, Mr. Cole. Tell me what you plan to do with it. Now."

The chief of Dusk police smiled. "As my ex-fiancée, though a very short lived one, Sara Eutim, knows very well I have such a horrible scar on my elbow. Being Mr. Jacob Harvey's fiancée at present, she must have seen the ugly scar on *his* elbow many times. The question is why she chose to make this show of strength now. Should I interpret it as a sign of your power, Sara?"

"To be honest, you should," the dazzling woman answered.

It was hot. The yellow thorns and tiny sand-colored flowers withered on their stalks, turning within seconds into brown dust that covered the stones. A short while ago, fierce winds plagued the valley, deep snowdrifts pirouetted in the distance, heavy masses of brown ice hung from the edges of the crags, but now the sun shone on Trun Chark and the mud in the stone cube mixed with the yellow dust of the dead flowers. The dark stone of the monument seemed to glow and emit opaque, scorching heat. Red clouds exploded in the sky of deep frightening blue.

"If we assume that the trio or trinity of individuals really exists, we should draw several conclusions," Professor Margaret Stan said, her eyes scanning the narrow valley, finally focusing on the young archaeologist. "There must be a bridge, or should I describe it as a *passage* which allows a man to move from the world of childhood to the world of adulthood or to old age. The child is Tony, who *found* the blackbird. The world of grownups is represented by Jacob Harvey, the archaeologist who *discovered* the Old Bulgarian Trun Chark song and leaked the secret about the Samodivas' place of safety and the four black holes, and John Cole. It transpires that the three elements of the trio, Tony, Jacob Harvey, and John Cole, are not only able to successfully coexist, but they also can join forces and pool resources to disclose information about the Samodiva civilization we don't care about and rub our noses in the dirt."

"You made yourself clear," John Cole said as he lit a cigarette.

"Being your ex-wife, though a short-lived one as you say, I learned to be keenly observant of details and gestures," Professor Margaret Stan retorted, watching the teacher's anxious expression. "Peter, you know he was my husband … an errant one, so you needn't worry about it." She smiled at her husband and squeezed his hand. "Being John Cole's ex-wife, I know very well that if he lights a cigarette, he's worried. He can sense something's brewing and doesn't know what it is." She paused, shrugging her shoulders.

"Go on," John Cole said.

"I assume that there is a bridge, leading from one world to another, from old age to childhood, or from adulthood back to the baby crib. *A Samodiva's eyes are a door to other worlds,* goes a famous saying in Dusk; one of the Samodivas is Death. If the Samodiva civilization is after pain, malice, and suffering, then I asked myself the question: what causes us extreme agony? My answer was: death. For us, ordinary human beings, death is synonymous with excruciating pain. So I think it is *death* that bridges the three separate worlds of childhood, adulthood, and old age. Probably, the Samodiva civilization knows how to use death to move from one world to another."

"And Samodiva civilization inhabits the subconscious mind of crazy human beings and thrives on their idiotic ideas," John Cole laughed. "Why should you think it is a civilization of agony?"

"Jacob Harvey wrote: *The loveliest Samodiva is Death, and if you have green dots, you may carry death,*" Ivan Georg said, watching the archaeologist's every move. "One of us present here, including me, carries death, or to put it plainly is Death," the young doctor added, licking his dry lips. "And if what Professor Margaret Stan has just said is true … I mean if death is a bridge between worlds, I am beginning to guess what John Cole's goal is," he was silent as he turned to face the pretty redhead. "Boya," Ivan Georg began, "you once told me, *You can learn to control your green dots by eliminating somebody, no matter who. Then your green dots disappear.* Now I understand. You simply give a man his death i.e., you offer him a bridge to another world."

Smiling, Boya Bagd touched Ivan's hand.

"Will you use death to transfer us all to another world, Mr. Cole?" she asked.

Thomas, Margaret Stan's son snarled. "If you do it, Cole, I'll be happy to accompany you and Boya to hell!"

"John Cole, Jacob Harvey, and Tony didn't writhe in pain when my wife let all of us listen to Killing Trun. So far, Tony and Jacob Harvey have never let anyone see their green dots," Peter Stan the teacher said. "These two can *control* their green dots. It means one thing: they have killed. They have *eliminated* men … Did you, Tony?"

"It might mean something else, old man," Boya Bagd said. "Perhaps Tony, Jacob and John Cole form the Trio of Death."

Sara Eutim touched the surface of the Samodiva's milk with her hand.

The black wings of the enormous stone bird seemed to flap. Crags, stones, and dust quaked. The thick mud-like liquid wobbled, billowed, and bubbled in the cube.

"I have a question for you, Sara Eutim," Professor Andrew Gils said. "You dipped your finger into the liquid, and the Samodiva's milk churned in the cube. You can make your green dots disappear." He peeked into her eyes. "This could mean one thing. Have you taken a man's life, Sara?"

It was extremely hot, yet Sara Eutim looked fresh and cheerful. She smiled at Andrew Gils, waved her hand, looking like an innocent dove against the indifferent immensity of the hill, and said, "Professor, I appreciate your interest in my public persona. Thank you for the time you spend thinking of me. It is just sheer luck that the chief of Dusk police is with us. He is the person in charge of murder investigations, and it is his responsibility to speak in favor or against me."

John Cole seemed unwilling to respond.

"We had a six-month courtship between us, Sara," he said. "Those were the happiest months in my life." The police chief bowed as Sara Eutim blew him a kiss. "I have seen a very interesting picture on your bedroom wall above your queen-size bed. It's a small canvas with a dead cherry tree painted on it." Sara kept silent. John Cole went on, "The trunk, boughs, branches, twigs, and stems are black and bone dry. This dead tree is heavy with big, juicy cherries. What is your interpretation of this picture?" John Cole stood gazing intensely at her. Sara Eutim, the famous writer, smirked to herself but held her tongue.

The police chief did something strange.

He burst into song, his sonorous voice a cracking whip in the hot air. *He threw his dots to the wind, and they don't protect him anymore. Why is the Tall Fellow so silly, Mommy? If pain wins, the Tall Fellow will destroy death.*

John Cole, alert and watchful, turned to Professor Stan. "Do you like this tune, Margaret? I've sung it to you a number of times." His words fell onto deaf ears, failing to impress the woman. The police chief shrugged and went on, smiling at Sara Eutim, "My ex-wife formulated an exciting hypothesis about the trios. If her assumption that death bridges different worlds is true, then your picture of the dead cherry tree, Sara, tells me something interesting: death is the symbol of life. Death is an insignificant checkpoint across the eternal river of existence."

"Death is the very symbol of life," Sara Eutim sneered. "And I'm the Queen of Egypt."

"And the Tall Fellow must stay hidden," John Cole hissed.

Chapter Forty-Four

"I cannot imagine how you look," the blind soothsayer said. "But I can see where you will go."

Her voice was steady, and it was hard to believe this exquisite woman was able to speak so firmly. Philip Mill, quiet and unobtrusive, supported her.

"John Cole, you told me you were Priest Dimo, but you were not a priest," Wanga said. "You cannot hide your green dots from me. I can see your green dots in that boy. I can see your green dots in the young man, too, all the time."

"What are you talking about?" the chief of Dusk police said.

"I told that woman," the seer's hand rose and pointed at Boya Bagd. "She has lost her dots. At the time she had them, she cared so much about a man who is with us now. He cares about her. He cares about her more than he cares about his blood."

"Who's this man?" John Cole asked. "Tell us."

"No," Wanga said. "He does not know."

Boya Bagd seemed relaxed, unaffected by these words.

"I told you," Wanga spoke directly to Boya Bagd now, her thin, almost transparent fingers touching the woman's pretty face. "You had not come to kill me the way you had said you would. You wanted to find out if I knew who Death was. I told you, *Philip Mill will kill me*. And he will."

"No!" Philip Mill cried out. "I love you, Wanga. I cannot live without you."

"You will live without me," Wanga said as she turned her flat blind eyes to Philip. Suddenly, she grabbed at the police chief's hand. "You believe truth will lead men from one world to another. *You cannot lie to anybody, Wanga, you said.*" She tilted her face up to his. "You said I was a New One and asked me if I knew another New One. I didn't understand what you meant." The blind woman blushed, pallor and her timid blood at war on her face as Philip Mill's lips touched her cheek.

Suddenly, the liquid swelled, rumbled, and billowed out of the stone cube.

"I heard what the other woman said about the trio," the blind seer pressed on. "She is right. Death is the path that leads an old man to childhood and a child to adulthood. And I can see your trio here ... the green dots of that man," she pointed at the archaeologist. "The child's green dots and yours, John Cole ... those dots are identical. Shame on you, liar, who tried to trick me into believing you were Priest Dimo." She paused and a second later, catching her breath, said, "Now I know what your trio is looking for." Wanga trembled, her hands, delicate, peaceful sonatas of light in the hot air. "You are looking for death ... death the passage, and death the bridge. Why do you think you can destroy it?"

Wanga fell silent, no trace of fear or anxiety on her pallid face. Philip Mill held her close to his heart.

"I'll not let anyone harm you," he whispered.

"You will bury me," she said.

The chief of Dusk police scanned the valley. The stones under his feet were scorching hot, and just a hundred yards away snowflakes whirled in the freezing air, ice and a heavy coating of rime covered the crags. Deaf Crags was a creepy place.

"Wanga is right. I am looking for Death," John Cole said. "And Death could be anyone among us, including me, a man or a woman who possesses green dots."

"You are worse than Death, John," the old teacher said. "You are a liar. You said you were my friend. No, you are not. A criminal, that's what you are."

"Peter, you *are* my friend, although you are far from being a smart man. I'd listen very carefully to what John Cole said if I were you. Then perhaps you could make the right decision." The chief of Dusk police came up to the teacher and tried to pat him on the back.

"Don't touch me!" Peter Stan snarled.

"Okay. Let's get down to business," John Cole said as he studied the faces in front of him. They all were closed and sullen, the only exception being Sara Eutim. She was smiling.

"The blackbirds were the first sign of trouble." John Cole began. "They were so heavy the pavement got damaged after they clawed at it." The police chief spoke in a brisk, matter-of-fact tone. "Sick people and injured dogs climbed down into the hole the birds had dug, and, lo and behold, both men and animals were back on their feet. Tony captured Ben, one of the birds, and Ben brought happiness to the boy and his mom. Boya Bagd destroyed the blackbirds. Tony's essay reveals they are nothing more than mechanical contraptions, generating joy. To cut a long story short, their heavy feathers did the same job. They made Tony and his mother happy. And before I forget, yes, I ordered Boya to destroy the clumsy, feathered songsters that couldn't sing."

He cleared his throat and went on. "The archaeological excavation on Gagarin Street: my not exactly brilliant friend Peter Stan was on the brink of death when he accompanied me to the shaft, leading to Trun Shrine as Jacob Harvey dubbed the place. Jacob is an ambitious archaeologist and, perhaps, an element of the *Trio of Death,* as my ex-wife Margaret came to unintelligently name it. Margaret is fond of prattling on about trios and triads, as you must have already noticed."

The chief of Dusk police frowned at Professor Stan, a wry smile cutting his face into two suspicious halves. "What is Trun Shrine remarkable for? First, the heaps of pans and stones look exactly like the ones in front of Wanga's hut which, in turn, closely resemble the heaps we all can see here, at Trun Chark. Second, on the front wall of the shrine, the archaeologists found a picture carved deep into the stone, a picture of a blind woman who I dare say closely resembles famous Wanga. We all have the honor of listening to what she has to say. Three, there is a map drawn on the front wall of Trun Shrine. This map helped Jacob Harvey, the archaeologist, to find Trun Chark. It is the map of Deaf Crags valley."

"Yes, I found Trun Chark, consulting this map, and I was interested in Deaf Crags because of the Old Bulgarian song you gave me, Father Dimo," Jacob Harvey said pointedly.

Sara Eutim's eyes settled on John Cole who pretended he hadn't noticed her and spoke, his voice fairly confident. "I hope you all like Deaf Crags. By the way, they are called *deaf* because the Samodiva's milk, that dangerous liquid in the cube, dampens all sounds and kills all noises we make."

"So, if your plan was to get rid of us, no one could hear our screams for help," Professor Margaret Stan said.

"Yes, you are right," John Cole commented, his face twisting into a grimace, "As always."

Professor Margaret Stan ignored him.

"Mr. Cole," she said. "I submitted all materials on my findings related to Killing and Healing Trun to the major television chains in Europe. I wrote an article on my *trio hypothesis*—or shall I now call it the Trio of Death hypothesis?"

"I have never doubted you are a sly girl, Margaret," the chief of Dusk police said genuinely amused. "These pictures on the wall in your room, the secrecy, the false clues, your plan, teeming in red herrings … Hats off to you for your cunning to mislead me," John Cole laughed. "*Burn the house down if someone comes in!* you'd ordered dear old Peter, and he, the poor devil, was about to set fire to his home when I arrived."

Peter Stan bit his lip in a silent rage.

"Poor simple-hearted Peter," John Coal continued. "My friend bent over backwards to photograph the pictures of the *monster*. Funny, isn't it? The ogre consisted of Tony's foot, Wanga's face, Margaret's hand and what else?" The chief of Dusk police chuckled as he went closer to Professor Margaret Stan. "Give me a kiss, dear. All misleading *signs* you tried to foist off on me! Your date of birth and date of death, making *clear* you could increase your and everybody else's life expectancy. Life expectancy, my foot, and congratulations, sly boots Margaret! Those pictures were all humbug. The only thing of real value was the series of the three pictures: the portrait of Tony, the big question mark, and my photograph. I saw them and I became aware you knew or at least had guessed what a trio would look like."

John Cole's frowning face was now close to Margaret's.

"Crafty girl!" he said.

"Am I right to assume you wanted me to guess that trios existed?" Professor Margaret Stan asked.

The chief of Dusk police did not answer.

Deaf Crags loomed large and dark in spite of the blazing sun that ripped the indifference of the horizon and seared the open blue sky. A stone's throw from Margaret, a blizzard raged, snowdrifts piled high and the shadow of the black monument seemed to weigh down the frozen valley.

"I wish I had set fire to the house," Peter Stan said. "Then you might have choked on your tongue in the flames, John."

"You didn't, but I tried to and failed, my friend," the chief of Dusk police said. "I studied the pictures on the walls, do you remember? Good old boy! I set fire to a heap of papers near the wall and surprise, surprise! The papers wouldn't burn. The wall produced Killing Trun instead. Margaret believes she outwitted me, don't you, Margaret?"

"I did," she said. "If the house was on fire, Killing Trun would go off, incapacitating the intruder. The only thing I was interested in was to find out who the intruder would be." Professor Margaret paused. "Now I can see your green dots, Mr. Cole," she said.

In the hushed silence, Wanga's voice sounded like snow crunching under heavy boots, "Everyone without exception has green dots."

"You are a New One and you cannot lie" Jacob Harvey said. "Tell me who can see the green dots the ordinary people have?"

"At times, I can," Wanga said.

"Perhaps the Tall Fellow can see them all the time?" Professor Margaret Stan asked. "I read about this character in Philip Mill's article."

"And who told you about the article?" John Cole purred, his words cold and slippery.

"You sound interested in the shadowy Tall Fellow, Mr. Cole," Professor Margaret Stan said. She studied the sulky expression on his face. "Or perhaps you are this Tall Fellow, John?" The police chief shrugged as Margaret Stan added innocently, "I've seen quite a few taller men than you, Mr. Cole; Peter for example."

It was the first time this afternoon the old teacher had smiled.

"Sara gave me the article on the Tall Fellow and I read it," the young archaeologist said. "The piece was well-researched, and I thought its author had done a good job." The archaeologist glanced at Philip Mill. "I've hated prophets and seers—like Wanga—all my life. They are all charlatans," Jacob looked so irritated he could hardly stand still.

A bank of clouds floated overhead, obliterating the sun, and a stiff wind cut through the valley. The four dark holes spewed silvery vapor that turned into rime within seconds. The heap of formless sharp stones quaked, and the earthenware pans—chipped, cracked, scratched—rang and shook. It was snowing heavily in the valley, and the dirt road had vanished under a thick white bandage of ice. Then suddenly the sun slashed through the clouds, its yellow face a scratch in the unending bruise of the sky. The stones were hot again, and Trun Chark's surface was strong and dark like the dead wings of the blackbirds.

"Does the Tall Fellow really exist?" Professor Gils asked.

No one expected Wanga's answer, and when she spoke, Philip Mill was the one who fidgeted, anxious and tense by her side.

"Yes," the blind woman said. There was a deafening silence as Wanga went on, "I know a fairy tale about a man who sacrificed his life for his brethren. Centuries later, Christians believed this man was called Christ. Christ rose from the dead because he was stronger than death. Other people called him simply the Tall Fellow. And he is one of *them*," the seer was whispering now. "He is one of the Samodivas, but he is humbler than me. I have green dots. He's given up his. They protected him and guaranteed his safety. Now anguish strikes his heart, and he groans in agony because mankind lives in pain and agony. He is a Samodiva …" her voice broke. She breathed with difficulty, her skin pale, Philip Mill by her side. "I …" Wanga's voice was a shadow of a dying bird. "I could feel his presence during the Dirty Days … long, long days when the *chark* did not work and nothing protected him. The most powerful among the Samodivas is *Death*. During the Dirty Days the *chark* sleeps, death is strong, thorns are weak, and many men shall cross the bridge to childhood."

"The thorns are weak? What do you mean, Wanga? Please tell us." Professor Margaret Stan said.

"She is very sick," Philip Mill whispered. "Leave her alone!"

"Thorns are weak during the Dirty Days," Ivan Georg said thoughtfully. "The Old Bulgarian word for thorn is *trun*," he said. "My brain surgery took place on a Dirty Day, Doctor Andrew Gils who operated on me was born on a Dirty Day; it was on a Dirty Day that I produced Healing Trun."

"It was on a Dirty Day that Killing Trun sounded for the first time and nearly killed me," Professor Margaret Stan said. "It must have been on a Dirty Day when Boya Bagd planted Killing Trun in my computer."

"Yes, this happened on a Dirty Day, 27 December," the beautiful woman said, looking John Cole in the face as she declared, "I took orders from a person who is among us now."

"I nearly died in a car crash on a Dirty Day, 22 December," Margaret Stan's son Thomas said.

"I met Jacob Harvey on a Dirty Day, 15 December," Sara Eutim chimed in.

"Wait, wait," Peter Stan said. "December 15, yes, it was 15 December when the flock of the blackbirds perched on the asphalt in our school yard, a Dirty Day again."

Silence thickened, devouring the sun in the ailing sky.

"During the Dirty Days pain and agony run loose ... if *they* don't make the *chark* good again ..." the blind woman whispered.

"Who are *they?*" Professor Gils asked.

"During the Dirty Days I don't ..." Wanga breathed. "I don't collect pans and stones. There's no *chark* to handle them," she paused, beads of perspiration glistening on her forehead. "Tell men not to go out after sunset throughout the Dirty Days."

The stones were warm. The boy went to the gleaming cube and whispered to the stones, "Stop it." He grabbed a pebble, threw it into the liquid and its glow died. The dark opaque surface contracted and bristled. Ripples ran through it as if a big animal swam there.

"Every human being is a lake of pain and envy," Wanga said. "There is no exception to this rule," she spoke, addressing no one in particular. "Happiness is a house, a wife and three kids. Happiness is a million dollars in a banking account. Happiness is a handful of rice, a child recuperating from a dreadful disease. Happiness is different for everyone. But pain ... oh, pain! Everyone feels it. No man is bigger than its horrible presence. Pain is Death's beloved son. Men create shortcuts to death, and malice paves the road to it. Jealousy is stronger than love. Pain is stronger than happiness. Trun is a lake, which transforms pain into peace. Peace is the father of joy." She coughed, took a shallow breath and coughed again.

"She's delirious!" John Cole said. "Philip, make her keep quiet!"

But the blind woman spoke on, her lips two colorless lines of agony. "He will be the death of me," she whispered as she caressed Philip Mill's hands. "I will die in less than an hour. I must tell you all … You have to know all I know. I'll bleed if I tell a lie. You have to be sure that what I speak is true."

"In other words, we can use you as a filter of truth, can't we, Wanga?" Sara Eutim scoffed. "You bleed; therefore, you lie. I think all this is pretty naïve."

"Few men can transform pain into unsurpassed beauty," Wanga went on. "In the prison of deepest misery, Beethoven created heavenly music; blind John Milton wrote *Paradise Lost.* These two were natural transformers. They absorbed agony and gave beauty and purity to the world."

Professor Margaret Stan's words had the effect of an explosion. "The Talented Ones," she said. "The Talented Ones in the Trun Chark song!" Her face darkened. "The song says the *chark* cannot help the Talented Ones. They have to go to the second hole." She stared at the mountain face, dark, cavernous, portentous in the unusually warm Deaf Crags valley.

It was snowing above the fourth, largest hole, but Deaf Crags glittered below it, every stone a thousand blazes of heat.

"I think that no Trun Chark song exists. You wrote it, Mr. Cole, didn't you?" Professor Margaret Stan's eyes fastened on the police chief's face. "You wanted to tell us about the civilization of green dots, the Samodivas, and Jacob Harvey gave me the song. Jacob Harvey's translation of the text was wrong. And I suspect that you John, and you, Jacob, wanted to hide something from us. You gave us a part of the whole, a half-truth. Through the Trun Chark song, you did tell us about four types of living beings: the Ordinary Ones; the Talented Ones who the *chark* cannot help, the Marked Ones i.e., the ones with green dots—the Samodivas—

who are men's only chance; and the New Ones who bleed to death if they lie to anybody."

Professor Margaret Stan smiled mirthlessly at the police chief.

"One of the Marked Ones, the most malicious and destructive Samodiva, the most beautiful, too, is *Death*. And death is the bridge between the different worlds—childhood, adulthood, and old age. Are you after death, John? Or perhaps you *are* Death?"

She didn't hear the hardly audible click of the stones beneath her feet; she was lost in thought.

"I think your goal is to understand how talent works, Mr. Cole," Ivan Georg said sharply. "I remember the email you sent me. You wrote that *talent* was a sign the experiment had failed because *Samodivas cannot live in the Talented Ones.* The green dots lost ground to men. It is only the Talented Ones who are able to transform agony into beauty, and there's not enough pain left for the *chark* to work properly."

"Human beings, men and women, can transform pain into joy. Mankind is a transformer of pain!" the blind seer's voice was tinged with emotion. "This is why *they,* the green dots, inhabit our subconscious mind, our thoughts. We constantly dream of happiness, but every day of our lives we give each other anguish and lies."

"You said that every man is a transformer!" John Cole spoke under his breath. "Wanga, you said it and you don't bleed!"

The blind woman ignored the chief of Dusk police.

"Like this man here," she blurted out as she turned to Ivan Georg, the doctor with the scarred face. "I could hear his voice as he let loose Healing Trun, the hectic tune that killed pain and drove away death. Death is the mysterious Samodiva, the path to childhood. The dust on this path is pain … This man," her thin finger pointed at Ivan Georg. "This man did something that only the Tall Fellow could do …" the seer gasped unable to control her shaking voice. "This man drove death away. This man closed the door to the worlds, and he was not one of *them.* He is human!"

Sara Eutim chuckled.

"I can imagine the commotion Doctor Georg's master stroke must have set up in Samodiva's neat civilization," she turned to John Cole. "I can also imagine how jealous the proverbial Tall Fellow was. Doctor

Georg, an ordinary man who barely survived brain tumor surgery, coped with a task, which only the highest authority, the tall chap, was able to accomplish. Doctor Georg drove away death? He drove away death, my foot!"

Wanga broke away from Philip Mill's hands and walked up to Sara. The beautiful woman took a step back, but the seer pushed forward, staggering towards the writer.

"Healing Trun, which the young man produced …" Wanga said as she turned her head toward Sara Eutim, "Healing Trun is life. It is a bridge to a place you wouldn't like to visit. Don't kill your brother or you'll land there. I told you once and I tell you again. Don't harm the man with the scarred face."

"I have no brothers," Sara Eutim said, but the blind woman took no notice of her words.

"If you ruin life, you'll ruin yourself. If life and death go away, only that place remains." Wanga stood bolt upright. "You don't want to go there."

Sara Eutim said nothing, did nothing, just listened, calm like ice, her eyebrows raised in a curious arc.

"She outwitted you," Wanga went on. "You were lucky she outwitted you."

"Who is she? Is she here now?" Sara Eutim laughed, but the blind woman's mind was elsewhere. "The Tall Fellow can see the dots in the Ordinary Ones. He can teach men to transform agony into peace and life." Wanga paused, a tear rolling down her cheek. "The Tall Fellow is the only one able to abolish death for good. Death's child is loneliness and Death's heart is sorrow. Death is not evil, Death, the poorest Samodiva! She absorbs all the pain in the world, collects all people's malice and opens the clean doors to the worlds … Poor Samodiva who is Death, poor, poor Death …" Wanga's voice broke. They all watched as she slowly brushed off the tiny tear then she said, "If the Tall Fellow abolishes death, truth will become the door to childhood, adulthood and old age … but truth is very weak now."

"Don't talk nonsense to us," said Sara Eutim.

"This time you are wrong, Ms. Eutim," Professor Margaret Stan said. "Wanga didn't bleed. She must be telling the truth."

Wanga turned her back on Professor Margaret Stan, her blind eyes searching, probing...

"She helped the sick man to live on after brain surgery. I don't know why she did it," the blind prophetess spoke like a puzzled child. "Why? Samodivas don't do this, but she did it. And he ..." she pointed her finger at Ivan Georg, "He drove death away because she gave him the Healing Trun path."

"Who is she?" Sara Eutim asked. "Or do you mean it was the Tall Fellow who gave Doctor Georg Healing Trun and saved his life?"

"I am not sure," the blind clairvoyant said as she raised her hand and pointed at someone, her head hanging low. "Her green dots seemed to have disappeared."

"I am waiting for your kind response," Sara Eutim said, but the seer was silent, her eyes closed, her lids bluish, her breathing shallow.

Professor Margaret Stan stood in front of the police chief.

"John Cole, are you the Tall Fellow?" she asked.

The chief of Dusk police said nothing.

"Then you must be Death, John Cole," Margaret Stan said. "You sent Doctor Ivan Georg an email: *You'll be the first one they will kill.*"

"You are digging your own grave now, my dear Margaret. You've been a serious obstacle all the way. This said, I hate it when I am far from you." The chief of Dusk police moved a step closer to Philip Mill and tapping him on the shoulder, said, "Philip, tell me: who gave Doctor Ivan Georg the Healing Trun *path?*"

Philip Mill ran his hand over his stubble then pushed John Cole.

"Where are your manners?" the police chief sneered. "Philip, do you think I don't know who Wanga had in mind?" The police chief tapped the journalist on the shoulder again, and a dangerous smile flickered across his face. "Boya, would you like to add something on this issue? I remember Doctor Andrew Gils had told me that you, the best occupational therapist, were on duty on the day Doctor Georg miraculously recovered from his complex brain surgery."

More ravishing than ever, Boya Bagd shook her head. "I have included all pertinent information in my report on the case, sir," she said.

"I strongly doubt it," John Cole said. "I am sure you will tell us about everything that happened between you and Doctor Ivan Georg during the week after his brain surgery i.e., the period when he recuperated from the operation. I am sure Ivan Georg will also make a clean breast of it, won't you, Doctor Georg?" The police chief said his tone of voice the dark calm before the storm.

The liquid in the stone cube seemed to simmer as it spilled over the sharp edges then, after a minute, Deaf Crags Valley was again quiet and deceptively peaceful. It was Sara Eutim's clear voice that interrupted the long silence. "Maybe the answer is buried in the inscriptions carved at the base of the four prodigious holes," she said. "My fiancé Jacob Harvey read to me—surprise, surprise—another Old Bulgarian song dedicated to these four eh … caves." She produced a folded sheet of paper from her coat pocket and carefully smoothed it.

"Isn't it strange you have an Old Bulgarian song on you all the time?" the police chief remarked.

"Yes, it is," Sara Eutim conceded with a sweet smile. "I have made multiple copies of it. Let's get down to brass tacks," she added, glancing at the young archaeologist. "The song that Jacob gave me says, I quote: *Every letter cut into the stone stands for a human being who died as he tried to find out the truth.* Interesting, especially if we do not forget what Wanga had just said, *Truth is very weak.* It seems that people tend to meet their maker if they are too keen on getting at the truth," Ms. Eutim, the renowned journalist, beamed a smile at Jacob Harvey. "There's another very stimulating line in this Old Bulgarian song. The anonymous poet says: *Only the New Ones are not afraid.* Shall I gather that if we go up there and read the inscriptions at the base of the four holes, we shall all kick the bucket—with the exception of the two New Ones among us—Wanga and that handsome young man whose face is smeared with his own blood, Professor Margaret Stan's son? Why don't we all go to the holes and check?" she suggested.

"I strongly advise you against doing this," John Cole said. "Remember that one of us here might be—or shall I say—one of us *is* Death?"

Sara Eutim's smile was so broad it touched the snowdrifts, towering over the dark holes in the mountain face.

"Then I wonder why my fiancé Jacob Harvey insisted on taking me to see the inscriptions," A gleam in Sara's eyes hinted at her amusement. "Was Jacob checking on me? Have you ordered him to kill me, John?"

The chief of Dusk police said nothing. It was the archaeologist who immediately took the floor, "Sara, another Old Bulgarian song of the thirteenth century, the one I gave you, says that Samodiva's milk churns only when Death touches it. Well, maybe it is not that important but … Trun Shrine dates back to the thirteenth century, and someone has carved a map of Deaf Crags valley in the front wall of Trun Shrine," the archaeologist's voice trailed off. After a second, he pulled himself together, cleared his throat and added, "Sara, when you touched the Samodiva's milk, the liquid churned and thundered."

Chapter Forty-Five

"Before we find out who Death is," John Cole started, his eyes on Boya Bagd, "We have to concentrate on the riddle of the thorn." The police chief narrowed his eyes. "Perhaps the thorn holds vital clues as to who the traitor among the Samodivas is, and I mean the Samodivas present here and now. I use the insulting word *traitor*," he said, his voice was a nest of writhing snakes. "And I use this word because Healing Trun was not supposed to leak through a crack and land in the hands of the malicious humans. You remember the legend of Prometheus, the Titan who defies gods and gives fire to humanity. Fire is laughably innocuous compared to Trun, i.e., the ability to abolish death, and Trun is a road that men can freely choose." He paused, cleared his throat, the poison in his voice stronger than before. "Wanga says that truth is feeble. No one is ready to obliterate death because the New Ones are weaklings incapable of acting. At this crucial moment, a Samodiva turned traitor and gave Healing Trun to mean, self-serving men who will not use Trun to ease the pain. The only thing they need is Killing Trun. Their goal is to stir up hatred, wage bloody wars to get rich quick. Our back-breaking work throughout the centuries will go to the dogs." The police chief chewed his lower lip. "We tried to help men escape from the trap of malice and greed. We built transformers. Yes, Trun Shrine and Deaf Crags are transformers of anguish. Men brought their pans and their stones and gave us their diseases and hate. They went home healthy and peaceful."

"You are not the Tall Fellow, John," Professor Margaret Stan said.

"What if I am?" John Cole said. "As you can see the Tall Fellow is not tall at all. He wanted to help the suffering men and women, so he focused on their tales of woe and failed to identify danger under his nose. A Samodiva stole Healing and Killing Trun."

"I don't believe you, Mr. Cole," Professor Margaret Stan interrupted him. "You can't be the Tall Fellow, a *creature* who sacrificed his dots the way Christ sacrificed his life on the cross to help mankind." She paused, watching him. "It is a selfless act totally out of John Cole's character. You are a selfish person."

No one made any comments on this brief statement. The light breeze touched stunned faces.

"If we solve the Trun mystery, Margaret, it won't be a pleasure for you to meet the Tall Fellow," John Cole said. "We will soon learn who Death is; however, I will be truly gratified if I lay my hands on the Samodiva that has turned traitor."

"You are *not* the Tall Fellow," Wanga said.

"You cannot be so sure," The police chief snarled.

"I am," the blind woman said.

All eyes were on her.

Nothing happened.

"We heard what you said on the so-called trios, Mr. Cole. You captured us all," Ivan Georg said. "You did your best to provide us with details about the Samodiva civilization and the four different types of human beings." He nodded as he added calmly, "We all know too much. I'd be the first one *they will* kill. You'll kill all the rest."

"Everything depends on Trun, the conundrum of the thorn," John Cole was smiling now. "The big thorn carved on the wall of Trun Shrine. Someone had cut another remarkable thorn here, in the mountain face above the Trun Chark, and yes, the word *trun* means thorn in Old Bulgarian." The police chief's eyes darted from face to face. "Trun is a word repeated over and over again both in Killing Trun and in its healing brother." The chief of Dusk police rubbed his forehead. "Before I forget … Everything about the two chambers at the bottom of Trun Shrine is fascinating. The walls of the first one are freezing cold stones; the walls of the second chamber are scorching hot. Jacob Harvey, the archaeologist, did an interesting experiment. He took a sample from the Trun Chark liquid and heated it. It hissed and, intriguingly, at exactly the same time, the stones Jacob had collected from Trun Shrine, which he kept on the table in his living room, became scorching hot. He cooled the liquid and the stones on the table in his living room were freezing cold within seconds."

"It happened exactly the way you had described this," the archaeologist said. "And I submitted the sample to Professor Margaret Stan."

"I had the samples analyzed, "Professor Stan said. "The analysis of the liquid Mr. Harvey labels *Samodiva's milk* proved it contains no dangerous additives. It was pure and simple muddy water," the Professor wrinkled her forehead as she added, "At that point, I doubted Jacob Harvey's integrity. His translation of the Trun Chark song does not contain a crucial detail: it pays no heed to the repetition of the number three in the initial four stanzas, and the emergence of the number two in the last, fifth stanza. Jacob Harvey sends me a Samodiva's milk sample, and it turns out it is just water. This 'water' boils and bubbles after Ms. Sara Eutim touches it." Professor Margaret Stan's eyes, as hard as flint, studied the young archaeologist's expression. "A while ago, we saw Sara Eutim plunge her hand into the liquid, and it remained absolutely unimpressed. I'd say, Mr. Harvey, you are trying to be economical with the truth, to say the least."

"I described what I had witnessed," the archaeologist began as Professor Margaret Stan turned her back on him.

"The truth will out," the chief of Dusk police said enigmatically. "The members of the archaeological team who discovered Trun Shrine were on the brink of dying. My wonderfully clever friend Peter Stan was about to cash in his chips as well. It turned out Trun Shrine meant death. It was powerful enough to kill its desecrators, the ones who had no green dots. Jacob Harvey too suffered from severe paralysis and was about to breathe his last …"

"Wait a minute, Mr. Cole," Professor Margaret Stan interrupted him. "Jacob Harvey has green dots and should be impervious to the influence of Trun Shrine. Jacob somehow managed to switch off his green halo i.e., Jacob Harvey could control his green dots. This might mean one thing: maybe Jacob Harvey is *Death*." Professor Stan glanced at the police chief, and there was mistrust and defiance in her gaze. "Is the whole *Trio of Agony* looking for Death among us now? A minute ago, you said you were the Tall Fellow. Wanga insisted you told us a fib. Why didn't you bleed to death then? I think Death is the Trio of Agony: Tony—Jacob Harvey—John Cole. I don't believe that your goal, Mr. Cole, is to find the Samodiva who has turned traitor."

John Cole beamed a sharp-toothed smile at no one in particular.

"Haste makes waste, Margaret," he said. "You'll have your luck run out when you need it most." he shrugged. "The Samodivas, or the ones having green dots, are *our last chance* as Wanga had told Philip Mill," he said, his eyes closed. "If my dear Margaret's hypothesis is correct as I believe it is, the dots are the only possible approach to making men understand that time does not follow a straight line. Time is not two simple directions: the future and the past separated by the elusive *present,* that a mortal would call their *life.* Time is everywhere. It has no beginning and no end, no depth, no height or width. One can be a child, a grown-up man and an old man at the same time. Humans do not *disappear,* leaving a bag of bones, a handful of dust and a grave behind them."

"And pigs will learn to fly," Thomas Stan jeered, his bruised face an eyesore.

"The only stable element that keeps the trio of different ages together," the police chief went on, ignoring Thomas altogether, "are the identical green dots, i.e., the Samodivas who live in the thoughts and dreams of man. The Old Dusk songs tell us that a Samodiva is a man's fate. A frightening detail: it is death that serves as a checkpoint along the border between different ages. Death is the whirlpool of agony one has to swim through of his own accord to become a child, an adult, or an old man." John Cole looked Professor Margaret in the eye. "Death is pain and suffering, and for this reason Margaret comes to the conclusion that Samodiva civilization, or the so-called *green dots,* thrive on pain and constantly drive human beings to wars, diseases, jealousy or malice. This is logical: human agony is, figuratively speaking, the Samodivas' *food.*"

"However," John Cole's voice went up, "the noiseless blackbirds took away pain and cured patients suffering from terminal diseases. Think about Healing Trun that helped thousands to fully recover and enjoy good health. Could we assume that Samodiva civilization has a special task to perform? Maybe a Samodiva is—let me put it figuratively—man's guardian angel, an entity aiding people in overcoming lies and vices that cause disease?"

"What would happen if hell froze over?" Thomas Stan said as he waved his fists in the air, the crust of dried blood a rusty mask on his face. "John Cole, you poisoned my parents' life. You humiliate Boya Bagd, the woman I used to care about. I'll break your head. I don't want to know how you'll crawl back to your dimensionless time. I don't care if you are Death, the Tall Fellow or the 'Short Fellow,' a grumpy old man or a street urchin."

A breeze rose, light and fresh.

"Thomas, I am your godfather, remember?" the chief of Dusk police said. "I am sorry you don't have the green dots, but this problem can easily be solved. Your mother learned how to acquire them. You have to listen to Healing and Killing Trun, cackling simultaneously, and you are an entirely new man." John Cole snickered at young Thomas. "On the other hand, my beloved Sara Eutim and Professor Andrew Gils procured their dots because they lived near Trun Shrine, on Gagarin Street. The same holds true for Boya Bagd. Don't forget that the shrine is a transformer of pain, which turns agony into sheer bliss."

"The shrine cannot defeat loneliness," Professor Gils said. "Loneliness is the father of arts."

The Samodiva's milk glowed in its stone cube, giving the quiet afternoon a brown appearance. A few yards away, the crags were high, covered with snow.

"Something happened to my mother. I witnessed her transformation," Professor Andrew Gils went on. "I don't have any explanation for what I saw. I pushed the Killing Trun button by mistake. My mother choked. I quickly switched on Healing Trun, putting an end to the murderous sounds. She listened to Healing Trun for no more than five minutes. After I switched off Healing Trun, my mother looked years younger. Our neighbors thought it was her daughter who had come to visit us." Professor Gils paused, stared at the mountain peak, and his voice came back, firm and matter-of fact. "Mr. Cole, I carefully read the emails you admitted you had sent to Doctor Ivan Georg and me. I was struck speechless by the following sentence in your email dated 18 February: *They do not know this code can transform the universe.* I think Killing and Healing Trun are the code you have in mind. My mother's transformation is a modest achievement."

It was Sara Eutim who was the first to speak. "I'd like to try your mother's experiment, Professor Gils," she said with a smile. "I think our prophetess here needs it too."

"Shut up, Sara," John Cole snarled. "A code capable of controlling the *universe!* These two diametrically opposed Trun series can tear a civilization apart." He cleared his throat. "Babies who lived near Trun Shrine on Gagarin Street either died young or had the dots. Were the paving stones on Gagarin Street excavated from Trun Shrine?" he chuckled. "As far as Wanga is concerned, I wouldn't run the risk of even trying to explain how she got her little green friends. The important thing is the dots make it possible for her to *see* everything within the flat, endless time." His voice was suddenly a guillotine. "Somebody has carved a picture of a blind woman into the front wall of Trun Shrine. Jacob Harvey tells me the woman in the picture bears a striking resemblance to Wanga."

The mud-like liquid in the cube was now black. It didn't glow.

"I can …" the blind woman gasped. "I can see her …" she staggered towards Sara Eutim. "I can see a little fair-haired girl. A beautiful girl, dying … You are that girl! But …" her face was beaded with sweat. "But … I cannot see you as an old woman. Where's the old woman? There must be an old woman in the trio. The fair-haired child and … and you … No old woman."

Sara Eutim said nothing.

"A little fair-haired child," Wanga muttered under her breath. "But I know you. I saw your mom and dad. They were sick with worry. They brought you to me … you! You, a grown-up beauty waited nearby, watching me. I should have guessed … there was no old woman … If there is no old woman, there is no trio." Wanga's lips were thin colorless threads that knitted dangerous words. "The child's pleading blue eyes …"

Sara did not try to retreat in the shadow of the enormous blackbird.

"Where did the girl go?" the clairvoyant asked, clutching at her elbow. "Where did *you* go?"

The soft breeze played with the shadows and swept over the rocks. The air hovered like a torn kite. The Samodiva's milk was a dark, malicious substance that seemed to glower at the valley.

"A little fair-haired girl," Ivan said. "Quiet steps and a sweet sad face … I was dying. After my brain surgery, I knew I was dying, and a girl, a small thing, entered my hospital room. Then she was gone," he looked up. "I don't know why I am saying this. I felt so sorry for her. She felt for me, she cared for me, and I liked her."

"I saw a little fair-haired, blue-eyed girl several times," Peter Stan said. "She walked alone in front of our house. It's strange," he added. "I met her when I thought Margaret would leave me for John Cole. I wanted to die. And I saw her blue eyes … so sad."

"Peter," Margaret Stan spoke softly, patting his hand. "I remember when you and I saw a little fair-haired girl, walking all alone. We were talking about the Tall Fellow and the impossibility to kill pain. Do you remember, Peter?"

The old teacher shook his head. "It's confusing, Margaret," he said, his lips moving as if he were struggling to read a sentence the thickening shadows were writing on the sky. "Margaret, I remember I saw the little child, her sad blue eyes. I saw her when John Cole dragged me out of the shaft. I thought I was dead. I was dying …"

"I saw a fair-haired girl, too. John Cole, she stood in front of your house," Sara Eutim said. "I asked you who she was and you told me you didn't know her. Do you remember?"

"That girl's green dots are the same as yours, Sara Eutim," Wanga said. "This means that you and that girl are one and the same … life-form."

Sara Eutim came up to the blind woman and stared at her face. The skin on the seer turned gray.

"What is it, Wanga?" Philip Mill whispered.

"She is here," the prophetess blurted out.

John Cole stared at her.

"I saw a little fair-haired, blue-eyed girl," Boya Bagd said evenly. "I was reading Tony's essay about the blackbird. The boy had given the bird crumbs, and I thought this was funny." Boya shivered. "Then I saw the child. The thought of her still gives me the creeps. Her eyes were cold, cruel. She asked me something I didn't understand. The chill I felt inside my bones! Her face was gray like … like hers," Boya pointed at the seer.

"I know the little girl Wanga speaks about," Philip Mill said. "I saw her and her parents. The man carried the child. He walked slowly, with difficulty. The kid was small and frail. I can still see her pained face. *I am going to die,* she lisped. Her parents were worried sick. I was sorry for them."

"Obviously, the girl survived," Professor Margaret Stan said. "And that young lady, Ms. Sara Eutim, author of articles I admire, possesses the same combination of green dots as the sad little girl. If what Wanga says is true," the Professor paused, studying Ms. Eutim, the famous scholar, the most beautiful woman among them all. "We should ask Ms. Eutim where the old woman of their trio is."

Sara shrugged as she flashed Professor Stan a radiant smile, "You produced the trio theory, Professor Stan," she said. "We still have no conclusive proofs if it is true or false."

Tony ran to the cube and threw a stone into the thick liquid. The mud-like substance contracted rapidly, the four dark holes grew darker, and a cloud of vapor crawled up the mountain, slowly hiding the peak under a shroud of fog. The rocks smoldered, warmer, more dangerous than before as dark-gray clouds sifted snow into the narrow gorge a dozen yards away from the cube.

"I saw a little fair-haired girl," Professor Andrew Gils said in a monotonous tone of voice. "It happened when the blackbirds attacked my house then Boya Bagd dragged me to her minivan," he pointed at the patch of even land where the vehicle was parked. "Yes, I saw the little girl by the minivan, and I thought I was going to die. I had seen this kid before, in the clinic. She looked so much like the girl who told me fairy tales in my childhood … She looked like you, Sara Eutim." He glanced at Boya Bagd. "At that time, I felt so lonely I didn't want to live. That girl seemed to take mercy on me. I was scared Boya would kidnap her, but fortunately she had not seen the little one."

"Of course, I saw her," the slim young woman said. "My task was to take you to Deaf Crags, Professor Gils, not the little girl," Boya stared the police chief in the eyes. "I am sure Mr. John Cole will be happy to confirm the accuracy of the statement I have just made."

Mr. John Cole glared at the stunning redhead as he cleared his throat and spoke in a flat, toneless voice, "I don't appreciate my orders being ignored. Ms. Bagd was in charge of the blackbirds. I expect Ms. Bagd will explain to us how and why the flock of blackbirds showed up in the schoolyard near Iztok Clinic. How come a *blackbird* entered Dr. Ivan Georg's hospital room after his brain surgery? Why did the black flock perch on the asphalt exactly in front of the high school where my *too-smart* friend Peter Stan had classes? We all know whose husband Peter Stan is. As for Tony, the boy who took the 'injured blackbird' home: in the light of the hypothesis put forward by Professor Margaret Stan, Tony is the youngest element of the Trio of Death, or shall we call it the Trio of Agony?"

In the embarrassing silence that ensued, Margaret Stan's voice was a savage épée that cut the horizon into two shimmering lines of fear.

"Speaking of the Trio of Death," she began, looking at no one in particular, "I'd like to draw your attention to a possible *incomplete* triad. One. Many of us present here have noticed the little fair-haired girl. Two. Sara Eutim, the famous writer and scholar who has green dots, had made the Samodiva's milk roar as Jacob Harvey told us. Three. I scrawled a big question mark on the wall in my room. Who is the third element in the Trio of Agony? Who is he or she?" Professor Margaret narrowed her eyes. "Four. The Old Bulgarian song: five stanzas, repetition of the number three in the first four stanzas. Number two emerges several times in the last, fifth stanza." Professor Margaret Stan looked up. "The little fair-haired girl and Ms. Sara Eutim are the only known elements to this trio, or should I describe it as a duo?"

All eyes were on Margaret Stan's face.

Chapter Forty-Six

"I hope we will soon find the third element of Sara Eutim's trio," the police chief said.

"I doubt it exists," Professor Margaret Stan's voice had a cold dangerous edge. "Remember that the number *two—not three!*—is repeated in the last stanza of the song. The last stanza is the end. What is the definition of *end?* The point where something ceases to exist." she said slowly. "If we believe that death is the door to the worlds of childhood, adulthood and old age, then perhaps the third element of Sara's trio has a special role to play in the tragedy which ..."

"I am after Death," John Cole cut her short.

"You are after the Tall Fellow," Boya Bagd objected. "You want to take everything away from him, his power and his influence!"

"I want what I want," John Cole said as he glowered at Boya, but the slim attractive woman didn't flinch. Her blue eyes trapped his and remained cold. "I have a bone to pick with you, Boya," the police chief went on. "I'm sure you know why." He grabbed her hand. "Boya Bagd, I have checked on you. You lived in a flat just a stone's throw from Trun Shrine. Another important detail: you had put someone on your reference list, so I invited you to work for me. Your records were brilliant, I give you that."

"I don't know what you are speaking about," Boya Bagd said.

"Oh, you do," he said. "Let us go back to the day when Doctor Ivan Georg lay dying after his brain surgery. Professor Gils informed me that, as a rule, patients hardly survived severe interventions of this nature. He believed Ivan Georg was going to pass away. A miracle occurred. Ivan Georg not only recovered his health, but also produced Healing Trun!" The police chief made a dramatic pause. "I admit I suspected Professor Andrew Gils: maybe he had administered the wrong medicine or had not performed the surgical operation in the way he should have. That was not the case. Dr. Georg's surgery was filmed, and I made sure leading experts studied the film. They found nothing wrong with Professor Gils' work." John Cole's eyes were on Ivan Georg. "Then I thought of Ivan Georg. Well, Dr. Georg was dying therefore he is above suspicion. Then I thought of you, Boya Bagd."

The slim young woman gave him a thin-lipped smile.

"Go on," she said.

"Old Boya Bagd," Thomas Stan chuckled. "She behaves as if the police chief worked for her ... haughtier and more arrogant than I remember her."

"Haughtier and more arrogant," John Cole repeated. "You are right, young man. It was arrogant and haughty Boya who entered Ivan Georg's hospital room after he had brain surgery. Arrogant Boya was in charge of the blackbirds. No one has seen the voiceless songsters for years, or would it be more precise to say ... centuries? Ivan Georg was dying and instead of a coffin, lo and behold! He came up with Healing Trun!"

The wind had died, the ailing sky was silent, and it was the sun—the old spider—that wove its cobweb in between the angry swollen clouds.

"The email you sent me, Mr. Cole, was a thought-provoking one." Professor Gils said, and all eyes were on him. "I am thinking of a curious detail," Professor Gils shook his head. "Ivan Georg gave us the key to changing the world. Interesting, isn't it?"

"I agree it is," John Cole said. "Boya Bagd was the only person the cameras—the ones installed above the front door of Ivan's room—had caught. There is no one else." The police officer's voice was harsh. "Boya Bagd was in charge of the benevolent iron-feathered songsters as heavy as hills. One of them mysteriously bluffed its way into Ivan Georg's hospital room. A tiny detail: Boya Bagd has green dots which, if we believe Wanga—and I cannot give you a reason why we should not trust the clairvoyant's judgment—Boya Bagd's dots had undergone a major alteration."

"Her dots were different when she came to kill me," Wanga said as she stretched out her arms towards Boya. "I felt their pattern exuded joy." Wanga's face looked strained as she added. "Now her dots tell me something else. They are upset."

"Boya Bagd," the police chief began. "I ask you again—what did you do to Ivan when you were in his room after his brain surgery?"

Boya Bagd was silent, unflinching, her eyes on the four black holes.

"Did you intentionally let one of the blackbirds fly into Ivan Georg's room?" John Cole asked as he grabbed Boya's hand.

"Yes," the red-haired woman said in a matter-of-fact voice.

"Did you send all the blackbirds to Ivan, to Iztok Clinic?" John Cole asked.

"I did not want him to die," Boya Bagd said as she shook her head.

The police chief tightened his grip on her wrist. "What else did you do to Ivan Georg?" John Cole whispered. "The blackbirds cannot defeat death. They can ease the pain or inflict excruciating agony but cannot stop the Samodiva that travels freely within the space of youth, adulthood, and old age. No blackbird can stop death or take men to their new home in the universe of flat time, Boya Bagd. But you managed to outwit death, and Ivan Georg survived lethal procedures. He has fully recovered."

"If you think the blackbirds cannot stop death, why did you order me to destroy them, Mr. Cole?" Boya asked.

"The blackbirds did kill the pain," the teacher Peter Stan said. "Why did you disable them, Mr. Cole?" Peter asked sadly. "You *killed* them because the Samodiva civilization enjoys human suffering!"

"I think the Samodivas feed on pain," Professor Andrew Gils said. "All major world religions denounce suicide as an act against God. Why? By committing suicide man refuses to be a reservoir of pain. Man rejects the prospect of absorbing agony for good. Man is stronger than Samodivas and will become more powerful than death."

"The blackbirds are an instrument which has proved unable to adjust to the consequences of death," the police chief said. "They killed too much pain." He paused, still squeezing Boya Bagd's wrist. "What did you do to Ivan Georg, Boya? Why did you do it?" He was silent for a while, thinking. His hoarse whisper had the effect of a gunshot. "I think I know you very well."

The statue of the blackbird cast a shadow over John Cole.

"My blackbird was my best friend," Tony, the boy who had been quiet so far, said as he hurled a big stone into the stone cube. The Samodiva's milk gobbled it up, glowing, deaf and mute. "I hate you!" the boy shouted at John Cole. "You killed my bird and I'll kill you. Don't forget that I will kill you."

"Tony, if Professor Margaret Stan is right," Ivan Georg said, watching the boy, "You cannot kill him. You are an element of his trio and killing him means that you commit suicide."

"I'll deal with you later, Tony. I will explain to you why it is impossible for you to kill me. I cannot kill you either," John Cole spoke slowly, releasing his grip on Boya's hand. "In the first place, I want to know why Boya saved Ivan Georg's life, and second, *how* she did it. I am waiting, Boya."

The attractive woman turned her back on John Cole as if he was no longer there. John Cole scowled and shook his head as he muttered something under his breath.

It was Jacob Harvey, the archaeologist, who declared stubbornly and clearly, "I think I know the reason behind Dr. Georg's recuperation." The archaeologist waited as he dramatically took a breath then went on, "The Old Bulgarian songs do not offer us a wide range of options. We have to consider two possible scenarios: a Samodiva saves a man's life either because she is this guy's mother or because she is head over heels in love with the man." Jacob Harvey turned to face Dr. Ivan Georg. "Doctor Georg," he went on. "Who is your mother?"

"My mother is a woman who refused to take care of me," Ivan Georg said. "I have not seen her for years."

"In other words, we cannot dismiss the possibility that some old woman, the element of Boya Bagd's trio, i.e., Boya Bagd in her old age, might be your mother?" the archaeologist insisted.

Ivan Georg raised his eyebrows, his face hard.

"To be honest, I don't put much faith in Professor Stan's theory," he said forcefully. "I would sacrifice my life to save that of Boya Bagd." His voice broke.

"I was ready to die for her too," Thomas Stan snarled. "Look at me now. My life was a shambles after she went away. She is a dagger wrapped in good velvety intentions. Mean, that's what she is. She'll kill you."

The red-hot air glittered under the dazzling rays of the sun. The monument of the blackbird seemed to wobble, the black claws digging the crag, the huge wings sweeping the sky as if the mountain was about to fly away.

"I am not Ivan Georg's mother," Boya Bagd said her words as dark as the wings of the blackbird. "The old woman of my trio is not his mother either."

"Then we can choose between two options: either you are Death," at this point John Cole's voice rose, strong and menacing, then was again even like the barrel of a gun. "Or ... Jacob Harvey has mentioned it already, *a Samodiva will do everything for a man she is head over heels in love with.*"

Boya Bagd said nothing. Her face showed nothing. Her eyes revealed nothing, beautiful eyes, depthless as the sky and as indifferent.

"Can you hear me, Boya?" The police chief said.

"Yes," she said.

"Her green dots have changed," Wanga said. "They *feel* much different now." The blind woman lapsed into silence. "I ..." she ventured. "What has happened to her? It is the first time I have witnessed a profound change like this ... like the change of seasons."

"A Samodiva turned traitor," John Cole snapped. "She gave the ordinary guys," he cleared his throat, his tone a stiletto. "She gave these arrogant, greedy, mean creatures ... gave them Healing Trun and Killing Trun. They have already turned Healing Trun into an article of trade. What will they turn Killing Trun into?" he was whispering. "The Samodiva who has turned traitor brings the end to the world."

"I will explain," Boya Bagd began coldly. "My green dots used to inhabit Ivan Georg. They stayed with him for years. Yes, I had grown attached to Ivan, got accustomed to his ways. I appreciated his kindness, and I did not want to walk away on him." The beautiful woman was calm, her clear skin glowing, soft like the breeze. "After he produced Healing Trun, my dots could not stay in his thoughts any longer." She sighed. "I found out that Ivan had become a Talented One, and my dots fled from his mind. This is the reason why Wanga feels they are different now."

The afternoon turned into silence as the deaf crags collided with the sky, pierced it, their brown edges smashing into its frightening depth.

"You were responsible for the blackbirds, Boya," the police chief said. "No one has let them loose since the Great Plague of London in 1666. It is against the rules. You were in charge of the flock, Boya, and the blackbirds flew to Iztok Clinic."

"I turned the flock loose," the slim red-haired woman said. "I sent it to Iztok Clinic because I wanted the blackbirds to save Ivan's life."

"You know the blackbirds cannot beat death," John Cole said.

"He was in pain," Boya said.

"You did something else, Boya," the police chief went on. "What was it? It was not the flock of blackbirds that saved Ivan Georg's life. It is only the Tall Fellow who can defeat death. Are you that tall one, Boya? Or are you, Death?"

The pretty woman said nothing.

"Ivan Georg got the better of death," John Cole went on. "No, I am wrong. A woman did it. You might have heard about the place where death will land if the Tall Fellow *destroys* it." For an instant, John Cole's eyes were on Tony. The boy sat close to his teacher Peter Stan. The old man patted him on the shoulder. "Tony, you will go to that place too, if you kill me," John Cole breathed. "I'll go there too, and Jacob Harvey will accompany us. The three of us belong together, you, Jacob, and me. If I kill you or Jacob, the three of us will go there. Time does not exist in that place. You'd better not kill me, boy, no matter how much you hate me."

"I still think that Ivan outwitted death," Jacob Harvey, the archaeologist, said. "He's alive and kicking now."

"Boya Bagd was smarter than death," John Cole said. "Or maybe Boya is just a path to old age. Maybe Boya is Death, the door men open as they collapse in agony while traveling to adulthood. Probably Boya is the end of us all. Or she is in panic because by now she's realized that the Tall Fellow is among us. The Tall Fellow is the only one who can shut the agony's door and keep it closed at all times."

"A Samodiva will save a man's life … if she … is in love with him," Thomas Stan whispered, his blood-stained face miserable, empty like a stretch of land scorched by fire. "I loved you, Boya. I gave you everything I had."

Boya Bagd did not look at him.

"Boya!" the police chief whispered. "How did you save Ivan Georg's life?"

Silence felt oppressive. The dark monument of the blackbird seemed to push Deaf Crags Valley towards the place where time did not exist.

"I injected Samodiva's milk into Ivan's vein," Boya Bagd said. "A minute later, he produced Healing Trun."

At that moment, no one was looking at the turbid liquid. No one noticed it was bubbling in its stone cube.

Chapter Forty-Seven

Wanga's voice was sand and sunset.

"I tell you again!" the clairvoyant wheezed. "Don't kill him!"

Sara Eutim stood behind Ivan Georg, the light breeze brushing her outstretched arms.

"He knows," Wanga went on. "Now the man with the scarred face knows what to do. *She* will inject Samodiva's milk into his blood one more time. He will find the path to the place where time is not an insurmountable wall."

Sara Eutim did not say anything, did nothing, her exquisite figure a shade of silver in the warm afternoon.

"I am talking to you, Sara, or shall I address you by your real name?" the seer asked slowly.

Sara Eutim ducked into the shadow of the enormous bird, a thick formless cloud of darkness, which had reached the stone cube and was playing with the Samodiva's milk in it. The blind woman lost her balance. In a split second, Philip Mill was by her side, holding her.

"I am speaking to her," Wanga went on, her bloodless lips invisible on her face. "You can kill him …" her voice trailed off, then suddenly seemed to spurt, soft and small, from the invisible pores of her skin. "Yes, you know you can, Sara. You will take me soon. I can see you doing it."

Sara Eutim tiptoed carefully, slowly, finally stopping behind the prophetess' back. Wanga turned around, spread her arms, her fingers sinking into the emptiness, sifting the breeze, powerless like feathers of a bird.

"His face is slightly disfigured. His mind is brilliant. If you destroy him, you'll destroy men. No one will remain under the sky, and no one will be scared of you. Samodivas will run dry. Remember: if you delete *the beginning,* there will be no end." A shudder ran through Wanga, her body a thin, loose thread in the air. "Sara Eutim, if you destroy him, you will be a deserted plain. Think of the pain that has eaten your bones … the horror you've been through … the eyes you've closed …" the seer went on, her words a jumble of mutilated sounds, an avalanche of fear, an abyss. "But he is here!" shouted Wanga suddenly. "The Tall Fellow can make you run dry."

"Is Sara Eutim Death?" Professor Margaret Stan breathed. "The Samodiva that takes men to the unexplored universe, the world beyond." Professor Stan paused, thinking. "I should have guessed. There are only two elements in what should be Sara Eutim's trio: Sara the little girl, and Sara the dazzling beauty. There is no Sara, the old woman. Death is space that does not grow old."

Lost in thought, at last Professor Stan said out loud, "Now, I see why the number two is repeated in the lyrics to that Old Bulgarian song. A trio cannot consist of *two* elements; the last stanza of life, death, is its third element."

The liquid in the stone cube suddenly rippled as it took a leap to the sky, the thin clouds squawking in a thousand broken voices.

"Sara!" Jacob Harvey shouted. "Sara, you touched the Samodiva's milk, and it roared the way it is screaming now. Sara! My dearest! Are you … are you … Death?"

"I am the way, the truth and the life," Sara Eutim said confidently as she grinned at him. "Death is different. Death is an everlasting universe."

"He is the life, the Tall Fellow!" Wanga gasped. "The Tall Fellow is here! Sara, after you close the earth behind you, the truth—and not death!—will be the door to the worlds of childhood, adulthood, and old age. There will be no pain," Wanga's voice collapsed. She fell onto the stones, her breathing shallow and labored.

Philip Mill cupped her face in his hands.

"You will take me to death, Philip," the seer whispered.

"Wanga! Dearest …" he started. "Don't …"

"You'll kill me," she said calmly.

Sara Eutim spoke in a flat voice, "Wanga, you said the Tall Fellow is here, with us. Do you know him?"

"No," the prophetess muttered. Her nose started gushing blood. Red drops gleamed on her cheeks.

"She's lying. Don't let her speak on!" Thomas Stan shouted, the brown crust of dried blood, dead embers on his cheeks. "She'll bleed to death!"

"The New Ones cannot lie to anybody," Professor Andrew Gils said. "Wanga is very weak." Then the professor added quietly. "Truth is powerless. Truth is unable to become the door to other worlds."

"Truth leads one nowhere!" Thomas Stan thundered.

"Truth led me to a better world!" Ivan Georg said. "Maybe Wanga is not only a New One, maybe she is Death's disciple. She knows who is going to die, dissolving in the mystic domains of childhood, adulthood, and old age."

"No," Wanga said.

Professor Margaret Stan said. "You capture and filter lies, Wanga." The professor pointed at John Cole and asked, "Is the police chief the Tall Fellow?"

Wanga was silent for a long while. Professor Margaret Stan waited, patient, insistent, adamant. The prophetess said nothing, her blind eyes dry wells, her cheeks glowing white like salt.

"John Cole …" Wanga mouthed. "John is not an Ordinary one," she gasped as the monument of the blackbird reeled in the air. "John is *not* a Talented One, not a New One either." A trace of a smile played across her pale lips. The liquid in the cube churned and hissed. "John Cole is a Marked One, but he is *not* the Tall Fellow."

The blind woman sat down on the hot stones, clutching at Philip Mill's feet, her eyes white as the snow that covered the narrow valley. The sun, an evil old man, curled up in the sky above the stone cube, its light unable to melt the clouds.

"Is he the Tall Fellow?" Professor Margaret Stan asked as she pushed her son Thomas to the clairvoyant. Wanga turned her eyes toward the young man's blood-stained clothes. Her fingertips, soft as cobweb, touched his bloody lips.

"Your son is a New One," the prophetess said. "Don't make him tell lies. But you are such a mulish woman."

"Thank you," Professor Margaret Stan said, her face a red, angry sunrise, a thunderstorm brewing in her eyes. "Is he the Tall Fellow, Madam?" the Professor's voice was abrasive as she sneaked to Professor Andrew Gils, grabbed his hand and dragged him to Wanga. "I am more than mulish, Wanga. Tell me. Is this man the Tall Fellow?"

The prophetess scrambled to her feet, her shadow a thin spindle as she turned her back on Professor Margaret Stan.

A voice as deep as Deaf Crags Valley sang, capturing the power of a dozen silver bells.

He threw his dots to the wind, and they don't protect him anymore.
How could the Tall Fellow be so silly, mommy?
He threw his dots to the wind, and now he can feel the pain
we feel, my pretty girl.
Why should he care about pain, that silly Tall Fellow, mommy?
If pain is everywhere, the Tall Fellow
will destroy death.

Jacob Harvey was singing, a tall, thin man.

"Sara, this is the song you've printed under the dry cherry trees in the picture you carried in your pocket everywhere you went ..." he stared at the hill with the black monument of a bird on its top. "The Tall Fellow gave up his *dots,* so he could feel pain the way ordinary men do. Christ died on the cross to save our souls. Do you believe the Tall Fellow can wipeout death?"

"I find this parallel quite entertaining," Sara Eutim said, a glimmer of amusement creeping into her eyes. "If the amazing Tall Fellow is here, and if what the venerable blind lady says about me is true—and it must be true because Wanga is a New One—then I should be Death, and the Tall Fellow is most welcome to destroy me here and now."

"You forget a tiny detail, Sara," Jacob Harvey said. "The Tall Fellow must stay hidden. Who knows what will happen if we find out who he is? Maybe another Trun might come into existence."

"Another Trun?" Professor Andrew Gils asked. "We have Healing and Killing Trun. What other Trun could there be?"

The words Wanga uttered made John Cole jump.

"Trun of death!" she said.

"What if death and the Tall Fellow are one and the same thing?" Ivan Georg asked. "What if Death decides to disappear? What if Death commits suicide?"

No one had noticed that the liquid in the stone cube had stopped glowing. Deep, gurgling sounds carried over the Samodiva's milk.

"Wanga, is Boya Bagd the Tall Fellow?" Professor Margaret Stan asked.

"She ... she is not an Ordinary One. Not a New One. Not a Talented one," the blind woman spoke slowly, her cracked lips hardly moving. "She is a Samodiva ... a traitor because of her infatuation with a man," the prophetess' finger pierced the air, looking for somebody until at last the cold fingertip touched Ivan Georg's forehead. "This man!"

"Am I the Tall Fellow, Wanga?" Professor Margaret Stan asked.

A wan smile crossed the blind woman's face.

"I said you were a mulish woman," Wanga said. "You are an Ordinary one who used her mulishness to learn how to become a Samodiva. You are not the Tall Fellow." The smile on Wanga's lips was genuinely amused. "You can capture the Tall Fellow if you set your heart on capturing him," the seer's thin hand hesitated as it finally touched Peter Stan's cheek. "This very kindhearted man calls your mulishness an *iron will!*"

"Thank you!" Professor Margaret Stan said dryly. Then her voice sneaked past her husband and crawled like a lizard towards the blind woman. "Wanga, are you the Tall Fellow?"

No one had ever heard Wanga laugh. Her laughter was quiet like the first drops of rain after months of severe drought. Her laughter was the uncertain steps of a toddler, it was the last ecstatic flight of a butterfly that had one more minute to live. It was happy laughter.

"Is he the Tall Fellow?" Professor Margaret Stan asked sharply as she took hold of Professor Andrew Gils' hand.

"Leave her alone!" Philip Mill snarled. "Wanga is weak. You have a stubborn streak, haven't you, Professor Stan?"

"This man is a Samodiva," Wanga whispered. "How much he loves her ... poor guy." Beads of perspiration glistened on Wanga's forehead. "He has not stopped thinking of her since the day she told him her first fairy tale in that big empty house on Gagarin Street. He has not stopped dreaming of her. Poor Samodiva ..."

Professor Andrew Gils' face glowed red-hot. He didn't know what to do with his hands.

It had stopped snowing. A gusty wind hit the mountain, and the air was light, warm with the sunshine.

"I wonder why the Tall Fellow must stay hidden," Jacob Harvey, the archaeologist, said. "This makes no sense."

"Think about what happened to Jesus after Judas gave Him the kiss of greeting," Sara Eutim said. "Or ask Wanga what will happen to the Tall Fellow. Perhaps she will be good enough to enlighten you on this topic."

"Leave her alone!" Philip Mill said darkly.

He wore a shabby faded shirt, and his black trousers were tattered. His beard, shaggy and bristling, looked horrible.

"Wanga," Professor Margaret Stan began quickly. "Is your boyfriend, Philip Mill, the Tall Fellow?"

The seer turned abruptly, her face a block of dry white salt on a dead riverbed.

"Philip Mill is not a New One," Wanga began. "Philip Mill is not a Talented One." She paused, the same genuine happy smile playing on her lips. At that moment, the blind woman looked beautiful. "Philip Mill is not a Samodiva ..." her voice trailed off.

"Wanga, stop!" Philip Mill cried.

"Philip Mill is an Ordinary One," Wanga continued firmly.

"No!" Philip Mill shouted, but blood was already pouring from her mouth, blood spurted from her nose and gushed from her ears.

"Wanga, Wanga, my dearest," Philip whispered. "Help her! Please help her! Please!"

"I ... love ... you ..." the blind woman gasped, the words specks of dust in the red fire of her blood.

The shadow of the blackbird touched her hands then crept onto her lips. She stopped breathing.

"Wanga!"

The wind died.

Philip's sobs dissolved in the blazing sun. "Wanga ..."

Chapter Forty-Eight

The murky liquid in the stone pool whizzed and spluttered, writhed and wiggled, waves rose and broke and crashed against the crags. Black billows of smoke poured from the stones, enveloping the knot of men and women, who had gathered around Philip Mill. Dark mud gushed from the cube. A gray stream surged up and hit the brink, crushed it like a nut, devoured the stones and flowed toward Wanga's dead body. The smoke smoldered as it closed in on all sides, engulfing Philip Mill. The thick gray slush licked his feet, clambered up, reached his knees, bit his stomach, smashed his fingers, and ate his chest. Philip Mill's hands burst into flames. His beard was a nest of iridescent sparks, sharp tongues of fire and bluish flames.

Sara Eutim's figure glowed, flared up, exploding into a dazzling waterfall of blazing, scorching light. For a split second, Philip Mill seemed to dwindle, a shrinking heap of melting bones and corroded skin. His hair burned. Blood oozed from his eyes. He raised his smoldering arms, spat and choked on his blood, threw his head back and laughed. He laughed so hard that turbid mud dripped from his arms and legs. The fire, eating his old shirt, burned bright and more frightening. Philip Mill laughed and could not stop. He laughed and tears streamed down his cheeks.

"Stop it, Sara," he breathed at last.

The black mud retreated to the crags, blackish-gray water ran back to the stones, the four dark holes glowered, the face of the mountain glowed, the blackbird was dead again, the liquid, a dangerous layer of murky molten substance, sprawled lazily in its cube beneath the agonizing blue of the sky. The smoke turned into brown dust that slowly settled on the crags. The terrible wings of the statue towered over the narrow sunlit patch of land, reaching the heaps of ice as huge and cold as the hills. The lifeless, eyeless liquid waited. Like a bolt out of the blue, a piercing, whining sound rent the air. A deafening roar of TRUN! … TRUN! … shattered the momentary silence that had lulled Deaf Crags Valley into a stupor.

Sara Eutim's body glowed no more. She stood by the dead blind woman, almost as thin as her, but much more beautiful, so beautiful that even Professor Margaret Stan held her breath, rubbing her eyes.

"You are the only one I have ever loved, Philip," Sara Eutim said. "You've known who I am all the time."

"Yes, I knew who you were," Philip Mill said. He knelt down by dead Wanga, a tear running down his cheek. "Where did you take her, Sara? Back to childhood or far away to lonely old age?"

Sara Eutim stared defiantly at him.

"I will not tell you, Philip." Her eyes were hard and dry. "Now, you will destroy me. I know." She paused, her voice heavy with bitterness. "I did my job well. I closed doors and eyes. I carried away children's last breaths. I took their pain and agony from them, Philip," she spoke slowly like an old woman who was climbing a steep hill and knew she wouldn't make it to the top. "I hated it when mothers cried for their sons I took. I was always alone. The one who opens doors to worlds can have no husband or children. I had many fiancés." She sighed. "I loved only you, Philip. This didn't seem right. I should have guessed you are the Tall Fellow, the only one who can turn me into a timeless place."

Slowly, gradually, the stones became colder, clouds gathered like a pack of wolves, biting off patches of the sky until grayish-white vapor swallowed the sun. A strong wind rose, then it started to snow, and within seconds, snowdrifts and heaps of ice jutted out by the stone cube.

"Now I know you are the Tall Fellow," John Cole said. "Philip Mill, the weakling, the pampered journalist I've despised." He squinted at the man with the shaggy beard and tattered, crumpled clothes. "I wanted to be the Tall Fellow," the police chief's words were daggers of ice meant to kill. "But the glory the Tall Fellow covered himself with disgusted me. Just imagine: Philip Mill, the wimp who escaped to Wanga to hide behind her back! The mouse I could hardly stand … is supposed to destroy death."

Philip Mill shook his head as Sara Eutim let out a shrill scream.

"Let her alone!" Professor Andrew Gils yelled, his arm outstretched, his face dangerously scarlet. He seized Philip by the throat. "I don't care who you are. Don't touch her."

John Cole ran to him.

"Shut up, Andrew!" he thundered. "I've known you ever since you were born. I've kept an eye on you ever since your mother brought you, scared stiff, to the candy man, to me. You saw green dots entangled in a blue-eyed girl's hair. She told you tales. You didn't know Death was telling you fairy tales, Andrew."

"Don't touch Sara, Cole!" Professor Andrew Gils growled.

It was suddenly so cold that the black liquid froze in a frenzy of sharp-edged ripples and gray, surging waves. Tony, still grieving for his lost blackbird, jumped to his feet, his cheeks purple in the wind.

"All these years I've been after Death," John Cole began slowly through his clenched teeth. "Every time a green-dots child was born, I suspected he or she was Death. I wanted to kill pain for good. I wanted to prove that the Samodivas didn't enjoy men's agony and malice. They thrive on truth! They live in thoughts that reveal truth! And truth, not death, should be the door to childhood, old age, adulthood. Truth is the shortest path between men's hearts. I should have been the Tall Fellow, not him … this is ludicrous … not Philip Mill!"

"Truth is feeble and sickly. Truth is unable to open doors!" Thomas Stan shouted. The gusty wind grabbed his words, and the snowstorm crushed them. Suddenly, Thomas' nose bled.

"He's a New One. He can't lie," his mother Margaret Stan groaned. "Don't say anything, Thomas. Don't speak!"

"He bleeds," John Cole said. "This means truth is strong enough."

Then John Cole's nose bled. Andrew Gils, Ivan Georg, Boya Bagd, Thomas Stan, his father Peter, the old teacher, Professor Margaret Stan, archaeologist Jacob Harvey, Tony the youngest among them, they all groaned, faces twisted, muscles contorted, limbs thrashing wildly in the snow, noses, mouths spurting blood.

"She … she's killing us," Margaret Stan breathed, pointing at Sara Eutim who stood motionless, her back turned on the heap of squirming bodies, dark pools of blood, gleaming red at her feet. It was snowing hard, and a small white hillock marked the spot where Wanga lay. Philip Mill stared at it, deaf to the storm, blind.

"She's killing us!" Margaret Stan shrieked, bloody froth concealing her lips like a layer of toxic scarlet dust.

Philip Mill staggered. The wind tore at his beard, opened his shirt, hit his chest. He faced the stone statue and spread his arms, then slowly, almost imperceptibly, raised his head, his eyes closed, his body a blur in the chaos of heavy, whirling snowflakes.

Sara Eutim screamed. It was a piercing, nightmarish screech. She collapsed on the snow, her fists shaking. Her beautiful face was flushed, her rapid breathing had turned into a net of desperate traces woven in the snow by a wounded animal. The heap of writhing limbs and bodies, bloodstained faces, hands, and horrified eyes slowly disintegrated. Panic gradually subsided, and agony was a shadow no one feared anymore.

"What happened?" Professor Margaret Stan asked at last.

"No one is in pain now," Philip muttered under his breath as he touched the tiny hillock and wiped the snow off Wanga's forehead. "Where did you take her, Sara?" he whispered, tears gleaming in his eyes." Back to childhood … Or did you throw her away in old age? I want to go with her. Take me there, Sara! Take me to her! Please."

"You, stupid idiot!" John Cole thundered. "You have to destroy death! Do it! Do it now! I have found Death for you! Come on! Choose between truth and death!"

The frozen liquid in the cube crackled into life. Rifts, deep as wells, opened up within the black surface, severing the sharp-edged crests of the icy waves. The wings of the statue glowed intermittently, and the four holes spat gray smoke that dissolved in the falling snow.

"We will all make a decision," Philip Mill said quietly. He took a handful of snow and kissed it, then slowly, carefully spread the snow on Wanga's cheeks. He squared his shoulders and spoke loudly and clearly, "Those of you who think I must destroy death, come to me and stand by my side."

Professor Margaret Stan scrambled to her feet first. She went to Philip Mill. Her husband Peter Stan followed her.

"You have to destroy death!" the police chief shouted, looking Philip Mill in the eyes. "Do you hear me?!"

Thomas Stan, his bloodstained face a wound that would never heal, staggered over to his father. "Truth is a failure," he muttered. "No. I'm wrong. Truth is the only path to eternity."

"Truth is an open door for everyone," Jacob Harvey said. "Truth will let the Samodivas live in the dreams of the Talented Ones," his voice broke—a rivulet of sad glowing sparks—then he coughed, gulped for air and blurted out, "I love you, Sara. I love you. Forgive me!" He strode to the Tall Fellow and hissed, "John Cole, I hate you. You've been shadowing Sara's steps all your life."

Tony was silent as he pressed a dark stone to his dirty coat. "It resembles my blackbird," the boy said as he tried to wipe the blood off his cheeks. "Death hurts," he added and stood by his teacher Peter Stan. "Truth hurts, too."

"I didn't believe you had the courage to be Death, Sara. I was sure Wanga was the bitter end of everything." Boya Bagd murmured. "I like you, Sara. But … I love … him."

Ivan Georg came up to Sara Eutim, took her hand and kissed it.

"Thank you," he said. "I remember the pain. It was horrible. You tried to save me from it … thank you!" He said nothing more, turned around and stood next to Philip Mill.

"No," Professor Andrew Gils said. "You have no right to destroy her! Sara, I love you. I always have." The freezing cold wind hit Sara Eutim, but she stood still, silent, magnificent. Andrew Gils took off his coat and gently, very carefully covered her shoulders with it. "I love you, Sara, dearest."

"She was about to kill us all!" John Cole hissed. "And she'll try to do it again. She's wicked. I understand her!"

Sara's body glowed, and the liquid in the cube soared up into the air. The heaps of snow on the brink melted within seconds. The crags whirred, the cube buzzed, chunks of black ice and stones spurted from the mud. The four holes roared, and the statue of the blackbird reeled. TRUN! TRUN! The whole valley quaked and swayed in the wind.

Everybody who stood behind Philip Mill were screaming in pain.

Andrew Gils, a strange smile on his face, shrieked, choking on his blood.

Sara Eutim towered over them, her eyes closed, her beautiful face expressionless.

"Destroy her!" John Cole bellowed in pain." Now!"

Philip Mill slowly raised his arms. The wind died then the dark liquid went to sleep in its stone cube.

"The pain ..." Peter Stan breathed. "It's gone."

"Don't let it come back," Boya Bagd pleaded. "Please, Philip, don't let it come back."

"Sara!" Andrew Gils whispered. "Dearest Sara!"

"Destroy her!" John Cole snarled. "Now!"

The wind came back, driving the ice and snow that closed in on all sides. Deaf Crags Valley had shrunk under the deep blanket of the storm.

Philip Mill watched the group of tortured men and women.

"Destroy her!" John Cole yelled. "Destroy her, you coward!"

"Destroy her?" Philip Mill murmured, staring intently at a vast snowdrift.

All eyes turned to what he saw.

Sara Eutim had vanished.

A fair-haired girl in a pink baby frock stood atop the snow. She was freezing. Her eyes were clear and blue. Tears ran down the child's cheeks.

"Sara ... is that you?" Andrew Gils whispered.

It started to rain. The little girl stood motionless, barefoot in the snow.

Philip Mill breathed ... "How can I destroy a child?"

About the Author

ZDRAVKA EVTIMOVA was born in 1959 in Pernik, Bulgaria.

She is a fiction writer and a literary translator in English, German and French. A native Bulgarian speaker, she is fluent in English, German, French and Russian. Zdravka holds a BA in English Language and an MA in American Literature from the University of Veliko Turnovo, Bulgaria.

Zdravka is married to Todor Georgiev. They have two sons and a daughter, and five grandchildren so far.

Her short stories have been published in 31 countries around the world, including the USA, China, UK, France, Germany, Switzerland, Japan, Canada, Vietnam, Argentina, Spain, Italy, Norway, Denmark, North Macedonia, Austria, the Netherlands, Slovenia, Serbia, Romania, and Greece.

BIBLIOGRAPHY OF TITLES PUBLISHED INTERNATIONALLY

United States of America

Asylum for Men and Dogs, novel, Fomite Books, 2022

You Can Smile on Wednesdays, novel, Fomite Books, 2020

In the Town of Joy and Peace, novel, Fomite Books, 2017

Parable of Stones, short story collection, All Things That Matter Press, 2017

Sinfonia Bulgarica, novel, Fomite Books, 2014

Carts and Other Stories, short story collection, Fomite Books, 2012

Time to Mow and Other Stories, short story collection, All Things That Matter Press, 2012

God of Traitors, novel, Bucks Publishing, 2008

Good Figure, Beautiful Voice, short story collection, Asremari Books, 2008

Somebody Else, short story collection, MAG Press, 2004

UK

Impossibly Blue, short story collection, Skrev Press 2013

Miss Daniella, short story collection, Skrev Press, 2007

Bitter Sky, short story collection, Skrev Press, 2003

Canada

Pale and Other Postmodern Bulgarian Stories, short story collection, Vox Humana Publishing Canada, 2010

Greece

Endless July, short story collection, Paraxenes Meres Press, 2013

Israel

Wrong and Other Stories, short story collection, Tiktakti Press, 2014

Pale and Other Postmodern Bulgarian Stories, short story collection, Vox Humana Publishing Israel, 2010

Macedonia

The Same River (Една иста река), Antolog Press, 2018

The Arc (Коработ), novel, Branko Tsvetkovski Publishing, 2017

Thursday, novel, Antolog Press, 2015

Italy

La citta della gioia e della pace (In the Town of Joy and Peace), novel, Slento Books, Besa, 2021

La donna che mangiava poesie (The Woman Who Ate Poetry), short story collection, Salento Books, Besa, 2019

Lo Stesso Fiume (The Same River), novel, Salento Books, subsidiary of Besa Publishing Conglomerate, 2017

Sinfonia (the Bulgarian title is *Thursday*), novel, Salento Books, subsidiary of Besa Publishing Conglomerate, 2015

China

Stories from Pernik, short story collection, Ningbo Publishing, 2019

Thursday, novel, Literature and Arts Publishing, Shanghai, 2015

Serbia

Thursday (new translation), novel, Antolog, 2021

Thursday, novel, Vaslaar Books, 2016

France

D'un bleu impossible (Impossibly Blue), Le Soupirail, 2019

Bulgaria

Reservation for Men and Wolves, novel, Zhanet-45 Publishing, 2022

The Good Side of Things, short story collection, Zhanet-45 Publishing, 2019

The Green Eyes of the Wind, novel, Zhanet-45 Publishing, 2018

July Stories, short story collection, Zhanet-45 Publishing, 2017

The Same River, novel, Zhanet-45 Publishing, 2015

Stories from Pernik, short story collection, Zhanet-45 Publishing, 2013

The Arch, novel, Ciela Press, 2007

Blood of a Mole and Other Stories, short story collection, Zhanet-45 Publishing, 2006

Thursday, novel, Zhanet-45 Publishing, 2003

Stories against Loneliness, short story collection, Narodna Mladezh Press, 1984

Zdravka Evtimova has won a number of literary awards in Bulgaria as well as internationally, which include the following:

Major Bulgarian Literary Awards

2020 Hristo Danov National Literary Award
> For contributions to contemporary Bulgarian literature.

2019 Zyapkov Literary Prize
> For her short story collection *July Stories.*

2017 Best Bulgarian Novel Award of Fund 13 Centuries Bulgaria
> For her novel *The Same River.*

2015 Best Novel of the Year National Award
> For her novel *The Same River.*

2015 Blaga Dimitrova National Fiction Prize
> For her short story collection *Stories from Pernik.*

2010 Golden Necklace Best Short Story of the Year National Prize

2005 Golden Necklace Best Short Story of the Year National Prize

2005 Anna Kamenova National Short Story Award
> For her short story collection *Blood of a Mole and Other Stories.*

2004 Gencho Stoev Literary Award for a Short Story by a Balkan Author

2004 Cosmos National Short Story Award

2003 Best Bulgarian Novel Award of the Union of Bulgarian Writers
For her novel *Thursday.*

2000 Razvitie Literary Award for Best Bulgarian Contemporary Novel

1984 Yuzhna Prolet Prize for a Debut Short Story Collection
For her short story collection *Stories against Loneliness.*

Major International Literary Awards

2022 Mihai Eminescu Prize for Fiction
For her work in fiction. From the International Academy Mihai Eminescu, Craiova, Romania.

2022, 2012, and 2006 Pushcart Prize nominations
For her short stories. USA.

2015 SINBAD international competition, second place
For her novel *Sinfonia.* Italy.

2014 Balkanika International Fiction Prize
For her short story collection *Pernik Stories,* best fiction work published in Albania, Bulgaria, Greece, Macedonia, Romania, Serbia and Turkey.

2007 Book of Europe nomination
For her novel *The Arch.*

2005, her short story "Vassil" was one of the ten award winning stories in the BBC worldwide short story competition. It was broadcast by Radio BBC UK in February 2006. In 2004, they had broadcast two of her short stories during their focus on Eastern European fiction.

2005, her short story, "It Is Your Turn" was one of the ten award-winning stories, which after a worldwide competition was included in the anthology *Dix auteurs du monde entier* (Ten Writers from All over the World). Nantes, France.

2005 Pushcart Prize nomination
For *Somebody Else,* a short story collection. USA.

Other Awards

2022 25th Annual Critters Readers' Poll Best All Other Short Story
For "For Dimitar—a Poet." USA.

2005 Best Short Story Collection of MAG Press by an Established Author
For *Somebody Else.* USA.

Of Interest

Her short story "Blood of a Mole" is included in high school textbooks in
Denmark and junior high school textbooks in the United States.

Zdravka Evtimova has won residencies for writers with her short stories and
novels as follows:

2021 Association Kurs from Split, Writers in Residence Program, Split,
Croatia

2019 Lu Xun Academy of Literature Program, Beijing, China

2018 Sun Yat-sen University, Guangzhou, China

2018 Stromstad, Sweden

2017 University of Bologna, Italy

2016 Tianjin Writing Program, China

2015 TRADUKI Program, Sarajevo, Bosnia and Herzegovina

2015 University of Bologna, Italy

2012 Shanghai Writing Program, China

2010 Translator's residency at the University of Rochester, Open Letter
Books Publishing, USA

2006 OMI Residency for writers, upstate New York, USA

2005 Chateau de Lavigny, Foundation Heinrich and Jane Ledig Rowohlt,
Switzerland

Editor's Note

Dear Reader,

When I received the manuscript for this novel from Zdravka, I knew that it would be good, I just didn't know how good. I often stand at my desk while working, but this time I promptly sat down to continue reading the manuscript. What really hooked me is the way in which Zdravka has created a modern masterpiece of fantasy, including robust elements of science fiction, by incorporating the fairy and folktales, the myths and legends of Old Bulgaria (of which I had known nothing). I think that this story is positively brilliant. Obviously, I'm hardly impartial, but I don't believe that a work of literature exists in the English language quite like it, certainly not in its original treatment of ancient Bulgarian folklore to construct the deeply enthralling and sophisticated fantasy architecture that we are presented with here, within which one of the wildest and most imaginative stories I've ever read plays out. I found it to be immersive and constantly intriguing, and its vivid imagery had me seeing green dots for days! I was stunned by the elements of science fiction introduced later in the story, original and tremendously creative, they provide a surprise twist that is the equivalent of an electric shock—one that creates a paradigm shift in the mind of the reader! Just superb. Zdravka has deftly and vibrantly interwoven the ancient and the contemporary, crafting a riveting and uniquely spellbinding work of fiction that boldly negotiates the fundamental questions and themes overarching human existence, and, magnificently, even provides some answers!

Ladies and gentlemen, take note, the fairy and folktales, the myths and legends of Old Bulgaria have arrived at the shores of the English-speaking world! Enjoy your reading and thank you for holding this book in your hands.

Here is the team of exceptional and marvelous talents who have brought this book to fruition. I thank each of them with heartfelt gratitude.

Thank you to Zdravka Evtimova, who is one of Bulgaria's foremost contemporary authors, for entrusting Starship Sloane Publishing with bringing this novel to the literary market. It has been an honor. Zdravka has had the patience of a saint with me throughout the entirety of the publishing process, for which I am most appreciative. The manuscript for this novel was the first ever received by this publishing house and it sang of promise. Zdravka's impressive and ever-growing body of literary work is richly deserving of the national and international accolades that it has garnered. I sincerely hope that this novel will also be very well received, accomplishing more literary success for Zdravka and further building her international name recognition and reputation as an author of great note. Cheers!

Thank you to Bob Eggleton, who has won the Hugo Award for best artist a remarkable nine times, for providing the gorgeous and haunting cover art, *Storm Coming,* a painting that was originally intended for a science fiction novel by a well-known author some two decades ago, but the book was not published and so it instead ended up hibernating in Bob's studio, waiting impatiently to hear the music of its new destiny. I found it quite fortuitously and the moment I saw it, I knew that it was meant to be on the cover of this novel—happily, Bob agreed! Is that not the little fair-haired girl that you see standing there in the field?

Thank you to Nigel Suckling, the author of more than twenty books and a bestselling tarot card with guidebook set, *The Dragon Tarot.* He is the winner of a Hugo Award and has collaborated with some of the biggest names in science fiction and fantasy (including Bob, so this is a reunion of sorts), in creating biographical, literary and artistic genre masterpieces. Nigel is deeply immersed in the world of fairy and folktales, myths and legends, and his exquisitely researched literary work is at the top of the field. Nigel kindly provided the foreword and generously offered to do a proofreading of the manuscript. The support provided was invaluable and much appreciated. We are in firm agreement that we have not read anything quite like this extraordinary story by Zdravka before. This sense of the work being unique added a certain energy to the completion of this publishing project.

Thank you to F. J. Bergmann for her expert and elegant book design work. I am very happy that she was able to take on this project. F. J. is an award-winning poet, having received the Rhysling Award for poetry, twice, and the Elgin Award for a chapbook of poetry, twice. In addition to book and magazine design, F. J. is a book and magazine editor. I also admire the webmaster work that she has done for one of my favorite organizations, the Science Fiction & Fantasy Poetry Association.

Thank you to the early manuscript readers, Tom Sloane, and another, who prefers to remain as mysterious as any Samodiva, for their feedback.

Thank you to Brent, Demi, Amber and the whole crew at Art Direct in Austin, Texas for the fine art scanning services that brought *Storm Coming* from the physical into the digital.

Finally, thank you to Jean-Paul L. Garnier, the editor of *Star*Line* and *Simultaneous Times* magazines, for graciously accepting my request—made at literally the last minute—to read the manuscript for a book blurb.

And again, thank you, dear reader.

All the best,
Justin T. O'Conor Sloane, Editor
October 2023
USA